THE BEST AMERICAN SHORT STORIES anthology was established in an era when *best* was a word used more sparingly than it is today. It has survived the literary storms and crosscurrents of fifty years in America and, through changing tastes and mores, it has maintained its tradition.

"As usual, in this long-established annual that always has a ready audience, both established writers and those less well known are included. Trends pointed out are the reappearance of the ghost story (the casual, matter-of-fact introduction of the supernatural into realistic fiction); the decline of chilhood themes; and the resurgence of interest in the 1930's. It's difficult to pick favorites, but outstanding are Brian Moore, Joyce Carol Oates and Carol Sturm."

—*Publishers' Weekly*

Distinguished Novels and Shorter Fiction From Ballantine Books

THE BEST AMERICAN SHORT STORIES 1966
    edited by Martha Foley and David Burnett $.95
An especially rich selection, with stories by William Maxwell, Shirley Ann Grau, Abraham Rothberg, Flannery O'Connor, William Faulkner, and fifteen other gifted writers. "The duds in this year's display are few. The successes light up the sky."
—*The New York Times*

A LEGACY, Sybille Bedford $.75
A novel of life among the rich and titled of Europe in the years before the First World War. "As richly satisfying a novel as has been published in years ... a work of art."   —*New York Herald Tribune*

AFRICAN STORIES, Doris Lessing $.95
A major writer's magnificent portrait of the loved and hated land of her birth. 672 pages. "A wide, diverse, and magnificently populated landscape."
—*The New York Times*

THE LONG DAY WANES, Anthony Burgess $.95
The brilliant "Malayan Trilogy" by the highly acclaimed author of *Tremor of Intent*. "One of the most revealing narratives about the East and the West since *A Passage to India*."
—*The New York Times Book Review*

THE MORNING WATCH, James Agee $.75
The celebrated early short novel by the author of *Let Us Now Praise Famous Men* and *A Death in the Family*. "A successful and satisfying *tour-de-force* ... first class writing."
—Oliver LaFarge, *Saturday Review*

For a complete list of Ballantine titles in fiction and nonfiction, write to Dept. CS, Ballantine Books, 101 Fifth Avenue, New York, N.Y. 10003

The Best American Short Stories 1967

and the Yearbook of the American Short Story

Edited by
MARTHA FOLEY
and
DAVID BURNETT

BALLANTINE BOOKS • NEW YORK

FIRST PRINTING C
COPYRIGHT © 1967 BY HOUGHTON MIFFLIN COMPANY

ALL RIGHTS RESERVED INCLUDING THE RIGHT TO
REPRODUCE THIS BOOK OR PARTS THEREOF IN ANY FORM

LIBRARY OF CONGRESS CATALOG CARD NUMBER: 16-11387
PRINTED IN THE UNITED STATES OF AMERICA

"The Promise of Heat" by Ethan Ayer. First published in *The New Yorker*. Copyright © 1966 by The New Yorker Magazine, Inc.

"A Place Not on the Map" by George Blake. First published in *The Literary Review*, Summer 1966. Copyright © 1966 by Fairleigh Dickinson University, Teaneck, New Jersey.

"The Wild Horses" by Kay Boyle. First published in *The Saturday Evening Post*. Reprinted by permission of Doubleday & Company, Inc., from *Nothing Ever Breaks Except the Heart* by Kay Boyle. Copyright © 1966 by Kay Boyle.

"Will You Please Be Quiet, Please?" by Raymond Carver. First published in *December* Magazine. Copyright © 1966 by Raymond Carver.

"One of the Boys" by H. E. Francis. Reprinted from *The Southwest Review*, Spring 1966. Copyright © 1966 by Southern Methodist University Press.

"Trepleff" by MacDonald Harris. Reprinted from the December issue of *Harper's* Magazine by permission of the author. Copyright © 1966 by Harper's Magazine, Inc.

"White Anglo-Saxon Protestant" by Robert Hazel. Reprinted by permission from *The Hudson Review*, Volume XIX, No. 4 (Winter 1966-67). Copyright © 1967 by The Hudson Review, Inc.

"Acme Rooms and Sweet Marjorie Russell" by Hugh Allyn Hunt. First published in *The Transatlantic Review*. Copyright © 1966 by The Transatlantic Review.

"The Heroic Journey" by Lawrence Lee. First published in *The Michigan Quarterly Review*, V (April 1966) and reprinted by permission of the author and *The Michigan Quarterly Review*. Copyright © 1966 by the University of Michigan.

"Search for a Future" by Arthur Miller. First published in *The Saturday Evening Post*. Copyright © 1966 by Arthur Miller.

"The Apartment Hunter" by Brian Moore. First published in *The Tamarack Review*. Copyright © 1966 Brian Moore.

"Andrew" by Berry Morgan. First published in *The New Yorker*. Copyright © 1966 by The New Yorker Magazine, Inc.

"Where Are You Going, Where Have You Been?" by Joyce

Carol Oates. Reprinted from *Epoch*, Summer 1966. Copyright © 1966 by Cornell University.

"Song of the Simidor" by Donald Radcliffe. First published in *The Literary Review*, Winter 1966-67. Copyright © by Fairleigh Dickinson University, Teaneck, New Jersey.

"The Surveyor" by Henry Roth. First published in *The New Yorker*. Copyright © 1966 by The New Yorker Magazine, Inc.

"Longing for America" by David Rubin. First published in *The Virginia Quarterly Review*. Copyright © 1966 by the University of Virginia.

"The Accident" by Jesse Stuart. First published in *The Saturday Evening Post*. Copyright © 1966 by The Curtis Publishing Company.

"The Kid Who Fractioned" by Carol Sturm. Reprinted from *Prairie Schooner*. Copyright © 1966 by the University of Nebraska Press.

"The Big Brown Trout" by Robert Travers. First published in *Argosy* Magazine. Copyright © 1966 by Robert Travers.

"House of the Blues" by William Wiser. First published in *The Kenyon Review*. Copyright © 1966 by The Kenyon Review.

This edition published by arrangement with
Houghton-Mifflin Company.

First Printing: April, 1968

BALLANTINE BOOKS, INC.
101 Fifth Avenue, New York, N.Y. 10003

Acknowledgments

GRATEFUL ACKNOWLEDGMENT for permission to reprint the stories in this volume is made to the following:

The Editors of *Argosy, December, Epoch, Harper's Magazine, The Hudson Review, The Kenyon Review, The Literary Review, The Michigan Quarterly Review, The New Yorker, Prairie Schooner, The Saturday Evening Post, The Southwest Review, The Tamarack Review, The Transatlantic Review, The Virginia Quarterly Review;* and to Ethan Ayer, George Blake, Kay Boyle, Raymond Carver, H. E. Francis, MacDonald Harris, Robert Hazel, Hugh Allyn Hunt, Lawrence Lee, Arthur Miller, Brian Moore, Berry Morgan, Joyce Carol Oates, Donald Radcliffe, Henry Roth, David Rubin, Jesse Stuart, Carol Sturm, Robert Travers, William Wiser.

To
Joyce Carol Oates

Foreword

AMERICA'S most distinctive and distinguished kind of writing has flourished during the past year. Thousands of short stories, more than in any recent year, were published. Hundreds of new writers appeared. Those who see only the handful of large-circulation magazines cannot realize that some literary magazines carry between ten and fifteen short stories in an issue. New magazines, proud of their short stories, recently have come into being. As a result the number of short stories found worthy of place on the Honor Roll and the list of Distinctive Stories in the Yearbook of this volume is unusually large.

The question most asked editors of this collection is, "What new trends in the short story have you seen this year?" Of course it is impossible to measure in only twelve months any great literary groundswell. In literature, as in nature, such phenomena are caused by distant forces. But there are always some immediate changes. Such changes may be temporary and not of lasting importance. Especially when they seem as bizarre as the one strikingly new note in the past year. The ghost story is back with us. Not as in the Gothic tale or in fantasy, the supernatural is being introduced casually and matter-of-factly in everyday and otherwise realistic stories.

Ghost stories have never lost their popularity in the British Isles. One is not surprised to encounter them in magazines and books there. But how could the ghost go west to America, land of modern pragmatism? Apparitions, haunted houses, second sight, returnees from the dead—in one tale a ghost dog, in another even a haunted suit of clothes—are appearing in our literary quarterlies, sophisticated magazines and slick periodicals. Shades of Irving, Poe and Hawthorne, the progenitors of the American short story!

Another noticeable development has been a new kind of formula story, not in the "girlie magazines" where you might expect it but in the more literary magazines. The old formula was boy-meets-girl, boy-loses-girl, boy-regains-girl and, in the worst examples, boy-gets-job-in-bank. In this freer age, the story begins in bed. Boy loves girl but for one reason or another loses his potency. There come terrific efforts to restore it, either on his part, the girl's part or on both parts. "How could he convince Helen he was potent?" one such story begins. Authors are running out of sexual positions. One desperate pair of lovers even tried having the girl stand on her head. There is a happy ending if the boy regains his potency in time. The unhappy ending is when the boy regains his potency too late. Now the girl will never know he really is a man. Not Irving or Poe or Hawthorne should be involved here but, because of the deadly seriousness with which such stories are written, the laughter of Rabelais.

Even more intriguing than the sudden resurgence of the supernatural in fiction is the new labeling in some magazines of narrative poems as "short stories" or fiction. In the past there has been writing which has been described by critics as prose poems. This has been understandable because of their melodiousness and imagery. It is startling, however, to find a piece of writing called a short story in a magazine's table of contents and turn the pages to find a poem.

"Are there many good stories about the war in Vietnam?" is a question frequently asked. These editors have not been able to find any. Great stories of all wars seem to come after their termination. Perhaps the oft-quoted definition of poetry as "emotion recollected in tranquility" applies equally to story writing. Perspective is needed before the full impact of a great dramatic event can be distilled into words.

The Thirties are now with us as the Twenties once were. Not only are they providing the background for much of the new fiction, but authors whose work has not been seen much since that decade are also reappearing. There are cycles in literary styles as in other fashions.

As during the past few years there are many stories of fathers and sons and their relationship. The number of anti-mom stories is waning. For a while impressionable girls could almost be frightened from maternity by the innumerable depictions of vicious mothers. Unlike other years this one has not seen an overabundance of child stories.

To any reader who is given a chance to compare them, selections from the smaller literary magazines necessarily far outweigh those from large-circulation publications. The quality of fiction in the latter has vastly improved in the last ten years, however. Sadly, some of the women's magazines which had also raised their literary standards have recently been lowering them.

We are grateful to the editors who have kept us supplied with their magazines and to the authors for generously granting reprint rights. The editor of any new magazine is invited to send copies to us.

The editors and staff of Houghton Mifflin Company are also entitled to gratitude for their help. Finally, tribute is paid to the memory of Edward J. O'Brien, who founded this anthology.

MARTHA FOLEY
DAVID BURNETT

Contents

THE PROMISE OF HEAT. *Ethan Ayer* From *The New Yorker*	1
A PLACE NOT ON THE MAP. *George Blake* From *The Literary Review*	15
THE WILD HORSES. *Kay Boyle* From *The Saturday Evening Post*	27
WILL YOU PLEASE BE QUIET, PLEASE? *Raymond Carver* From *December*	41
ONE OF THE BOYS. *H. E. Francis* From *The Southwest Review*	75
TREPLEFF. *MacDonald Harris* From *Harper's Magazine*	95
WHITE ANGLO-SAXON PROTESTANT. *Robert Hazel* From *The Hudson Review*	113
ACME ROOMS AND SWEET MARJORIE RUSSELL. *Hugh Allyn Hunt* From *The Transatlantic Review*	135
THE HEROIC JOURNEY. *Lawrence Lee* From *The Michigan Quarterly Review*	173
SEARCH FOR A FUTURE. *Arthur Miller* From *The Saturday Evening Post*	185

THE APARTMENT HUNTER. *Brian Moore* From *The Tamarack Review*	201
ANDREW. *Berry Morgan* From *The New Yorker*	215
WHERE ARE YOU GOING, WHERE HAVE YOU BEEN? *Joyce Carol Oates* From *Epoch*	221
SONG OF THE SIMIDOR. *Donald Radcliffe* From *The Literary Review*	241
THE SURVEYOR. *Henry Roth* From *The New Yorker*	273
LONGING FOR AMERICA. *David Rubin* From *The Virginia Quarterly Review*	293
THE ACCIDENT. *Jesse Stuart* From *The Saturday Evening Post*	317
THE KID WHO FRACTIONED. *Carol Sturm* From *Prairie Schooner*	329
THE BIG BROWN TROUT. *Robert Travers* From *Argosy*	343
HOUSE OF THE BLUES. *William Wiser* From *The Kenyon Review*	357
Biographical Notes	377
The Yearbook of the American Short Story	383
Roll of Honor, 1966	384
Distinctive Short Stories in American Magazines, 1966	387
Addresses of American and Canadian Magazines Publishing Short Stories	397

THE
BEST
AMERICAN SHORT STORIES
1967

ETHAN AYER

The Promise of Heat

(FROM THE NEW YORKER)

CERTAINLY THE ARBOR in the garden was not the place to get the grape leaves to decorate the chair. There weren't enough of them at the moment, and the ones there were had a sort of pox on them that made them look catching.

Bruce didn't like getting up at seven in the morning, but today it was hot enough, even that early, to make sleep difficult. "The promise of heat." That's what people called it, but what they really meant, his mother said, was that the promise had already been kept. When they said "It's going to be a hot day," it already was one, like today.

The dew on the cobwebs and the morning mist on the river were features of the landscape that Bruce seldom noticed, even on his walks to the garden. For him, the beauties of nature were simply adjuncts to the human scene, like the leaves to decorate the back of his mother's chair. Leaves were not the only thing he was going to decorate the chair with, of course; there would be flowers, too, from the cutting garden—gladiolas and snapdragons, mostly. And phlox. The fireweed in the meadow between the garden and the river was always a temptation, but it was to be resisted. Fireweed began to droop the minute it got indoors.

Bruce pulled a double handful of the mangy leaves from the arbor. He felt guilty and lazy about it, even though the arbor looked no worse for being thinned. Bruce felt that he should have found another arbor somewhere—perhaps in a neighbor's garden?—with better grapes. But he was lazy. He wondered if he had the right to steal on his mother's birthday. The Larcom property was about one hundred and twenty acres. Did he, who had so much, have the right to steal at all? Did he have any rights at all?

Bruce was a good five feet seven at the age when most of his contemporaries were five feet nothing. His height put him above and therefore beyond them. He was always sitting down, and though he was alone, he sat down now. As he did so, he heard some footsteps on the gravel of the garden path behind him.

"Going to be a hot day," the gardener said. Bruce could tell it was the gardener by the voice.

"It already is," Bruce said.

"Wilting already," the gardener said then as he made his way to the handle that turned on the watering pipes that rose like great long croquet wickets over the long lines of flowers. Bruce looked up from his double handful of grape leaves to the gardener. Thin streams of water rose from the perforations in the pipes into the air.

"I was going to get some gladiolas, too," Bruce said.

The gardener was a red-faced Scotchman who did not speak lightly or often. Long pauses were the essence of his conversation. They made Bruce nervous. He always thought he had in some way offended him. The gardener's name was MacIntosh. "Tosh" for short.

"Them leaves," Tosh said now, pointing to them with his whole arm.

"Oh," said Bruce, "I thought you meant me."

Tosh began to walk away. His legs worked all together, like his arms, as if they were incapable of bending. Bruce supposed Tosh must sometimes sit down, but he had never really seen him. In a minute, he was back again. "Basket," he said, leaving one beside Bruce on the ground. Tosh always walked away when he was being thanked, so Bruce didn't bother to thank him. He just put the leaves in the basket, got up , and reached in his pants for the pruning knife.

It was the era of knickerbockers for boys, and there was a particularly bad style of them made from a cloth that looked like silver burlap. They were equipped with tongues and buckles at the knees, and were never known to stay either under or over stockings longer than the first strenuous motion. All the kids hated them, but they all wore them, because they were expendable. High-laced Keds sneakers and a sleeveless shirt customarily completed the unlovely costume. Into his silver-burlap pocket Bruce reached his right hand for the pruning knife. He pushed down. His hand kept on going. The imbalance of his pants released the buckle on his left leg, his left stocking subsided, and a mosquito bit him. The night before, he had had a vision of the pleasure this errand, this flower-gathering, would be for him. Every year, Bruce and his brother and sister decorated their mother's chair on her birthday, and their father's on his. This was the first year he had come down to the garden alone. He hadn't wakened his brother and sister. They had been up all night the night before at a dance, and were tired. Anyway, he saw this flower-gathering as a personal tribute to his mother, to the flowers themselves, even to the summer. Now, as his hand came up empty from his right-hand pocket, he saw why it was empty. The pocket was bottomless, torn. It was not a pocket at all, and the knife was his mother's, a rather pretty knife with ivory sides, two folding blades, and one permanent ivory tongue that emerged from one of the steel ends. The purpose of the tongue was to break the stems of the flowers.

Bruce now saw himself as a thief, as many a borrower has before who has not been able to repay. He knew he would not be able to find the knife. It had had all the way from the pen tray on his mother's desk to here to get lost. Even if it was found, there would first have to be a search. And what would he have to show for it? A few wilted leaves. A few massacred gladiolas. Some ragged snaps. Some phlox.

Bruce hiked his pants up, and in so doing released the right-hand stocking, which subsided on his ankle. The cold metal of the dangling buckle was against his skin. Both stockings were down now. Bruce picked up the basket and started toward the gladiolas. He was crying. He always cried when he was angry, and he started to pull the flowers up by the roots. After he had stripped the third from its surrounding leaves like an ear of corn, he became aware that he was again in the red-faced and rigid presence of Tosh. Tosh was holding out a knife. A plain, small, wooden-handled one. Tosh and Bruce looked at each other.

"She don't want the roots," Tosh said. His voice was always carefully bled of all expression. It had none of that lilting madness that was part of the way of talking of the Irish maids in the house.

"I lost her knife," Bruce said. He didn't sniffle or choke. Five feet seven was too old for that. Besides, he was sweating—it was going to be a hot day all right—and sweat and tears in him were frequent enough to be indistinguishable.

There was a terrifying pause while Tosh considered his crime.

"You'll find it," Tosh finally said.

Everything, with Tosh's words, now became dependent on his finding the knife. The freshness of the flowers that they picked and put into the basket, and of the fireweed, which Tosh said would look all right braided through the lattice in the back of the chair, became dependent on the fact that he was a thief. There had to be an act of expiation. The rightness of all the ceremonies of the day, even of his lonely ascent to the house, depended upon that. He had to find the knife before there was a search for it.

The house was one of those stone dreams with arches and towers given to the world by the architectural office of H. H. Richardson. It had awnings at all the windows, and looked as if it were going to fly right off the top of its high green hill. Bruce went in the back way, across the drying yard and through the back door, and put his basket on one of the zinc-covered wooden tables in the big brown and yellow kitchen. The pendulum wall clock said seven-thirty-five, which gave him not very much time to arrange his offering—

for offering it was now more than ever, because there must not be a search. If there was a search, he had somehow got it into his head, the flowers would fade, and the flowers must not fade. He filled the huge old steel sink with water and dumped the flowers in. And the leaves. Then he went into the dining room for the Chinese Chippendale armchair that his mother sat in. It looked like the arbor—all bits of wood at odd geometric angles to each other and a little pagoda on top of the back rail. It was very delicate. He must not break it. He carried it into the kitchen.

"Ain't them lovely," the cook said as Bruce started to wind the grape leaves through the lattice.

"Just look at them flowers," the waitress and the kitchen maid said.

Bruce's brother and sister came into the kitchen.

"Hurry up," Larry said. He was practicing his long jaw so he would look more grown-up.

"We only have ten minutes," Bets said. Her jaw was already the right length, but she wouldn't have minded if it hadn't been.

"It's lucky I'm not old enough to go to dances yet," Bruce said. Then Larry and Bets began to help. Through the kitchen windows they could see the big Packard limousine being brought up for the day. They could see Beaulieu, in his uniform cap, at the wheel.

The heat was already getting to the ice in the bucket standing beside the wooden, zinc-lined kitchen icebox. Cornelius would put it in when he came up from the cellar with some coal for the stove. The stove was already going, but birthdays were always big days and you needed a lot of coal. Cornelius was the man in the house. Beaulieu was the man in the garage. Tosh was the man on the place. The knife had belonged to Bruce's grandmother—something she always carried in the pocket of her whipcord suit as she made the rounds of her acres and servants and flowers. In the same pocket she always carried an ivory whistle, to call the numerous dogs—the Great Danes, the Persian gazelle hound, and the whippet—that all lived in places they called home in the huge Tudor house in Ipswich, two miles upriver. The whistle had a hole in it, just under the hole you were meant to blow through. The hole was made the day his grandmother was thrown from her horse and a little dead branch poked right through it in the forest where she fell. She was killed by the fall, and Bruce's mother went every day to have lunch with his grandfather and take him for a drive in her car. Grandfather was nervous about driving with anyone else but Snodgrass, the family chauffeur, or Bruce's mother. But Snodgrass was dead. He had died, Bruce's father had said, of a broken heart, because he could no longer get parts for the old car. Snodgrass and the Pierce Arrow, Bruce's mother and the Lincoln coupe. Tosh on the place, and Cornelius in the house, and Beaulieu in the garage, and of all these, while Bets and Larry helped with the flowers, only Snodgrass and the Pierce Arrow had perished. Everything on a birthday was a ritual, and so with a minimum of quarreling—it was too hot to quarrel—the three of them finished the chair and carried it into the dining room.

"They say that flowers are for remembrance," Mrs. Larcom said when she saw the chair. It was the first thing she said, and the most important.

Mr. Larcom was always embarrassed by praising anything. He took the flowers for granted when it came time for his own birthday, and he could still blush. He sat down now in his own chair. Bruce and the others sat down, Mrs. Larcom gingerly so as not to crush the flowers. The butter was beginning to melt in the cut-glass butter dish on the lazy Susan. The ice in the dish had already melted. What a contrast they were, the Larcoms. His tall mother, with her oval head and hair pulled straight in a bow at the back, her tanned face and hands, and the riding suit of the inevitable morning family rodeo. His father, in his sports shirt and jodhpurs, the rimless glasses, the air of aggressive concentration as he bent over the morning paper, just as if this were an ordinary day and he were off in a few minutes for Boston and the office. His sister, Bets, with her dark hair only just up from a braid, and his brother, Larry, fair and already losing his.

"Who has a knife to open the presents with?"

Mrs. Larcom had a straight, not very flexible, but deep-toned voice that was always pleasant to hear when it was saying pleasant things. Only to Bruce was this simple question not pleasant—knives just then were not a pleasant subject. He reached for his pocket, but Bets had already got up. "I'll get your pruning knife from the desk," she said.

Not only had Bets put the phlox so it completely obscured the fireweed that was meant to be a backdrop for it but now she was about to spoil the whole occasion. Bruce's mother didn't take a tally every day of all her personal possessions, but Bruce knew that the pruning knife and the ivory whistle were valuable to her. They had always lived in the same pocket. They were his grandmother's life, and his grandmother's death.

"I can't find it," Bets said, returning from the living room.

"Never mind."

"Here," Bruce said, producing Tosh's knife from his pocket. Not until he produced it did he think of reaching for it, and not until his mother began to open her presents with it did he remember that he had pocketed it.

All that day, the events seemed to Bruce to work backward from the knife. It was as if all history were bound up with it. And the promise of heat became a kept promise, indeed, as they all went horseback riding, and then picnicking on the river, and then to Grandfather's for supper. Between all these diversions, Bruce looked at the flowers, his father looked through them, his mother looked at Bruce, and Bets and Larry looked at each other. The flowers did not fade. There was nothing wonderful about this, perhaps, to those who take flowers for granted. Bets and Larry did. Mr. Larcom did. Flowers were not parties or newspapers. They had no language. They had no sex.

"They are just there," Bets said on the river, "to be cut or to be thrown out." Bruce was paddling stern, since he was the heavier of the two, and he could see the dark, so recently braided hair of his sister glint in the sudden highlights made by the sun as it filtered through the overhanging trees.

"But they are pretty," Bruce said.

"Not if you have to arrange them."

Bruce hated paddling stern. He had never learned to steer.

"I love to arrange them," he said.

"You lost Mother's knife, didn't you?"

"You knew that when you went looking for it."

"What d'you mean?"

"I can't explain. It's all backward."

"But I didn't," Bets said, turning round. "I didn't know anything."

"Look out," he said, but they ran into the bank anyway. The other canoe, with Larry and his father paddling and his mother in the middle, was disappearing around a corner.

He said, "Are you going to tell?"

"She knows," Bets answered him. "Wasn't that one of Tosh's knives we opened the presents with?"

"Would she recognize it?" Bruce asked.

Brother and sister looked at each other.

"If I borrowed his, why would she think I borrowed hers?"

Bets shipped her paddle. She was still looking at him.

"Because you pocketed his," she said.

"I might have been absentminded."

"You were," she said.

"It might have been anyone," he said. "It isn't only a *pruning* knife, you know. Anyone could have taken it. For any reason."

"Not that early in the morning."

"Did she know it was there yesterday?"

"Did you?"

"All right," he said, "it was a silly question."

"I will look for it when we get back," Bets said.

"For God's sake, don't," he said.

"Why?"

"I can't explain."

"Is there something wrong with you?"

"Probably."

"I'm trying to help you."

"D'you think Mother'll be mad?"

"What do you think?"

"No. It's her birthday. But that isn't a reason."

"Don't you want me to help you?"

He told her about the flowers' fading if there was a search. "But then," he said, "maybe the knife has already been found. Maybe Tosh has found it."

"But Mother already knows," Bets said.

"The search would spoil everything," Bruce explained.

"The search has already started," Bets said. "I started it. And if you had looked for the knife, you would have started it."

She began to push the canoe away from the bank with the paddle.

"It's all over with," she said.

"You see," Bruce triumphantly said, backing water, "you did know it was me that lost it when you went looking for it."

"I can't explain," Bets said, pushing violently against the river-bank.

"It's all backward," he said.

She refused to turn around to look at him, even though his eyes were boring holes in her back.

They were catching up with Larry and their parents when Bets said, "Why do you always feel you have to give somebody something to get something you want? Don't you ever feel that anybody owes you something?"

"I have to get something I want if I want to give somebody something," Bruce said.

"What do you want for your birthday?" Bets said.

"A pruning knife like Grandma's."

"Mother gave me a party when I was your age," Bets said.

"I'm not a girl," Bruce answered.

They paddled a little while in silence. The heat, even with the river breeze, was overwhelming. A haze rose over the water, and the yellow pond lilies rose on snakelike stems from the lagoons. Dragonflies flashed over the canoe into the increasing shadows. Treacherous grass promontories and islands of grass had marked the beginning of their trip, but now that the day was more than half over the trees grew thicker and thicker, and very soon they would reach Grandfather's landing in Ipswich, where, instead of having their mother to lunch, he would have them all to supper. These suppers were not easy occasions, but Bruce never failed to be impressed by the big house, with its endless shadows and silences, its chiming clocks, and its shafts of sunlight almost palpable in the surrounding distances. Also, its incredible population of bronze statues, mostly of animals, and ghostly reminiscences of the wintergreen that had been sprayed over the doggy carpets so often that it clung even now that the dogs were dead.

"Are we going home to change?" Bruce asked his sister.

"No. Beaulieu is bringing our clothes when he comes with the car."

It was the time-honored arrangement. Beaulieu always picked them up at Grandfather's landing and took the two canoes back on the roof of the beach wagon to the Larcom landing, where the trip started. Sometimes he took the Larcoms, too, but this time, evidently, they were to change at Grandfather's. Bruce loved this arrangement, as it meant he could bathe in the huge Crane bathtub, and change in the big bedroom that was furnished with tables and chairs and sofas just like a sitting room, and had a double bed with a high, arcaded headboard and a pair of big pillows with starched white pillow shams embroidered with raised initials. (Years later, when he was taking a last, long look at his favorite room in his favorite museum in Paris, a guard was to say searchingly to him, *"Cela vous est important, n'est-ce pas, monsieur?"* The Larcoms had always had French governesses, and they all would have understood the question. But Bruce was the only one who would have answered, "Yes, all this is important to me. The whistle is important. The knife is important. The flowers are important.")

He was glad that the possibility of a general search for the knife was reduced to this evening, if it took place at all, and to the house, since it would be dark when they got home. Not to spoil the day, that was the important thing, even though the day was spoiled.

"It was a good play," his mother was saying at supper at Grandfather's over the tablecloth and crystal, "even if the last act wasn't up to the others."

Grandfather was owlish and had beautiful hands. He kept taking off one pair of glasses and putting on another one and then another all during the meal. When he wasn't doing this, he was piling up the salad and entrée forks and then laying them side by side, and then the soup and dessert spoons and doing likewise. His conversation was a little bit like that of Tosh's. "Then it wasn't a good play," he said.

Bruce had rather settled something with Bets this afternoon on the river, and now, for the first time, Grandfather's pronouncements, all in low key and couched, as it were, under the moustache, made sense to him.

"A bowl," his grandfather said, "may be a good bowl, but not if it has a hole in it."

There was a cut-crystal glass of cold raspberry juice at everyone's place in concession to the heat, and the great casement windows of the dining room with their glittering diamond panes had been left open and the curtains drawn back.

"There was a promise of heat in the air this morning," Grandfather had said at one point.

"When people say it's going to be a hot day, that means it already is one," his mother had said.

Bruce looked at his grandfather and his mother. He had not cried since this morning. He was too old to cry. But a feeling came to him now that things had finally been either taken out of his hands or put into them—he could not have said which. Larry and his father ate their soup in silence, Larry's fair hair thin on his forehead, his long-jawed grown-up expression on his face, his father's glasses brilliant as the windows, his eyes as blank as the dark behind them.

It was like the dragonflies on the river, Bruce thought. Somebody said that they only lived for a day, and yet they were beautiful. Somehow, their beauty was over before it was begun, like finding the knife before there was a search for it.

"It could be a Lowestoft bowl, Father," his mother said.

"Or a work of art," Grandfather said.

"A bowl has to be broken sometime," Bruce said. He was eating soup, but he had put his spoon down to speak, and he had all their attention.

"Curious," Grandfather said, "how Lowestoft has taken over. In my day it was Minton. And in the days of Bernard Palissy, it was Bernard Palissy."

But as he spoke he looked at Bruce—possibly, Bruce felt, for the first time.

On the way home in the station wagon, with Beaulieu at the wheel, Bruce's mother sat in the back with Bruce. The two other children sat in the middle seat, and Bruce's father up front. It was one of those beach wagons made of wood, with roll-down isinglass curtains, and seats around the sides and back like a paddy wagon. A year later, it was to be driven by Beaulieu to the top of their hill and left there without being sufficiently braked, and was to plunge down and wreck on one of the two stone cairns that served as gateposts to the driveway. There would not be enough left of it to hold a single memory.

Not a single one.

None.

Bruce's mother said, "It doesn't matter about the knife."

"How do you know about it?" Bruce asked her. He reviewed in his mind all Bets' reasons, but for some reason of his own rejected them.

"Because you had a knife," she said.

"It was Tosh's."

"Was it?"

"Yes. You know, he always uses those knives with thick wooden handles and thin blades."

"Does he?"

Bruce, hearing the deep tones of his mother's voice in the darkness, knew from the sound that this conversation was not going to be the round robin he had had in the afternoon with Bets.

"Yes, he does," Bruce said.

"And what do you use?"

Bruce began to cry. The second time today. He knew she was looking at him in the dark. "An ivory whistle," he said.

There was a long silence between them. Bruce wondered if Bets was listening. There was enough silence in the car for everybody to be listening.

His mother put her arm around his shoulders. "You don't like things to be broken, do you?"

"Or lost," he said.

"Or faded," Bets put in.

His mother tightened her arm. "It was a lovely birthday. The flowers were lovely."

As they pulled up to the house, Bruce made out a figure outlined in the light that came from above the great stone arch of the front door. It was Tosh. As they got out of the car, he held something toward them in his hand.

"You know what the promise of heat is, don't you?" his mother asked Bruce. Bruce again sensed something beyond the round robin.

"Heat," he said.

His mother pushed him gently toward Tosh. "He has something for you," she said.

A Place Not on the Map

GEORGE BLAKE

(FROM THE LITERARY REVIEW)

"You can take the ferry to Pedreña and walk to Las Horas," I told him. "When you get to Las Horas you will see the mountain very close. There is a lake at the foot of the mountain, and you can go for a swim on the way back."

"It looks pretty high," Henderson said.

We sat in the shade of the umbrella in front of the Café Pollo. The *Sierra Andrea* rode at anchor in the Gulf. Across the Gulf were the red tile roofs and square white houses of Pedreña. Beyond Pedreña in the mist was the outline of the mountain.

"No. It is really only a rather high hill, and in Las Horas there is a *cantina* where you can buy cheese, bread and wine."

"She probably won't want to go," he said, "and we might get lost. We're always getting lost. You won't change your mind and come?"

I told him again that I was going to Somo. "But the ferry stops first at Pedreña. I'll be going that far with you."

"I wish you'd change your mind," Henderson said.

"Look," I told him, "if you're going over to climb the mountain you better eat something. If you take the ten-thirty ferry you'll be back here by seven tonight. You can drink all the wine you want when you get back. You can drink all night."

"I'll have some coffee," Henderson said. "All I really want is some coffee. You order for me. I feel like a fool not speaking the language. But don't order anything else. All I need is some coffee."

I waved the waiter over and said, *"Café con leche, por favor."*

"Pan con mantequilla?"

I told him only the coffee and cream.

"Fruta?" he asked.

"You want some fruit, Henderson?"

He was looking across the Gulf toward the mountain. He shook his head. "It looks pretty high to me."

"No fruta," I told the waiter. "It's not even a mountain," I told him. "You'll climb it in two hours."

"She probably won't want to go anyway," Henderson said.

"Why don't you go alone?" I said.

"I want to be with her every minute," he said. "But it's been hell. Ever since we found out. I wonder if I've done the right thing. For God's sake watch what you say. Here she comes."

She was a young, tired, not quite pretty girl, but her eyes were frank and a lovely shade of blue. When she sat in the shade under the umbrella her eyes were violet. She didn't look like a Bryn Mawr girl, but it had been quite a long while since I had seen a Bryn Mawr girl. She spoke like a Bryn Mawr girl though.

"Why did you come to Santander?" she asked. The waiter came over and she ordered coffee and cream, bread and butter, reading the words very crisply from her Spanish Phrase Book.

"Because no Americans come here. I wanted to come because there are no Americans here."

"But we're here," she said.

"I know," I said. "You're here."

"Do you want to go over to the mountain this morning?" Henderson said.

She didn't answer him. She spoke to me. "Oh, I couldn't. I'd tire. I tire very quickly, you see. Because the doctor in

New York at Medical Center said I would die before next Christmas, and the doctor in Lisbon said the same thing, and the doctor in Madrid said it would be before next Christmas. I asked him about Thanksgiving, but he didn't know that holiday. I told him about the Pilgrims and the turkey and he was very kind, but he didn't understand. No, I couldn't possibly climb the mountain."

She spoke as though it were far away like a childhood illness. I wouldn't have believed her if I hadn't known. Looking at her fine eyes and tan arms and face and remembering the lovely way she walked, it was difficult to believe her.

"Are you going over to the mountain?" she said.

"He doesn't want to go," Henderson said. "He's going over to Somo."

"Somo?"

"Nobody goes to Somo," I said. "It's a very long, deserted beach. The tourists go to the beach here in Santander but not to Somo. There's nothing to do over at Somo. There is no café. There are no gardens. There's nothing to do. You walk along the beach and don't see anyone, and then you rest on the dunes and watch the gulls."

"Oh!" she said. "How lovely! No, I mean it sounds quite lovely! Do let's go to Somo!"

"You wouldn't get tired?" Henderson said.

"But I could rest on the dunes!"

"Maybe he doesn't want us to go to Somo with him."

"We wouldn't populate the lovely deserted beach too much?"

I glanced at her. She smiled wonderfully. "Don't be absurd," I said.

"I'm never absurd," she said, half smiling.

"I'll go back to the hotel and get our things," Henderson said. "Do you want me to get your bathing suit?"

"There's no place to change," I said.

"There are the dunes," she said.

"Yes," I said. "There are the dunes."

Three curve-prowed fishing boats had docked while we talked, and now four old women in black were crossing the Square of the Broken Column carrying the headless bonitos. They carried the fish by their tails. The old women walked in a row, and the fishes' red gore dripped onto the blue and white tiles. The first woman went into the Café Pinchero on the other side of the Square.

"He's very good to me," she said. "He's very sweet. And his wife is wonderful about it all. I hope my talking this way doesn't embarrass you, but I know he's told you everything."

"We met only last night," I said.

"I know, but I know he tells everything. But he's very sweet. He's very kind."

I didn't say anything.

"And it's not that he feels sorry for me. No, he agreed to meet me in Lisbon before he knew about it. I wouldn't even have told him in Lisbon, but I was sick and then he knew. We stayed at the Mundial. Do you know the Mundial?"

"Yes, but I didn't stay there." I told her where I had stayed.

"Oh, near the American Express off the Avenida de Libertad? But we didn't stay long at the Mundial. The Mundial was horrid. We went to Guincho. It was lovely! The wild surf! And then Sintra, we stayed at Sintra! The carriage rides! Lord Byron's house!"

She had a lovely voice, soft and frank and utterly controlled.

"I know I talk a bit. I didn't used to. But I do now. I don't know why. That's not true. I do know."

"I don't mind," I said. I don't think she even heard me.

"And I know I say everything is lovely. But it's because everything seems so. This café! The sea! The sun!" She held her slender hand beyond the umbrella's shade in the sunlight.

"Ah, here he is. My, what a lot of things he has! Blankets! And a bottle of wine!"

"I think I've got everything," Henderson said.

"And my lovely straw hat!"

"It's almost ten-thirty," I said. "Let's go down to the ferry."

There were always priests on the ferry, and they sat very straight holding their black, wide-brimmed hats on their knees. They sat turned from the waist with their faces into the breeze. The old women in black sat with their hands folded, not looking into the breeze. Between their knees hung the limp sacks empty of potatoes and onions, which they had sold at the back doors of restaurants and cafés when the mist was still on the Gulf. The old women had brown worn hands, and sitting next to them on the slatted benches you smelled the garlic and the onions. The old priest at the end of the bench uncorked his green bottle of wine and drank, tilting the bottle so that the green of the glass and the purple of the wine were hectic with the sun's yellow, and then he passed the bottle to the young priest who refused and passed it again along the bench until it came to Henderson's girl. She tilted the bottle with her tan slender hands, afraid that it would fall, her face arched toward the sun which silently exploded into myriad suns in the wine. She turned, her face flushed, her lips wet and red, smiling. "What's left is yours." I drank and passed the bottle back to the old priest.

He smiled gravely and said, *"Buena vida."*

"Isn't he sweet!" she said. "Isn't he lovely!"

"I'm glad you're my girl," Henderson said.

"I wish I were your woman," she said.

"No, you don't, not really," Henderson said.

"No, I really wish I were your woman," she said.

"You're just saying that," Henderson said. "And it doesn't matter. I don't care."

She turned toward me and almost smiled and then looked straight ahead toward the mountain.

Henderson whispered to her, and she said, "I feel fine, I really do." Henderson whispered to her again, and she said, "You mustn't worry. Why do you worry so? I'm really fine, I feel splendid, and I don't want you to worry. It makes me nervous when you worry. Don't, please. You promised."

Henderson continued to whisper, and I felt her move away from him against my shoulder with each gentle sway of the ferry. The mist was no longer on the Gulf or the hills or the mountain now. You could see the mountain sharp and hard beyond the houses of Pedreña and the hills which led to Las Horas. You could not see Somo. Somo was in the bay.

"Do we get off here?" Henderson asked.

"No. You can't see Somo. It's in the bay."

The old women got off, and as the ferry backed off from the stone dock you saw the old women start up the dusty road past the white church. An old man sat fishing at the end of the dock. Beside him lay four small bonitos. A yellow cat hunched, staring at the fish. When we turned into the bay the old women were moving black dots far beyond the white church, and the cat was something motionless and yellow at the end of the dock.

The priests got off the ferry first and then Henderson, and he held her hand as she stepped from the deck onto the rocks. She walked between us down the dusty road. Henderson carried the blankets and the bottle of wine and her blue Pan Am bag. I pointed out the path through the cork grove, and we were for a short time in the shade of the trees. It was hot. Piles of cork bark were piled along the path. You smelled the cork. It was very hot under the trees. The sea was coming closer. Suddenly there was nothing but dunes and sharp sand grass and the sound of the surf. We walked down toward the surf. There was nothing but the wind, the taste of salt in the spray, and the sea.

"It's lovely!" she said. "It really is! I feel very involved!"

Henderson didn't say anything.

"I mean I really do! And I think I'll change immediately!"

"Where you going to change?" Henderson said.

"Why, behind the dunes," she said.

Henderson handed her the Pan Am bag. "We won't watch," he said.

"Watch?" she asked. "Of course not. But why should you? But I wouldn't care. I really wouldn't, it's so lovely here."

Henderson followed me down toward the surf. He sat down beside me on the damp, darker sand and uncorked the bottle. It wasn't the same. There had been no Americans in Santander. Then I met Henderson at the Pinchero. Now Santander wasn't the same. Now even the Pinchero wasn't the same. I shook my head.

"Go on and take a drink," Henderson said.

"All right," I said.

Now Somo wasn't the same. It would be all right back at the the café. You could sit in a crowded café and be alone. The café was always crowded at night. It was always better at night.

"Here I am," she said.

She wore a modest pink and white suit. Her hair was loose. The wind lifted her long hair as she ran toward us.

"Why haven't you changed?" she said. "I want to go right in!"

"I don't think you should," Henderson said.

"You change and I'll wait. I'll only go in up to here." She held her hand's edge against her knee.

"I don't want to go in," Henderson said. "You go in with her."

I changed behind the dunes where her things lay, and she was waiting and we walked into the surf.

"Don't worry," she said. "I'm an excellent swimmer."

I didn't say anything.

"I'm timing you!" Henderson called. "Ten minutes and then you come out and rest!"

We didn't speak. We knifed through the first breaker. We swam in the hollows of the waves. We didn't speak. She moved through the water with absolute control. Her arms were blond, freckled blades. Each time she turned her face to breathe I saw her happy, shining eyes. We moved almost touching side by side, rising on each swell, feeling the body of the sea beneath us.

I heard Henderson again. This time he stood in the surf, waving the empty bottle. She didn't stop. We were way down the beach from him. He ran toward us. He waved the empty bottle and yelled.

"We better go in," I said.

She didn't answer. She kept on swimming. I followed behind her, and then she turned in the direction of the shore. She stood in the foam, glistening and tan, and when I came up to her she said, "If I come to Somo every day I won't die, will I?"

I didn't know how to answer.

"I won't, will I? I can't die if I come every day, can I?"

I took her fine hand. "Let's go up and rest," I said.

"I wouldn't, would I?"

"Nobody would," I said.

Henderson was angry at her and at me. She was very sweet to him, and he kept saying, "You'll see, you'll be sick tonight."

She was. It only seemed that she was abruptly tired on the way back under the dark green leaves of the cork trees. By the time we were on the dusty road Henderson had said several times, "I'll carry you," and then she didn't pretend anymore. He passed me her blue Pan Am bag and the blanket. He threw the empty bottle over the bank into the field. Geraniums nodded red on the bank, and she was very quiet, cradled in his arms, very small, with her head on his shoulder. Her eyes were not always closed. She smiled at me with her eyes and I smiled back.

The girls from the farms dressed in bright dresses sang all the way back on the ferry. The yellow lights of the *Sierra Andrea* were multiplied on the water. She fell asleep on the way back. The girls sang all the way. They got off first and went immediately to stroll in twos back and forth past the cafés.

Henderson took her immediately to the hotel. He carried

her under the street lights among the umbrellas of the cafés. He didn't want any help. I watched him for a while and then went to my room above the Pinchero. There was another desperate letter from my wife.

I packed and changed. I carried my bag and Henderson's blanket and her blue Pan Am bag downstairs, went into the restaurant and paid, and then went across the Square to the Café Pollo. I was surprised to see Henderson. He didn't sit.

"Here's your blanket and her bag," I said.

"Blanket?" he said. "Who cares about the blanket."

"How is she?" I said.

"You shouldn't have urged her to go to Somo," he said.

"I didn't," I said.

"It was you," he said.

I thought, What the hell. "How is she?" I said.

"You urged her to go and tomorrow she may begin to feel the pain," he said.

"She's not in pain now?" I said.

"Almost. She said, 'I feel it waiting to come.'"

"She's a fine girl," I said. "She's a wonderful girl. I hope the pain never comes."

"Oh, it'll come, it'll come."

"Do you want a drink?" I asked. "I'm catching the Taf in an hour, but we have more than enough time. We have enough time for a bottle."

"I want her hat," he said. "I only came to get her hat. She woke up and wanted that crazy hat. I want the hat for when she wakes up in the morning."

"There's the blanket and her Pan Am bag," I said. "I think we left the hat over in Somo. I think it's on a dune over in Somo."

"What'll I do if she wakes up and wants it? I mean, what'll I do?"

I didn't say anything.

He sat down abruptly. "I think I will have that drink."

"No, you better go back in case she wakes up," I said.

He didn't say anything for a moment. The café was filling.

All the women had dark hair and dark eyes and were attractive in that way. The gentlemen were all very polite. There was much kissing of ladies' hands. The old waiter and the young waiter were very busy among the umbrellas. From inside the café you could hear the radio. At the yacht club on the terrace over the water couples danced in the blue light. You heard the violins from the yacht club when the music from the café radio ceased and the announcer spoke rapidly in Spanish.

"They play the same songs over here," he said. "You can't get away." Then he rose and walked hurriedly away and then hurried back to the table. "I want to thank you," he said. "You've been very kind." He spoke very formally.

"I'm sorry about the hat," I said.

"It's quite all right," he said.

We shook hands, and he went away among the umbrellas across the Square to the hotel next to the Pinchero.

The blanket didn't matter. Her crazy floppy straw hat apparently mattered, but that was lost over at Somo. Her blue Pan Am bag didn't matter, but I couldn't leave it on an empty seat in the night in Santander, Spain. I took it along. It was with my bag on the rack above my seat on the silver Taf. But I forgot to take it when the train stopped in Madrid. I took a cab to the Pension Susana on the Marqués de Cubas. I slept until noon, changed and shaved, paid the bill, got my bag and took a cab to the Ritz. I ate a splendid meal beautifully served at the Ritz. They told me at the Pan Am office in the Ritz that I couldn't get a flight out until tomorrow. That was all right. Around eight o'clock I phoned my wife. I lay across the bed with the receiver in my right hand and a cigarette in the other waiting to hear her voice. On the wall over the dresser was Goya's "Lady with Masked Men."

The first words she said were, "What did they say at the Lahey Clinic?"

"I'm flying out tomorrow morning," I said. "I'll phone you when I get into Kennedy."

She asked the same question again. I answered her question.

"Then why didn't you go out to the Mayo?"

I told her.

"But they can't be sure," she said. "They're never really sure. And why in heaven's name did you suddenly go to Spain?"

"I don't know."

"You don't know!"

We talked a little longer, but it all went like that. And then we hung up. I went over to the Club 31 for dinner. I took a long time dining. I was the last one to leave. I lay in my room in the dark for a long time. On the wall was Goya's "Lady" deep in the forest, and the four men still had their masks on. It was probably over in the Prado. I wouldn't have time to visit the Prado.

The next night I sat with my wife out on the patio in the close suburban dark. The boys were in bed, but not asleep, and we could hear them talking.

"You've got to stop worrying," she said. "You've got to believe what they told you at Medical Center. You're fine. You haven't got *it*. Do you think they'd lie to you? Do you think I'd lie to you? You must believe me. Remember Fred Stratton?"

Fred Stratton had thought he'd had *it*. He shot himself last spring.

"I'm not Fred Stratton," I said, "and I believe you."

"Oh, you must," she said. "You must!"

And then she went on about *it* and how I must believe her, but I wasn't thinking of whether or not I had *it,* but about Henderson's girl, and I found myself telling her very slowly and seriously about it all.

"I don't believe you," she said.

"Wait till I finish," I said.

"I don't want to hear," she said.

"Please," I said.

"I don't want to hear," she said. "But now I know why you ran off to Spain. There was this girl and you—!"

It wasn't any good. She wouldn't let me finish. I sat out on the patio alone for a long while. When I came in she said, "I knew you were lying. Here, look."

I took the atlas.

"See," she said. "It isn't even on the map. There's no such place."

"You need a larger map, one of those big atlases," I said, stupidly.

"Don't be silly," she said.

"Look, let me finish."

"I don't want to hear. It's quite plain. You're not telling me what really happened in Spain. I'll never really know."

She closed the atlas, covering the place that didn't show on the map where I had been with Henderson's girl.

"Let's go up," I said.

And we did. But it wasn't any good. I lay in my darkness, and she lay in her darkness, and later we began to touch the familiar geography of each other. But we didn't go into each other's country. We lay touching the borders.

"You're not going to die," she said. "Please, please, don't do what Fred Stratton did."

"I won't," I said. "And I believe you."

"Do you? Do you?"

"I feel fine, and I do believe you."

And lying there, I almost did.

I slept not dreaming of Somo or Henderson's girl or anything. It was a good sleep. And the whole day went by before I remembered to worry about whether or not I was really going to live.

KAY BOYLE
The Wild Horses

(FROM THE SATURDAY EVENING POST)

DAN MINOS WAS a boy who collected all kinds of odd information from the newspapers he read—bits and pieces of things that had already taken place, or were still taking place, here and there in the world—such as the report that an octopus in Berlin, Germany, was devouring itself at the rate of a half inch of tentacle per day. One of the aquarium officials had stated that the octopus was suffering from some emotional upset, and if the situation continued, it would certainly be dead by the end of the month. The boy read this and looked at his own gnawed fingernails, and then looked quickly at something else.

Once he read about how scientists are trying to dilute the venom in the stings of jellyfish that drift along the eastern seaboard like fringed umbrellas (as the paper put it), pulsing in and out among the bathers, with limp, curved handles hanging under them, while the tide, or some unseen hand, opens and closes them continuously. This poison, went the story, is stored in cups along the umbrella handles, and it acts in the same way as the stuff South American Indians tip their arrowheads with, causing paralysis, failure of the respiratory organs, and death in the case of small sea animals. Another time there was a half-page report on the remarkable navigating abilities of the green turtle, saying that the U.S. Navy was financing a study of how this large seafarer finds the pinpoint island of its birth.

When Dan's mother came back to their Brooklyn apartment at night, she would bring some newspaper or other with her that a customer had left behind on a table in the restaurant where she worked. Some nights it might be the *Herald Tribune* or maybe *The New York Times* that she carried with her handbag into the kitchen; other nights it might be the *Journal-American* or the *Daily News*. But whatever paper it was, Dan would go through the pages of it in his room before he went to sleep, not noticing the name of the paper or the date, but, reading the columns eagerly, as if in search of some final communiqué that would tell him how either beast or man had coped with the predicament of circumstances; as if seeking in the silent doom of animals without knowing precisely what he sought, some indication of what his own vocabulary might one day be.

If you have come to the conclusion that Dan Minos speculated on these things he read because the world of newsprint was the only world he functioned in, you are wrong; for he had as well the daily world of high school, and he had major-league baseball to follow, and television to present to him as reality the myths of power by which America lives. It was more that he carried the news items he read like a kind of shield between himself and others, a shield that was never emblazoned with any likeness of himself, but with that of aquarium official, or of scientist isolating the sting of jellyfish, or naval experimenter tagging green turtles at Ascension Island. Once it was the likeness of a German priest he carried, a priest who had been sitting in the front row of the circus when the lion tamer clutched at his heart and fell to the floor of the enclosed arena. The wild beasts had slunk down from their perches, the newspaper item said, and moved stealthily toward the fallen lion tamer while the spectators watched with bated breath for what was absolutely certain to take place. And then the priest had run forward, pulled open the door of the cage, warded off the lions with a chair, and dragged the stricken man to safety. (Whether or not the lion tamer died of his heart attack, the newspaper did not say.)

It was only the story of the harness-racing horse that went

berserk in an airfreighter eight thousand feet above the ocean that Dan couldn't put to any immediate use.

"Sometimes I've thought of being a pilot, a commercial pilot," Dan said to his mother that evening when she came home, "but then I read this thing about the horse in the airplane and maybe I don't feel the same about pilots any more."

"If my opinion was to be asked," his mother said, "I'd say go ahead and be a commercial pilot, and forget about the horse." She worked as a waitress, and she never gave him any real trouble except when he came in so late at night that, for hours, she'd have been walking her high heels sideways up and down the street outside. Sometimes it was three o'clock when he'd come home, and she'd be walking back and forth on the Brooklyn street without so much as a Kleenex to stop her crying, complaining about him to anyone passing by. "He doesn't know five o'clock in the afternoon from midnight," she'd say to anyone at all. "I don't know how he gets along. He can't tell good from bad." Or she'd give a description of him, in case someone had seen him, saying, "He's nearly six foot tall, and his shoulders are broad, and he's nicely built, the way his father was. He'd be good-looking if he went and got his hair cut every now and then."

She got up now from the kitchen table and crossed the room and took a can of beer out of the refrigerator, and she swore under her breath as the new-type, built-in-the-can opener tore a piece out of her nail. "But my opinion isn't worth anything to anybody, living or dead," she said.

Dan looked at her dark orange hair and her face bleached white as a china cup, with the various features painted carefully on it. "There were six horses in the plane," he said, thinking of this thing that had taken place yesterday or maybe the day before, "and this one, this champion, he panicked. He'd been winning harness races everywhere— Australia, New Zealand, all over—the paper said. He was worth seventy-five thousand dollars, and he was kicking and rearing like at a rodeo."

"All they had to do was turn around," the mother said, drinking exquisitely from the can. "Planes can always turn around and go back, the way cars can't. You get yourself on a thruway in a car, and if you're heading west you have to go to Chicago whether you want to go there or not."

"This plane was going to Montreal," Dan said. "They couldn't go back."

"What's so special about Montreal?" the mother asked, her small cherry, upper lip moustached with foam.

"The handler, he said they'd tried cutting the sling around the horse's ribs so they could get him to lie down," the boy said. "There were three of them trying to quiet him, but he threw them off, and his front legs were hanging out over the side of the stall. He was smashing against the cockpit, like trying to get to the controls. The other five horses had started acting up, so that's when the pilot told them what to do."

"I don't want to hear what they did," the mother said, taking another swig of beer.

"You can't change it by not listening," Dan said. "It happened. You can't make things different by just looking the other way."

"If you drank a can of beer every now and then, things would look different to you, whether they were or not," his mother said. "It would relax you. It would do you good."

"The pilot of the airfreighter said the horse had to be destroyed," Dan said, perhaps not even having heard her speak. "That's the word he used," he explained. "But they didn't have a gun."

"They could have pushed the horse out the hatch," the mother said. She got up from her chair and carried the empty beer can across the kitchen to where it had to go. "For a horse worth seventy-five thousand dollars they could have afforded a parachute," she said, daintily pressing her foot, in a bedroom slipper trimmed with gilded feathers, on the pedal of the garbage pail. When the white lid gaped open, she dropped the beer can inside. "Can't you see that horse parachuting out of the plane, pulling the rip cord and everything?" she said, and she gave a little scream of laughter. Then she took another can of beer from the refrigerator and walked carefully back to the table in her wedge-soled slippers and sat down. "So this time maybe you'll open it for me," she said to him as she had said it on so many other evenings.

Dan took the can in his narrow fingers and twisted the flat metal tongue from its misted top. "I bought another pair of eyelashes today. Better quality," she went on. "Real dark long ones, with a new kind of stickum on them. If I go to the show tomorrow night, maybe you'll help me put them on."

"So when the flight engineer got the word from the pilot about what to do, he grabbed a fire ax," Dan said. He was seeing it exactly as it must have been.

"Stop it!" his mother cried out with sudden ferocity. "I don't have to hear it! I have a hard enough time working myself to death on my feet all day!"

"You have to hear it," Dan said. He looked at her small, bright, trembling mouth and her quivering chin, but he did not seem to see her. "If you don't know whether you're on the side of the horse they killed or on the side of the pilot, there's no sense trying to work out your life. You have to decide that first," he said.

"On the side of the horse or the side of the pilot? You're crazy!" she cried out in fury, her hand too agitated now to lift the can of beer.

And then, two nights later, on Christopher Street, in Greenwich Village, Dan made the acquaintance of the girl. It could have been any month and any Saturday, with no extremes of any kind in the bluish New York air. It had not yet begun to go dark when Dan saw the old man lying across the curb near the corner of Seventh Avenue, lying flat on his thin back with his legs sticking out into the street, so that the passing traffic had to swing around them. His ancient trousers were slashed as if by a knife, and his shoes were split by the bunions and corns he had carried around with him for a half century or more. His small head, economically crowned with a crew cut of the purest white, lay in a semblance of ease and comfort on the sidewalk paving. The same white bristled without hostility along his jaws, and his cheekbones were bright as apples on either side of his short, scarlet nose. Beside him, in a black sweater and slacks, the girl squatted, her face masked by a swinging curtain of long, straight, almost tinsel-colored hair. She was trying to raise the old man by his shoulders, and she was trying to push her bracelets and the black sweater sleeves back on her forearms, to get these encumbrances out of the way. "Repeatedly striking with force between the horse's eyes"—the newspaper line kept going, for no good reason, through Dan's mind as he stooped down—"the flight engineer brought the frenzied pacer to its knees, and the ordeal of terror for man and beast was over."

"He looks as though he's been here a week," the girl said.

"I'll get his shoulders," Dan said, and the girl shifted out of his way, on the heels of her loafers.

The mottled-tweed jacket the man wore was soft and expensive to the touch; but however good it had once been, and whatever tall and elegant stranger had worn it once with grace, frayed wool now hung like feathers from the cuffs and from the jaunty lapels. As Dan drew him up onto the sidewalk, the girl moved on her heels beside them, her knees in the tight black slacks almost touching her chin, her bracelets ringing musically when she placed her palms beneath the old man's head. The three of them might have been quite alone in the crowded street. No one slackened his pace, no one turned to look in their direction, perhaps because of the sad, sharp odor of grieving dreams and rotted teeth that lay in an aura around the sleeping man. Dan knew that aura well. It was there winter and summer, in snow or in rain, in the gutters and alleyways of the city streets he wandered. It lay in stupor under the park benches in the early mornings when drunks sobbed aloud to grass and stone the furious accusations of their pain.

"You'd better get that pint out of his hip pocket," Dan said to the silky lengths of the girl's hair, knowing, too, the exact size and shape the flask would be. "Sometimes when they fall, it cuts them up right through their clothes."

"You're sharp, aren't you, kid?" the girl said. For the first time now she looked up at him, and he saw that her eyes were wide and dark and stormy, and her brows and lashes were smudged like charcoal across her face. "I happen to live in this city," she said. "I happen to live right on this street."

Dan still held the little man under the armpits, and as he looked down at the girl he thought of the things that might be of interest to say. He might tell her that in Japan a drunk is called *otora-san*, which means "Honorable Mr. Tiger," and that there are over a hundred and fifty sobering-up stations over there called "Tiger Boxes." He could even give her the statistics, saying that just last year one hundred and twenty-eight thousand and ninety-seven drunks had been taken by the police to "Tiger Boxes" to sleep it off. But he had got the little old man in a sitting position, with his neat head fallen forward on his breast, and it did not seem the moment to speak.

The girl reached into the little man's back pocket and took out the gold-and-red-lettered bottle that had clung so perilously to his hip. "Two houses up, there's an alley where he can lie down, where the fuzz won't see him," she said. She slipped the half-empty flask into the depths of her black shoulder bag, her bracelets ringing like sleigh bells as she moved.

They were walking now, the little old man held upright between them and Dan thought of the Potawatomi Indians on Michigan's Upper Peninsula drinking for solace, as one newspaper had said. The professor who made the report had been drinking for two years with them, and he said that alcohol now substituted for the tribal customs and rituals that had disappeared from their lives. Alcohol, the professor stated to the press, had given them the illusion that their ancestral rights had restored to them the high status that Potawatomi men had held until the white man had come upon the scene. "This professor said drinking was a way for them of asking for pity," Dan wanted to say to the girl, but he didn't say it. Nor did he tell her that in Brazil the police let sleeping drunks lie as long as they didn't block the sidewalk. With the little man propelled between them, they had come to the alleyway, and there seemed no reason to speak of things that were taking place so far away.

"Get him to the end, back there behind the garbage cans," the girl said, and the pigeons who had been pecking at the paving stones hurried aside to let them pass.

The girl lowered her half of the little man to the ground, and Dan could not see the back of her neck because of the window shade of hair drawn down across her shoulders. But he saw her slender waist and her narrow hips and the long, slim, tapering legs in the black slacks, and he could not look away.

"I'll put my jacket under his head," he said, once the little man lay flat on his back in comfort.

The girl waited until he had folded it under the neat head, and then she drew the old man's right hand free of the elegant frayed sleeve and laid it, palm down, on his breast.

"Give me the other one," she said to Dan. It lay as if cast off, as if forgotten, on the alley stone, and Dan lifted it while she took the whiskey flask out of her bag. Then she bent the old man's will-less arm so that his two hands lay upon his heart, and she closed his fingers around the flask so that he—this ancient, malodorous infant in his asphalt crib—would find it there in solace when he awakened. "Regulations," the girl said. "Orders from the top."

She stood up now, and Dan saw that she was not tall, and that her hair was parted in the middle, and that she had no lipstick on her mouth. "This is my job. I get paid for it," she was saying, and a look of singular shrewdness was in her stormy eyes. "I've got quite an important position. I get paid by the city," she said.

"If they're hiring people, I'd be free to work every night," Dan said. They walked down the alley together, past the last of the pigeons hastening back and forth in the beginning of dusk, their eyes cocked sharply in their smooth, gray-feathered skulls. And every word that he and the girl exchanged seemed as reasonable to him as the story of that other, foreign pigeon who had hopped a hundred and sixty miles across Denmark with its wings bound. The newspaper had said that it crossed two rivers, nobody knew how, to get back to where it came from. "I'd like a job like that," he said.

"You have to be twenty to work for the city," the girl said. "You look too young." As they entered Christopher Street again, the street lights came on in the early evening and she shifted her black bag higher on her shoulder, walking now with that sort of frenzied dedication that takes people across deserts and prairies, not caring about food or drink or sleep, driven toward some final destination that had no geography or name. "You have to know Spanish and French and Puerto Rican, and a lot about history," she said.

"I know about things like that," Dan said, keeping step beside her. "I read a lot." He thought of the green turtles' knowledge of the currents of the sea and the beaches they came back to, not every year but whenever they could make it, sometimes navigating more than a thousand miles to reach the hot white sands where they had been born. "The green turtles' lives are something like history," he said. "Anyway, Columbus left written records about them. I read about how they come swimming in to these beaches and dig their holes and lay their eggs. Columbus and the other explorers, like Leif Ericson and everyone, they used to eat the eggs."

"Did they eat them fried or boiled?" the girl asked sternly. "These are the things you have to know."

"That wasn't in the paper," Dan said, and his voice was troubled. They had come to the corner of Seventh Avenue, and the girl turned left without any hesitation, and Dan followed where she led. "They have something like a compass inside them—the turtles," he went on saying.

The girl and he were moving through the electric blue and yellow and red of the café lights, and through the spaces of city dark, and his head was turned to watch the side of her face changing as the lights and the diluted darkness changed. "I think I have something like that, too," Dan said. "I bet I could find New York wherever I was. I could come straight back cross the country without needing maps or roads or anything like that."

"What country?" the girl asked, with the sharp edge of something different in her voice. "What country are you talking about?"

"Well, this country. The United States. I mean, America," Dan said, as if not quite certain of the name.

"You're pretty weak on geography," the girl said. She was stepping down from the curb, over rotting orange peels, over onion tops that had once been green, and over flattened grapefruit rinds. "We haven't got a country. Wise up, kid. We've got New York," she said.

They crossed this street as they had crossed the others, moving through the altering sections of dark and light. Wherever the girl was taking him was of no importance, and the impatience of the words she spoke was transformed to gentleness by the sight of the curve of her cheekbone, and the delicacy of her temple and brow when she swung back her hair. They were entering warehouse territory now, and high above the traffic hung the letters of a sign not written in neon, but only faintly alight with the dying glow of bulbs set in its frame. VOLUNTEERS OF AMERICA, the sign read, and Dan knew that a queue of men would be standing beneath it, standing night or day, crippled or upright, sober or drunk, and, no matter what time of year it was, waiting to pass through the double doors.

"They're waiting for something to eat," Dan said.

The girl did not take the trouble to turn her head and look

at him. But she said, "They're waiting for me. I make a report on them every night. I'm the only one in the field the city trusts." And even this Dan did not question, believing as he did that everything she said was true.

Just this side of the slowly moving queue of men she slipped, without warning, into the shadows of a warehouse doorway, and flattened her shoulders and her narrow hips against the wall. "Don't let them see you," she whispered, and Dan stepped in beside her. "If they start running after me, don't move. Stay out of sight. Some of them are still very strong, even though they're old. If they once get hold of you, they squeeze you terribly in their arms," she said, her voice still hushed, "and they push their chins into your face."

"About us not having a country," Dan said. He was standing so close to her in the darkness that he could hear the breath running in and out of her mouth. "Did you read that in the paper, that we only have New York?"

"Oh, the paper!" she said in irritation.

"Sometimes there are interesting things in the paper," he said. "Last night I read about the artichoke war they're having in France."

"Do you speak French?" the girl asked quickly. "Sometimes I need it. Some nights there're Frenchmen standing in line, sailors who jumped their ships and haven't any place to go. I have to get their names. I have to make an official report on them."

Dan waited a moment, thinking of this, and then he said, "Do you report back on these men? Is that the kind of work you do?"

"You're very handsome," the girl said softly, her breath running gently in the darkness, her voice turned tender and low. "I like your hair and the way you talk, and everything, but you don't seem to understand things very well. I'm paid by the city to call them back from where they are. I'm the only one that can do it."

And this might have been the whispered password, the

valid signal given that would cause the sentries to lower their guns and let the trusted through, for now the girl stepped out of the doorway, and her bracelets rang as she made a megaphone of her hands. "Oh, Daddy, Daddy, Daddy!" she cried out in almost unbearable and strident despair, and some in the slowly advancing queue turned their heads, as if aroused from sleep, and some did not. "Oh, Pa*pa,* Pa*pa,* Pa*pa!*" she cried as a daughter from a foreign country might have cried out from the sucking undertow before the final music for the drowning played. "Oh, Daddy, Daddy, Daddy, help me!" she cried. "Oh, Popio, Popio, here I am! I'm here!" And now that she had summoned them four times, a wail of anguish rose from the throats of those who had broken from the line and stumbled back through the darkness to where she was.

Brenda, Shirley, Mary, Barbara were the names they called out as they tried to run in other men's cast-off shoes, in the outsized bags of other men's trousers, and could not. Jean, Amy, Pat, Ann, the muffled voices sobbed like foghorns, and the men in whose throats the hoarse names rose fumbled their way past light poles and fire hydrants, felt their way like blind men along the warehouse walls toward the sound and the flesh of all they had mislaid in the desert of their lives.

"We'd better get going," the girl said to Dan. She was standing beside him again in the shelter of the doorway, her breath coming fast. "Just run, just run," she whispered, and she pulled him out onto the sidewalk, her fingers tight around his hand.

They did not stop until they had reached the flight of subway steps, and there she let Dan's hand drop. As she threw back her head to look up at him in the wash of the street light, she shook her bracelets savagely.

"You were faster than any of them," Dan said. Without warning, the vision of the racing horse gone berserk plunged through his thoughts again. As it reared in terror, hammering the cockpit of the airfreighter with its frantic hoofs, Dan touched the girl's silver hair with uncertain fingers, saying, "But you'll have to stop running soon, before you get too tired."

"No, no!" the girl said, whispering it quickly. She stood close to him, looking up at him with her wild, stormy eyes. "You have to get somewhere, don't you?" she said. And then she put her arms in the black sweater sleeves tightly, tightly, around Dan's hips, tightly, as if forever, with her head pressed fiercely against the beating of his heart.

It was only for a minute, and then she was gone, running like crazy across Seventh Avenue. The green light turned to red as Dan got to the curb, and the beams of headlights poured between them, and he waited, understanding now with singular clarity the urgency of the choice to be made between horse and pilot, man and man. He could see the white of the harness pacer's eye, and the features of the airfreighter pilot's face, and he knew what should have been done in that interval when the election of either life or death hung in the balance eight thousand feet above the sea. He could not hear the pilot's voice saying *quiet, quiet* to the stampeding terror. He could not hear it naming the destination to which they were—man and horse—committed, as the course of turtle and pigeon-with-its-wings-bound named it louder and clearer than catastrophe. Instead, the pilot's voice, not only heard but visible, as are the words contained in comic-strip balloons, pronounced *destroy*, thus summoning death as witness to his fear. *We are not turning back. We shall complete this flight as scheduled*, he might have said, but he did not say it; and, standing waiting at the curb, Dan felt the failure of all men in the pilot's failure, and he whispered, "Quiet, now, quiet," to the horse or the girl or the traffic passing by. When the light changed again and the cars halted, he crossed, running, in the direction the girl had fled.

But she was not in the alley off Christopher Street. The little old man was gone, and only his empty flask and the garbage pails were there. At the VOLUNTEERS OF AMERICA, the sign had gone dark, and for once the street was empty. There was no queue of derelict men waiting at the door. It was growing cold, but Dan did not think of this as he walked up one street and down another, searching among the faces that passed in twos or threes through the lights from the cafés, and searching among the solitary others that lingered in the intervals of dark. If he did not find her tonight, still it would not be the end, he kept saying to himself, for he could come back every night, whatever the weather, and on one of the streets, around one of the corners, he would hear her bracelets ringing or see her tinsel hair. If it was not tonight, it would be the night after, or maybe three nights later, or else at the end of the week; and after they had put the drunks to sleep, they would sit down on a curbstone together, and he would say, or try to say, "Don't call the lost men back from where they are. Don't make them remember. Just let them go." He would tell her about things that were taking place in other parts of America, beyond New York; about the Middle West, for instance, where seven university professors had made a tape recording proving that you can hear corn grow.

It was four o'clock in the morning when he got back to Brooklyn. His mother was walking up and down outside, complaining loudly enough about him for any neighbors who were awake to hear.

"Your jacket!" she cried out when she saw him coming up the street. "You had your good jacket on when you left the house! Oh, God, oh, God!" she wept.

Above them, as they went into the apartment house together, the morning star was fading from the sky.

RAYMOND CARVER
Will You Please Be Quiet, Please?

(FROM DECEMBER)

1.

WHEN HE WAS 18 and left home for the first time, in the fall, Ralph Wyman had been advised by his father, principal of Jefferson Elementary School in Weaverville and trumpet-player in the Elks' Club Auxiliary Band, that life today was a serious matter; something that required strength and direction in a young person just setting out. A difficult journey, everyone knew that, but nevertheless a comprehensible one, he believed.

But in college Ralph's goals were still hazy and undefined. He first thought he wanted to be a doctor, or a lawyer, and he took pre-medical courses and courses in history of jurisprudence and business-law before he decided he had neither the emotional detachment necessary for medicine, nor the ability for sustained reading and memorization in the *Corpus Iuris Civilis*, as well as the more modern texts on property and inheritance. Though he continued to take classes here and there in the sciences and in the Department of Business, he also took some lower-division classes in history and philosophy and English. He continually felt he was on the brink of some kind of momentous discovery about himself. But it never came. It was during this time, his lowest ebb, as he jokingly referred back to it later, that he believed he almost became an alcoholic; he was in a fraternity and he used to get drunk every night. He drank so much, in fact, that he even acquired something of a reputation; guys called him

Jackson, after the bartender at The Keg, and he sat every day in the cafeteria with a deck of cards playing poker solitaire, or bridge, if someone happened along. His grades were down and he was thinking of dropping out of school entirely and joining the air force.

Then, in his third year, he came under the influence of a particularly fascinating and persuasive literature teacher. Dr. Maxwell was his name; Ralph would never forget him. He was a handsome, graceful man in his early forties, with exquisite manners and with just the trace of a slight southern drawl to his voice. He had been educated at Vanderbilt, had studied in Europe, and later had had something to do with one or two literary magazines in New York. Almost overnight, it seemed to him, Ralph decided on teaching as a career. He stopped drinking so much and began to bear down on his studies. Within a year he was elected to Omega Psi, the national journalism fraternity; he became a member of the English Club; was invited to come with his cello, which he hadn't played in three years, and join in a student chamber music group just forming; and he ran successfully for Secretary of the Senior Class. He also started going out with Marian Ross that year; a pale, slender girl he had become acquainted with in a Chaucer class.

She wore her hair long and liked high-necked sweaters in the winter; and summer and winter she always went around with a leather purse on a long strap swinging from her shoulder. Her eyes were large and seemed to take in everything at a glance; if she got excited over something, they flashed and widened even more. He liked going out with her in the evenings. They went to The Keg, and a few other nightspots where everyone else went, but they never let their going together, or their subsequent engagement that next summer, interfere with their studies. They were serious students, and both sets of parents eventually gave their approval of the match. They did their student-teaching at the same high school in Chico the next spring, and went through graduation exercises together in June. They married in St.

James Episcopal Church two weeks later. Both of them held hands the night before their wedding and pledged solemnly to preserve forever the excitement and the mystery of marriage.

For their honeymoon they drove to Guadalajara; and while they both enjoyed visiting the old decayed churches and the poorly lighted museums, and the several afternoons they spent shopping and exploring in the marketplace (which swarmed with flies), Ralph secretly felt a little appalled and at the same time let down by the squalor and promiscuity of the people; he was only too glad to get back to more civilized California. Even so, Marian had seemed to enjoy it, and he would always remember one scene in particular. It was late afternoon, almost evening, and Marian was leaning motionless on her arms over the iron-worked balustrade of their rented, second-floor *casa* as he came up the dusty road below. Her hair was long and hung down in front over her shoulders, and she was looking away from him, staring at something toward the horizon. She wore a white blouse with a bright red scarf at the throat, and he could see her breasts pushing against her front. He had a bottle of dark, unlabeled wine under his arm, and the whole incident reminded him of something from a play, or a movie. Thinking back on it later, it was always a little vaguely disturbing for some reason.

Before they had left for their six-week honeymoon, they had accepted teaching positions at a high school in Eureka, in the northern part of the state near the ocean. They waited a year to make certain that the school and the weather, and the people themselves were exactly what they wanted to settle down to, and then made a substantial down-payment on a house in the Fire Hill district. He felt, without really thinking about it, that they understood each other perfectly; as well, anyway, as any two people could understand one another. More, he understood himself; his capacities, his limitations. He knew where he was going and how to get there.

In eight years they had two children, Dorothea and Robert, who were now five and four years old. A few months after Robert, Marian had accepted at mid-term a part-time position as a French and English teacher at Harris Junior College, at the edge of town. The position had become full-time and permanent that next fall, and Ralph had stayed on, happily, at the high school. In the time they had been married, they had had only one serious disturbance, and that was long ago: two years ago that winter to be exact. It was something they had never talked about since it happened, but, try as he might, Ralph couldn't help thinking about it sometimes. On occasion, and then when he was least prepared, the whole ghastly scene leaped into his mind. Looked at rationally and in its proper, historical perspective, it seemed impossible and monstrous; an event of such personal magnitude for Ralph that he still couldn't entirely accept it as something that had once happened to Marian and himself: he had taken it into his head one night at a party that Marian had betrayed him with Mitchell Anderson, a friend. In a fit of uncontrollable rage, he had struck Marian with his fist, knocking her sideways against the kitchen table and onto the floor.

It was a Sunday night in November. The children were in bed. Ralph was sleepy, and he still had a dozen themes from his twelfth-grade class in accelerated English to correct before tomorrow morning. He sat on the edge of the couch, leaning forward with his red pencil over a space he'd cleared on the coffee table. He had the papers separated into two stacks, and one of the papers folded open in front of him. He caught himself blinking his eyes, and again felt irritated with the Franklins. Harold and Sarah Franklin. They'd stopped over early in the afternoon for cocktails and stayed on into the evening. Otherwise, Ralph would have finished hours ago, as he'd planned. He'd been sleepy, too, he remembered, the whole time they were here. He'd sat in the big leather chair by the fireplace and once he recalled letting his head sink back against the warm leather of the chair and starting to close his eyes when Franklin had cleared his throat loudly. Too loudly. He didn't feel comfortable with Franklin anymore. Harold Franklin was a big, forthright man with bushy eyebrows who caught you and held you with his eyes when he spoke. He looked like he never combed his hair, his suits were always baggy, and Ralph thought his ties hideous, but he was one of the few men on the staff at Harris Junior College who had his Ph.D. At 35 he was head of the combined History and Social Science Department. Two years ago he and Sarah had been witness to a large part of Ralph's humiliation. That occasion had never later been brought up by any of them, of course, and in a few weeks, the next time they'd seen one another, it was as though nothing had happened. Still, since then, Ralph couldn't help feeling a little uneasy when he was around them.

He could hear the radio playing softly in the kitchen, where Marian was ironing. He stared a while longer at the papers in front of him, then gathered up all the papers, turned off the lamp, and walked out to the kitchen.

"Finished, love?" Marian said with a smile. She was sitting on a tall stool, ironing one of Robert's shirts. She sat the iron up on its end as if she'd been waiting for him.

"Damn it, no," he said with an exaggerated grimace, tossing the papers on the table. "What the hell the Franklins come by here for anyway?"

She laughed; bright, pleasant. It made him feel better. She held up her face to be kissed, and he gave her a little peck on the cheek. He pulled out a chair from the table and sat down, leaned back on the legs and looked at her. She smiled again, and then lowered her eyes.

"I'm already half-asleep," he said.

"Coffee," she said, reaching over and laying the back of her hand against the electric percolator.

He nodded.

She took a long drag from the cigarette she'd had burning in the ashtray, smoked it a minute while she stared at the floor, and then put it back in the ashtray. She looked up at him, and a smile started at the corners of her mouth. She was tall and limber, with a good bust, narrow hips, and wide, gleaming eyes.

"Ralph, do you remember that party?" she asked, still looking at him.

He shifted in the chair and said, "Which party? You mean that one two or three years ago?"

She nodded.

He waited a minute and asked, when she didn't say anything else, "What about it? Now that you brought it up, honey, what about it?" Then: "He kissed you after all, that night, didn't he? ... Did he try to kiss you, or didn't he?"

"I didn't say that," she said. "I was just thinking about it and I asked you; that's all."

"Well, he did, didn't he? Come on, Marian, we're just talking, aren't we?"

"I'm afraid it'd make you angry, Ralph."

"It won't make me angry, Marian. It was a long time ago, wasn't it? I won't be angry ... Well?"

"Well, yes," she said slowly, "he did kiss me a few times." She smiled tentatively, gauging his reaction.

His first impulse was to return her smile, and then he felt himself blushing and said defensively, "You told me before he didn't. You said he only put his arm around you while he was driving."

He stared at her. It all came back to him again; the way she looked coming in the back door that night; eyes bright, trying to tell him ... something, he didn't hear. He hit her in the mouth, at the last instant pulling to avoid her nose, knocked her against the table where she sat down hard on the floor. "What did you do that for?" she'd asked dreamily, her eyes still bright, and her mouth dripping blood. "Where were you all night?" he'd yelled, teetering over her, his legs watery and trembling. He'd drawn back his fist again but already sorry for the first blow, the blood he'd caused. "I wasn't gone all night," she'd said, turning her head back and forth heavily. "I didn't do anything. Why did you hit me?"

Ralph passed his open hand over his forehead, shut his eyes for a minute. "I guess I lost my head that night, all right. We were both in the wrong. You for leaving the party with Mitchell Anderson, and I for losing my head. I'm sorry."

"I'm sorry, too," she said. "Even so," she grinned, "you didn't have to knock hell out of me."

"I don't know—maybe I should've done more." He looked at her, and then they both had to laugh.

"How did we ever get onto this?" she asked.

"You brought it up," he said.

She shook her head. "The Franklins being here made me think of it, I guess." She pulled in her upper lip and stared at the floor. In a minute she straightened her shoulders and looked up. "If you'll move this ironing board for me, love, I'll make us a hot drink. A buttered rum: now how does that sound?"

"Good."

She went into the living room and turned on the lamp, bent to pick up a magazine by the endtable. He watched her hips under the plaid woolen skirt. She moved in front of the window by the large dining room table and stood looking out at the street light. She smoothed her palm down over her right hip, then began tucking in her blouse with the fingers of her right hand. He wondered what she was thinking. A car went by outside, and she continued to stand in front of the window.

After he stood the ironing board in its alcove on the porch, he sat down again and said, when she came into the room, "Well, what else went on between you and Mitchell Anderson that night? It's all right to talk about it now."

Anderson had left Harris less than two years ago to accept a position as Associate Professor of Speech and Drama at a new, four-year college the state was getting underway in southwestern California. He was in his early thirties, like everyone else they knew; a slender, moustached man with a rough, slightly pocked face; he was a casual, eccentric dresser and sometimes, Marian had told Ralph, laughing, he wore a green velvet smoking jacket to school. The girls in his classes were crazy about him, she said. He had thin, dark hair which he combed forward to cover the balding spot on the top of his head. Both he and his wife, Emily, a costume designer, had done a lot of acting and directing in Little Theater in the Bay Area before coming to Eureka. As a person, though, someone he liked to be around, it was something different as far as Ralph was concerned. Thinking about it, he decided he hadn't liked him from the beginning, and he was glad he was gone.

"What else?" he asked.

"Nothing," she said. "I'd rather not talk about it now, Ralph, if you don't mind. I was thinking about something else."

"What?"

"Oh ... about the children, the dress I want Dorothea to have for next Easter; that sort of thing. Silly, unrelated things. And about the class I'm going to have tomorrow. Walt Whitman. Some of the kids didn't approve when I told them there was a, a bit of speculation Whitman was—how should I say it?—attracted to certain men." She laughed. "Really, Ralph, nothing else happened. I'm sorry I ever said anything about it."

"Okay."

He got up and went to the bathroom to wash cold water over his face. When he came out he leaned against the wall by the refrigerator and watched her measure out the sugar into the two cups and then stir in the rum. The water was boiling on the stove. The clock on the wall behind the table said 9:45.

"Look, honey, it's been brought up now," he said. "It was two or three years ago; there's no reason at all I can think of we can't talk about it if we want to, is there?"

"There's really nothing to talk about, Ralph."

"I'd like to know," he said vaguely.

"Know what?"

"Whatever else he did beside kiss you. We're adults. We haven't seen the Andersons in . . . a year at least. We'll probably never see them again. It happened a long time ago; as I see it, there's no reason whatever we can't talk about it." He was a little surprised at the level, reasoning quality in his voice. He sat down and looked at the tablecloth, and then looked up at her again. "Well?"

"Well," she said, laughing a little, tilting her head to one side, remembering. "No, Ralph, really; I'm not trying to be coy about it either: I'd just rather not."

"For Christ's sake, Marian! Now I mean it," he said, "if you don't tell me, it will make me angry."

She turned off the gas under the water and put her hand out on the stool; then sat down again, hooking her heels over the bottom step. She leaned forward, resting her arms across her knees. She picked at something on her skirt and then looked up.

"You remember Emily'd already gone home with the Beattys, and for some reason Mitchell had stayed on. He looked a little out of sorts that night to begin with. I don't know, maybe they weren't getting along . . . But I don't know that. But there were you and I, the Franklins, and Mitchell Anderson left. All of us a little drunk, if I remember rightly. I'm not sure how it happened, Ralph, but Mitchell and I just happened to find ourselves alone together in the kitchen for a minute. There was no whiskey left, only two or three bottles of that white wine we had. It must've been close to one o'clock because Mitchell said, 'If we hurry we can make it before the liquor store closes.' You know how he can be so theatrical when he wants? Softshoe stuff, facial expressions . . . ? Anyway, he was very witty about it all. At least it seemed that way at the time. And very drunk, too, I might add. So was I, for that matter . . . It was an impulse, Ralph, I swear. I don't know why I did it, don't ask me, but when he said, 'Let's go'—I agreed. We went out the back, where his car was parked. We went just like we were: we didn't even get our coats out of the closet. We thought we'd just be gone a few minutes. I guess we thought no one would miss us ... I don't know what we thought ... I don't know *why* I went, Ralph. It was an impulse, that's all that I can say. It was a wrong impulse." She paused. "It was my fault that night, Ralph, and I'm sorry. I shouldn't have done anything like that, I know that."

"Christ!" the word leaped out. "But you've always been that way, Marian!"

"That isn't true!"

His mind filled with a swarm of tiny accusations, and he tried to focus on one in particular. He looked down at his hands and noticed they had the same lifeless feeling as they did when he woke up mornings. He picked up the red pencil lying on the table, and then put it down again.

"I'm listening," he said.

"You're angry," she said. "You're swearing and getting all upset, Ralph. For nothing, nothing, honey! ... There's nothing else."

"Go on."

"*What* is the matter with us anyway? How did we ever get onto this subject?"

"Go on, Marian."

"That's all, Ralph. I've told you. We went for a ride ... We talked. He kissed me. I still don't see how we could've been gone three hours; whatever it was you said."

He remembered again the waiting, the unbearable weakness that spread down through his legs when they'd been gone an hour, two hours. It made him lean weakly against the corner of the house after he'd gone outside; for a breath of air he said vaguely, pulling into his coat, but really so that the embarrassed Franklins could themselves leave without any more embarrassment; without having to take leave of the absent host, or the vanished hostess. From the corner of the house, standing behind the rose trellis in the soft, crumbly dirt, he watched the Franklins get into their car and drive away. Anger and frustration clogged inside him, then separated into little units of humiliation that jumped against his stomach. He waited. Gradually the horror drained away as he stood there, until finally nothing was left but a vast, empty realization of betrayal. He went into the house and sat at this same table, and he remembered his shoulder began to twitch and he couldn't stop it even when he squeezed it with his fingers. An hour later, or two hours—what difference did it make then?—she'd come in.

"Tell me the rest, Marian." And he knew there was more now. He felt a slight fluttering start up in his stomach, and suddenly he didn't want to know any more. "No. Do whatever you want. If you don't want to talk about it, Marian, that's all right. Do whatever you want to, Marian. Actually, I guess I'd just as soon leave it at that."

He worked his shoulders against the smooth, solid chairback, then balanced unsteadily on the two back legs. He thought fleetingly that he would have been someplace else tonight, doing something else at this very moment, if he hadn't married. He glanced around the kitchen. He began to perspire and leaned forward, setting all the legs on the floor. He took one of her cigarettes from the pack on the table. His hands were trembling as he struck the match.

"Ralph. You won't be angry, will you? Ralph? We're just talking. You won't, will you?" She had moved over to a chair at the table.

"I won't."

"Promise?"

"Promise."

She lit a cigarette. He had suddenly a great desire to see Robert and Dorothea; to get them up out of bed, heavy and turning in their sleep, and hold each of them on a knee, jiggle them until they woke up and began to laugh. He absently began to trace with his finger the outline of one of the tiny black coaches in the beige tablecloth. There were four miniature white prancing horses pulling each of the tiny coaches. The figure driving the horses had his arm up and was wearing a tall hat. Suitcases were strapped down on top of the coach, and what looked like a kerosene lamp hung from the side.

"We went straight to the liquor store, and I waited in the car till he came out. He had a sack in one hand and one of those plastic bags of ice in the other. He weaved a little getting into the car. I hadn't realized he was so drunk until we started driving again, and I noticed the way he was driving; terribly slow, and all hunched over the wheel with his eyes staring. We were talking about a lot of things that didn't make sense ... I can't remember ... Nietzsche ... and Strindberg; he was directing *Miss Julie* second semester, you know, and something about Norman Mailer stabbing his wife in the breast a long time ago, and how he thought Mailer was going downhill anyway—a lot of crazy things like that. Then, I'll swear before God it was an accident, Ralph, he didn't know what he was doing, he made a wrong turn and we somehow wound up out by the golf course, right near Jane Van Eaton's. In fact, we pulled into her driveway to turn around and when we did Mitchell said to me, 'We might as well open one of these bottles.' He did, he opened it, and then he drove a little farther on down the road that goes around the green, you know, and comes out by the park? Actually, not too far from the Franklins ... And then he stopped for a minute in the middle of the road with his lights on, and we each took a drink out of the bottle. Then he said, said he'd hate to think of me being stabbed in the breast. I guess he was still thinking about Mailer's wife. And then ... I can't say it, Ralph ... I know you'd get angry."

"I won't get angry, Marian," he said slowly. His thoughts seemed to move lazily, as if he were in a dream, and he was able to take in only one thing at a time she was telling him. At the same time he noticed a peculiar alertness taking hold of his body.

"Go on. Then what, Marian?"

"You aren't angry, are you? Ralph?"

"No. But I'm getting interested, though."

They both had to laugh, and for a minute everything was all right. He leaned across the table to light another cigarette for her, and they smiled at each other; just like any other night. He struck another match, held it a while, and then brought the match, almost to burn his fingers, up under the end of the cigarette that protruded at an angle from his lips. He dropped the burned match into the ashtray and stared at it before looking up.

"Go on."

"I don't know ... things seemed to happen fast after that. He drove up the road a little and turned off someplace, I don't know, maybe right onto the green ... and started kissing me. Then he said, said he'd like to kiss my breast. I said I didn't think we should. I said, 'What about Emily?' He said I didn't know her. He got the car going again, and then he stopped again and just sort of slumped over and put his head on my lap. God! It sounds so vulgar now, I know, but it didn't seem that way at all then. I felt like, like I was losing my innocence somehow, Ralph. For the first time—that night I realized I was really, really doing something wrong, something I wasn't supposed to do and that might hurt people. I shouldn't be there, I felt. And I felt ... like it was the first time in my life I'd ever *intentionally* done anything wrong or hurtful and gone on doing it, knowing I shouldn't be. Do you know what I mean, Ralph? Like some of the characters in Henry James? I felt that way. Like ... for the first time ... my innocence ... something was happening."

"You can dispense with that shit," he cut in. "Get off it, Marian! Go on! Then what? Did he caress you? Did he? Did he try to feel you up, Marian? Tell me!"

And then she hurried on, trying to get over the hard spots quickly, and he sat with his hands folded on the table and watched her lips out of which dropped the frightful words. His eyes skipped around the kitchen—stove, cupboards, toaster, radio, coffeepot, window, curtains, refrigerator, breadbox, napkin holder, stove, cupboards, toaster ... back to her face. Her dark eyes glistened under the overhead light. He felt a peculiar desire for her flicker through his thighs at what she was leading up to, and at the same time he had to check an urge to stand up yelling, smash his fist into her face.

" 'Shall we have a go at it?' he said."

"Shall we have a go at it?" Ralph repeated.

"I'm to blame. If anyone should, should be blamed for it, I'm to blame. He said he'd leave it all up to me, I could ... could do ... whatever I wanted." Tears welled out of her eyes, started down her cheeks. She looked down at the table, blinked rapidly.

He shut his eyes. He saw a barren field under a heavy, gray sky; a fog moving in across the far end. He shook his head, tried to admit other possibilities, other conclusions. He tried to bring back that night two years ago, imagine himself coming into the kitchen just as she and Mitchell were at the door, hear himself telling her in a hearty voice, Oh no, no; you're not going out for liquor with that Mitchell Anderson! He's drunk, and he isn't a good driver to boot. You've got to go to bed now and get up with little Robert and Dorothea in the morning ... Stop! Stop where you are.

He opened his eyes, raised his eyebrows as if he were just waking up. She had a hand up over her face and was crying silently, her shoulders rounded and moving in little jerks.

"Why did you go with him, Marian?" he asked desperately.

She shook her head without looking up.

Then, suddenly, he knew. His mind buckled. *Cuckold*. For a minute he could only stare helplessly at his hands. Then he wanted to pass it off somehow, say it was all right, it was two years ago, adults, etc. He wanted to forgive: *I forgive you*. But he could not forgive. He couldn't forgive her this. His thoughts skittered around the Middle Ages, touched on Arthur and Guinevere, surged on to the outraged husbandry of the eighteenth-century dramatists, came to a sullen halt with Karenin. But what had any of them to do with him? What were they? They were nothing. Nothing. Figments. They did not exist. Their discoveries, their disintegrations, adjustments, did not at all relate to him. No relation. What then? What did it all mean? What is the nature of a book? his mind roared.

"Christ!" he said, springing up from the table. *"Jesus Christ.* Christ, no, Marian!"

"No, no," she said, throwing her head back.

"You let him!"

"No, no, Ralph."

"You let him! Didn't you? Didn't you? Answer me!" he yelled. "Did he come in you? Did you let him come in you? That s-s-swine," he said, his teeth chattering. "That bastard."

"Listen, listen to me, Ralph. I swear to you he didn't, he didn't come. He didn't come in me." She rocked from side to side in the chair, shaking her head.

"You wouldn't let him! That's it, isn't it? Yes, yes, you had your scruples. What'd you do—catch it in your hands? Oh God! God *damn* you!"

"God!" she said, getting up, holding out her hands. "Are we crazy, Ralph? Have we lost our minds? Ralph? Forgive me, Ralph. Forgive—"

"Don't touch me! Get away from me, Marian."

"In God's name, Ralph! Ralph! Please, Ralph. For the children's sake, Ralph. Don't go, Ralph. Please don't go, Ralph!" Her eyes were white and large, and she began to pant in her fright. She tried to head him off, but he took her by the shoulder and pushed her out of the way.

"Forgive me, Ralph! *Please.* Ralph!"

He slammed the kitchen door, started across the porch. Behind him, she jerked open the door, clattered over the dustpan as she rushed onto the porch. She took his arm at the porch door, but he shook her loose. "Ralph!" But he jumped down the steps onto the walk.

When he was across the driveway and walking rapidly down the sidewalk, he could hear her at the door yelling for him. Her voice seemed to be coming through a kind of murk. He looked back: she was still calling, limned against the doorway. My God, he thought, what a sideshow it was. Fat men and bearded ladies.

2.

He had to stop and lean against a car for a few minutes before going on. But two well-dressed couples were coming down the sidewalk toward him, and the man on the outside, near the curb, was telling a story in a loud voice. The others were already laughing. Ralph pushed off from the car and crossed the street. In a few minutes he came to Blake's, where he stopped some afternoons for a beer with Dick Koenig before picking up the children from nursery school.

It was dark inside. The air was warm and heavy with the odor of beer and seemed to catch at the top of his throat and make it hard for him to swallow. Candles flickered dimly in long-necked wine bottles at some of the tables along the left wall when he closed the door. He glimpsed shadowy figures of men and women talking with their heads close together. One of the couples, near the door, stopped talking and looked up at him. A box-like fixture in the ceiling revolved overhead, throwing out pale red and green lights. Two men sat at the end of the bar, and a dark cutout of a man leaned over the jukebox in the corner, his hands splayed out on each side of the glass.

The man is going to play something. Ralph stands in the center of the floor, watches him. He sways, rubs his wrist against his forehead, and starts out.

"Ralph!—Mr. Wyman, sir!"

He stopped, looked around. David Parks was calling to him from behind the bar. Ralph walked over, leaned heavily against the bar before sliding onto a stool.

"Should I draw one, Mr. Wyman?" He had the glass in his hand, smiling.

He worked evenings and weekends for Charley Blake. He was 26, married, had two children, babies. He attended Harris Junior College on a football scholarship, and worked besides. He had three mouths to feed now, along with his own. Four mouths altogether. Not like it used to be. David Parks. He had a white bar towel slung over his shoulder.

Ralph nodded, watched him fill the glass.

He held the glass at an angle under the tap, slowly straightened it as the glass filled, closed the tap, and cut off the head with a smooth, professional air. He wiped the towel across the gleaming surface of the bar and set the glass in front of Ralph, still smiling.

"How's it going, Mr. Wyman? Didn't hear you come in." He put his foot up on a shelf under the bar. "Who's going to win the game next week, Mr. Wyman?"

Ralph shook his head, brought the beer to his lips. His shoulders ached with fatigue from being held rigid the last hour.

David Parks coughed faintly. "I'll buy you one, Mr. Wyman. This one's on me." He put his leg down, nodded assurance, and reached under his apron into his pocket.

"Here. I have it right here." Ralph pulled out some change, examined it in his hand from the light cast by a bare bulb on a stand next to the cash register. A quarter, nickel, two dimes, pennies. He laid down the quarter and stood up, pushing the change back into his pocket. The man was still in front of the jukebox, leaning his weight on one leg. The phone rang.

Ralph opened the door.

"Mr. Wyman! Mr. Wyman, for you, sir."

Outside he turned around, trying to decide what to do. He wanted to be alone, but at the same time he thought he'd feel better if other people were around. Not here though. His heart was fluttering, as if he'd been running. The door opened behind him and a man and woman came out. Ralph stepped out of the way and they got into a car parked at the curb. He recognized the woman as the receptionist at the children's dentist. He started off walking.

He walked to the end of the block, crossed the street, and walked another block before he decided to head downtown.

It was eight or ten blocks and he walked hurriedly, his hands balled into his pockets, his shoes smacking the pavement. He kept blinking his eyes and thought it incredible he could still feel tired and fogged after all that had happened. He shook his head. He would have liked to sit someplace for a while and think about it, but he knew he could not sit, could not yet think about it. He remembered a man he saw once sitting on a curb in Arcata: an old man with a growth of beard and a brown wool cap who just sat there with his arms between his legs. But a minute later it snapped into his mind, and for the first time he tried to get a clear look at it; himself, Marian, the children—his world. But it was impossible. He wondered if anyone could ever stand back far enough from life to see it whole, all in one piece. He thought of an enormous French tapestry they'd seen two or three years ago that took up one wall of a room in the De Young Museum. He tried to imagine how all this would seem twenty years from now, but there was nothing. He couldn't picture the children any older, and when he tried to think about Marian and himself, there was only a blank space. Then, for a minute, he felt profoundly indifferent, somehow above it, as if it did not concern him. He thought of Marian without any emotion at all. He remembered her as he had seen her a little while ago; face crumpled, tears running off her nose. Then Marian on the floor, holding onto the chair, blood on her teeth: "Why did you hit me?" ... Marian reaching under her dress to unfasten her garter belt ... She raises her dress slowly as she leans back in the seat.

He stopped and thought he was going to be sick. He moved off onto the edge of a lawn. He cleared his throat several times and kept swallowing, looked up as a car of yelling teenagers went by and gave him a long blast on their musical horn. Yes, there was a vast amount of evil loose in the world, he thought, and it only awaited an opportunity, the propitious moment to manifest itself ... But that was an academic notion. A kind of retreat. He spat ahead of him on the walk and put his heel on it. He mustn't let himself find solace in that kind of thinking. Not now. Not anymore, if he could help it. If he was going to think about it—and he knew he must, sooner or later tonight—he must begin simply, from the essentials: with the fact that his wife had let herself be fucked, yes, fucked, by another man. And this, this he *knew* was evil: he felt it in his bones.

He came to Second Street, the part of town people called Two Street. It started here at Shelton, under the street light where the old rooming houses ended, and ran for four or five blocks on down to the pier, where fishing boats tied up. He'd been down here once, two years ago, to a second-hand store to look through the dusty shelves of old books. There was a liquor store across the street, and he could see a man standing outside in front of the glass door, looking at a newspaper.

Ralph crossed under the street light, read the headlines on the newspaper the man had been looking at, and went inside. A bell over the door tinkled. He hadn't noticed a bell that tinkled over a door since he was a child. He bought some cigarettes and went out again.

He walked down the street, looking in the windows. All the places were closed for the night, or vacated. Some of the windows had signs taped inside: a dance, a Shrine Circus that had come and gone last summer, an election—Vote For Fred C. Walters, Councilman. One of the windows he looked through had sinks and pipe-joints scattered around on a table. Everything dark. He came to a Vic Tanny Gym where he could see light coming under the curtains pulled across a big window. He could hear water splashing in the pool inside, and the hollow echo of voices calling across the water.

There was more light now, coming from the bars and cafés on both sides of the street. More people, groups of three or four but now and then a man by himself, or a woman in slacks walking rapidly. He stopped in front of the window of one place and watched some Negroes shooting pool. Gray cigarette smoke drifted around the lights over the table. One of the Negroes, who was chalking his cue, had his hat on and a cigarette in his mouth. He said something to another Negro, looked intently at the balls, and slowly leaned over the table.

He walked on, stopped in front of Jim's Oyster House. He had never been here before, had never been to any of these places before. Over the door the name was in yellow light bulbs: JIM's OYSTER HOUSE. Above the lights, fixed to an iron grill, a huge neon-lighted clam shell with a man's legs sticking out. The torso was hidden in the shell and the legs flashed red, on and off. Ralph lit another cigarette from the one he had, and pushed open the door.

It was crowded. A lot of people were bunched on the floor, their arms wrapped around each other or hanging loosely on someone's shoulders. The men in the band were just getting up from their chairs for an intermission. He had to excuse himself several times trying to get to the bar, and once a drunken woman took hold of his coat. There were no stools and he had to stand at the end of the bar between a coast guardsman and a shrunken-faced man in denims. Neither of them spoke. The coast guardsman had his white cap off and his elbows propped out in front of him, a hand on each side of his face. He stared at his glass without looking up. The other man shook his head and then pointed with his narrow chin two or three times at the coast guardsman. Ralph put his arm up and signaled the bartender. Once, Ralph thought he heard the shrunken-faced man say something, but he didn't answer.

In the mirror he could see the men in the band get up from the table where they'd been sitting. Ralph picked up his glass, turned around, and leaned back against the bar. He closed his eyes and opened them. Someone unplugged the jukebox, and the music ground to a stop. The musicians wore white shirts and dark slacks with little string ties around their necks. There was a fireplace with blue gas flames behind a stack of metal logs, and the band platform was to the side, a few feet away. One of the men plucked the strings of his electric guitar, said something to the others with a grin, and leaned back in his chair. They began to play.

The music was country, or western, and not as bad as Ralph had imagined. He raised his glass and drained it. Down the bar he could hear a woman say angrily, "Well there's going to be trouble, that's all I've got to say about it!" The musicians came to the end of the number and swung into another. One of the men, the bass player, came to the microphone and began to sing, but Ralph couldn't understand the words.

When the band took another intermission, he looked around for the toilet. He could make out some doors opening and closing at the far end of the bar, and headed in that direction, staggering a little. Over one of the doors was a rack of antlers. He saw a man go in, and he saw another man catch the door and come out. Inside, waiting in line behind three or four others, he found himself staring at the penciled picture of a huge pair of female thighs and pubic area on the wall over the pocket-comb machine. Underneath the drawing was scrawled, Eat ME, and a little lower down someone had added Betty M. Eats It—RA 52275. The man ahead of him moved up, and Ralph took two steps forward, his eyes still fastened on the drawing. Finally, he moved up over the bowl and urinated so hard it was like a bolt going down through his legs. He sighed luxuriously when he was through, leaned forward and let his head rest against the wall. His life was changed from tonight on. Were there many other men, he wondered drunkenly, who could look at one singular event in their lives and perceive the workings of the catastrophe that hereinafter sets their lives on a different course? Are there many who can perceive the necessary changes and adjustments that must necessarily and inevitably follow? Probably so, he decided after a minute's reflection. He stood there a while longer, and then he looked down: he'd urinated on his fingers.

He moved over to the wash basin, ran water over his hands without using the dirty bar of soap. As he was unrolling the towel, he suddenly leaned over and put his face up close to the pitted mirror, looked into his eyes. A face: that was all. Hardly even familiar. There seemed nothing fixed or permanent about it. His nose just hung there, occupying a space, spotted with several tiny blackheads he hadn't noticed before. His skin was slightly chapped on the inside of one cheek. His lips . . . like any other lips. Only his eyes under the narrow eyebrows seemed out of the ordinary, like shiny glass objects. They moved as he moved, followed him around the mirror, looked out at him steadily when he looked straight in. He put his finger up to the mirror and touched the glass, moved away as a man tried to get past him to the sink.

As he was going out the door he noticed another door he hadn't seen at the end of a short, narrow corridor. He went over to it and looked through the glass plate in the door at four card-players around a green felt table. It seemed still and restful inside. He couldn't hear anything, and the silent movements of the men appeared languorous and heavy with meaning. He leaned against the glass, watching. One of the men at the table, the man dealing, looked up at him and stared until he moved away. He weaved back to the bar and thought how the scene reminded him of Cézanne's Card-Players. But did it really?

There was a flourish of guitars and people began whistling and clapping. A plump, middle-aged woman in a white evening dress was being helped onto the platform. She kept trying to pull back and was shaking her head and laughing. Finally she took the mike and made a little curtsy. The people whistled and stamped their feet. He thought of the scene in the card room. No, they didn't remind him of the Cézanne; that was certain. He suddenly had an enormous desire to watch them play, be in the same room with them. He could watch, even if he didn't play. He'd seen some empty chairs along the wall. He leaned against the bar, took out his wallet, keeping his hands up over the sides as he looked to see how much he had. He had eighteen dollars—just in case he was asked to play a hand or two. Without thinking anymore about it, he worked his way to the back. Behind him, the woman began to sing in a low, drowsy voice. Ralph stepped into the corridor, and then pushed open the door to the card room.

The man who'd looked up at him was still dealing.

"Decided to join us?" he said, sweeping Ralph with his eyes and looking down at the table again. Two of the others raised their eyes for an instant then looked back at the cards flashing around the table. As they picked up their cards, the man sitting with his back to Ralph, a short, fat man who breathed heavily through his nose, turned around in his chair and glared at him, and Ralph moved back a step.

"Benny, bring another chair!" the dealer called to an old man sweeping under a table that had the chairs turned up on the top.

"That's all right," Ralph said. "I'll just watch a few hands."

"Suit yourself."

He sat down in a chair against the wall, a few feet away from the table. No one spoke. The only sounds were the *clat-clat* of the chips as the men dropped them into the center of the table, and the shuffle and sharp flicking of the cards. The dealer was a large man, thirty or so; he wore a white shirt, open at the collar, and with the sleeves turned back once exposing the forearms covered with black, curling hair. But his small hands were white and delicate-looking, and there was a gold band on his ring finger. Around the table a tall, white-haired man with a cigar, the fat man, and a small dark man with a gray suit and a tie. An Italian, Ralph thought. He smoked one cigarette after another, and when he swallowed, the tie over his Adam's apple moved up and down. The old man, Benny, was wiping with a cloth around the cash register near the door. It was warm and quiet. Now and then Ralph could hear a horn blare out in the street. He drew a long breath and closed his eyes, opened them when he heard steps.

"Want anything to drink?" Benny asked, carrying a chair to the table.

Ralph said he'd have something; bourbon and water. He gave him a dollar and pulled out of his coat. Benny took the coat and hung it up by the door as he went out. Two of the men moved their chairs and Ralph sat down across from the dealer.

"How's it going?" he said to Ralph, not looking up.

For a minute Ralph wasn't sure whether it was directed at him. "All right," he said.

Then, as Ralph watched the other men play their cards, the dealer said gently, still not looking at him, "Low ball or five card. Table stakes, five dollar limit on raises."

Ralph nodded, and when the hand was finished he bought fifteen dollars' worth of blue chips.

He watched the cards as they flashed around the table, picked up his as he'd seen the tall, white-haired man do; sliding one card under the corner of another as each card fell face down in front of him. He raised his eyes once and looked at the expressionless faces of the others. He wondered if it'd ever happened to any of them. In half an hour he had won two hands and without counting the small pile of chips in front of him, he thought he must still have fifteen or even twenty dollars.

Benny brought a tray of drinks, and Ralph paid for his with a chip. He took out his handkerchief and wiped the perspiration from his face, aware how tired he was. But he felt better for some reason. He had come a long way since that evening. But it was only ... a few hours ago. And had he really come so far? Was anything different, or anything resolved?

"You in or out?" the fat man asked. "Clyde, what's the bet, for Christ's sake?" he said to the dealer.

"Three dollars."

"In," Ralph said. "I'm in." He put three chips into the pot. "I have to be going though ... another hand or so."

The dealer looked up and then back at his cards.

The Italian said: "Stick around. You really want some action we can go to my place when we finish here."

"No, that's all right. Enough action tonight . . . I just have to be going pretty soon." He shifted in the chair, glanced at their faces, and then fixed upon a small green plaque on the wall behind the table. "You know," he said, "I just found out tonight. My wife, my wife played around with another guy two years ago. Can you imagine?" He cleared his throat.

One of the men snickered; the Italian. The fat man said, "You can't trust 'em, that's all. Women are no damn good!"

No one else said anything; the tall, white-haired man laid down his cards and lit his cigar that had gone out. He stared at Ralph as he puffed, then shook out the match and picked up his cards.

The dealer looked up again, resting his open hands palms-up on the table. "You work here in town?" he said to Ralph. "I haven't seen you around."

"I live here. I, I just haven't gotten around much." He felt drained, oddly relaxed.

"We playing or not?" the fat man said. "Clyde?"

"Hold your shirt," the dealer said.

"For Christ's sake," the white-haired man said quietly, holding onto each word, "I've never seen such cards."

"I'm in three dollars," the fat man said. "Who's going to stay?"

Ralph couldn't remember his hole card. His neck was stiff, and he fought against the desire to close his eyes. He'd never been so tired. All the joints and bones and muscles in his body seemed to radiate and call to his attention. He looked at his card; a seven of clubs. His next card, face-up, was an ace. He started to drop out. He edged in his chair, picked up his glass but it was empty.

"Benny!" the dealer said sharply.

His next card was a king. The betting went up to the five dollar limit. More royalty; the Queen of Diamonds. He looked once more at his hole card to see if he might somehow have been mistaken: the seven of clubs.

Benny came back with another tray of drinks and said, "They're closing in ten minutes, Clyde."

The next card, the Jack of Spades, fell on top of Ralph's queen. Ralph stared. The white-haired man turned over his cards. For the first time the dealer gazed straight into Ralph's eyes, and Ralph felt his toes pull back in his shoes as the man's eyes pierced through to, what seemed to Ralph, his craven heart.

"I'll bet two dollars to see it," the fat man said.

A shiver traced up and down Ralph's spine. He hesitated, and then, in a grand gesture, called, and recklessly raised five dollars, his last chips.

The tall, white-haired man edged his chair closer to the table.

The dealer had a pair of eights showing. Still looking at Ralph, he picked ten chips off one of the stacks in front of him. He spread them in two groups of five near the pile at the center of the table.

"Call."

The Italian hesitated, and then swallowed and turned over his cards. He looked at the dealer's cards, and then he looked at Ralph's.

The fat man smacked his cards down and glared at Ralph.

All of them watched as Ralph turned over his card and lurched up from the table.

Outside, in the alley, he took out his wallet again, let his fingers number the bills he had left: two dollars, and some change in his pocket. Enough for something to eat. Ham and eggs, perhaps. But he wasn't hungry. He leaned back against the damp brick wall of the building, trying to think. A car turned into the alley, stopped, and backed out again. He started walking. He went past the front of the Oyster House again, going back the way he'd come. He stayed close to the buildings, out of the way of the loud groups of men and women streaming up and down the sidewalk. He heard a woman in a long coat say to the man she was with, "It isn't that way at all, Bruce. You don't understand."

He stopped when he came to the liquor store. Inside he moved up to the counter and stared at the long, orderly rows of bottles. He bought a half-pint of rum and some more cigarettes. The palm tree on the label of the bottle, the drooping fronds with the lagoon in the background, had caught his eye. The clerk, a thin, bald man wearing suspenders, put the rum in a paper sack without a word and rang up the sale. Ralph could feel the man's eyes on him as he stood in front of the magazine rack, swaying a little and looking at the covers. Once he glanced up in the mirror over his head and caught the man staring at him from behind the counter; his arms were folded over his chest and his bald head gleamed in the reflected light. Finally the man turned off one of the lights in the back of the store and said, "Closing it up, buddy."

Outside again, Ralph turned around once and started down another street, toward the pier; he thought he'd like to see the water with the lights reflected on it. He wondered how far he would drop tonight before he began to level off. He opened the sack as he walked, broke the seal on the little bottle, and stopped in a doorway to take a long drink. He could hardly taste it. He crossed some old streetcar tracks and turned onto another, darker street. He could already hear the waves splashing under the pier.

As he came up to the front of a dark, wooden building, he heard someone move in the doorway. A heavy Negro in a leather jacket stepped out in front of him and said, "Just a minute there, man. Where you think you're goin'?"

As Ralph tried to move around him, frightened, the man said, "Christ, man, that's my feet you're steppin' on!"

Before he could move away the Negro hit him hard in the stomach, and when Ralph groaned and bent over, the man hit him in the nose with his open hand, knocking him back against the wall where he sat down in a rush of pain and dizziness. He had one leg turned under, trying to raise himself up, when the Negro slapped him on the cheek and knocked him sprawling onto the pavement. He was aware of a hand slipping into his pants-pocket over the hip, felt his wallet slide out. He groaned and tried to sit up again as the man neatly stripped his watch over his hand. He kicked the wet sack of broken glass, and then sprinted down the street.

Ralph got his legs under him again. As if from a great distance he heard someone yell, "There's a man hurt over here!" and he struggled up to his feet. Then he heard someone running toward him over the pavement, and a car pulled up to the curb, a car door slammed. He wanted to say, It's all right, please, it's all right, as a man came up to him and stopped a few feet away, watching. But the words seemed to ball in his throat and somthing like a gasp escaped his lips. He tried to draw a breath and the air piled up in his throat again, as if there were an obstruction in the passage; and then the noise broke even louder through his nose and mouth. He leaned his shoulder against the doorway and wept. In the few seconds he stood there, shaking, his mind seemed to empty out, and a vast sense of wonderment flowed through him as he thought again of Marian, why she had betrayed him. Then, as a policeman with a big flashlight walked over to him, he brought himself up with a shudder and became silent.

3.

Birds darted overhead in the graying mist. He still couldn't see them, but he could hear their sharp *jueet-jueet*. He stopped and looked up, kept his eyes fixed in one place; then he saw them, no larger than his hand, dozens of them, wheeling and darting just under the heavy overcast. He wondered if they were seabirds, birds that only came in off the ocean this time of morning. He'd never seen any birds around Eureka in the winter except now and then a big, lumbering seagull. He remembered once, a long time ago, walking into an old abandoned house—the Marshall place, near Uncle Jack's in Springfield, Oregon—how the sparrows kept flying in and out of the broken windows, flying around the rafters where they had their nests, and then flying out the windows again, trying to lead him away.

It was getting light. The overcast seemed to be lifting and was turning light-gray with patches of white clouds showing through here and there. The street was black with the mist that was still falling, and he had to be careful not to step on the snails that trailed across the damp sidewalk.

A car with its lights on slowed down as it went past, but he didn't look up. Another car passed. In a minute, another. He looked: four men, two in front, two in the back. One of the men in the back seat, wearing a hat, turned around and looked at him through the back window. Mill workers. The first shift of plywood mill workers going to work at Georgia-Pacific. It was Monday morning. He turned the corner, walked past Blake's; dark, the venetian blinds pulled over the windows and two empty beer bottles someone had left standing like sentinels beside the door. It was cold, and he walked slowly, crossing his arms now and then and rubbing his shoulders.

He'd refused the policeman's offer of a ride home. He couldn't think of a more shabby ending to the night than riding home in the early morning in a black and white police car. After the doctor at Redwood Memorial Hospital had examined him, felt around over his neck with his fingers while Ralph had sat with his eyes closed, the doctor had made two X-rays and then put Merthiolate and a small bandage on his cheek. Then the policemen had taken him to the station where for two hours he'd had to look at photographs in large manila folders of Negro men. Finally, he had told the officer, "I'm sorry, but I'm afraid everyone looks pretty much alike right now." The man had shrugged, closed the folder. "They come and go," he'd said, staring at Ralph. "Sometimes it's hard to nail them on the right charge due to lack of proper identification. If we bring in some suspects we'll have you back here to help identify." He stared at Ralph a minute longer, then nodded curtly.

He came up the street to his house. He could see his front porch light on, but the rest of the house was dark. He crossed the lawn and went around to the back. He turned the knob, and the door opened quietly. He stepped onto the porch and shut the door. He waited a moment, then opened the kitchen door.

The house was quiet. There was the tall stool beside the draining board. There was the table where they'd sat. How long ago? He remembered he'd just gotten up off the couch, where he'd been working, and come into the kitchen and sat down ... He looked at the clock over the stove: 7:00 a.m. He could see the dining room table with the lace cloth, the heavy glass centerpiece of red flamingos, their wings opened. The draperies behind the table were open. Had she stood at that window watching for him? He moved over to the door and stepped onto the living room carpet. Her coat was thrown over the couch, and in the pale light he could make out a large ashtray full of her cork cigarette ends on one of the cushions. He noticed the phone directory open on the coffee table as he went by. He stopped at the partially open door to their bedroom. For an instant he resisted the impulse to look in on her, and then with his finger he pushed open the door a few inches. She was sleeping, her head off the pillow, turned toward the wall, and her hair black against the sheet. The covers were bunched around her shoulders and had pulled up from the foot of the bed. She was on her side, her secret body slightly bent at the hips, her thighs closed together protectively. He stared for a minute. What, after all, should he do? Pack his things, now, and leave? Go to a hotel room until he can make other arrangements? Sleep on the extra bed in the little storage room upstairs? How should a man act, given the circumstances? The things that had been said last night. There was no undoing that—nor the other.

There was no going back, but what course was he to follow now?

In the kitchen he laid his head down on his arms over the table. How should a man act? *How should a man act?* It kept repeating itself. Not just now, in this situation, for today and tomorrow, but every day on this earth. He felt suddenly there was an answer, that he somehow held the answer himself and that it was very nearly out if only he could think about it a little longer. Then he heard Robert and Dorothea stirring. He sat up slowly and tried to smile as they came into the kitchen.

"Daddy, daddy," they both said, running over to him in their pajamas.

"Tell us a story, daddy," Robert said, getting onto his lap.

"He can't tell us a story now," Dorothea said. "It's *too* early in the morning, isn't it, daddy?"

"What's that on your face, daddy?" Robert said, pointing at the bandage.

"Let me see!" Dorothea said. "Let me see, daddy."

"*Poor* daddy," Robert said.

"What *did* you do to your face, daddy?"

"It's nothing," Ralph said. "It's all right, sweetheart. Here, get down, Robert, I hear your mother."

Ralph stepped into the bathroom and locked the door.

"Is your father here?" he heard Marian ask the children. "Where is he, in the bathroom? Ralph?"

"Mama, mama!" Dorothea exclaimed. "Daddy has a big, big bandage on his face!"

"Ralph," she turned the knob. "Ralph, let me in, please, darling. Ralph? Please let me in, darling. I want to see you. Ralph? Please?"

"Go away, Marian. Just let me alone a while, all right?"

"Please, Ralph, open the door for a minute, darling. I just want to see you, Ralph. Ralph? The children said you were hurt. What's wrong, darling? . . . Ralph?"

"Will you please be quiet, please?"

She waited at the door for a minute, turned the knob again, and then he could hear her moving around the kitchen, getting the children breakfast, trying to answer their questions.

He looked at himself in the mirror, then pulled off the bandage and tried gently with warm water and a cloth to wipe off some of the red stain. In a minute or two he gave it up. He turned away from the mirror and sat down heavily on the edge of the bathtub, began to unlace his shoes. No cowardly Aegisthus waiting for him here, no Clytemnestra. He sat there with a shoe in his hand and looked at the white, streamlined clipper ships making their way across the pale blue of the plastic shower curtain. He unbuttoned his shirt, leaned over the bathtub with a sigh, and dropped in the plug. He opened the hot water handle, and the steam rose.

As he stood naked a minute on the smooth tile before getting into the water, he gathered in his fingers the slack flesh over his ribs, looked at himself again in the clouded mirror. He started when Marian called his name.

"Ralph. The children are in their room playing . . . I called Von Williams and said you wouldn't be in today, and I'm going to stay home." She waited and then said, "I have a nice breakfast on the stove for you, darling, when you're through with your bath . . . Ralph?"

"It's all right, Marian. I'm not hungry."

"Ralph . . . Come out, darling."

He stayed in the bathroom until he heard her upstairs over the bathroom in the children's room. She was telling them: settle down and get dressed; didn't they want to play with Warren and Jeannie?

He went through the house and into the bedroom where he shut the door. He looked at the bed before he crawled in. He lay on his back and stared at the ceiling. *How should a man act?* It had assumed immense importance in his mind, was far more crucial and requiring of an answer than the other thing, the event two years ago . . . He remembered he'd just gotten up off the couch in the living room where he'd been working, and come into the kitchen and sat down ... The light ornament in the ceiling began to sway. He snapped open his eyes and turned onto his side as Marian came into the room.

She took off her robe and sat down on the edge of the bed. She put her hand under the covers and began gently stroking the lower part of his back. "Ralph," she murmured.

He tensed at her cold fingers, and then, gradually, he relaxed. He imagined he was floating on his back in the heavy, milky water of Juniper Lake, where he'd spent one summer years ago, and someone was calling to him, Come in, Ralph, Come in. But he kept on floating and didn't answer, and the soft rising waves laved his body.

He woke again as her hand moved over his hip. Then it traced his groin before flattening itself against his stomach. She was in bed now, pressing the length of her body against his and moving gently back and forth with him. He waited a minute, and then he turned to her and their eyes met.

Her eyes were filled and seemed to contain layer upon layer of shimmering color and reflection, thicker and more opaque farther in, and almost transparent at the lustrous surface. Then, as he gazed even deeper, he glimpsed in first one pupil and then the other, the cameo-like, perfect reflection of his own strange and familiar face. He continued to stare, marveling at the changes he dimly felt taking place inside him.

H. E. FRANCIS

One of the Boys

(FROM THE SOUTHWEST REVIEW)

EVERY NIGHT I waited for Millie to say it: "Will you see Red tonight?" And I would think: Don't resent it, she can't help it, maybe she's even trying to give you a little of that freedom she's heard men complain they never have, and she's Red's sister, I'm glad she cares that much about him.

But I was *not* going to Dom's place, though I might walk past, I might look in, I might even see Red . . .

Red is one of the boys. You can see them any night at Dom's, a few standing at the end of the bar, Wag and Buff at the dartboard, the others huddled in a semicircle, their feet hooked on the stool, their voices constantly erupting as they talk, argue, laugh—and in the midst of it Dom, whose mammoth Greek head is perched on a walrus body that can barely lumber its weight along behind the counter, who would be unhappy without a world of men. Dom tends his own bar. After a long, sickly childhood he has at last found his health in the lithe athletes whose out-of-doors world comes to life as the boys recreate the games play by play. Night after night, wreathed in their own tobacco laurels, their voices louder as the night grows shorter, they help Dom live his unlived youth.

That late August afternoon when I first walked in, the boys were all there. Nobody paid much attention to me—the usual flick of eyes with that casual and imperturbable condescension which customers acquire when their long-standing business gives them proprietorship. After all, I was the interloper.

I took out my handkerchief and mopped. I felt the blowers but I was still hot. Outside, a sheer crystal sea poured up from the Atlanta pavements, and the sun blinded. So for a few seconds inside I couldn't see—the figures were simply ashen silhouettes before the darkness dissolved and they dropped one by one into my eyes and made that living tableau that I see even now. For a moment I thought I was back in the service, that it was war, a world of men, and there were no women. I can't go through that again, not that, I thought. And I would have turned and gone out, but Dom said, "Yours?"

"Bud," I said.

I am not an afternoon drinker, but I blame that beginning on the heat. Like some impersonal force which was not chance or fate, but simply itself, the heat had driven me in with a prodding insistent hand, and even inside it seemed to hold and cement us together in that room on a particular afternoon that could never be undone.

But of course, then, nothing happened.

I sat at the bar, put both my hands around the glass and closed my eyes to let the coolness of the beer run up into them, then drank it straight down.

It was that bottoms-up that made the boys turn because Dom spoke again.

"You wanted that bad, hey?"

"Yes, I wanted that bad," I said, and laughed. An old man just beyond me laughed too—and I could see him in the mirror almost head-on—and two of the gang around the end of the bar looked curiously but they didn't laugh. I knew at once it was that proprietorship again: you don't give a stranger the advantage. That would admit him. Okay, I thought, okay, I get the message.

But the shorty—five feet two maybe, with red hair in a coxcomb that added two or three inches to him—stared a minute. I heard him too: "Creep." Okay, I thought. Wait.

So I listened to them, the sweat subsiding after a while, as Atlanta burned outside, and this den cooled like an earth hole despite the smoke coils above and the beer and sweat inevitable between the cleanest walls that are crowded with drinking men and vats and nicotine. And it was two hours just sitting and watching, listening to them wind up the old plays, argue about scores:

"Hey, Dom—get the almanac."

"Now wait a minute. Buff's right. One forty-eight runs."

"Get the *al*manac." The oldest one. "*I* can remember. You guys are too young."

"Too *young!*"

"*Get*—the—*almanac.*"

"Cut it down, boys. I got other customers, you know." But he brought them the almanac. "Here."

"Okay, Dom."

"Yeah, look. *Look,* I tell ya. One forty-three. *Three,* get it? Now I'll take that beer. Hey, Dom—one draft on Tom."

Laughter.

Maybe, after the hectic irregularity of my affair with Lettie, it was the reliable reputation that made me feel at home at Dom's, the slow habit of hearing the same phrases, the same arguments from the same voices until after a while you expect them with a regularity of sound that grips you slowly and which you begin to long for so that looking at your watch at a certain hour of night you say, It is almost time, and then, It *is* time, the boys will be there, and you grab your jacket—

Lettie was sick that afternoon; she did not want me around. Besides, she had quarreled with me before her illness, so it was only kindness—no, why should I lie to myself? *duty*—that made her see me then. She kept saying she wanted to break it off; she wanted to try somebody else, for its own sake, until she was sure; she didn't trust me, herself, sex; she named her friends, how bad marriage had turned out for them; on and on . . . It was tedious. Yes, I felt sorry for her. Yet I wanted more than sex, I wanted to touch her *inside,* just to let her hand touch me and me her in a place our sex did not touch. But she misunderstood. "I'm sick, damn it," she said, "sick." "You don't understand," I said. "I understand everything." "Everything!" I said, angry, though I didn't want to be, I didn't want to upset her more.

Our trouble was more than illness. She was edging away from me toward a precipice which she would soon fall off. I could not save her. No amount of begging did that; and pleading tenderly, kindly, and then angrily only agitated what I had thought to soothe into submission. To tell the truth, we had both been too easy with too many people and knew it; in the back of our minds there was a remote, mutual disrespect. Our break tore our habits; it left loose nerve ends. And I walked in a crooked line with no magnetism at the other end, so I reached out for habits—

"Go then. Go!" she shouted when I went back to try once more that afternoon. I did not return or call after that. We both used pride as the excuse, I know, a lie to cover up our freedom for a new enslavement.

So I went back to Dom's place. I sensed all along that it was what I would do. I felt I had found something familiar in myself that I couldn't define, but I recognized that I had to find out what it was—because it was in Buff and Dick, Tom, Eddie, and Line—and Red. Mostly in Red. And in what Dom's place was to them.

It was Red who began it. He stood next to my stool at the bar, just outside the circle of raw light that encompassed the gang, and he could not help hearing me talk to Dom about England.

"Hey, you guys—he been to England," Red said. He had sidled into the light; it spilled into his red hair, which quivered like a menace. Those faces behind him turned to glance with diffident scorn at England in the flesh. So I played it by ear. "Yeah," I said. Not *yes*. "Yeah." And his eyes froze an instant, with jarred stillness, and then made a suspicious roam over me.

"Bet you play darts too, ahn?" As accurately as your eyes

do, I thought, and I felt them all penetrating me. But I didn't answer.

"Suhmatter? English too good for us, uh?"

I had thought silence would cool him off, but the others stood up in support of him, a circle of controlled alien faces. I still didn't speak, but I did get up—perhaps it was the way I did it that saved the night, I don't know—and held out my hand for the darts. It didn't shake.

Buff handed them to me.

"Okay. Who with?" I said.

There was an instant's silence before anyone moved. And then it was Eddie.

"I'll go you," he said.

"Me too," Tom said.

Line made a fourth. We paired off—or Eddie paired us off. What was strange was that Red hadn't offered to oppose. He leaned his arm on the bar, high and awkward for him, and watched us all the while. He was then just beginning to grow fat, his stomach sloppy over his belt, his chest a bit sagged, and he had that habit of tucking his thumbs into his belt, arms akimbo. His pants were too long, the cuffs creased with a crippled look at his ankles, and dragged. You expected him to turn any minute and walk pathetically, with Charlie Chaplin scuffing, down the aisle, out the front door, and into the distance.

As it turned out, Line and I won the first game and Red could not even say, "Thanks to *Line*," though his eyes glowed with hope when we lost the second. We played until closing and our team carried the day, thanks to Oxford pubs and the boys at Pemmie during my Fulbright year.

The victory was enough to make me go back the following Saturday night. Red wasn't in sight, and the boys scarcely spoke. I was still the once-a-week stranger. I sat alone a good while before anyone spoke to me.

"Hey, shark—" It was Red. He'd been in the Den. He was very drunk, which meant he must have been drinking hard because he was a veteran beer holder, and he was smiling warmly with rheumy eyes. "Shark, I want you to meet my sister. *C'mon,* shark."

She was sitting alone at one of those huge oak tables for eight or ten people, which made her look small and lonely and very much self-conscious and afraid, though she wasn't.

"I've heard about you all week," she said, taking my hand. She didn't let it go; it rather guided me to the chair next to her, and Red closed in—he dragged a chair around tight between us.

"He's the cham*peen,* Millie. Y'oughta see those throws."

She was gazing at me, her face rather wistful, and did not reply, yet her green eyes were alive with a strength that reinforced the tight clasp of her hand, as if she and I had (and both instantaneously realized it) something to cling to in the quiet storm that always goes on about us, as if we were two of the islands of this world she was to speak of, which will be swallowed up by something that crouches and waits beyond the horizon toward which we slip day by day. Between Red's praises, surprising in themselves after Saturday's silent treatment, came gradual powerless little grunts. The alcohol crept into the regions of his body so that we could watch one after another the parts of him die for the evening. Behind his wet, half-open eyes there was only the remotest recognition, which came out in ribald, smiling twists of his mouth and weak grunts, between which—or instigated by them—she tried to explain.

"Partly it's the times too. You feel that? The atom and all. The islands are still here, but they're people. People are the only things we have to reach out to. These days we depend so much on touching, but when your hands *can't* touch any longer, you can't find people, you get frantic, you flounder, you want to shout for something bigger than you to take you up and hold you, and even that's not there, it's dispersed like everything else, and you *want* to cry out, you *try,* but you don't have the strength, it dies in your throat—like Red's— and the worst thing is you begin to forget anybody's there

. . ." She at last let me go. My hand felt so empty and I wanted to cry out—she must have seen that on my face because even as she reached over and touched Red ever so tenderly so that he felt it, so that he sat up and stared with what seemed like a tremendous effort to comprehend where he was and what was happening, so that he recognized us and smiled, she did not take her eyes off my own face, and I was sure in her own way she was trying to tell me she had not let go, she was still touching me.

"What are you doing *here?*" I said—in a bar with a brother who hung with the boys and left her alone in this enormous Den, where college kids and locals whooped it up nightly so that the very noise drove your loneliness goading back into you.

"He doesn't get drunk very often. He drinks a lot, he knows how, but sometimes . . . well, I just know when the times are. You understand? I come—just to be here, I guess."

"He's got the boys."

"They can't go as far. There's a certain point they can't go beyond, even when they want to—you understand? They're . . . useless, I guess."

I got up feeling a bit like them, useless, and I said, "Yes," and stood there.

"Ohhh—I didn't mean . . ." She too rose, both of us standing awkwardly almost against each other.

"No, I didn't take it that way," I said. "You misunderstood." I hadn't taken it personally either, but now her saying it *made* me take it personally.

"It's just the way things work, I guess," I said.

Red lolled in the chair, his small kangaroo arms hooked over the side. His head balanced awkwardly on his right shoulder, his lower lip clutched over his upper, and the scraggly thick red hair fell over his ugly face. I say ugly, but I mean that bizarre grotesquerie which makes sad clowns out of some of the homeliest of men.

"Well," she said. "We've got to go. He's in no condition to stay."

"My car—"

"No," she said, rather emphatically I thought, until I said, "Well, then, the boys—"

"No!" she said more emphatically. I did not understand. Was she putting herself between me and Red, without reason, and between the boys and Red?

"I only meant that if *I* offered, the boys might be offended. After all, he's their—" I didn't know how to say there was a code at work in these things.

"That's too primitive." She laughed and, bending over, took Red's face between her hands. "Red. *Red!*" Her voice roused him like a conditioning which spoke beyond his immediate mind, and she managed to get him up and guide him out and left me standing there like a fool, feeling—and why?—a peculiar inadequacy but—worse—a resentment that she had made me feel that way.

Even now I am not sure if it was to eradicate that resentment that I wanted to see her again, though I told myself it was. So, rather awkwardly, I began to stop by after work, about eight, to pick up Red on the way to Dom's place. I went more often, I got to know the crowd, and on the nights that Millie came along she rode with me; after closing we lingered in the Impala. And sometimes, after she was gone, I could hear her soft breathing beside me, or waking that night the same soft breathing, until I clamped my hand on my chest, like trying to hold her, make her *me*, interrupting the sound with a start at discovering that it was my own; but the breathing would creep back into my head until I could only hear the one, mine and hers, and then Red's too, and the boys', everybody's, until it flooded over me, all at the same time, from one big body ... After that, I would sleep.

With Millie beside me, I forgot about Lettie most of the time. I acquired something I had never had before, a link with life, I was held *in* life, saved from being out of it as an observer watching Red, the boys, Dom, life itself. And now I knew I could not stand *not* to have that. So when I touched her, when finally my hand was on her thigh and her hands tore over my back and we sucked and bit, it was not simply sex at last—it was that I had got *to* her beyond that resentment; we had fought—we were fighting then—and we both knew it but could not say that it was the struggle itself that we wanted because our conflicting wills made us live.

"What about Red?"

"Red? Why . . . I could never leave him." She was incredibly matter-of-fact.

"I know that," I said. But why thrust him onto me? I thought, yet I couldn't imagine what it would be like if she had not. "That needn't change things. We're getting married anyway."

"Yes. And Red will live with us—or maybe, if you want to, we'll stay here, and you can move in with us."

"No—" It was somehow the one condition I'd have fought for. "We'll find a bigger place, a place of our own, with a good-sized room for Red."

"You really want that? You'll do it?" She smiled, almost too pleased at that. Yet there was a perceptible antagonism in her voice.

"For you. You know that."

I was not then thinking of the boys—not that they had fully accepted me. A good shot at the dartboard and the approval of a few members of a club are not enough to make you belong. There is a trust which comes from years of anchoring in another's habits, and I knew, the moment Red came into the apartment a few days before we began to move to the new flat, that beyond the surface a tumult was at work. I did not know how subtle the workings in Dom's place were.

"I got me a place around the corner," he said finally. "McCorkell's. You know the house, Mill. Her husband's got the wheel-chair, sits in the sun parlor all day."

Millie's silence was worse than the fiercest sun—for an instant I thought she would cry out, so taut was she. But she worked on until she subsided, then she said, 'It's McCorkell's then?"

At the table his hands edged the cloth. "Aw, come on, Mill. What'd you expect? I mean, a guy can't let somebody else—"

"You'd be paying your own way. I always made you do that," she said calmly. "But obviously you won't be." It was his dismissal, though he didn't go at once. Abruptly he turned to me. "You! What the hell you think you're doing anyway?" And he left.

"Red!" I called, but only the stubborn sounds deep in the stairwell reverberated, then the shut door, and hollow, irregular steps down the street.

"He'll come back—he will, won't he?" she said, and for the first time in weeks I sensed a loss of that touching, because she was reaching to something beyond me, to some need I couldn't and she couldn't supply. "He will, won't he?"

"I don't know, Millie," I said.

That night she did not really have to plead with me, though I'm sure she thought that was the reason I finally went to Dom's to talk to Red. It ended with a kind of pleading on my part—for her, I said. That gave him importance and a triumph which he lorded before the boys: "See that—I told ya she'd come after me." I sensed a different rhythm among the boys as they played darts, talked, joked, fought over reputations and scores. Something of the old status quo had been reestablished. The boys retreated into the circle of light, and I was the ignored stranger again. I was angry; I felt I saw them for what they were: a self-contained bunch of peacocks, ex-athletes living on ex-games, with thick waists, drooped breasts, beer-swollen jowls, and bleary eyes blind to the world outside. There was only one thing missing: Millie, their audience of one. And she was mine now.

"You shouldn't feel as bad as I do, but you do, don't you?" she said.

Her insight startled me, for I did feel bad. Something had been torn away from me too. Red was fixed on an opposite bank from us, and as long as he was there we were broken, all three of us. Millie was disrupted; her lost routine wrenched her out of socket; naturally it was impossible to plant her years-old fixation for Red in me. She fretted. I saw the loss in her face even when she didn't say anything to me, when she turned inquiringly to me as I entered the apartment, that happy but frightened look of disappointment, the brief constriction from fear of permanent loss which separation brings.

"You seeing Red tonight? *Are* you?" she'd say, and I had to sit beside her, I had to say, "Millie, don't you understand— now you and I are the same thing to him. What's you he identifies with me. He's going to react the same way with me as with you."

"But you could *try*. He's my brother." It grew then to a new stage—she would begin to cry, taut, soundless tears. I could not get close to her. She made me feel what islands we are, how we can't stand what islands we are. And I would promise, "Tonight, Millie. Tonight I'll talk to Red."

Returning late, I knew she would speak out of the darkness: "You talked to Red?" Sometimes in my first silence she knew: "He won't come . . ." I couldn't understand her. I wanted to say, "You're not married to Red. You're married to me, Millie, *me*." Immediately I regretted thinking it. How small I was. Never once did she reproach me for the few times I drank too much with Red, or after Red had gone, though occasionally when we were downtown, when she did say, "You don't really want a drink, do you?" I felt a probing in her understanding, and as I looked at her, reproach must have been hard in my eyes because she would say, "I'm sorry, I *am*." At such times I was aware of how she knew there are, simply, inexplicable presences which cement others together, without which what was can't exist again in the same way. But whoever stops if he does believe that?

Finally I succeeded: whether Red was actually lonely for her or whether his own resistance, even with the support of the boys, was not enough to sustain his own broken routine or his emotional dependence on her, he decided to come to dinner on Wednesday night. Cautiously, to fortify himself, he wangled an invitation for Line and Buff, perhaps to show he had the boys' sanction, perhaps to hold back her onslaught, or more typically ("primitively," she would say) to hide a man's fear of acting alone.

Millie was beautiful that night. She glowed with the strength of a hidden source of energy that compelled every move. Red's face as he came into the room registered his pleasant shock as he stared at her. She laughed.

"Red!" she cried as if she hadn't seen him in years. In her laughter the timbre of happy tears resounded so strongly that Red himself could scarcely speak. The boys felt it too. For a while they enjoyed it like a sound aimed at each of them separately. They had a brief, breathless look into a happiness they hadn't yet known, an inkling of what woman, marriage, home might mean. It kept them quiet for a time, just watching, until Red started talking and laughing spontaneously, already steeped in the apartment, not at all a stranger. His pleasure was a threat, and in Line and Buff something happened, some animal secretion at the scent of danger threatening their species, and Buff said, "You sure got it cozy here, Millie, just like I had before I left the house. My mother, she drove me to it—ya know? That's the way they all are." He slipped comfortably down into the chair, long and, if a little too heavy, still lithe, and strummed the endtable in quick rhythm—he used to play the snare drum, you never forgot that. He kept glancing at his watch and it made Millie nervous, she laughed at nothing, especially with Red joining in because he was getting a little high on the wine, which he seldom drank except on special occasions. Line said, "You put too much of that away, Red, and you know that beer at Dom's won't mix, you'll wind up pretty sick."

"Oh, *Line*—" Millie reproached. Something of the glow left her.

"Well, *you* know, Mill. You don't want him sick, do you?"

"Yeah, Mill. You don't want me sick." Red pushed back the wine. Buff looked at his watch. He smiled at Red. "You all right, Red?"

"Why shouldn't he be all right? Of course he's all right," she said.

"Aw, Mill, I didn't mean anything."

"Of course you didn't." Her lower lip loosened, down, as when she argues with me.

"Well, I didn't, Mill. You know that."

"All right, all *right!*" she said.

"Come on now, Millie. Don't get upset. Buff only meant—"

"Yeah—" Buff said.

"I *know* what Buff only meant!"

"Well, if you're gonna take it that way, Mill—" Buff rose. Like a shadow, Line rose too. Red scuffed his chair back. "Look, Mill—"

"*I* know. You don't have to tell me. These are your *friends.* Go ahead—*say* it: 'These are my friends.'"

"Well, they are!"

"Who'd ever guess?" she muttered.

"Okay. *Okay*—'f that's the way you feel..."

"That's the way I feel."

Red turned at the door. "Okay, Mill...," he said, but she turned away from him. She did not look at me. She stood there, keyed up but not trembling, contained as stone; she did not move until after the door below closed and a torn laugh sounded down the street. Then her hands hooked up, helpless, at the air; she trembled with anger, tears came, and a thin tight cry in her throat. "Millie..." I drew her close. "It's all right, Millie." She let herself flow into me, her tears hot against my chest, her pulsing like my own; and I had a queerly perverse gratitude to Red for making me feel this. But it was *not* all right. No matter what I felt, the minute she broke away I knew again that if Red had thrust us together for that moment, the separation was greater because he was gone.

"I can't give him anything, that's the trouble," she said. "You can only go so far with somebody else—*he* doesn't know that, and you don't. He's a sweet, ugly little man. If he had a wife, he'd understand, our relations would be serene, he'd know then why I can't leave him alone. He may never know. *Think* of that—he may never know. He can't go on like this always. Can he?"

And I saw the boys at Dom's with her eyes: night after night for a whole lifetime, drinking, laughing, throwing darts, arguing about baseball scores, their athletic frames gathering paunches, their faces fading with a more open desperation, their heads gray and oily with baldness—

"*Can* he?" She searched me, but her eyes went beyond me, and I thought, Jesus, Mill, what *is* it? How much do you want?

"Why not?" I said, and I have to confess that at her startled look and the way she arrowed "Paul!" at me, there was a shock in my words for me too. "What do you mean?" And I didn't know then. But her question was thrust back at me after what happened Saturday night: because I left her alone—she wanted that, actually argued it, thinking I might bring Red back or give him back some of our companionship and relieve his loneliness, which she grieved about day and night. I hadn't seen Line or Buff or Red since Wednesday, so I was not really prepared for what happened: they smiled at me, first one then the other. "Hey, Paul—" Buff said. Buff never said "Hey, Paul" to me like that—quick, spontaneous, without the reserve of a minority group that sized you up for a whole evening before it acknowledged you verbally. Silent Tom actually condescended to grunt and Eddie talked a blue streak though it wasn't aimed at me. It was Buff who finally egged me into the Couples' Den.

"Hey, Paul. Come on 'n sit. There's plenty-a-room." He strolled into the Den and sat facing me. "Dom did a good thing opening this here new room," he said, scrutinizing me. And then I saw her—he *knew* I saw her—and the insidious look of pleasure on his face communicated it to the bar, because I heard their soft, undertoned laughs behind—

"You know *her?*" he said.

She was sitting at the table behind him and I could see her over his shoulder. I half rose ... *Lettie*— And Buff rose too, smiling that treacherous, knowing smile which coated me dirty inside with its implications.

I went over to her table and sat. "Hello, Lettie."

"Paul—" she said with a look of near pain, as if the word hurt.

In a way I was pleased to see her and I told her so.

"I knew you would be," she said, but she had misunderstood.

"I mean—"

"I know what you mean," she said. "After all is said and done, I know, and I had to satisfy my instincts—to see you in the flesh just to see if there's some change, if it's that girl—Millie?—you really want, what it's done to you."

"Wait a *minute,* Lettie. You're going too fast for me."

"I always did, didn't I? But I was right, you see—you're not changed, you're just Paul, you don't even look 'right,' you just look like ... Paul."

"What in hell did you think I'd look like?" Certainly I did not want to become exasperated—ours had been a history of exasperation—that would only confirm whatever her feelings were.

"It's not what I thought you'd look like—different somehow, and whole, with that smug self-satisfaction a married man at least ought to have. Well, you haven't got that self-assurance."

"Who has it for long? It comes and goes in anybody's life."

"Now you're throwing barbs."

"I didn't mean it that way. *You* had to live through things to make up your mind too."

"I have," she said. Her look was wrong, too confident, filled with some pity poured out to me; and I felt if I held out my hands I'd catch it, she'd touch me. I dug them into my pockets.

"Lettie," I whispered, aware now of the shadows, the heads on the floor at my feet, beside my chair.

"I *have*," she shrilled with the faintest hysteria in her whisper.

"It can't ever be," I said. "I'm married. I'm committed—"

Then I felt the presence of Red beside me. He laughed. I can see the beer in his hand, yellow, close to my face, the foam like slops, spraying up and over the edge, over his hand, dirtying it, making me feel dirty; and the heat of his hand touched me—

"Committed!" he said, with an excruciatingly painful edge to his own voice. "So that's what you are with my sister—"

Behind him Buff laughed, and there was a muffled echo, a guffaw, and someone stamped a foot. The darts struck unusually hard in a rapid three into the cork.

"Red, I didn't mean—" His eyes, redwebbed and tired, glared with a petty triumph I didn't want to see him descend to, and I felt sorry for him. I wanted to grab his hands and tell him, Red, Red, I didn't do anything to you, I didn't take anything away from you, I'm trying to give you something, when Line (I once thought him the kindest of the lot) stepped forward. "Aw, come on, Paul, give the lady what she came after." His voice nudged sharp as an elbow in me. There were only a few people in the Den—they were discreetly talking—but the boys all heard Line, they laughed, yet they were tense too; it was in the air, in the still, hard way they blew their cigarette smoke. I simply wanted to get out before the release. Somebody was out to destroy something, and nobody—I am convinced of it—knew what it was. But they would go on, and I stood there.

"Yeah, what's the matter with you, Paul?" Eddie said. They all laughed again. At the other end of the bar, Dom, unaware of what was going on, smiled and waved to me.

And then Red seemed to come to—things were now going in the wrong direction. He turned on them. "Hey, fellas, *wait a minute*—" But they laughed again. Buff thumbed at him. "Millie's my sister," Red said.

" 'f I had a lonely girl, wowee—" Buff said. Shamed now for Lettie, and angry, insulted, and feeling Red on my side, with a fast wild pulsing in me that struck my temples, coursed in my breathing, I said, "Then you *got* one, boy—go ahead, I dare you." I edged close and looked up at Buff, and then at the boys. "All of you," I said, grabbing Lettie's arm. "What the hell *would* you do? Well, here's your chance, you dart throwers, you goddamned strong-man clique. All talk and no action. That's what you are—talk talk talk. For the next fifty years that's all you'll do. No women and no life, just this cozy little bunch of deadheads. Why the hell don't you do something *useful!* Why?" And I shoved her forward. She knew what I was up to better than I did, and for just a second a smile flickered over her face before the fear set in it.

The stillness was deathly—in that brief interval before they realized what the words meant in this unstudied vacuum I had set them in, before Eddie's lightning fist plunged out and struck me in the left shoulder, I saw Red in the mirror: he was staring into his own image, dead still. His face had a raw, peeled-away look; his arms hung, and his stomach sagged absolutely inert over his belt. "*Red*—" I said, instantly ashamed, but he didn't move until I struck the bar and rolled over and Buff jumped me and dragged me up again. "*Hold it, Buff!*" Red shouted and leaped at him. The whole gang tensed, ready for Red and me when Dom cried out, "What's the matter with you guys!" probing his way down the aisle. He grabbed Buff's shoulder. "Now let's cut it out! You wanta make trouble for me?" Loosed, I sprawled against the wall. I thought it was over then, but for Red, who gripped my jacket, his beety face thrust against my chest. "Now you listen—" he said, realizing that I had set him against his own crew. "You caused enough trouble. Now you get out. Leave us alone, *alone*—you hear?"

"Red," I said. His action was the last thing I had expected, but the boys began, at first with a sheepish softness, to back him: "You tell him, Red."

"Alone!" Red shouted. *"Hear?"* And maybe I was the only one to see his wet eyes and hear his hard breathing.

"Red, please—" But I knew it was futile, I could not ask what it was that moved him—because I had exposed the boys? set the rift deeper between him and Millie and me? told some truth about us all?

"Get out!" he cried. Not even Dom protested that.

I turned and went out, and Lettie followed. I heard her behind me. I didn't look, I was standing on the street in front of the glass window, between the letters C and A of the word DELICATESSEN spread over the pane.

"I'm sorry, Lettie. That was a rotten thing for me to do."

"It was my fault. I shouldn't have come."

"No. It would have happened sooner or later. It was bound to come."

"I know that too," she said. "You had to learn it."

"Yes." And in that instant I could have taken her hand and told her I realized it now, but an interval is sometimes too late, and I heard her steps round the corner and then her car door slam and then the ignition.

After she had gone, I looked into the pane. Through my own image, a faint ghost of a man in the glass, the boys were gathering around the bar again. They took their glasses. From their midst Red looked my way . . . For just a moment his face quivered, then froze— He stared at me and I at him as if we were caught in each other. If I reached through my own shadow I felt I might touch him. The pane was between us, but I'd got inside him and he inside me, and we couldn't get out. I was ringing with the discovery. And then he laughed, the way the defeated do under the guise of triumph, and he goaded the others—they all began to laugh, I could hear it through the fan vent. Laughs. Laughs. But the laughter didn't matter now. They were all alone. The laughter made them feel together. How multiple and subtle our treachery is. I didn't need them anymore—because I'd been one of the boys all the time. I was alone, like them, and Lettie, and Millie. *Millie*— I had to hurry back. She would be waiting ...

She was sitting at the kitchen table, and she asked the inevitable question: Did you see Red?"

I gazed at her.

"Well?" The still way she looked up, I could tell she knew something had happened to me.

And I said, "Yes."

She waited, her vigilant eyes expectant.

"I stripped him," I said abruptly. "I *did*. I told them all what they were. I didn't mean to, Mill, but now ... I'm glad." I looked out the window in the direction of Dom's—it was so far away in the darkness, but I felt closer to the boys than I ever had before.

"And I'm sorry for them, for everybody—because they're alone."

I heard her get up. And for the first time she touched me.

"I know," she said.

"You know?" I saw her beside me in the pane. She was smiling. And then I saw her night after night sitting alone in this apartment, I saw all the nights of her waiting for me, waiting for my confrontation with Red, with myself, knowing it would happen, trying to *make* it happen to free me, waiting alone while I pursued Red and myself.

And now she knew her waiting was over.

"Millie ..."

She clutched me. I could feel her behind me, her hand against my neck, her arms slipped around my chest. There was nothing to separate us now. We were all the same, Red and Lettie and the boys and Millie. And I could feel her blood pulsing against me, and her touch, like that laughter, bridging the islands we are. Let us have this, I thought, covering her hands as I looked out into the darkness. And I could see our hands in the pane, I could see Lettie and Millie and Red and the boys, I could see them in my own eyes.

MacDonald Harris

Trepleff

(FROM HARPER'S MAGAZINE)

THE THEATER WHERE the rehearsals were held was a little building that had been a cabinet shop before it was acquired by the Players. It had no ceiling and if you looked up into the roof you saw a labyrinth of beams and wooden props, rather amateurishly fitted with lights from which festoons of wiring hung down. Perhaps because it had been a cabinet shop the building always smelled of freshly cut wood. The rehearsals took place in the afternoon, after the students who were taking classes were out of school. At precisely three o'clock Egon would burst into the theater exuding energy, his corduroy jacket unbuttoned to display his waistcoat. Odor of cologne, bass voice, ears with small black tufts of hair growing out of them. Amethyst on third finger of perfectly manicured hand.

"Stage, stage. Places, everybody. Where's Trepleff? Nina ... Pauline ... over here. Where's Madame Arkadina?" Mme. Arkadina, in real life the wife of an Ann Arbor dentist, was in the bathroom, which served for both sexes. "Irina Nikolaevna, get the hell out of the can." His voice could be heard all over the building, through walls and inside the deepest closets. He always called us by our stage names and sometimes I wondered whether he knew our real names. At first we were Trepleff, Sorin, or Mme. Arkadina and then when we got on more intimate terms he began addressing us in the Russian fashion with first name and patronymic: I was Konstantin Gavrilovich, Sorin was Pyotr Nikolaevich, and so on. The Stanislavsky method as practiced by Egon was incredibly demanding and took all our concentration. He made us live the parts, not only in the theater but down the street in the café drinking coffee, at home, on our dates, on weekends.

I had just come out of the hospital, where I had spent six weeks recovering from infectious hepatitis and reading Sinclair Lewis' *Arrowsmith*, and in my weakened condition I was probably more susceptible to this kind of suggestion than the others. Somebody told me the Orchard Players were going to do *The Seagull* and still hadn't cast several parts, and I thought it would be good mental hygiene, which was about as wrong as you could get. It wasn't long before Egon had us all in a state of semi-delusion about our identities. For instance he set us to writing essays on what we (our Russian selves) were like as children. I (as Trepleff) wrote a schoolboy theme which I had allegedly composed in a *lycée* at the age of sixteen. In its juvenile style it rather ingeniously anticipated certain things that were later to recur in the poem Trepleff writes for Nina in Act I, for example the solitude of the universe and the struggle between spirit and matter. Egon was quite pleased with it. There was a good deal of this kind of homework. But mostly it was a matter of Egon cajoling and browbeating us until we were harried into our Chekhovian selves. For instance he would turn to Nina, in real life a grave and somewhat prim girl named Syd who always rehearsed in leotards and a heavy white ski sweater. "Nina—what is Nina?" he would growl at her, holding out his hairy hands, palms turned upward, elbows against his stomach. "Innocence. Grace. Not intelligence but intuition. A longing for—what? She doesn't know. Something here." He would lay the palms of his hands flat on his chest. "Nina— feel, feel!" He made Nina put her own hands on the same place on the white ski sweater. "There's something there—a desire—a melancholy, graceful, very feminine, elusive longing. Nina is a seagull. Something in her soars, floats over the world, but she never finds what she is looking for. Trepleff brings her a dead seagull which he has shot. She says, 'This seagull, I suppose that's a symbol. Forgive me, but I don't understand it.' That's the essence of Nina. She doesn't understand—she feels *here*." Again the two hairy palms on the pectoral region. "And Nina—that day after Trepleff offers you the seagull—what do you do when you go home?"

"It isn't in the play."

"Of course it isn't in the play. But what do you do? You're Nina. Only you know what you do. What do you feel like doing?"

"I don't know. Some sewing perhaps. Or read a book."

"Sewing." He raised his clenched hands and made a goatlike sound of contempt. "No, no no no. Listen. You open the window. You look out. What do you see?"

She hesitated. "Birches. Fields. The water beyond. And— over the lake, gulls."

"Exactly!" Finally he drove us into understanding what we would do even in the parts of our lives that Chekhov hadn't written. "The gulls over the lake. Sunset, a voice calling, music from the other shore. A melancholy, a faintly pleasant melancholy. Now you are Nina, now you are feeling it, fine."

Striding up and down the stage, he would turn suddenly on me. "Trepleff! What are you? A visionary. But the thing you see is not God but the gulf of human loneliness. You love and pity others because you love and pity yourself. You kill a seagull, you murder it and bring it to Nina, but you say, 'Today I was low enough to kill this seagull. I lay it at your feet.' You are a criminal in order to lay your crime at the feet of others, out of compassion for them. Essentially you are a weak character, and yet there's a saintly streak in you. The Doomed Saint. This is very Russian! You are not only out of Chekhov, you are also out of Dostoevski. Trepleff! What have you read of Dostoevski?"

"*Crime and Punishment. Karamazov.*"

"But you must read the rest of it!" he would bellow,

thrusting his arms toward me with palms up, trembling as though he were holding a heavy log. "Read it all, read everything in the library! On Monday bring me a list of what you've read!"

I would spend the weekend staying up until four in the morning, reading Dostoevski until my eyes were red. On Monday Egon would have forgotten all about Dostoevski. He would point one hairy hand in my direction and demand, "Trepleff. Where did you go to the university?"

I was damned if I knew. I decided that since I was a citizen of Kiev I would have gone to the University of Kiev. None of us knew whether there was a University of Kiev, but Egon succeeded in convincing me I had gone to it.

"And what did you study at the University of Kiev?"

I was getting the hang of it now. I had studied German philosophy, literature, and a little medicine. Mostly, however, I had read Dostoevski.

"Ah, Dostoevski. And what character in Dostoevski are you most like?"

I pondered for a moment. "Prince Myshkin."

"Right! Wonderful! Myshkin, the saint, but also a little of the criminal in him. He too could kill a bird and say, 'Today I was low enough to kill this seagull.' He too is capable of laughing with his face wet with tears. And Trepleff—my friend, please allow me to call you Konstantin Gavrilovich. Konstantin Gavrilovich, my friend, please tell me." His voice dropped to a confidential rumble. "Please tell me, when you were a little boy, how did you think of your mother?"

"My mother?"

"Your mother, Madame Arkadina. How would a little boy think of a mother who was a famous actress?"

"Well." I hadn't expected this. I had to grope a little. "How old am I?"

"Three."

"Well, uh. She seemed to me—a strange angel. Glitters, sequins—smelling good—but distant, unattainable—where I couldn't reach her."

"Splendid! A little boy whose mother is always away, traveling, appearing before audiences in Moscow and Petersburg—and when she comes home!"

"She passes through the nursery—" As I spoke I began to see the scene clearly now, as clearly as though it had been my real childhood. "She bends over my crib, there is a glitter of jewels and a scent of patchouli—she says, 'My Kostya, little prince, my angel, don't cry now, ah look, he has porridge on his face, how disgusting—nurse, Avdotya! take him off and wash him—Kostya, my star, angel of my heart, farewell, I'm off to'—where the hell is she off to?"

"Yaroslavl. Splendid, but patchouli is for old ladies, Konstantin Gavrilovich. Madame Arkadina would wear—" he raised his arms and didn't know himself. "Irina Nikolaevna! what would you wear?"

The dentist's wife was brought forth and decided she would wear jasmine. There was a pause while we all imagined her bending over my crib and smelling of jasmine. Egon went on stalking back and forth on the stage.

"So your mother is always in Yaroslavl, in Moscow, in Petersburg, playing in theaters. You grow up longing for a human touch, an affection to replace that of your mother. And gradually you learn to pity others who long for a human touch, and because you pity them you love them. And yet, and yet—you love them not as ordinary men love, but with the love of a criminal, who is also a kind of a saint—h'm?"— our eyes met and I nodded, a little wildly—"a saint who lies under a special curse, that for him the souls of others are transparent."

I looked around me and it was true, the souls of all those students and dentists' wives were transparent. At that moment I must really have looked doomed, because Egon stared at me with a strange smile and exulted, "Splendid, splendid!" The hairy arms spread in an expansive gesture and then swung back together until he embraced himself. "Konstantin Gavrilovich, I congratulate you! You are becoming yourself!"

Egon, of course, was Trigorin. Nina and Trepleff were one thing. Ah, but Trigorin! Trigorin was a famous author, his name in the papers every day, his books translated into foreign languages. The darling of the public, beloved of a million sentimental women, and what was he interested in? Work! Only in work! And what was his work? To create people, characters, human beings! And for this, of course, it was necessary for him to live, to have experiences. He was capable of shooting a seagull, but not to lay it at the feet of someone out of pity. Merely to see what it felt like to kill a seagull, in order to put it in a story. But what a man! Not a human being at all but a machine for work, a machine for living, lusting, feeling, knowing, in order that it could all go into his art! Egon really dug into the part, the character of Trigorin touched something in him that released a flood of energy. Or else he had practiced the Stanislavsky method for so long that he really became Trigorin even to himself, as he wanted us to do.

His voice took on a Russian intonation, the way Chaliapin would perhaps talk if he spoke English. He strode up and down the stage with hands thrust out and his elbows on his stomach, a gorilla but an elegant gorilla in a checked shirt and burgundy waistcoat, exhorting, pleading, chastising, wheedling, browbeating us in his hairy bass. "Please, everybody. Places! Let's start from the beginning, since nobody with the possible exception of myself seems to have grasped yet what this play is about. It's about the Russian soul, melancholy, flowers, poetry, loneliness, death!" He held out his fierce hand, the bass voice shook and there was a catch in it almost like a tear. "Soul! Flowers! Loneliness! Everybody think soul, flowers, and loneliness. Everybody! Act one, scene one. Masha, Masha. Little turtledove, listen. I love you with all my heart and soul, but please. When they ask you why you're wearing black and you say, 'I'm in mourning for my life. I'm unhappy.' You know that line? You haven't forgotten your lines? Good. If you can't learn to act, at least try to focus your tiny little brain on learning your part. But you can learn to act, little turtledove, my sweet. When you say that line, please, for me, for the sake of my rather delicate nerves, do not say it as though somebody had stuck a hatpin into your behind. Say it quite simply. Yet with tremendous emotion! But the emotion is underneath! It does not consist in making little trills and screeches."

Masha was a pretty sophomore girl with brown eyes who was not used to being treated this way. "First you want more emotion, then less emotion," she quavered. "How can you say something quite simply and yet with emotion?"

"It is necessary to distinguish between emotion and hysteria. First, however, it is necessary not to be a half-wit. In this respect I admit you have a certain handicap. I do not ask of you anything beyond your powers. All I ask is that you do your best, and that means DOING EXACTLY AS I SAY!"

Masha collapsed in tears and it was some time before anybody could calm her down. Egon took no part in her consolation. He turned his back contemptuously on her and made another of his gestures: he cupped his hands and moved them slowly up and down in front of his chest, as though he were holding two grapefruit and trying to decide which was the larger. When he looked around they were mopping up Masha's tears with a handkerchief and patting her on the back. He rubbed his short stiff beard and sighed. Finally she got up, they pushed her onto the stage, and Medvedenko asked her, "Why do you always wear black?" "I'm in mourning for my life. I'm unhappy," she intoned monotonously like a sleep-walker. But with terrific emotion underneath. It was exactly what Egon wanted. He could be heard rumbling softly to himself, "Ah. Ah."

I was unhappy too but in a different way from Masha. It was a beatific, poignant, philosophical kind of unhappiness that consisted of loving Syd or did I mean Nina? I was a little confused on this point but in any case loving the creature with slender legs, boyish manner, cool elfin grace whose life was so intimately intertwined with mine on the stage as well as off and yet who managed to elude me in some mysterious way in both realms. My love was hopeless, purified, and utterly devoid of selfishness. It would be wrong to say it was devoid of fleshly desire, but it was an odd fleshly desire, passive and resigned, that lingered like a sadness in the bones. It made me an excellent Trepleff. She wasn't cold or unfriendly toward me, in fact we were together frequently and there was even a certain intimacy between us but she was the same with the others and it was only the easy and superficial camaraderie of the theater that would end when the play was over, or so I concluded in my pessimism. My Russian, Trepleffian pessimism. I had never been pessimistic before but now it seemed a part of my nature. I had dug into my part too, I had dug into it tooth and nail until the dirt was over my head and I had forgotten my way out into the air again. Trepleff was my grave. The funny thing was that in some goofy spiritual self-exacerbating way I liked it down there under the ground. It fitted me, it was restful.

Anyhow there we were, Trepleff and Nina, walking back to the women's dorm on a frosty Michigan night. It was December now and so cold it made your teeth ache. I walked at a distance of five feet from her down the tree-lined paths of the campus, never daring to touch her or say anything of what I felt. It was enough to be with her, and I even liked the bitter cold because it provided an appropriate physical misery to go with the misery of my soul. When she left the theater she still wore the heavy white sweater and leotard but she added a black scarf that went two or three times around her neck and was still long enough to reach almost to her knees. Once I asked her if she was cold and she said, "All that's relative, I think." I was unable to find out even the most innocent physical fact about her. Perhaps she had learned to talk this way at Wellesley where she had gone before she came to Ann Arbor or perhaps she merely preferred not to discuss her physical sensations with a member of the opposite sex. Because she did think of me as a male, that was apparent from various small signs. And so? What next? Nothing. I was totally blissful in my misery as it was.

Sometimes I even had a kind of a date with her, so to speak; that is, after rehearsal we would go to one of the student cafés on the edge of campus and drink coffee. We dutifully called each other Trepleff and Nina, as per instructions. But it didn't seem to me that Syd, or Nina, had dug quite as far into her part as I had. For one thing she hadn't been sick. And then she was a drama major and thought of herself more consciously as an actress. But it seemed to me also that she had got interested in the theater for the wrong reason, like most college students who get interested in the theater. She liked the paraphernalia of it, the slightly risqué camaraderie, the rehearsing late at night in leotards and ski sweaters, the feeling of thinking of yourself as an actress. Whereas according to the Stanislavsky method she wasn't supposed to be an actress, she was supposed to be Nina. And Nina was quite simple, an intelligent, lonely, and unhappy girl, a victim. We discussed this several times when we went out for coffee, but she said of Nina, "She's an idiot." This sounded almost like sacrilege to me. She *was* Nina. I was Trepleff. Should I tell Egon? What was I talking about? I was really getting unhinged.

Perhaps the trouble was that she was badly cast for the part. I had thought it was a good piece of casting at first but now I wasn't sure. Above all Nina was unhappy, and considering her background and general attributes it would have been very difficult for Syd to be unhappy. It might have made her unhappy if Egon had browbeaten her as he did the others, Masha for instance, but he never did. He might criticize the way she delivered a line but he never told her she was a half-wit or accused her of chewing gum. The two of them seemed to communicate without talking very much; in fact she seemed to have some kind of a special relation with him that excused her from being barked at like the rest of us. Sometimes after rehearsal it was Egon who took her to coffee at the student joints, or at least he took her somewhere. He would come out with a little twisted smile over his beard, looking like Henry VIII in the well-known portrait by Holbein. "Nina, pigeon, am I wrong or are you mine this evening?" She would smile her own little Wellesley smile and follow him silently out the door. Through the thin walls of the theater we would hear the boogle-boogle of his Jaguar starting, then a long whir as it pulled away.

On those nights when she went to drink coffee with Egon I would walk home alone to my boardinghouse, my hands deep in my pockets, wrapped to the nose in scarves and mufflers, the cold like a knife pain in my lungs, miserable in body and soul and loving my misery. I was drunk on cold, love, poetry, and unhappines. Overhead the bare branches of the trees were distorted and a little wild against the starry sky: a landscape of Edvard Munch. Ann Arbor was Moscow, Petersburg, Stockholm, a city of white nights and frozen abstract demons; the campus lanes were the Nevsky Prospekt. White nights! I had finally thought of a name for my insomnia. It was the title of a novel by Dostoevski. The world of artifice was real, the real world flimsy and contemptible. Through the artifice of Egon, that genius we loved and hated, I was in love not with some Connie or Martha but with a girl named Nina Mikhailovna Zarychny.

Sometimes I would walk through the frozen campus until four o'clock in the morning. It was very bad for someone who was recovering from hepatitis. The infrequent people I passed, milkmen, students going home from dates, probably didn't even know who I was. I was Trepleff, crushed under the weight of his solitude, all-pitying and all-loving, the Doomed Saint. The stars overhead winked indifferently, the cold too bit my face without understanding who I was. Finally I would go back to my rented room. Standing half-undressed in the middle of the floor I would say, "Today I was low enough to kill this seagull. I lay it at your feet." Then, smiling, I would get into bed and go to sleep.

With the possible exception of Nina, we all dug into our

parts in this way and the play was a tremendous success. We played for nine nights and every night we were left exhausted, emotionally drained, unable even to talk to each other, bumping into each other clumsily and silently on our way to the dressing rooms. The audience was as hypnotized as we were. When the curtain came down there was a strange numb pause of perhaps thirty seconds and then they began to clap, a scattered fusillade that soon rose to a roar. It went on for ten minutes.

When we took the curtain calls Egon didn't even bother to smile at the audience. He detested audiences. Over the applause he could be heard growling "Yah. Yah," to himself like a gorilla. Egon took no pleasure in success. It was *making* the thing, wrenching all these students and dentists' wives and bright little coeds out of their miserable personalities and making them do as he wanted, that interested him. It didn't interest him, it obsessed him. He was addicted to manipulating other human beings the way some people are addicted to alcohol. This had been apparent before, but I only grasped the full force of it that night after the play was over.

There was a cast party, but Syd and I didn't go to it. When I came out after ungluing the wispy little Trepleff-beard and changing into my street clothes I found her still sitting on a stool on the darkened stage. In the play she wore a simple cotton dress with a wide skirt, but now she had changed back into her leotard and ski sweater. When she saw me she smiled, faintly, one side of her mouth lifting so that it made a small hard crease in her cheek.

"Waiting for somebody?"

"No."

"Going to the party?"

"No."

"Then?"

Without answering she sighed, got up off the stool, wandered around the darkened stage for a while, and finally stopped in front of me and gave me a strange look. Then I became aware that she was bending her head slowly until at last it was resting on my shoulder. It was very unlike her. There she stood with her head on my shoulder and I found that in some manner my arms were around her. Not knowing what to do, I patted her awkwardly, consolingly, in the middle of the back. The sweater was rough under my fingers but inside it her form was slight, almost unbelievably fragile.

After a moment of this she broke away and turned her head, not looking at me. "Take me somewhere."

I feverishly put on my overcoat, she wound the black scarf three times around her neck, and we went out. I didn't know what was wrong with her but I was filled with a terrific sense of impending joy, a joy that was a melancholy kind of joy on the surface because she was melancholy, but at a deeper level was exultant because in her melancholy she had for some reason, inexplicably, needed me. I realized now she had been waiting for me.

We went down the street and turned in the first place we came to and ordered coffee and pastry. As it happened it was a place called the Pit because it was supposed to specialize in barbecue, but the ventilation was so bad that everybody called it the Armpit. The barbecue was terrible but the pastry came from a Danish bakery across the street and it was the one thing in the place that was good. She took a bite of her pastry, chewed it once or twice, and then unexpectedly bent forward and propped her forehead in her hands. Great tears welled in her eyes and trickled down her cheeks and fell onto the table. After a few moments she mastered herself, got out a handkerchief and dried her cheeks, and then began mechanically mopping up the tears on the table.

All this without a sound. Finally she made a little sigh that was almost half-humorous. "Masha, that half-wit. That Kewpie-doll. I never thought it would be Masha. I knew it would be someone because that's the way he is. It lasted even longer than I thought. But Masha. That little idiot with her turned-up nose and her two eyes like raisins in a rice pudding." The tears still welled in her eyes but her teeth were clenched now in a fierce small expression of determination. "I wish I could go off quietly and die somewhere. No I don't, I want to stay around until he realizes she's a little plaster Betty Boop, the kind you win by knocking down milk bottles at carnivals."

It was characteristic that even with her throat so tight she could hardly speak, she called Masha by her name in the play, as Egon had made us all do.

"It isn't as though I didn't know it would happen," she went on, exhaling and talking a little more calmly. "I knew he was selfish, egotistical, cold. No, that's wrong, he's not cold. He's like a huge big locomotive full of passions, but his passion is all inside himself. He needs women——" In spite of her teeth-clenching the tears were beginning to well again: "He needs women the way he needs handkerchiefs to blow his nose in. After he's done with them he throws them away. The kind of handkerchiefs he likes are too fine to be laundered."

Her own handkerchief was sturdy Irish linen, expensive but durable. It was rapidly becoming saturated and I passed her my own. She thanked me by nodding, unable to speak, or at least unable to speak about anything but Egon.

"He's not interested in love. He has nothing against it, you understand. It just doesn't fit in with his métier. He wants to *drive* people the way you drive a car. He wants to make them cry or laugh or be angry at him or fall in love with him, it doesn't really matter which. If he saw me now he'd be pleased, because he's making me feel some emotion. He's a genius in his way. He's not really an egotist, you know. An egotist is satisfied with himself but he's never satisfied. He always has to prove it all over again. Do you know what he is? He's a man—man—" With the tightness in her throat it was difficult for her to get the word out but finally she managed it—"a man-*ip*-ulator."

There was a brief silence while I imagined Egon in his apartment with Syd, driving her the way you drive a car. But mental pictures of this kind were pointless and instead I tried to offer some constructive advice. "Forget him. It's all over now. He's not worth it."

"Oh, he's worth it," she said in a weak voice, almost to herself.

"But if you knew all these things—"

She lifted her shoulders and almost smiled. "Egon has a new term for giving in to temptation. He calls it not saying no to life. Does that shock you? I'm sorry. I was an idiot. Do you know why I really did it? Because he made me into Nina, and Nina is an idiot."

It didn't shock me exactly. It simply made me understand what the knot of unhappiness was that had been collecting in my stomach for weeks; it made me realize that you can know something and not know it, until somebody finally forces it up into the front of your mind by putting it in words as she was doing now. I was like a man who has been going around all day feeling miserable and not knowing why and finally he realizes he has a toothache. But it was simple, teeth can be pulled out! I was ready with the forceps of my youth, my love, my spirit of feverish self-sacrifice. The more the tooth hurt the more I anticipated the joy of it slipping easily and scientifically out of its socket.

"So here I am. What am I going to do?" I heard her inquiring more to the air around her than to me.

"Do nothing. Forget he ever existed. Simply go on as you were before."

"Yes, but you see, I can't exactly go on as I was before. Because, even if I forget him, in due time a certain in-evitable event will occur."

She didn't look at me, but in spite of the fact that her voice was barely audible it was not devoid of a certain irony. It was a queer moment, pathetic and yet slightly farcical. It was clear that she would rather have been run over by a truck, pulverized by a meteorite, that at least would have been dramatic, anything except this old-fashioned and ludicrous predicament which only happened to maidens in Victorian novels. "O, that Nina, what a fool she was," she gritted to herself after a moment.

Oof. This jeering little mannikin, the relic of Egon's driving lesson, was growing inside the elf I had loved so chastely from a distance? But even this I took in my stride. I hadn't anticipated it, even my premonitory knot of pain hadn't gone that far, but if you were going to pull out a tooth it was just as easy to pull out a whopping big one. I reached across the table and pulled her hand away from her chin and covered it with my own hand. "Look. Why not cheer up and be practical? We're not living in a play. It's the age of modern science. These things are the simplest thing in the world to take care of." I had no idea how they were taken care of but I thought I could probably find out.

She seemed to be ready to leave the details to me. She slumped in her chair and almost smiled. "Don't tell anyone what I said about Masha being a Kewpie-doll, will you? That was stupid, stupid, stupid."

And so there in the Armpit, at a wooden table that smelled of ketchup and sour coffee, my life changed direction and shot off at an obtuse angle toward other reveries and other goals. In Syd's despair, I realized, lay my own happiness. But it was another kind of happiness from the sentimental melancholy happiness I had known when I had walked the lonely campus thinking of her, in the time when she had been pristine and unattainable. Now I saw that the thing was simple, much simpler than I had ever dreamed. I didn't have to be Trepleff. I didn't want to be Trepleff. Why had I let that gorilla in a waistcoat walk all over me? I had been sick—that was the only explanation of it. I had been sick the whole time. I had rehearsed and played the whole damned play with a fever and it had made me susceptible to the manipulations of that provincial Svengali. The Doomed Saint! What stupidity. Nobody was doomed, I wasn't doomed and neither was Syd. All we had to do was stop acting like a couple of idiots and do the practical thing and we would be happy like everybody else.

Syd herself was in no mood to do the practical thing. She had fallen into a curious passivity which was perhaps only a biological reflex of females in her predicament, intended to stimulate the sympathy and protection of the nearest male. Anyhow it worked. I found myself in a position where I had to save her, or rather I found that the sheer and unalloyed happiness of saving her had somehow fallen to my lot. Means were found to remove the unwanted token of Egon's esteem from consideration. After some searching a suitable doctor was located in the nearby town of Ypsilanti, which was popularly deemed more appropriate than Ann Arbor for such squalors. The horrid deed was actually performed in a motel. Syd was just sick enough for me to feel protective and for her to feel grateful, and not sick enough to frighten either of us. She hemorrhaged a little more than she should have and the Ypsilanti doctor showed me how to give her plasma, being careful to get all the air out of the tube and observing sterility precautions. I watched her all that night; I hadn't slept for what seemed like a week but the fatigue only left me keen, piercingly awake, and even more competent, although I noticed a slight tendency to hallucinations of a harmless sort. (Voices kept saying, "You're doing fine, fine, everything is sterile.") From time to time she woke up and I applied cool cloths to her brow, fed her soup with a spoon, and read her Gerard Manley Hopkins. She smiled at me a little weakly, still with wry irony at finding herself the Sadder But Wiser Girl in the song. Weak in this way, passive and drained of the energy that had been her most charming quality, she was less pretty but I loved her more. When she went to sleep I read Hopkins myself ("It is the blight man was born for, it is Margaret you mourn for") or just sat and smoked cigarettes.

Sometimes when she woke up I would find her staring at me silently with tears in her eyes, and I would smooth her hair and talk in a quiet voice to her. I was in command of the situation, medically, psychologically, and emotionally. I was no longer sorry for myself and I didn't hate anybody. I didn't even hate Egon, or Trigorin, or whatever the hairy ape wanted to call himself. Egon-Trigorin had needed the experience for his art; he was a machine for having experiences and Syd had got caught in the machinery. It was an unfortunate mishap but one without sentimental significance, an industrial accident. As for the so-called moral aspects of the situation, to hell with them. I didn't consider Syd any more guilty than if she had got her skirt caught in a threshing machine. This was partly because I loved her but partly because in my new role as Arrowsmith I was totally objective about suffering and its causes. I knew my mission now, it was to solace the victims of industrial accidents and make them happy again, and be happy doing it.

The next morning I took Syd back to her dormitory. The house mother in the dorm never knew about it. The house mother thought she was visiting her parents in Evanston. Her parents never knew about it. Her roommates in the dorm never knew about it. Nobody knew about it.

A couple of weeks after that we were married. She had tears in her eyes the whole two weeks, tears of gratitude at first and then tears of real love. I knew it was real love because Syd would have preferred to conceal the emotion if she could. But it was too much to conceal and it came out in the tears and in various other signs that in my Arrowsmithian objectivity I recognized as unmistakable. She was in a weakened condition just as I had been with the hepatitis, but I was well now and she was the one who had emotions. And yet I loved her as much as I ever had or more, I was very gentle with her, understanding, solicitous, consoling, and didn't touch her for several weeks except to kiss her lightly. I waited patiently while the broken pieces of her womanhood healed, and left to herself in this way she finally came to such a high fine pitch of desire that I was practically overwhelmed, one night, with one arm still in my shirt. I had suffered a long time, through all the Dostoevskian white nights and walking on the banks of the Neva, but it was worth it. She was cured and so was I. It was as though all the rest of it, Egon, the Orchard Players, *The Seagull,* and the whole goddam sophomoric thing, had never happened. I had saved her, and we were young and in love in a rented room with gas plate in Ann Arbor, Michigan. The cynics were wrong and virginity could be restored.

ROBERT HAZEL

White Anglo-Saxon Protestant

(FROM THE HUDSON REVIEW)

HERE COMES HAMPDEN now, on his way to kill me. He staggers past Minetta's Tavern, the long red and white banner of the Gaslight Café, the green oval sign of the Kettle of Fish. Now Rienzi's Coffee House with its disarrayed chessboards and miscegenous couples drooped in the scummed windows, and the Funky Antique Shop. And now the Folklore Center where a crowd of students have collected, filling the steps and eddying out to the old granite curb of MacDougal Street: young partisans of Joan Baez and mourners of Medgar Evers, with their guitars, wearing jeans, boots and checkered flannel shirts, Negro boys and girls with a certain gravity, and self-conscious Jewish kids hugging banjos—all ready to go down to Cambridge, Maryland to protest segregation on the Eastern Shore. They appear sixty percent excited and scared, thirty-nine percent honest, and one percent crazy out of their young heads, all reminding me of myself as an undergraduate when I told my professors I was of the religion of Socrates, Jesus and Gandhi, and wrote a petition to the British Crown to free India. How young I was, how young they are!

Yesterday Nathan came to me, his professor, a Kentuckian with an accent, and Nathan wanted to know about going to Maryland. I said, "Yes, I know. They will hate you in particular, Nathan, because you're a New York Jew Communist and the Klan is looking for you." Nathan grinned, looking noble and frightened and curious. I said, "Nathan, those people have a strange religion. The morality is all King

James *Old Testament*, but the conscious ethic is all *New Testament*. It's their way of embracing the Chosen People and denying this pack of Jews in the same breath. In the South, Moses doesn't even cut any ice because he was an Egyptian nigger. It's all New Dispensation, all Jesus. And in the South, Jesus is a German. Have you seen those calendar pictures of Christ that hang on the walls of parlors and bedrooms all over the South? No? Well, Billy Graham looks like all of them in composite. There's a real case of life imitating art. Jesus is a real Luftwaffe Ace, as in Dali's insane painting of the last supper. It was actually hung in the National Gallery of Art in Washington, you know." I paused and stared at Nathan. "And, Nathan, don't go down there with any illusions about Southern cowardice. The Southerners aren't any more afraid of you than you are of them. They believe their cause is just, too. They really believe that Negroes are inferior creatures, an inferior species—the way you and I don't keep dogs on leashes because we're afraid of dogs. We just want the power to compel obedience from an inferior creature, and the leash secures that power for us." I waited a moment, then said, "Nathan, there's a bitter thing to dispose of, by action and imagination. When I was your age the enemies were Harry Bennett's company police clubbing the workers, and then fascism. Good luck. Watch yourself. And when you get back, bring Rama up for coffee."

Nathan is standing down there near the red door of the Folklore Center. I watch this tall, courageous, excited and false posture: false by a small fraction only because he is in love, as only a nineteen-year-old boy can be, with the daughter of a famous Negro expatriate. Rama is a startlingly pretty girl and Nathan is very handsome. They are too beautiful for tear gas, fire hoses, and dogs.

And here comes Hampden, reeling past the Folklore Center. He is near enough now for me to see his skewed tie, the coffee blotted shirt, the jacket and slacks that don't match, pulled on in a drunk hurry, the slacks with a dark river down the left leg where Hampden has pissed himself; see the thin, neat hair, the expensive pipe jutting from a frayed pocket; even see the creases of distaste near his Mississippi-Puritan mouth as he walks in brisk spurts, in confused surges, past the line of Negro and white students. Hampden shoulders some of them, not accidentally, on his way to the Golden Pizza parlor directly across the street. Hampden, my old friend, an editor with Aegean House, a stolid pipe-smoker, a spouter of conservative publishing maxims in what he considers a crooked and opportunistic publishing house, calmly affirming the freedom of authors, the wisdom of scholars, deploring the recent "tawdry" under-the-table deals between reprinters and hard-cover firms which turned traditional publishing upside-down; Hampden the rational-seeming proper man who is also consumed by Rimbaud, Wolfe and Dylan Thomas, an editor who believes in the Maxwell Perkins myth of Creative Editorship, a man with an attractive and intelligent wife, a ten-year-old son who batted .580 in the Little League in Merrick, an energetic Deep South hunter and fisherman who takes five-mile walks in a tweed jacket rough as a Kentucky cob, with the gait of an Englishman, toe before heel, who swallows a hundred bottles of assorted vitamins and proteins, whose belts are of the thickest English leather, who does thirty pushups before breakfast and who is not convinced that Westbrook Pegler doesn't still have "something of the old verve."

And here he comes down the swingingest block in the Village, down MacDougal between Minetta's Tavern and the San Remo, jostling "the cheap integrationist bastards" in front of the Folklore Center. Hampden puts shoulder to shoulder, cagily scuffing ever so little, as if feeling out his enemy, as he jars past. Both Negroes and whites that he brushes wheel involuntarily, change faces quickly, but do not follow to trample the drunk white man. Nathan's face is alert, almost hostile, but open to doubt, because Hampden has jostled cannily, as a drunk man will who is shot through with hatreds too strong to become obvious until he wants to turn back, at some moment, and scream them. Hampden is on his way from Merrick, hungry beyond recall of eating, weakened, sick, stumbling toward the Golden Pizza to spend twenty cents for a slice of dough, tomato and rubbery cheese, trying to remember, I guess, why he feels he has to come up here to kill me. It is because he thinks I made a pass at his mistress.

Hampden had, by intelligence and judgment, worked up to a good spot on a man's magazine, then jumped to Aegean House, without even three hours of college credits. Then his wife spent four years getting a Columbia Ph.D., with an excellent dissertation on Alexander Pope. Hampden had spent his boyhood pleading for pennies from a sluttish mother in the town of Bucksnort, Mississippi. Then his wife tried to give him dollars from fairly well-to-do parents on Long Island. My girl and I were constant guests at Hampden and Regina's place, an apartment sticky and sterile as antlers with Danish modern furniture, given them by her parents. We saw the struggle begin.

From a confident, pipe-smoking, hi-fi-playing man who enjoyed his skill at chess, at carving a duck for his friends, Hampden became a wife-slayer who made laconic disparagements of Regina in our presence, in small asides which she was sure to overhear. After all, Pope was a hunchback, and any woman who would choose to do research on a hunchback—the inferences were clear. If Regina went out of her way to try, with all pathetic concentration, to bake Southern cornbread, Hampden mentioned in a too-quiet tone, that, of course, if one doesn't have water-ground meal, the bread is not to be compared with the original Mississippi Choctaw bread in food value and flavor. If Regina put records of folksingers on the hi-fi, Hampden rejected the disks with a mechanical click that could be heard all over the room, a hard silence, a punctuation mark for his wary and quiet speech about young Communist folk-singers, and that *anyone* knew if the words Lincoln or People were mentioned in song titles, the songs were Red, "the latest Bronx Renaissance." Puffing vigorously on his straight-grained Algerian briar,

Hampden looked deeply at his wife, a Yankee, and at Fauna, who lives with me, and remarked as if musing to himself, "Funny how all my Liberal friends are putting their kids into private schools. They won't say it's because there are too many goddam stupid lawless niggers in the public schools. No. They talk about better math instruction and 'development opportunities.'"

Fauna set down her after-dinner brandy with a loud clatter, a feminine disagreement with Hampden. But Hampden had a sure Southern weapon against Fauna: he considered her much too beautiful to talk seriously to. Hampden could express his hatred of Fauna by shutting her mouth with a chocolate mint and assuming, with slyly gentle gestures, that she was much too feminine *ever* to disagree with him. With Fauna it was not so much a matter of taking Regina's side as it was simply loathing this man Hampden, who sat there drawing on his pipe in patriarchal grandeur, too much like her own unbending Spanish father, too perfectly encased in his own defenses, too unreachable.

When Regina began her research on Pope, Hampden began to cultivate a young woman author who, as it turned out, was a fine translator of German, one of the best in America. Hampden edited two of her books. She is Margery Parsons, and she is the reason why Hampden is coming up here to kill me. Last night after Hampden left his "other apartment" here in Manhattan where he shacks with Margery, I dialed his home number out in Merrick. Regina answered. She told me she was moving out and taking their son to her parents' house at the far tip of the island. I had to phone Margery Parsons then because I knew if Hampden wasn't back up there with her, he would be down on the East Side, drunk and challenging the retired fighters in Lulu's Bar on Second Avenue, and the old fighters not even glancing up when Hampden gave the trite, bellowed challenge, "I can lick any man here!" and the heads of the fighters not even moving, bored, and Hampden diminished to nothing, standing there crazily drunk and wishing: wishing for cut eyes and a dislocated jaw, a masochist in heat like a bitch for assault by other men. I knew they wouldn't even accord him a nod of manhood, wouldn't knock him into a coma but would grin at him, if anything, with the curious kind of pity that men who have been hit give to men who want to be hit. And there he would be in Lulu's Bar, stifled absolutely, or with his translator of Rilke, his sex relations with her only a stab at his recognizably intellectual wife—and how could a high school boy from Mississippi try to kill the spirit of a wife who had a Ph.D. except to lay a lady-scholar whose translations and essays were "definitive"?

Going there in the winking cold lights of the Golden Pizza, Hampden holds all the darks and lights of honesty and deceit, tenderness and murder on his shoulders. If one of his friends was ill, Hampden would phone eight times a day. He would bring medicines, food, books. I could not begin to catalogue his spontaneous gifts to Fauna and me, ranging from Turnbull's *Letters of Fitzgerald* to a smoked fish. Fauna was suspicious of potato salad and fish. She said, "He just wants to patronize me because I'm Jewish. He just wants to get me out of the way so he can lay you, Richard." I said, "Darling, could you just try to believe, for five seconds, that he simply thought you might like the food?"

Often at night I hear Italian sausages frying there in the Golden Pizza, turned lazily and expertly by a fatbellied boy who serves a greasy sausage and a smear of fried onions and peppers on a soft roll. He makes small talk, New York illiterate small talk with all the unescorted girls who come in: "Eh, ya dun remember me, eh? Out to da beach, yeh, Joneses Beach last summa, yeh. Ya hadda straw hat on." At night I often wake up, hearing the hiss of frying sausages in my own kitchen. It is just an echo off the tenement wall.

But to see an old friend who is drunkenly burning his mouth on a slice of pizza just to get the energy to come up here and kill me—and all because I had to phone his mistress to try, at least, to find out where he was so I could keep him out of Lulu's Bar and the nut ward at Bellevue? Margery made the mistake of telling Hampden that I had phoned. When he got in touch with her from a phone booth at 14th and 2nd Avenue, she had cooed, "Richard is *so* concerned. Are you *drinking* again?" Then Margery had to report to me that Hampden said the *awfulest* things, like I'll kill the treacherous bastard! And Hampden had taken my call to Margery as an attempt to cut his balls and throw them out into the winter snow, as he and I had cut pigs in our Southern boyhood. He would have been flattered, Fauna said, if I had made a pass at Regina. He could have swept such a pass away with a good-humored, superior, buddy-buddy gesture, as a way to caress him, too, through Regina's body. I said to Fauna, "Or maybe in an even more destructive way, with this wife and mistress bit, like the way a farmer will allow you to kick a mare he already owns, but not one he is going to buy."

Hampden seldom drank during the years of his increasing success as an editor. Instead, he read hungrily—as a matter of fact, he is better read than either Regina or me—and he exercised strenuously to stave off a potbelly. He teased me constantly about putting on weight, and when I pointed to his flab he sucked in his breath and declared, "But my muscles have *definition* underneath." Quickly he became a food faddist. He chewed lean sirloin, swallowed the blood and spat out the pulp. He claimed that was the way Marciano had dieted on the eve of a fight. He became exaggeratedly concerned about his appearance. Once when he visited his mother in Mississippi, he brought back a mysterious bottle of clear liquid that he doused on his hair; and, incredibly, the whisk of white on his temples was black again. A Chickasaw formula. He spent more money than he could afford on tailored clothing. His record collection was large, but not so impressive as it was meant to impress us. I thought he had a lot of middling-to-poor stuff, but when I told him so, he didn't take it well, but very seriously declared that my academic taste, my formal education with its stultifying degrees had destroyed my ability to sense and feel genuine music. His pipes, expensive, handsome, varied in size and design, glowed in their walnut rack on his hi-fi stereo cabinet. Hampden teased me about sticking to my boyhood tastes for fried pork, hot bread and pies, and for my habit of downing double bourbons, "a poison which attacks the cells of the brain directly." He kept a generous bar, but there was a twinge of superiority in his gestures as he poured for Regina, Fauna and me. Once when I lost a train of thought after six drinks, Hampden remarked that he was glad he didn't require an alcoholic coma for a sense of well-being, that he preferred to keep his wits about him. And suddenly, as I lolled my head in amazement, Hampden dived to the floor, did a dozen fast pushups, stood erect, inhaled deeply and announced, "I won five hundred dollars on the first Schmeling-Louis fight. Any well-conditioned German can take a nigger." The fact that Hampden was about six years old when that fight took place didn't appear to faze him at all. After that, he sat popping chocolate-flavored protein pills into his mouth, chewing slowly and pontificating about the low condition of education. Columbia had gone downhill fast. Everybody knew that New York University was a joke. How could I teach there? Didn't I recall Wolfe's disgust with The Factory and its little Jews? Hampden could ask me this even in Fauna's presence, knowing she is Jewish but genuinely forgetting it because, to him, Fauna was a good Jew because I loved her, so automatically she was removed from his disparagement. When I said, "Goddam it, Hampden, will you cut out this shit?" He was only momentarily rebuked. He seized the word and spun into a long digression about how everybody knew that academic degrees were a lot of shit. Didn't we know that Ph.D. meant piled higher and deeper? Regina was embarrassed. Quickly she served coffee and cake. Hampden, without realizing it, ate two huge wedges of chocolate cake with fudge icing, while delivering me a lecture on my "perverse consumption of pork gravy and bourbon, with all those calories and saturated fats."

Hampden drank once a year. Yearly he went to his doctor

for a checkup. After the data on lungs, heart, blood pressure, etc., were out of the way, the doctor asked Hampden how much he smoked. "I smoke a pipe." "Oh, that's nothing. How much do you drink?" "A quart per year." "Oh, that's nothing to worry about." "But I drink it in twenty minutes." Hampden could not resist the thrust. He wanted to see the doctor swallow painfully. What the doctor didn't know was that once a year Hampden not just got bombed out of his mind but prowled the streets, provoking fights, got badly beaten and was scraped up by the police from some walk or doorway in a dark part of town, and wound up in Bellevue Hospital, ill and penitent under Regina's solicitous gaze. He needed her mutely accusing, tear-filled eyes that he resented and loved. His allergy to alcohol was so severe that even on two beers he became belligerent. Walking out of a bar, he would say, "Dick buddy, I think I could take you." I'd say, "Hell, you don't want to take me. You're tough and hard, and I'm out of shape." "Yeh, yeh," Hampden would say happily, until his tension built again in another fifteen seconds and he would say, "I think I could take you, Dick buddy." When I assured him again of the mismatch—though I could have tilted him into the gutter with a finger—Hampden only sustained his frustrations which ran across his brain in little jerky ups and downs like a scrawl of a seismograph recording earth tremors.

Until Hampden fell off the wagon twice, nearly losing his life the second time, I didn't realize what a corked-up bottle of unflowing violence he was 365 days of the year. His resolves, disciplines, defenses of a rural Southern combat infantryman in Normandy were the cork in the bottle whose label read: I am the whitest, strongest, most intelligent, industrious and virile man in a city of polyglot, weak-willed, lazy, tax-supported parasites in history. And inside the opaque bottle lay the preserved foetus of a Mississippi waitress who had left her brutal husband for a horse trainer. And the alcoholic father wandering in a kind of dazed, uncomprehending sorrow from the ragged pine flats of Mississippi to the sour 50-cent beds in Manhattan's Mills Hotels for transients, and from those wire-mesh cages to his cobblestone deathbed under the cold iron lattice of the 3rd Avenue El near a Chinatown mission.

A faint smile on his smooth face with its large forehead under slickly combed hair, Hampden carved our Thanksgiving turkey. He praised Regina's stuffing—just the proper amounts of salt, pepper and sage, particularly the sage, which he said was the true test of a stuffing. It was a good beginning. Regina was flushed from the kitchen, her nicely done hair coming loose a little bit, attractively, her generous smile warming the room. Fauna had sipped three martinis and her thin face glowed gold-brown with little beads of sweat and oil and her flecked brown eyes had gone fiercely soft like those of a puma. Fauna had let her hair fall down her back "to revive an old lover," she teased. "And besides, besides, Richard, I'm too old for a ponytail, and besides, I'm tired of being the picture of a healthy animal. I want to be a sick intellectual like you!" She pounced down onto my knees. Her small dancer's body felt tight and expansive at the same time. I asked, "Why is it that most dancers get knotty muscles but you stay fluid like a swimmer?" Fauna put her nose against mine and stared, comically cross-eyed. "Because my body *sings,* you funny man." Regina teased, "Well! Do you two want to go upstairs before dinner?" I had had four drinks and loved Regina and Hampden and Fauna, loved myself even. But I became aware that Hampden had begun a sort of dreamy soliloquy, talking to himself again, but demanding that we hear it, just loud enough to register over the Montavani record on the player.

Hampden kept up a sardonic commentary on the writers, painters, lawyers he knew, and books he was editing. I didn't have to listen very closely to notice, actually to hear the pressured vapors of hate escaping thinly past the cork in the bottle: Mailer's tragedy was to have discovered sex at the age of 36. Woodstock didn't paint; he masturbated on canvas. Wealthy teenagers had torn up a Back Bay mansion.

They ought, all of them, to be lined up naked and have their cocks sliced off by their homosexual Scoutmasters, and their loss bewailed by a chorus of seven-year-old nigger virgins—at eight, of course, nigger wenches wouldn't be virgins. Eisenhower should have gone into Cuba and swatted Castro like any other dirty fly, not play dead like that drunken Irish boy in the White House, *which reminds me* that history has a curious way of making events turn out for the worse. Hitler, a man of clean habits, of great personal purity, who could have unified Europe and made Napoleon's dream come true, who could have unified Europe against the Communist threat, was defeated by a semi-literate American paralytic and an alcoholic British Tory.

Oiling the bowl of his pipe by rubbing it against the wing of his nose, rapidly chewing another protein pill, Hampden described what, to him, was the final ludicrous breakdown of a soft, liberal society. It involved a current newspaper campaign for safe driving to save the lives of children, and it had been touched off by the deaths of two children who were run down by cars in Jackson Heights. Hampden spoke with slow gravity. "That's the soft society for you. It tampers with survival of the fittest. Remember, Dick, when you and I were kids and our parents told us to stay off the streets, we obeyed. We were intelligent enough to stay out of the path of cars. Any kid who is too stupid to stay out of the street isn't worthy to survive." And Hampden appealed to me for confirmation, as one old country boy to another, which was embarrassing in the immediate chatter of protest from Regina and Fauna. Then Hampden drove another nail. "Remember your friend Marty. Marty was a cheap little fag nut who had to drown himself in his own bathtub because he was a Liberal and Liberals have no reason to survive."

Fauna bristled. She had loved our friend Marty, whose tumultuous life and early suicide had echoed her own sense of brevity and terror. Regina rebelled because her husband was guilty of "a stupid generalization." Fauna cried, "That's *cruel* of you, Hampden. You know that Marty wasn't killed by any creed. He was killed because he couldn't find out who he was. He was the Little Prince. And there's no world for little princes." And Hampden grunted, "I distrust books by French writers who write delicately about wind, sand and stars. I'll take an American like Jim Farrell who belches, farts and screws women."

That evening turned out badly, worse than usual. When Fauna made a retort, Hampden let his resentment of her come into the open. He called her a pseudo-intellectual slob who read Max Lerner and worshipped Eleanor Roosevelt and *dabbled* in faggy dances produced by Charles Weidman from an Ohio humorist whose fables "reeked of homosexuality." When Fauna determinedly told him that art is no respecter of persons, that talent has no sex, that any number of persons with talent, be they male, female or neuter can build something beautiful, Hampden still could not back down without trying to construct another platform. Regina had turned on a television documentary about the Hungarian Uprising. Events had reached the stage where a Catholic priest was gunned down by Heydrich's elite troopers because the priest had hidden a few rebels in the basement of his church. At this point Hampden said briskly, "He ought to have been disrobed first, or unfrocked, or his *dress* taken off, or whatever those corrupt bastards in the Church call it. He was unfit to be a priest. He knew the Laws of the Occupation. The trouble is these gypsy Hungarians have no respect for law. Just like the Jews and niggers. Always breaking the law, then yelling when they are justly punished, *which reminds me* of a lousy book I had a hand in publishing. It was called *Rosaries and Rice,* or something. Lousy book about how when the Red Chinese took over a village where there was this nunnery, they made a rule that the nuns were not to play their radios for a certain period of time. A simple rule. So the nuns played their radios. So the local commander politely reminded them of the rule and requested that the good sisters comply. So, naturally, the nuns, taking orders only from Jesus Himself, turned on their radios again. So the commander quite properly confiscated all the radios. But this nun, this Mother Superior, this Chief *Dyke* or whatever she's called, yelled bloody murder just as if an atrocity had been committed, just as if she hadn't known the law. No civilized man," Hampden said, "could help sympathizing with that poor commander, confronted, as he was, by a plague of locusts on cultural loan from Rome!"

Hampden turned off the TV and put a record on the hi-fi. Regina sort of bubbled with her outraged lips. Fauna started to make a speech. Her father is Catholic, and though she hated him, she had made a kind of hazardous compromise with his faith by getting involved with Dorothy Day's brand of Catholic action. But Fauna was too upset to cope with Hampden. His unrelieved needling had reduced her to a stutter of nerves. She was sweating and short of breath. All she could do was gasp, "Vicious—hateful—vicious!" and try to knife Hampden with her eyes. I said, "Come off it, Hampden. Tell us something you *love*, for a change." Hampden tamped his pipe. He muttered around the stem, "I love truth. I love justice. I was just trying to state certain facts, *which reminds me* of what Pound said about—" and he was preparing to take off on another trap-play up the broken middle of logic when I shot him a glance and said, "Yes, I know what Pound said about Confucius, Roosevelt and the Virgin. What else you got?" Hampden grew silent, morose, and went to change the Montavani record for one by Nelson Riddle.

Fauna and I had lived together for about a year and a half. We weren't what anyone would call happy: either we were ecstatic or in agony, too high or too low, eating apples in bed and whispering or throwing them and yelling accusations. I'm older than Fauna and have sort of run out of hope, lost enthusiasm for many things that excite her, like sitting up all night in a cafeteria on Sixth Avenue, reading the Sunday *Times,* talking with our friends about "the nature of creativity"—all these futile things that the very bright and the very young delight in doing, these beautiful creatures of twenty who haven't yet discovered they will die. And the constant strain of having to try to make everything I said sound like an insight—I was Fauna's hero as well as lover—had got to me, especially since I ran out of money from the novel I had published and had to take this teaching job. I was teaching all day and writing half the night, and Fauna was bringing me coffee or bourbon, whichever, but growing restless about being nothing but a "dutiful beast of burden," as she called herself. When I was working, I would reach out as she passed my table and touch her thigh, not really paying her the attention she craved, and say, "You're such a perfect sensualist, perfectly oriented around food and physical movements." Fauna would retort, "All we have is passion. I'm so utensible! Is that a word, Richard?" Fauna would cuff my jaw and demand a kiss.

Before I took this job, I reacted completely to her spontaneity. We would be munching knishes on Houston Street and Fauna would say, "Richard, let's go ride the Staten Island Ferry. I want to see all that dirty water turn white!" It might be five degrees above zero, but off we'd go, blue in the face, I in a sheepskin and Navy watch cap, Fauna in her latest garb imitative of the wool garments of Peruvian women, and a long shawl. When the wind slapped the wool against her face, and she was about half-shot on Scotch and Drambuie, Fauna said irritably, "Shawls can get *very* mad for having wind blow them in people's faces!" Brushing the tassels away like flies, Fauna looked very comic, very young, very dear. She liked to make up malapropisms that imitated her mood exactly. Squinting her eyes against the cold white foam in the boat's wake, Fauna cried, "I must go to an optimist and get some glasses." I laughed, "You want an electric skillet, too?" And coming back, half-frozen through the rough, dirty four o'clock morning streets of lower Manhattan, she murmured desolately, "I can't face it, Richard. This place perjures me."

But after I began to teach I didn't have many ways to

indulge Fauna's whims and random motions. I couldn't go to bed at four and teach at nine very many weeks in a row. We had built up some tension, anyhow, about a year ago when she slept with a guy, a painter I knew. She had brought home a camera he gave her, and wanted to take my picture with his camera on Christmas morning. I needed fidelity from her, so I kicked her out. She went to San Francisco with her dance group and several weeks later, when she got back to the city, I felt guilty about booting her out—and besides, Fauna and I love each other more than either of us can care for anyone else, by far—so I found out she was working in her spare time for Dorothy Day's projects, like the *Catholic Worker* and the charity farm on Staten Island. I found Fauna and took her back.

Hampden had had to spend several weeks on the West Coast, trying to make big promotional deals, tie-ins between his publishing house and a movie studio—something he detested; he was certain that the Hollywood hucksters and the rich, ignorant Texans were soon going to own New York publishing and dictate policy—and he had flooded me with picture postcards, usually scenes of swank hotel swimming pools garlanded with "starlets," which, he explained, meant beauty contest winners from Missouri and Nebraska who have to blow moguls. I wrote back, "Dear Hampden, I have read *The Deer Park*." A day or two later, a short letter came. Hampden was at a manic peak:

Hey, Dick!
    According to my mythical lady, a Vogelweide is literally a bird-meadow, and vögeln, in the vernacular, is "the bird," or as we would say, "to employ one's bird," possibly in a meadow. Now a small bird such as yours makes a very small impression in a meadow; however, an enormous bird with magnificent plumage such as mine makes every blossom quiver with its flight.
                                       Ho!
                                       Goethe

Hampden's glee about his mistress's publication was not simply boresome. He had called Margery Parsons his "mythical lady." He had become fixed on a little boy's pride in the size of his genitals. I began to worry, and decided to write him a long ramble, more or less just to keep him company while he was out there in Los Angeles, but also to tell him about how Fauna and I came together again.

Dear Hampden,
I went to one of these absurd cocktail parties that publishers give to launch new books by writers who sell exceptionally well. This party was for Golding, and the fad is still on, all out of proportion to his accomplishment. Golding takes a thin slice of Conrad's decay theme and exploits it artificially. But I guess the Ivy League sophomores who have made Golding a bestseller haven't got around to Conrad. Before Golding it was Salinger, then Roth, and now it's Updike whose balloon floats over the city. Calder Willingham is going to puncture that one.
At any rate, I went to the party, and there was the standard young promotion whore who does publicity, etc., holding a martini out to me, with a professional smile. Did I want to meet Francis Brown of the New York *Times*? Did I wish to meet Mr. Golding? Would I like another drink? Oh, *yes* Aegean published your novel. It was a very big success, wasn't it, yes. I *knew* I had heard of you, though I haven't read your book yet, something to look *forward* to.
As you know, I was with Golding at the Queenstown Arts Festival last fall, and he was very Englishcharming, and his wife, too. But it's difficult to try to talk with someone whose work you don't admire. And I had no reason to want to meet Sir Francis Brown of the worst-best middlebrow review we have. (But I'd still rather read the old ladies' bookclub *Times* crap than the pretentious *New York Review of Books*, with its Robert

Lowell orientation, for Christ's sake.) But after a third martini—it was about 4:30 P.M by then—I had only one thought: to go back downtown to the Village and get my beautiful faithless Fauna back.

I don't really care, Hampden, if you feel it was good riddance when she left. I understand what you mean. But you must realize that you have a damn cruddy antagonism toward Fauna because she fights back when you attack her, just as your Regina does. But you don't have to carry your battles with Regina into Fauna's house. Fauna is an energetic kid of 20 who has to do three things at the same time. She has to love me, has to dance, has to pick up stray poetic con artists like a kid who never had a puppy or a kitten. She has to distribute the *Catholic Worker,* has to boycott schools if LeRoi Jones says so. There's a starved quality to Fauna, and I've run short of food.

But there are many good hours, days, months even, left for Fauna and me, and I'm going to take them because I want her more than any other woman I've ever known. When she becomes restless again, and goes, she will yell and hiss and spit and grab a steak knife, which I'll take away from her, and that will be her way of saying, I love you, Goddam you! Hell, I can see it all, but I want it and I walked straight into it again last night.

Before I got Fauna back last night, I had no way to see, to feel, no way to think and feel the same way at the same time. Too much university and strangeness of new situation with trivial details to absorb like cotton taking up blood, my blood. I need her to feel alive, to know myself. As we used to say in the country, I need her like grass needs horseshit. So there you are. Anyhow, I left that stupid party and went down to the corner of 6th Avenue and 8th Street where she was hawking the *Catholic Worker*. Years ago I met Dorothy Day, who runs the publication and the *Worker* farm where she tried to rehabilitate rummies, etc., you know, Save the Unemployed Union Men, Save the Negro from Slavery, Save the World from War; she's a fine and beautiful-souled woman right out of Bernard Shaw. And the only flaws in her greatness are (1) that she has a religion, and (2) she is optimistic about people who have to destroy themselves; so she has a priest bless the food passed out to these poor guys who have dedicated themselves, beyond recall, to their own deaths.

It was Friday, about 5:00 P.M., and snowing, and the *Catholic Worker* was out—a very good issue which has some excellent reviews of books on the Montessori method of letting children grow up freely (My God, how you and I could have used some of *that!* As children we never heard of freedom, much less felt it); it's about the Italian *casa del bambini* experiments by Dr. Maria Montessori; and there's also a good article by Thomas Merton in this issue. Anyhow, there on the corner in the snow, looking like a Dreiser waif, was Fauna, without makeup, looking thin, but cheerfully freezing her ass to peddle papers for one cent, one penny, because she believes in what she's doing. Fauna held out a paper. I stood to one side, out of her direct view. She was looking straight ahead, passing out papers, taking in pennies, aware of the presence of somebody, but not wanting propositions from strangers, only to distribute the *Worker*.

Only one cent?

Yes, one cent, sir.

This is a pacifist paper, isn't it?

Well, uh, we promote peace.

I teach in a university. Suppose I get caught reading this?

Well, uh—

(I felt her disgust with an academic square.)

Give me a paper, please, miss.

She gave me a copy and I paid the one cent.

Are you a pacifist, miss?
Yes, sir.
To what lengths would you go to pacify me, miss?
(I saw her shudder slightly and was afraid she had recognized my voice, or my corny humor, or both.)
Her voice was shy.
Why don't you come to one of our meetings, sir? We have meetings every Friday evening on Chrystie Street.
The address?
It's in the paper, sir.
You're a pacifist, miss. You admire Lord Russell. Tell me, do you personally disarm?
What, sir?
If I were to assault you, would you unilaterally disarm and smother me with loving peace?
You really should come to one of our meetings, sir.
I will, if I can buy you a unilateral espresso afterwards.
(She smiled in confusion and irritation at a square, a hick, a simple con man, a recognized antagonist, a mocker.)
I stepped in front of her.
Honey, all you need is a red cap and a little iron pot.
Fauna clutched the papers to her stomach.
You? You? Oh, God!
With one thin arm she pointed at my face and began to laugh.
I started laughing, too. We stood there, laughing uncontrollably.
People passing by gave quick curious glances, as if watching two lunatics convulsed and about to collapse in the snow.
You! she cried.
No, *you!*
Richard? My own Richard?
She had stopped laughing.

Come on home, Fauna.
Take me home, Richard. Oh, God, take me home!
And that's how we got together again. And, Hampden, if she has to leave her "cruel Richard" I hope it won't be soon. I love her.
When will you return from the fleshpots of California so you and Regina and Fauna and I can resume some good habits, like going down to Mott Street for Chinese food?

Ever,
Dick

I read over the letter to Hampden. It didn't sound good, at all. I had pleaded my weaknesses. I had pleaded for understanding. I saw myself as a very tired man, excusing my failures in advance. I had identified myself with certain of Hampden's attitudes toward Fauna. But this was not really quite true. It was too pat, too facile to be the whole truth. I know I love Fauna. I know I love Hampden. I know I love Regina. I know I love my student Nathan, who is going to Maryland to protest segregation. I know I love his girlfriend Rama, too. I know I am a loving and desperate man.

Since Fauna came back we have had a lot of good talk, good food, good music—like Horace Silver at the Village Gate, Cecil Taylor at the Five Spot, and Coltrane uptown. Evenings when I have to mark student papers, Fauna reads, waters the plants I bring home to her, dreams of living in the country. She wants to get pregnant and go to Kentucky, and me grow vegetables and her cook them, wants to "know the soil." I realize it's only her new kick. She says, "Give me pleasure. Give me pleasure and babies, Richard. They'll have my skin and your brain."

Watching, listening, I can't keep from loving her. Her hair swirling on a pillow while she reads, her hands trying inexpertly to cook Spanish dishes, her unique creation of a mystifying chaos: a loaf of bread on the flush tank in the bathroom, the sink sponge and her panties stashed in the refrigerator along with frozen shrimp and ice cubes veined with vodka, her clothing in a trail from bathroom to bed as if she were a pioneer woman captured by Indians and leaving bits of cloth for me to follow to rescue her, her eyes sulky and refractory, her face expectant when I come home, her rushing out into the hall to meet me, springing into my arms, locking her legs around my waist, kissing, saying, "Play horsey with me, Richard. I have a good seat, or a good saddle—how do Kentucky girls say it?" I play with her. We horse around, eat at 11:30, play chess until 1:00, play blackjack for dimes until 3:00. By that time I have drunk enough not to care if I have to teach early because Fauna has become magic and her dreams almost believable. If I could believe Fauna, we will have children and eat wild berries and buds and roots and dandelions and live on a mountainside where thrushes sing at dusk, and eat groundhogs and rabbits. Christ, I can see her face if I ever brought her a rabbit I shot, the head pulled off against my boot, the raw carcass skinned and filmed with blood. The poor girl would wet her pants, then puke. But, hell, I'll let her live in an unreal world for as long as she can. I love her too much not to try to keep her happy.

But within a month Fauna began to complain about being the body-servant for a "Goddam professor" who demanded coffee every half hour. "You don't talk to me anymore," she said. "You don't take long walks with me anymore. Why did you take this stupid teaching job, Richard?"

She pushed my papers aside and sat on my lap.

"I can give you a year off right now, with my dancing bit, a whole *year*, Richard. We've got the money."

"I can't just resign, honey. I can't just up and quit this job after a few weeks. You know that."

"Job!" Fauna said. She clenched her hands. "All I know is you're killing yourself with this job. You don't write well anymore. You don't talk anymore. You come home dead. Listen. Listen, Richard. You remember what Behan said

Dylan said to a cat who told him he had a good job. He said there's no such thing as a good job. A job is death without dignity."

"That's true, I guess. Don't you think I have cursed my poor white ancestors in their Goddam cheap pinebox coffins a million times?"

"Richard. Richard, let's get out of here. You don't need this teaching bit. We've got money enough for a whole year in Kentucky."

"But, honey, what then? It's not just this job. If I walk out of here now, I'll never be able to get another teaching job in any college. And what other kind of work can I do that gives me summers off? The summers are what I have to live for. Then I'll come back to life, and work."

"No, Richard. No, you can't die nine months a year just to live the other three! Listen, Richard. You *said* we could get by in Kentucky, in the mountains, in a little farmhouse on fifteen hundred dollars a year. For both of us, and a baby, too, you said. Listen—"

"But, honey, we don't have money saved up ahead. We can't just go out there for a year and at the end of the year stare up at the sky and pray for manna."

"Listen. Listen, Richard. We have over eighteen hundred dollars in my savings account. Here. Here, I'll show you!"

Fauna leaped from my knees and danced to her dresser and took out a small blue book. She studied it fiercely.

"Honey," I said quietly, "we spend that much a year on Heaven Hill and Liquid Prell shampoo."

"Don't be sarcastic, Richard. We have the money. See? See? Right here."

Her fingernail dented the last figure in a column.

"Please, oh, please, Richard!"

I said, "You have the money. I have a job."

Her face turned gray as lead.

Communication dwindled rapidly after that. Fauna kept a cheerful mask on her face. I tried, too. Each morning I got up, showered, shaved, and before I left to walk across Washington Square Park to the university, I put my lips on her sleeping face and kissed and pressed gradually until she was half awake, just conscious enough to know who it was kissing her face. I didn't wake her completely—her dance rehearsals were at 4:00 P.M.—but just made her aware of my love before she lapsed again into deep sleep. She would phone me at the university and ask, "Richard, did you kiss me this morning? I think so, but I *have* to know. Richard, did you take your sandwich I made you? I put fresh Italian bread with the leftover steak and lettuce and mashed potatoes and some cottage cheese, just the way—"

"Mashed potatoes and cottage cheese in a sandwich?"

"But, but, Richard, I know how you love them!"

"Honey, please put the tomato juice in the refrigerator instead of the toilet paper, will you, next time?"

"But, Richard, I *like* cold toilet tissues. And in summer I put my panties in the refrig. It's so cool and reassuring."

"Honey, go back to sleep, will you?"

"Do you love me a little?"

"Yes."

"You evil man! You're supposed to say a *lot!*"

"Yes, honey."

"I love you, Richard. When can you come home? I can't wait to talk with you and fuck with you. When you kiss me I get all these crazy things going. I'm Pavlov's bitch. When you ring your bell, I'm ready to go."

"Fauna, my darling."

That was the way it went. I'd get up and find notes stuck on the refrigerator door, the stove, the bathroom mirror—stuck with Scotch tape or masking tape.

Richard,

When you get home I will be at the A & P (a big sale) for some steaks and artichokes. Should be home about 7:00 latest.

Richard's Fauna

P.S. Had some day at Carnegie. Kicked some creep in

the balls. He was lying on the floor in the wrong position.

and

Mah dahling Sugah,
Where did I get that from, I wonder!
I'll be at the laundry, the FUCK IT YOURSELF kind. Back about 7:00. I stole a bill from you. Your change is on the table.
I love you so very much today, all day—you'll never know, unless you touch me and talk to me.
"Titty-Boo ME," Lil Old, ah mean.

and

Dearest,
Even if we could not communicate last night, I still would like you to know there is coffee in the refrig, and that I love you. Why don't you wake me up, so we can talk???
Fauna Lawrence

I was getting up slowly in the mornings, dreading the spiritless winter days of lecturing huge groups of students—sometimes 140 at once—in a dingy old theater, a microphone hung on a string around my neck. William Butler Yeats and William Carlos Williams? I had begun to hear myself repeating things into the scratchy microphone. I had no communication with the students, either. And the bundles of papers, wound with rubber bands, were heavy under my arm. Home through the snow to find Fauna curled on the couch, fresh-looking, her hair washed and brushed, bringing me a drink, Fauna, hopeful of the kind of talk and nuance and careful warm touch that we had had months ago. It was pathetic, futile. I could not bring spring to her blood. She could not wait for my summer. I was learning the value of silence. She was beginning to learn the mysteries of speech.

One morning there was no note. I wondered about the last one, signed Fauna Lawrence. She had added my last name. I looked at her pillowed head, her Botticelli face. I walked over and knelt beside the bed and listened to her breath. For one moment I was about to raise the window, throw all the student papers down into MacDougal Street, make a phone call to the university that I had tuberculosis and was going to Arizona, and undress, and crawl back into bed again, and cradle her in my arms, and say, when she sighed and fed me into her, Love me now. And when you wake up, my darling, you can pack a bag for Kentucky. I kissed her nose, got up, went to the closet for a necktie, combed my hair, dropped three sets of keys into my pocket. I had been shown the cities and riches of the Earth, and I was dressed and tonsured for death. Sick, I walked to the table to pick up books and papers for a nine o'clock class. On the coffee table I saw a packet of cards, imitative of IBM cards, with staggered perforations. Fauna had gone into the garish little booth recently set up two doors north by some Times Square con men, and had her "scientific character analysis" clicked off on cards by a computer.

GRAPHOMETER		
	FAUNA LAWRENCE	
Address	Nowhere	
Street	*City*	*State*
Occupation	Nothing	No. 032850

I flipped the packet of cards. They read:

OFTEN YOU WANT TO BE CENTER OF ATTRACTION
EXPRESSIVE WITH A VERY ACTIVE IMAGINATION
YOU ENJOY HIGH STANDING IN SOCIAL GROUP
YOU SELDOM REFUSE A CHALLENGE
YOU ENJOY THE COMPANY OF THE OPPOSITE SEX
YOU PREFER A CAREFREE UNHURRIED EXISTENCE

And beside this crazy packet of little cards was a notice of the school boycott, scheduled for today, February 3. It was published in mimeograph by the Greenwich Village, Chelsea Branch of the NAACP.

The first name I saw was Rex Tolliver. Fauna and I had met him, admired him, talked with him in Queenstown a few months back. We had all his records. We felt Rex was the best of all the horn men going, better even than Miles. There had been a bad scene. All of us were boozed up and I thought Rex had made a pass at Fauna, or they had made passes at each other, or whatever, and I had taken Rex's trumpet away from him and hit him with it. Fauna thought I had slugged Rex because he was a Negro. I guess Rex thought so, too. Trouble, trouble. Naturally I hadn't heard from Rex.

And now he was at the Village Gate again. I buttoned my collar. It was too tight. I went to the university and hung the little black cord of the microphone about my neck.

It was three days before Fauna came back. She marched into the apartment, not even buzzing but using her key. She said, "Hello, Strom Thurmond, how are you today? How's lil old you, Sugah? Still killing time with the college kiddies?"

She was happily, belligerently drunk.

"No doubt you have been celebrating the defeat of the Yankee Germans, Irish, Italians and Swedes in the Civil War—excuse me, I mean the War Between the States. Where are the pigs-feet, Baby? I expected a real barbecue with white whiskey. Or have you been celebrating your great SINS by washing your socks? That's the way the mansion molders, Baby!"

Fauna went to the cabinet and poured me a double Heaven Hill.

"Here, Richard Bilbo Thurmond Byrd, son of Mighty William Faulkner, have a touch. Does that *scan* like 'Hiawatha'? Poet. Poet, my ass. You're dead and you know it!"

She examined her flowers on the windowsill.

I asked, "How's Rex?"

"Rex? Oh, he's great. You should catch him at the Gate before he splits. You should water my plants. Why haven't you watered my cactus—I mean my cacti, Richard?"

Fauna poured herself a thick drink on the rocks and gave me another. I had not eaten all day, and the booze became an angry electricity in my head and stomach.

I said, "You cheap shit, you cheap little whore, I can see you going helter-skelter for three days and nights!"

"Oh, me!"

"Yes, you, you with your whore's habit of walking insolently before strangers, letting your whore's eyes linger. You, you'd crow over any bastard's cock any morning. I can see you!"

"Oh, can you now?"

"Can I ask honesty from you? No. You always imagine you're on stage. I can see you, you with your simple whore's pride, you can climb on the merry-go-round and hold on to a wooden horse's mane with chipped paint, with your own chipped and peeling soul. You think this is *excitement,* you with your whore's dream of the brass ring, with your childish fist full of candy you never had before. So wear paper money in your hair. Tape it to your breasts. Go ahead. Be Queen of the Carnival in a white dress, you in your flimsy parachute drop at Coney Island, you with your hi-fi mind in your plastic skull!"

"You—" Fauna began contemptuously.

I interrupted, "You don't tell me *nothing,* for Christ's sake. I can see you."

She brought me another bourbon, and I went back to work on some student's paper on Yeats' Crazy Jane poems.

"Can I stay here tonight, Richard?"

"Stay any place you like. Stay with Cardinal Spellman. Stay with Rex Tolliver. Anywhere you want."

Fauna went into the bathroom. I heard a bottle drop, and a short cry. When I went in, she had two rubber bands looped around her elbow, burrowing into the flesh, making the veins strut. She held a spoon with some white powder and a few drops of water in it. She was trying to warm the white solution in the spoon with a match. I threw the spoon into the sink and broke the rubber bands from her arm. I shook her.

"Who turned you on this junk? Who the hell gave you this junk?"

She held herself against me, sweating, cooing, with hungering mouth and thighs. I imagined her, for the past three days, going from man to man, the half-baked poets, the sleazy painters, the far-out jazzmen.

Fauna murmured, "Yours, yours, Richard, forever and ever."

"Yes, until tomorrow," I said.

Fauna jerked her head back. Her hair fell out in dark rays. Her mouth was dry and blue.

Fauna shrieked, "You Goddam tight-assed bastard! You're just like Hampden! You *are* Hampden!"

She ran to the kitchen and drew my hunting knife out of its leather sheath. She whirled and ran at me with the blade. I turned her arm, the knife fell, her thin body crashed into the window. I took her in my arms. All at once she grew quiet. A half-moon of glass had fallen from the pane. Like two sleepwalkers we picked up the shattered glass and laid the pieces in a saucer. I led Fauna to the bathroom and washed her wrist with white soap, toweled it dry and stretched a Band-Aid across a small cut. I kissed her wrist, fingers, forehead, eyes. I took Fauna to bed and pulled her long hair smooth on the pillow as I entered and felt her ankles come to rest, crossed on my back. After she had come, whispering, "God! God! Oh, Richard! Oh, God!" she fell asleep. I got up quickly, poured a cup of black coffee, and gazed back at her, her mouth still except for small puffs of breath, her high clear forehead where black hair flowed like tar, the sharp little triangle of pubic hair, musky and curled, and her ankles that I could reach around with thumb and finger—all fragile, ill, her head full of father and me, father-Richard, and full of Thomas and Cummings and Ginsberg and Jones, all mouth and vagina, all ingestion and puking, all garlic and whiskey, terror and love. I had never loved and hated anyone so much.

I woke up about 4:00 A.M. A cold wind was driving snow through the broken window. I took a grocery bag and stuck it to the pane with masking tape, dressed quickly and wrote Fauna a brief note to leave her key on my worktable. Then I went out and rode the subway uptown and downtown between the 4th Street and 125th Street stations, back and forth, until it was time to go to the office.

When I got home in the evening, there were Fauna's keys, as I had asked, and a fresh pot of coffee—her good-bye gift. Fauna left a letter under her keys on my table.

My Richard,

What is your day like? Mine is rejection like it was going out of style. But I know that we're good, if we just could be. *Some* contact is better than none, even if we just touch the same piece of paper. No one can touch, I mean muss up the place in me where the real words go and leave their placenta(s?). Fuck/hate/love. Do you know what I mean, my Richard? Because if you don't, nobody else can or will, and I will be too alone, I mean really *loneless*. Is that a word, Richard?

I went in your wool robe downstairs to the candy store and bought a green balloon. I swung the balloon across the street, but nobody saw it. It went up and up, and you were not here to catch it. Is this a terrifying play of/or life?

You keep me more than I can say or stay, but I *want*

to stay. You are the only man I always wanted to present me to, like a gift. You are where I can keep from being a shit.

You have your bourbon to come home to, and your old cardboard box of photographs of your poor white parents. But I don't have any of this like you do. All I have is my Richard. I mean all I have is I am more than *sometimes*. Grass implies greenly soon, even under this snow we pile on each other. I mean I want us to be happening/happy.

Please water my plants. Please listen to our Trane albums. Please buy me a thermometer I can stick up my ass so we'll know when our beautiful fucking will make a son for you. Please phone me at OR 4-7200.

Fauna

P.S. William Carlos Williams died today. I don't think he cares.

I made a note to phone her late this evening. Then I went to the closet for a coat, to go downstairs and wrestle Hampden out of the Golden Pizza, drag him up here and drench him with coffee. If he had a weapon to kill me with, I'd have to pin his arms and yell for a cop to help me handle him. I went back to close the window against the snow. I saw Hampden come out of the pizza shop and take off, in a stumbling trot, after a Negro boy.

The Negro boy, about nineteen or twenty, was drooling drunk, and he was following a white girl, pleading with her to talk with him. Twice the girl turned and threw off his awkwardly pawing hand. The third time she stopped stiff-legged and cursed him, her head thrust out like that of a furious goose, hissing at his pained and dejected face. The pity was that I could see he wanted only to talk with her, to be recognized as a human being, a man, a person worth talking to. That was when Hampden caught up with him. Hands clinched, arms stiff at his ribs, body rocking forward, Hampden began to shout.

"You black sonofabitch, where do you come off? You Harlem bastard, just because you're in the North, where do you come off? Do you think you can proposition a white girl on the *streets?* You Goddam black-assed CORE hero! Just because you can knife white subway riders and get away with it, do you think you can get away with grabbing at a white girl on the Goddam street? Where do you come off? Haven't you ever heard of Emmett Till!"

When Hampden attacked the young man, the crowd from the Folklore Center, and a dozen passersby, surrounded them. By the time I ran downstairs and pushed through the crowd, Hampden lay by himself on the walk near the curb. His shirt was soaked with blood, and he was bleeding from the mouth. I took off my coat and folded it under his head. I heard the hooves of a mare that a mounted policeman rode.

"Hampden?"

"Dick? Dick buddy? Dick, they had all these basketballs. They kept dribbling all these balls between my legs and yelling Junior Globetrotters! Dick—"

When I realized Hampden was dead, I felt around for the wounds. He had been stabbed several times. But the young Negro boy hadn't done it. He was sitting on the curb, head in hands, in a pool of his own vomit. The policeman dismounted, came over and helped me carry Hampden's body under the awning of a liquor store. I gave the cop Regina's parents' phone number. I told him that I would take charge of the funeral arrangements in the morning. In about three minutes MacDougal Street was flooded red by the circulating lights of police cars and a police ambulance. A dozen policemen dispersed the crowd. On the walk Hampden's weapon lay, a small bone-handled penknife that he used to scour the bowls of his pipes. That was what he had fought his enemies with, and that was what he was going to kill me with, too.

I stood up, looked up. My students Nathan and Rama were staring at me. Nathan, with his anxious white face, Rama, in her subtle passive darkness, her octoroon shadow lightening and darkening as the lights swept across her face.

Nathan asked, incredulous, "Professor?"

I said, "Forgive him, Nathan. And forgive whoever killed him."

Their faces were tight, cold, unanswering.

I asked, "Will you have coffee with me? It's another forty minutes before your bus leaves for Cambridge."

Nathan said, "No thank you, sir."

The sir sounded underlined.

"We were old friends," I said. "At least you could try to respect that."

I took a call from Regina. Between sobs she told me she had phoned a Veteran's Administration official at his home in Queens. The VA were going to fire rifles over Hampden's grave because he was a combat infantryman. I phoned Margery Parsons. She did not intend to go to the funeral, but was full of excusing words: "My husband and I have been *terribly* concerned about Hampden." I phoned the Department secretary at her home that I would not be in for the next two days and arranged for graduate assistants to take my classes.

It was after dark already. I put on my black suit and went downstairs again and sat in front of the *No Loitering* sign on the stoop, waiting. I took out Hampden's penknife and pared my nails.

It is impossible to know what is going on here. Certainly no one person knows. Probably it cannot even be found in the experience of all the people here. There is too much that nobody ever wanted or wished for, but somehow happened.

Some drunk Ivy League brat in a cashmere coat is burning up a beautiful TR 3 across the street. A weekend bohemian on the way uptown to pick up his girlfriend at the Plaza. A car moves through MacDougal Street: Chrysler convertible, New Jersey cream-colored tags; six lesbians coast on a pathetic-lively weekend excursion, phys ed teachers from some small New Jersey college (anyone for tennis?); a tough baby at the power-steering wheel, a bob-haired, full-fledged AFL-CIO dyke, leading a little colony through the hog-sausage and 20-cent pizza alley of MacDougal Street. God is their eunuch. God is the radiator ornament, a smooth chromed bird without a cock. Among Bronx guitar players, those callow descendants of Nashville and Hazard, the Chrysler glides, stops, moves, stops—you can't get through here on the tourist weekends—among the fat white girls on the arms of Negro folksingers, the lean Negroes and the enormous-thighed white girls from the Bronx and Nebraska with their ribby-proud Negro men who want to be white, in their dirty jeans, the sullen Negro guys who play guitars badly and moan interminable imitations of Belafonte and Ray Charles. And the bob-haired bull-dyke in the cream-colored Chrysler nervously gooses the accelerator, rocking through MacDougal Street. She tries to park for hog-sausage sandwiches with stale fried onions and peppers heaped on buns. She cannot even get close to the curb until the neighborhood boys with spotless leather jackets and tapered black trousers clear the way. The dyke makes a poor stab at parking. One of the Italian boys leans ominously, grinning hugely, and gives directions: Cut, cut, atta baby, cut. When the rattled dyke brings the Chrysler lurching in, all the Italian boys clap hands like rifle fire, and cheer loudly. The lesbians are aware that they are being ridiculed; they grab sausages and pizzas and hasten away, edging the long car out into traffic again, led by the eunuch God on the hood, back, by the Holland Tunnel, to Jersey. The outing has been pointless, the tension created is the juicy necessity to get back to the campus housing project where they can fight to exhaustion over the prettiest field hockey girls, the sleekest tumblers, the swimmers in the Olympics Trials, the flat-chested breaststroke babies of sixteen, smelling of chlorine and one-piece wool-crotch swim suits.

MacDougal Street has begun to fill up for the weekend. More out-of-town kids drift in: white boys with delicate bangs, tight jeans and sandals; girls with dirty hair, great wallowing buttocks and hanging breasts—they tumble out of old Nashes and Plymouths, sit on the dented fenders and tune their guitars. They sing loudly and off-key: "Ain' gonna study war no more ... gonna bury that atom bomb right on the White House lawn ..."

Two fairies weave through the crowd. The older, brasher fag puts his arm around the younger fellow's neck, sneaks his hand down and pinches a nipple. The young fag, with a huge mass of carefully sculptured curls above a petulant face, chirps, "Don't be so indis*creet* in public. Now *sthop* it!" He leaps away from his lover, curtsies a few paces ahead, waves a white handkerchief daintily. "Well, come on, come *on*," he calls. He continues, though, to walk about four paces ahead, waving the kerchief. As he passes the candy store, the neighborhood boys cheer loudly: "Yay! Yay!"

As blond and bland as a calendar Christ, a long-haired and bearded boy in black turtleneck sweater beneath his denim shirt, and wearing faded jeans and rawhide boots, saunters self-consciously up and back through the block. He knows he is pretty as a picture and is more than willing to be looked at, his fair medallion profile and pale skin luminescent in the cold wind: Jesus, by Salvador Dali.

A little girl, directly in front of me, calls in a forlorn voice, "Glo-ree-uh! Glo-ree-uh!" There is a pause, then the tousled head of a middle-aged woman appears five flights up, beside her a delicate little girl about eight, her face wearing city-pallor, dying into death early, the little hands and scrawny hair. "Can Glo-ree-uh come down?" The woman's city-voice bellows, "Haf an howah!" The little girl disappears. A boy about six appears beside his mother. The woman takes him into her flabby arms, presses him to her rotund face. She sucks the little boy's ears, mouth, eyes, neck. He struggles but cannot escape. In a moment two girls of eight are turning a dirty rope, one end tied to the No Parking sign. Tourists and natives, indulgent, walk in the gutter among precise coils of dogshit so the little girls can keep the rope turning: "Step on a crack. Break ya mothah's back": girl-chants, city-rhymes for rope skipping, the thin stiff legs awkward, missing the beat, the rope slapping against dirty-fresh girl flesh, skinny, white, dirty.

A beautiful Negro girl idles by, eating a caramel sucker half the size of a paperbook. The Negro driver of a laundry truck slows the machine to a crawl, leans out and calls softly, "You gonna give me a bite?" The girl, obviously flattered, affects contempt. "I give you a bit on you ass!" He grins, asks, "You wanna pull my pud?" She puts him down. "You ain' got 'nough for me to pull on!" She returns the caramel sucker to her mouth. The driver laughs quietly and nudges his accelerator.

A Jewish boy and a Negro boy in their early twenties stop near the stoop where I sit and gesticulate frantically, arguing:

"Become a Marxist or you'll never get your freedom!"

"I don't want your help. You're passive. You can be appeased by the capitalists you pretend to hate. They will give you money, but they won't give me my civil liberties. They buy you off so you keep kicking *me* for *them!*"

"Okay. If you don't want my help, try to do it yourself. You'll see. You won't get your freedom until you come to socialism."

"Socialism! Huh! You're doubly passive. You're a Jew *and* a socialist. You won't help me!"

They move on, still gesturing, toward the San Remo.

Two Negro men, middle-aged, poorly dressed and carrying a jug of red wine, pass. One says, "I hate 'em all. I hate all the bastards!" The other says, "No, man. I'm a good nigger. I'm a friend of the white man."

In a repainted, salmon-colored Cadillac, two young white couples, the men with open shirts, the girls with gaudy scarves tied over orange-dyed hair full of curlers, brake to a cushiony stop. The driver hits the horn. Above the two-tone horns, a rock-and-roll singer on the full-blasted radio yells:

Let's get drunk and rock all night!
All right, sweet daddy, all right!
Let's get drunk and rock all day!
Okay, sweet daddy, okay!

The neighborhood boys have closed in on the candy store. When a pretty girl who is walking alone approaches, they form a line across the walk, blocking her way. If she moves toward the curb, they move in front of her. They touch her hair, her breasts, her buttocks. Apparently the girls know the rules of this game. If they give the guys a free feel, the line sags, an opening appears, and they can go through. If they fight, they are in trouble. There are several dark doorways near the candy store. Some of the staircases lead to the tarpaper roofs. The girls know this, and they simply turn and twist and slap lightly and make remarks, but they don't make the mistake of becoming too obviously angry.

After a girl is felt and let pass, the Italian boys seize a little kid, a boy about twelve. They practice mass attack. One guy pinions the little boy's arms while another fakes punches to his head and stomach, and kicks to his groin. There is no quaint idea of "honor" here, of one-against-one. They are in the real jungle where a pride of lions will attack a lone zebra. The little boys learn quickly. In front of the candy store the leather-jacketed, slim-pants guys fake punches, wheel, fake, grab, feint—and laugh.

A Negro boy about sixteen pedals up on his delivery bike. It is a three-wheeled contraption, a big metal box on springs, with a bicycle frame and seat behind. Two of the neighborhood boys casually walk out to the curb and stand on the springs of the delivery cart. Jumping up and down, they break the springs, which fall on the left front wheel. Another boy goes up to the seat and crowds the Negro boy away. The Negro boy is paralyzed, afraid to say a word. He knows what he would get. The Italian boy wants to "see how the seat fits." He "fixes" the seat. Meanwhile two other guys in the gang break the right axle of the grocery cart. Without a word, the Negro boy climbs on his wobbling bicycle seat. The cart limps off like a crippled duck, scraping iron and rubber. The jeering calls follow him: "Dun it work bettah dis way? Da wheels is *even* dis way. Din I tell ya it works bettah dis way?"

I got up and crossed the street to the Golden Pizza. I needed cigarettes. The big-gutted boy in charge makes small talk with unescorted girls who come in. He has a tic which makes his head jerk sideways every three seconds. He jerks his head, makes wisecracks, scratches his head, scratches his crotch, scratches his ass, then slices an Italian sausage. He says, "Da guy had five stab wounds. Yeh. Yeh. Right in fronta da Folklore Centah!" In unhurried moments he counts a box of Trojans under the counter.

On the lamp pole in front of Minetta's Tavern, somebody has pasted a crudely drawn cartoon: two Amos and Andy-type Negroes are kissing the cheeks of a white girl between them. The caption is: New York *Post* Legislates Morals. Under the caption somebody else has chalked: Fascist Bastards! On the glass wall of the telephone booth outside the drugstore there is a huge advertisement for the latest widescreen spectacular. And written across the heroine's exposed breasts is the legend: She Sells More Damn Pussy the Bitch.

In a doorway two small boys are exploding red rolls of caps with pieces of brick. As each one explodes they shout an accompanying "Pow!" Seeing me, they spring up and point six-gun fingers and scream, "You die! You die!" Their pale faces glisten with excitement. I sense the unreleased torture, anguish, murder in their young bodies. In their dark prison of bricks and criminal insanity, I walk past the wet smirch on the cement where Hampden's body lay a few minutes ago. New life has closed around that spot, its cancerous cell that will grow again, rapidly.

Nobody knows what is going on here. No man can make any sense of even his own life for the past week, let alone anyone else's. Less than a week ago Fauna and I sat, holding hands, in the Loeb Student Center of New York University where Erich Fromm gave a lecture, during which he said: ". . . violence is the experience of human impotence to change things and persons by means of reason, love and example . . . violence is the reaction of those who feel incapable of using their constructive human powers . . ." I know that within three blocks of the lecture hall, while Fromm was speaking, somebody was being assaulted, right then, any *then,* in any moment as it transforms itself from now to then and is lost; it is lost in violence. In their vivid, hypnotic glee, the little boys shout, "You die! You die!"

I was raised in rough country. I've been shot at. The first time was when I ran up on a guy who was stealing muskrats out of my traps. I was sixteen then. Three days a week, I hang a microphone around my neck and lecture about poetry. I am thirty now. I come home in the evening, drink, dream. Every time I dream, I think I am alive. Every time I remember a dream, I think I have lived. But then I wonder. The disaster of life. Is it beautiful, as I had hoped?

My secretary at the office has a boyfriend who slugged her, blacked her eye, then threw her on the floor and kicked her ribs. That was less than a day ago. I saw her bruised face under the carefully applied makeup. Assault and murder are common forms of love. I think of the young woman crying for help, being kicked by her lover. I think of the poor Negro boy who simply wanted a white girl to talk with him. I think of Hampden, skidding away in the police ambulance, already dead. I think of a young man with a kinife that went in five times, running from the police, who will catch him, or not.

I am tired of violence, and that means I am tired of people. People hide under the shadow of the world *inhuman.* But all acts are human. To knife a man is as human as to kiss a child. I am growing tired of people, and that means I am fed up with myself, with my own criminal impulses. I am tired of the horror of everyone and myself. I am full of the horror of people. We are too beautiful and too horrible. Once, in Kentucky, I had a gamecock that won five straight fights in the toughest pits. I retired him to the run. He was a magnificent bird, simple, clean, brilliant of feather. He was life clearly put. His internal principle, his purpose, was to kill and procreate. After that comes the vacuum of politics and psychology. Governments and doctors fail. I fail. Fauna fails. Hampden fails. The yet uncaught man who killed Hampden fails. Everywhere the failure spreads like waves from a single rock dropped into a pool. Love, the very ridiculous idea of love, fails. I do not think people will learn, not love, but the very least kindness to each other in my lifetime. I do not think I will talk about poetry again.

I bought two packs of Pall Malls at the Golden Pizza and came back up here to the apartment.

I lean on the sill in illusory light. In a random pattern other heads darken the old buildings. The snow is falling harder. About eight feet above the rusted cornices of the tenements a three-quarter moon looks motionless and scarred, not yet shining. In the street below there are many blurred shouts and cries. Across the street an old Italian couple live in their only window. The old man wears a white stocking cap indoors. Man and wife trim each other's nails, laboriously, attaching importance to the act, as the old do. I feel surgically removed. I try to inhale the odor of life, feeling a brief sense of being alive when Fauna gives me that dark-eyed unfathomable glance of the chronic New York waif with thin face, herself cold, frightened, her long hair and brown eyes gold-flecked, flaring, diminishing like lights in a theater.

At 10:00 P.M. there are insistent bongos, guitars, shouts, falling bottles. The long sadness of Catholic bells begins. The old couple pause in their single window and cross themselves. Bells from Father Demo Square. Night in a place far from Italy. Without their prayers, without their grief, the God of Peter would become sad as they.

The street boys in their black tapered pants, their black loafers, their white shirts open at the throat, begin to catch huge wet snowflakes. They begin to catch the snowflakes on their tongues. They field them as if the flakes were baseballs, pivoting with comic grace to catch a flake that burns out in one cold spot on the tongue, for a fraction of a second. They watch way up, to follow a flake as it enters the downdraft of the brick canyon, and trace it all the way down to a car top or the pizza parlor awning. If it falls free, they take it on their tongues and laugh in crazy innocence below the huge snowflakes they take as sacraments on their tongues.

One boy breaks from the gang and begins to dance in the snow. The others set the beat, very fast, with clapping hands. It is not like anything you ever saw at City Center, or in the phony *West Side Story* acrobatics. His dance is alive, real, final.

Somehow, maybe with lookouts, they know when a cop is coming. All the neighborhood boys disappear into the candy store, into the doorways. When the cop walks by, juggling his stick artistically, nobody is there.

The two Negro men, ignored by the thinning lines of people carrying limp slices of pizza, black guitar cases, umbrellas, are setting up their strange instruments under my window. One has a homemade drum, the head secured by strips of rubber cut from an old inner tube. The other has a heavy string tacked to a pine slat and fastened to the middle of a galvanized washtub. Bass and drum. They get all set up, then nod to each other. They play and sing "Route 66" and "Come On to My House" and a few other upjump things. Then they get serious, pause, as if they were in a club or concert hall, to consult about the next number. Slowly, bluely, they begin to play "Sunday Kind of Love."

Nobody pays any attention to them, or to the coffee can they placed on the sidewalk for coins. They play the song in the snowy street without coats or hats, just as if everybody were hearing, or if only they are hearing. It doesn't matter. Their music rises to my window. Their sadness is slow, quiet, sure. They are dead before they start. They know that. We are all dead in this place: white, Negro: dead.

I try to imagine a time of love and goodness. I try to

imagine God, or at least imagine a time when God may have lived. There is always a feeling that a human being ought to be more than a brick with an obscene word scraped into its face in an old wall. That a man ought not be in despair, alone, to die in the street, as Hampden did, or die standing up, listening to music, as I do now.

HUGH ALLYN HUNT

Acme Rooms and Sweet Marjorie Russell

(FROM THE TRANSATLANTIC REVIEW)

A PUCE ROMANCE, this is. Small towners hover round, for this romantic message comes to you straight from the hinterland heart of fields, farm houses and gentle, leafy communities of less than 20,000. These words figure to be nostalgia-laden, memory-aimed. Youth and love, those ever-warm states of being and mind, are about to be reheated. Sit down and prepare an indulgent smile for rural, boyish things recalled.

My town has exactly 16,548 easy-going, rather unanxious folk in it at the time all this takes place. It's bigger now, but this was far-away in the days of my youth, four thousand years ago in 1949. We're not, of course, going to deal with *all* those people. Just about a dozen or so.

For a helpful point of identification, I'm the long, skinny, flax-headed kid hinching his shoulders nervously over there at the drugstore counter. Notice this is not the usual adolescent cliche: I am *not* plagued by acne; beneath my straw sloshes a green river, *not* a coke; my levis, *not* corduroys or khakis, are hooked lethally low, the belt loops sliced off and the bottoms carefully cut the right length with a razor blade. I do have to admit to a letter sweater, but there's a switch-blade knife in my pocket to offset this. The sweater and the blade, incidentally, more or less typify a division of opinion within myself at this time. With normal high school aplomb, I am supporting two opposing and totally unintegrated points of view of the world. It is the co-presence of these two incompatible attitudes that, I think, I sincerely hope, will provide the dramatic tension of this purple-hued reminiscence.

Around me, in similar stagged pants, sweaters and lazily drooping cigarettes, stand my fellow adolescents. There are six of us, all of different sizes, everyone an eleventh grader and to a man sixteen.

If our sallow and fatigued features seem to indicate that we are plotting unspeakable degradations, good. For after all, the most significant and exciting hours of the day are just commencing: after school. Moments given completely over to teen-age evil. We are here at this particular hour—four o'clock in the afternoon—too, because it is between the end of basketball season and the beginning of track season. All of us at this counter attend Catholic high school and in this Protestant town we fish-eaters are known as deadly, fanatical competitors—not especially good, but competitive. At the moment, our six pallid faces are open testimony to the dissolute relief we're taking from months of tendon-stretching athletic combat. In a very brief time we've worked hard to relax, getting little sleep, losing our spending money at the poolhall, breathing numberless cigarettes and doing other things.

In plotting our boyish iniquities we have, naturally, come across such unimaginative things as getting into fights and stealing automobiles. But such things are not it; not what we are after. What we are seeking with undeviating singlemindedness, has to do with girls. We call it many things, most of them fanciful and extravagant. It is, of course, *sex*. Mysterious, furtive, condemned and immeasurably fascinating.

At sixteen, all of us have had our initial and incomplete little grapplings in cramped back seats. It is, in fact, this minor kind of experimentation that emboldens several of us (me, for instance) to keep an old American myth alive—that we are rampant swordsmen, that we've "gone all the way" with this or that girl, long ago last month—carefully selecting for these lies older females, usually recently graduated from public high school, who possess well-known reputations and who are totally removed from the possibility of knowing any of us. Against this unsatisfactory behavior and this unsurprising dishonesty, we relentlessly prepare and verbally rehearse keen teen orgies. What we impatiently seek now is the raw, unclothed act, fact, confrontation, the great entwined spasm. We are at the counter, behind our emerald drinks, waiting—nervously.

One other community or municipal (if you will) fact should be pointed out here. My home town is at the time of this story a division point for a Midwestern railroad and as such possesses the remarkable total of thirteen whore houses. There's really little more to add about this at the moment, except that ours is no sin city. The houses, regulated by the mayor and the city council, are quite sedate and rather spectacularly unobvious.

"Look," I tell Jerry Donovan, working hard to keep my cigarette balanced at the side of my lip and grab the position of chief evil-artist of the group at the same time, "what we'll do is pool all our loot, get two cases of beer, go up, ask for a big room and for as many girls for as long as we can afford." It is a long sentence for me and I am confused. I end by nodding rapidly, persuasively.

Jerry, who tries to be swift and clever, but is really good-natured and kind of slow, quickly wags his broad head and grins. "Yeah, yeah. Two blondes, a brunette and three redheads." He rubs his hands together hungrily. When and how he has worked out this ratio, I don't know, but every time girls are mentioned lately he offers this ambitious numerical proportion. Since he's agreeing with me, I agree with him.

"Sure," I tell him, trying to sound authoritative. "If we've got enough money. Now, how much loot do we all have?" The five permaturely worn faces around me turn childishly reticent and doubtful at this. Like small grade-schoolers they tug hesitantly, almost shyly, at their pockets.

Tom Murray finally flips out fifty cents and suggests cockily: "How about making up a pot and I'll go down to the poolhall and double it, huh?"

"Not my money, by God," Jerry squeezes his fist shut. Tom Murray is our school's hotshot football player, really pretty good, and this leads him to believe he's the world's greatest everything. Actually, he's an erratic pool player who usually loses all his money if he plays very long. Usually, he loses to Don Brandon or me. Now, belligerently, Brandon reaches over and punches Tom on the arm with wicked force.

"You couldn't win a game of slop from a blind, back-busted whore." Don has a thin, prisoner's face with a slit mouth. The first time I met him, I was immediately frightened. At eight years old, he was the only child I'd ever seen who looked as if he might at any moment, coldly, premeditatively, murder a close relative—his mother, say. He wasn't that tough at all, though he worked awfully hard to live up to that grim face of his.

Between the six of us, we place on the counter an unpromisingly small pile of gritty coins and a single faded bill. Acting as temporary treasurer, I count it. "Four dollars and seventy-three cents. Not even a buck apiece. God. What a bunch of duds." I shake my head. "What the hell do you think this is going to be, anyway—a sodality meeting, for Christ's sake? We need..., well...." I don't really know how much we need. "At least five bucks apiece for the whore house," I say recklessly, immediately appalled by the vast fortune that must be mounted to bring this orgy off.

"Damn," murmurs Curly Franklin. "That's ... that's thirty dollars." Curly is the mathematician in our group. There is a long silence as the monumentality of this sum sinks in.

"OK, how many want to chicken out? Say so now, before we get started," I challenge them, abruptly able to do so for the first time in the many years of our boyhood lives together. Compulsively, I am pushed to this exceptional brashness, this ferocity, by the dazzling, lustful visions writhing in my imagination, refusing to be dimmed or stilled by something so minor as thirty dollars. I sneer at my companions so unpleasantly that no one says a word. We all order another green river and ponder how we're going to get more money.

"A dice game," announces Tom Murray who has never been in one.

"You're nuts," says Jerry fretfully.

"We could steal it," Don Brandon grins, trying to be evil.

"Crap," Curly Franklin tells him. "Crap. We'll have to work for it." This announcement depresses us even more and silence wades through our ranks.

"Work," someone murmurs incredulously. "Wow."

"We could borrow it," says Franky Shea suddenly.

"Sure." Curly nods. "Just walk up to the bank teller and say 'We want thirty dollars to go to the whore house, how much is the interest on that?'"

"Yeah," says Frank disheartenedly. "I don't know anybody that'd lend it to us."

"Look, it's about five bucks apiece. Now each of us ought to be able to scrounge up that much some way." I'm still flexing my newly discovered and unfamiliar organizational abilities. "What things can we do to make money?" I ask. "That's the way to approach it." But unfortunately that's a hard question to answer. It's mid-school year and most of the after-class and weekend kind of jobs are already in the anemic grip of creeps that don't go out for sports. Then too, there is the fact that we are in a terrible hurry, both because we're impatient and sweaty to get to those simmering, purchasable female bodies, and because track season will start next week.

"Let's cop something to sell," says Don Brandon, still trying to live up to his face. His unlipped mouth smiles criminally, but we know he'll do nothing unless we all tag along to help.

"Look," says Curly, pretending to be smart and logical and, I think, maybe trying to ace me out of my just-gained foothold on temporary leadership. "Look," he says solemnly and I've already got three good reasons why whatever it is he says is wrong. "There are little things like, let's see. . . ." He's playing it big, pretending to think. "Like collecting bottles and selling them—"

"Oh, man, man," both Jerry and Don moan in unison. "You're kidding."

That's good, that's practical, I think. Maybe Curly and I can make a team. "Fine, fine," I declare with as much superiority as I can master in a hurry. "What else?" Generously giving him the lead, but thinking fast now that there's a challenger. "Maybe hook a job as a grocery boy after school this week," I say before anybody else can get it out. "Or mow lawns, do yard work." Here I lose momentum because the grass isn't growing that fast yet; it's just spring, not summer. But my brain joggles and spins out a better one: "Con your parents into paying you to do something around home. Clean the garage, the basement, something."

Curly nods his head in admiration. The challenge dies and I suck noisily at my straw, then calmly light a butt. "This is Monday," I snap in a company commander's voice, imitating the infantry captain in the movie I've seen over the weekend. "Friday is five days away. By then we should have it. That means we've got to come up with a buck a day. All right?"

"No sweat," declares Tom Murray, easing his fifty-cent piece out of the sandy pile on the counter.

"Anybody showing up without a full five dollars is out. Right?" I glare at them like a two-star general. They all agree: "Sure, sure." After that, I don't really know of anything else to say and neither does anybody else. Silently, we wonder about the money, chew the melting ice in our glasses and then, finally, split up, each going his acquisitive way, elaborate financial schemes sprouting in his head.

Skating with infinitely lewd dreams jerking my limbs toward the rear door of the drugstore, I spy blond and pink Marjorie Russell snuggled in a back booth with other public high school girls. I slow my pace, lecherous hopes losing their evil focus, changing to something I can't quite grasp. My pulse and breath maintain the same rambling race, but some hidden mechanism has shifted ever so slightly. My speed diminishes, my path wavers and I casually lope over to Marjorie Russell's booth, draping myself with careful ease across the back of it. "Hi," I grin with the sensible face of an idiot since the presence of a lot of girls confuses me. "Hi, Marjorie." I want to let the others know they don't exist, not for squishy emotional reasons, I think, but for convenience.

Marjorie is sipping a cherry phosphate demurely and can only nod. To fill the silence, I snarl at her companions and sardonically light a cigarette.

"Hi," she says at last. "How are you?"

I mumble rudely and blow smoke at her. For a moment I grit my teeth. Marjorie's nice, I like her and am anxious to do things with her, but she often says these very formal, stupid type things that drive me nutty. Like "How are you?" For Christ's sake, I just saw her last night. I'm fine and whatever trouble I've got she knows it.

Sawing my head up and down, I try to signal her out of the crowded booth, but she just giggles a little and blinks. The other girls laugh and I flinch at their pitched syllables. Behind a fog of smoke, I poke Margie's shoulder and growl: "Hey, I want to talk to you." At this she glares and turns away. Irritably, I flick ashes on the splotch-faced girl next to her. "Come on Marjorie," I plead, weary already. "Please. Just a minute."

At this, signaling her friends she has won, she simpers, smirks into her phosphate and considers my request. In my private presence, she is not like this at all, and while she makes me wait for my answer, I puzzle this curious adolescent warfare of the sexes. Finally, slowly, she comes out of the booth, sighing wearily as if it were costing her dearly, plopping books down, asking friends to stand up, at last stepping into the aisle with a very public expression of condescension on her girlish features. At the moment, I could easily strangle her and wish wildly for Don Brandon's cruel face with which to frighten them all. Instead, I grab her hand

and stalk to the telephone booth for our intimate exchange. At once, dumped unceremoniously onto the booth seat, she is demure, quiet, no longer simpering. Such changes jostle me, and I stand in the doorway squinting, my brow undoubtedly doubled, for she asks: "What's wrong, honey?"

"Jesus, Jesus," I say to that pretty face and blond hair, abruptly unable to explain why I'm angry. Marjorie is wearing the soft, pale pink sweater I like so much and within it her small, round breasts press gently outward. That is Marjorie: small and round and smooth. My alternate opinion of the world: soft, poignant, immeasurably emotional, infinitely hushed and gentle—Marjorie. My other astigmatic affliction. "Marjorie," I say, neither beginning nor ending a sentence. Then: "Look, let's walk home, huh?"

I wait at the telephone booth as she goes back and picks up her books, laughs at someone's joke and says good-bye to her friends. Outside in the street, I take her school things and put my hand around her plump, childish fingers. This is my girl, and as I ramble on about school and tease her easily, now that we are alone, I am troubled by the contrast between my whore-house plotting and the dreams I have for Marjorie. Though I know intimately how Marjorie's small breasts feel, I do not know what they look like and I have never made successful explorations elsewhere. Though we are not going "steady," we date no one else and I believe we have ambitious plans for one another, romantically. Marjorie's present physical reticence does not offend me outrageously, really. I'm infatuated with her, I cherish her and am trusting the future—tonight, tomorrow, the next night—to provide the opportunity, the right responses so that our romance may be consummated. I am young and incorrigibly American. I have little real evidence how she feels about our sexual destiny, nor am I clearly positive how I feel about it at this exact second, but nervously, jerkily, I believe we both think it's a certainty. I want to believe that, need to. As we stroll along, I saunter and strut, grimace and boast, entertaining her. I nip her ear and tell her how much I love her. On her porch, I've become so nervous that I kiss and hug her quickly even though her mother stands watching in the doorway. Then, embarrassed, I run off shouting back that I'll call her later. Instead of seeing her after dinner tonight, I will be busy launching my fund for carnal purposes.

All week long opposing instincts within me cut across each other. I dream of Marjorie in soft colors: pinks, faint blues, lavender—and she is cuddly, vulnerable, innocent yet passionate. In my other, darker dreams, I ruthlessly, coldly drive with abandon into the faceless, twitching bodies of dark-haired women, my passion there as close to rage as my unwieldy love for my dreamt Marjorie is to a kind of physical prayer. During the long hours of emptying the family garage of five years' accumulated junk, of running endless errands for my mother, for neighbors, of doing fifty odd little jobs, these two warring fantasies clash behind my sweaty brow. And diminish only slightly each night as I count the dimes and quarters. By Wednesday I am determined to get enough for a case of beer. My own. And Thursday afternoon I rush away from school and begin cleaning the back yard of a neighbor, bruising my sore hands with rakes, shovels, hoes, brooms. Then from the yard I go on to the next, pocketing with secret greedy glee the money these women pay me. From female to female these coins will pass, I think with exultant cynicism.

That night, after a hurried and rattled call to Margie, I count my money. I know, almost to the penny, how much is there, but I must count it, nonetheless. All the dimes I arrange in careful columns, side by side, the nickels, quarters, fifty-cent pieces, the few pennies. I smooth out the bills, turning them all green side up. There are ten amazing, potent dollars marching in little totem rows across my desk. I gloat. I giggle and clutch my sides and glee hiccups loose. At the locked door, my mother knocks and asks what's wrong, am I sick? Painfully suppressing my bouncing spirits, I gasp as calmly as I can: "No. No. Everything's fine." Indeed, it's glorious, uproarious. Troubled by my sniggering and gurgling, she stands outside my door as if waiting for prolonged cries of illness. But finally, with a sigh, she leaves and I topple onto the bed, burying my hysterical head in the pillow.

The endless moments of sunny Friday morning crawl by with incredible slowness. By ten o'clock, I've fretted and fidgeted myself into a state of near exhaustion. At the break, we feverishly confer, interrupting each other, demanding to know if everyone's brought their money. But the really big question is, where's Don Brandon? He isn't in school. Is he chickening out? He can't. We'll go to his home and get him, pull him out of bed if he's pretending to be sick. Nobody cops out. Standing in the crowded school hallway, squirting down cokes and peanuts, we curse Brandon for his cowardice. Then, we count the money. I put down my five. Everyone has theirs, except Franky Shea. He has only three dollars and twenty cents. I curse him and then Tom Murray slugs him, starts slapping him, venting his rage at Don on Franky.

"Hey, hey," I yell. "Maybe the girls are cheaper than we think. Anyway, if he needs some more money, I'll loan it to him." This surprises all of us, especially Franky and me. We both know I don't really like Franky that well. But at times like this, I dislike Tom more than enough. So. . . .

Gravely then, with uneasy glances flickering between us, we recount the money and speculate on exactly how much we'll really need. That's the unknown quantity—how much does a girl cost? A whore? Standing in the close hallway of this Catholic high school, we can think of no one who knows such facts.

Then, evil-leader of them all, I announce: "Hell, I'll call them. They've got a phone, haven't they?" I grin smugly, proud to have thought of it first. But the bell rings and we have to wait until lunch time to call.

At noon, across the street from the school, I sit in a service station telephone booth, carefully looking up the number of Acme Rooms—all such places of business hide behind this ingenious disguise. I find the number, write it neatly in my palm, open the door slightly and murmur to my friends: "Bless you my sons. When was your last confession?" They all grin and I close the door and theatrically dial.

An indifferent feminine voice answers and replies to my question. "All rooms here are five dollars, mister." There is a click as the connection is cut.

"Five," I announce solemnly as I climb out of my confessional. The remainder of the afternoon, we plot vengeance against Brandon and wish time, time, time would hurry. We are not going to the Acme until after dark, seven o'clock. As I listen to talk about parallelograms and side-angle-side, I wonder doubtfully how we'll ever last until seven. My muscles are fluttering and jumping.

At three-thirty, as we race with relieved shouts and ragged laughter out of school, Don Brandon is waiting for us across the street, a patronizing smirk fixed on his thin lips. Before we can grab him, accuse him, he waves a five-dollar bill at us. He's got more, he declares. Since six this morning he's been driving a truck for a dollar an hour. As soon as he'd earned eight dollars, he'd quit. He has a total of ten, he brags, and is not going to lend *any* of it to *any*body. "Beer," he grins thirstily. "Beer and broads, bring them on." And all of us, wrestling and punching one another, chant "yes, yes." Passersby stare at us. We leap down the street, pent excitement jerking our limbs, voices, thoughts. We are anxious for the Big Game.

At the drugstore we swarm into a booth, crowding each other, smoking, arguing, ordering, sipping, hoping time will disappear. Behind our bright, agitated eyes we are all planning just how we're going to act with the girl we'll buy at seven o'clock. Cool and steady, I direct myself. And unrushed. Get your money's worth, is my basic consideration.

As other students come and take booths about us, we eye them with open superiority. They instantly become objects of our scorn, pitifully unsophisticated and innocent. Dull, unimaginably clean-minded, they sit around us mindlessly munching their cokes and sundaes. We laugh outrageously and they look up, puzzled by our outbursts and this drives us to further hilarity. Those pathetically sinless, bewildered expressions. The manager comes back and asks us to please be a little quieter and we grin false obedience at him.

Then I see Marjorie. As I stand up my companions hoot and yell, kidding me, warning me in merciless, loud voices to be careful, not to become too exhausted before we meet at six-thirty. Luckily, Marjorie doesn't understand any of this as I hurry off to the counter in front. There, I buy her a phosphate and smile with exaggerated innocence. "Margie, uhn, the track team has a meeting tonight at about seven at the gym, so I guess I can't make it over." Intently, I concentrate on my drink.

"What about after?" she asks. For a week I have devised elaborate excuses for not seeing her. By now she is becoming hurt and distrustful. I can't blame her. I just hope she holds on until after tonight.

"Sure, if it's not too late." I try to be positive, yet vague.

Solemnly, she finishes her drink. Then, with exceptional quiet, she watches me. Doesn't say anything, merely looks at me steadily. Immediately, I begin hitching my shoulders and scratching and wiggling.

Pretty soon, Marjorie breaks the silence: "Are you going to come over tonight or not?" That's all, just that simple question.

"Yes. Yes, I am," I promise—both her and myself. "But it might be kind of late."

"Are you *really* going to a track team meeting?"

"Yes, I am," I lie and grit my teeth. In spite of my recent desire to be sinister, I dislike lying to Marjorie. Once more, she gazes silently at me with her smooth, little girl's face. Scratching my ear, I grin back, senselessly. After a moment, she picks up her books.

"I'll walk you home," I tell her.

"No. I'm meeting Mom over at the dime store. I'll see you tonight. OK?"

"Sure." I grab her hand and squeeze those small, doll-like fingers.

Six-thirty, six-thirty, six-thirty, I tell myself giddily. By the clock at the back of the drugstore, it now *is* six-thirty—rendezvous hour for the Sinister Six. Cleverly, I have fortified myself for the ravages of this evening with a healthy supper and eight multi-vitamin pills . . . which make me belch. Presently, I am watching the clock and holding my breath, hoping to cure the belches.

Spang. In burst my fellow evildoers, shouting. They are practically rubbing their hands in anticipation. Spilling nervous excitement about us, we huddle and count the money again. Don has relented and contributes part of his ten dollars for the beer, as do I.

When we arrive at the Acme Rooms, we scurry almost soundlessly up the steps to the door and, as chief evil-one, I press the buzzer. A little nervously, I set myself for this first, peripheral encounter. For tonight's occasion, I have carefully dressed in my adventurous best: a blue and white polka-dotted, long-sleeved shirt, pressed levis, white sweat socks and newly shined shoes. With a clever flair for the needs of the evening, I have worn no underwear. The polished door before me opens slightly and a woman stares at me. "Just a minute," she says and I can hear her trundle away.

"What the hell," mutters Curly Franklin impatiently. "What's going on?"

Then the door swings wide and a plump, henna-haired woman of about forty-five or so, examines us. "Well, boys, what can I do for you?"

"Girls," cries Brandon. "Girls, girls."

The woman chuckles. "How old are you boys, anyway?"

"Old enough," I tell her with ingenious brashness and move into the doorway. My companions hoot and laugh approvingly at this.

"Looks like you've come prepared." She flicks a red fingernail at the case of beer under my arm.

"Did you bring any money?" she asks with a smile.

We all wave dollar bills at her and she stands back, inviting us in with a generous gesture. Like eager children, I'm afraid, we crowd in, gawking around with immense, unrestrained curiosity.

"Hey, hey," chants Jerry Donovan, pushing past me, snapping his fingers in time to some personally heard music. "Hey, hey."

With an amused expression, the woman takes us into a parlor-like room furnished with a couch, several chairs and a jukebox. "Hey, hey," Jerry cries and pushes a quarter into the machine.

There is no one in the amber-lit room and we all look at each other a little nervously, disappointedly. To indicate we mean business, I slap the case of beer down on the couch and tear it open.

"Girls," Tom Murray says. "We'd like to see some girls, huh?"

Nodding, the woman counts us and hurries out.

Then, as Jerry's quarter begins to work and music comes bouncing out of the jukebox, we hear spiked heels in the hallway and swing around in a single, intent group. The girls—they are women, to my surprise—are all dressed in short, fluffy costumes. Like chorus girls, I think dimly. But the material is awfully thin and you can easily see their breasts through it. We stare. We stare with great intensity. Here it is. This is *sex*. The women we'll possess in a few moments. The confrontation threatens for an instant to become almost grim. Then, thumb and forefinger clicking nervously, Jerry whispers: "Hey, heaayh." And we all grin at the lightly clad women across the room.

For a moment, I wish the lights were just a little dimmer, that we were each alone with a girl, that it was more ... more romantic, I guess. But the long-checked lust coiling hungrily in my stomach, rapping impatiently at the base of my skull, overcomes all hesitations and I leer eagerly at the women. For an instant, I vaguely remember our plans for a mass orgy, my particular aim to select the best-looking, most gorgeous, most appealing whore in the world. But these are misty, evanescent thoughts, vanishing as one of the young ladies steps toward me and, with rather candid charm, smiles and administers a pleasant, professional caress. That is it—all my planning, my careful considerations disappear. There is really nothing at all in my mind, just the clotted web of blank desire. That's all. Sensation, but no thought. Laughing gently, she leads me from the parlor and, two doors down a carpeted hall, into a small room.

The room, I vaguely notice, has a table, a lamp and a single straight chair. Plus the bed, of course. The girl is quite merry and whispers something appealingly obscene in my ear. I don't really understand her, but I grin anyway and comment that the light is awfully bright.

"All the better to see you with, honey," she smiles and touches me again. As she unbuttons me, I ask what her name is.

"Shirley," she says and with warm water swabs me off. Squinting with embarrassment, I watch her pink-nailed fingers move efficiently over my skin.

"OK. Now, if you'll give me the money, I'll be right back, sweetie."

"Uh," I shrug uneasily. "How much is it?"

"What? Oh, haven't you been here before? My, my," she grins and squeezes my arm. "It's five dollars a round, sweetie. More, if you stay longer."

Rather blankly, I blink at her, wondering if she's overcharging me. Then automatically, I nod and hand her the money.

"Just take off your pants, baby. I'll be right back."

All these cold, directional remarks are reviving me from my trance and I stomp resolutely back down the hall into the now empty parlor and get a couple beers. Back in the room, I take off all my clothes, draping my polka dotted shirt over the lamp, dimming it provocatively, I think. Then, naked, I open a beer and lay back on the bed, momentarily in command of myself.

"Hey," Shirley exclaims when she comes in. "You've got

all your clothes off." Unzipping her dress, kicking off her shoes, she grins at me. "You're not bad looking, for a kid."

"I'm not a kid," I correct her. "You want a beer?"

"Well say, you know if you're in here too long, it's going to cost you more."

"Fine."

"OK, I'll take one." She gets a glass off the table and sits down beside me. She has rather long, pale brown hair and a wide, friendly mouth. Opening the beer for her, I stare at her breasts. They seem nice—I really have few comparisons, books, primarily. And below her navel her hair is black. This seems disturbingly incongruous to me and I realize that her long, light hair is dyed.

She takes the beer and, with a slim hand on my thigh, drinks.

"Humm, that's nice." Quickly, she finishes her glass and leans over me. "Come on, honey, let's go," she purrs roughly.

And then, then, with a deft, practiced movement, she runs her tongue from my ear downward, downward ... I'm sure I groan, at least, for I'm close to crying out in surprise. Sensations totally unexpected break in on me and after a moment she skillfully pulls me over on top of her. Desperately trying to clear my head, to refocus my vision, I blink against the red, clogged web of turbulence and amazement—totally without result. And then, easily, still smiling, she eases me off and steps away from the bed. Quite numbly, quite bereft of any feeling at all now, I blankly study the ceiling above me. What has happened? I ask myself. What has really taken place? What did I really do—I mean, feel? I don't know. I haven't the slightest idea. A stirring numbness is the only impression reaching my mind.

"OK, honey. Better get up and into your clothes," Shirley announces with that ever-present grin in her voice. Did she experience anything? I wonder. No. Whores aren't supposed to. Then, in spite of her indifferent, abrupt instructions, I have a difficult time believing Shirley is really a whore. I have the impression that she'll now get dressed in street clothes and we'll walk out of this place together, preferably hand in hand. She's become my girl—even if I haven't felt anything, nothing that I can remember, at least. This fact and the money I gave her doesn't matter. The act does. That makes her my girl. Watching as she stoops, picking up her little dress, I see her breasts sag and as she bends beside the lamp, wiggling a foot into a shoe, the light cuts unbecoming lines beneath her eyes and all at once I understand that she is older than I, much older. She is, well, maybe almost my mother's age.

"How old are you, Shirley?"

Frowning, she glances at me, then shrugs carelessly. "Oh, about twenty-seven."

Eleven years older than I am, maybe even more. Slowly, I get up and dress. In the hallway I pull myself along despondently, wearily. From the parlor comes the clatter of my friends' noisy banter and as we enter, I put my hand on Shirley's loose flank, wondering silently if I'll ever see her again.

Laughing at the girls, patting them familiarly, we tumble with our beer down the stairs. On the street, we exultantly brag to one another, replacing old lies with new ones. Elaborately, we gesture and giggle how it was with the whore we had. Confidently, we tell each other we're coming back as soon as we have another five dollars. Great, it's absolutely great, we all declare, agree.

Then, as we approach the corner, I unaccountably, fiercely, feel I must see Marjorie—immediately. Handing the remaining beer to my companions, I leave them, offering no explanation and their jeers echo down the sidewalk as I hurry away.

In the front room, she is waiting for me. As I say hello to her parents I am certain they can see the stains of my lechery, my wantonness, my new strangeness on my face, hands. Insistently, I pull Marjorie out onto the porch, away from her parents' eyes.

"Margie," I say with a big breath. "It's good to see you.' And I try to kiss her.

"Is your meeting over already?" she asks coolly.

"Yes." I hunch my shoulders and look out at the lawn. "Margie, uh, you know ... that I like you. You know that, don't you?"

Her blond hair swings softly and I want to touch it.

"After last week," she says crossly, "I don't know anything. I mean," her voice arches unhappily, "I mean, what's going on, anyway?"

"Nothing." I want to reassure her. "Nothing at all. Really. Just this track thing. It's all over now." At this moment, I am ready to tell her any fantastic lie I can think of. Now, close beside me, the warm scent of her floating around us, she's infinitely more real, more *possible* than ever before; both abruptly close and very far from tonight's experience. "Margie, I love you. I really do." This is not a lie, I realize at once. Yet, I am not sure it is the truth. It is something I feel, a lush unstoppable longing reaching my limbs, startling my fingertips. It is something, something absolutely new. For an instant I possess a totally unfamiliar confidence that I know much more about her than she can possibly know about me. In that moment, as our bodies lightly touch, I understand what it is I desire; that portion of her, of me, is no longer frightening and thoroughly dangerous. I want to share my total physical discovery, the immense freedom of it with Margie. And tell her much, more more. How this emotion I feel for her now is a gift of the *instructive,* nerveless lust that broke over me in that room at the Acme. That there is no longer any reason to be afraid of one another.

Immediately, I sense that these things will only frighten her. Besides, I have no truly accurate words for it. Instead of saying any of this, I touch her velvet hair, the deep curve of her cheek and whisper the word love, love, love, helplessly, happily—my alternating dual dreams of the world narrowed, abruptly, to one.

LAWRENCE LEE
The Heroic Journey

(FROM THE MICHIGAN QUARTERLY REVIEW)

WE COULD HEAR the strange, not-quite-human bawling through the rain as soon as the ship was tied up at the dock to let some of the passengers off at the island of Syros. In the darkness something was afraid or in distress. The bellowing could be heard above the spattering of the storm on the decks and on the whitewashed stones of the wharf about which shone the streaming lights of the town. We were both standing inside the passageway that led onto the deck. We could see the town and we could see the wheelhouse of a smaller ship close to ours.

"What's that sound?" Margaret asked. "Is something crying?"

Neither of us knew. Margaret only wanted the reassurance of human speech.

"I don't know," I said. "It sounds like something that's afraid."

For a moment a great noise engulfed the lesser sound. Thunder crashed into the naked wet stones of the ridge of the island and diminished in a rumble among the white houses stacked against the hill and the lighted streets running with rain. It muttered briefly through the confusion of the crowded, blind harbor. Then it ended in silence over the sea, invisible beyond the outer lights.

Margaret stepped onto the deck. I followed. Water ran noisily through the scuppers. The boat deck half protected us from the downpour. The town, its lights blurred in the rain, was as filled with confusion as the harbor. Café tables were abandoned. Blue-striped canvas chairs were empty and drenched. Some had blown over and were lying on the drowned stones of the wharf.

An orthodox priest hurried from the storm toward the closed door of a lighted café bar. The tube of his black hat, with the flat black disk of the wider top, was wet. His face and beard ran with drops of rain. The full gowns of his priestly garments whipped like loose black sails about his body, above his black shoes and wet ankles.

The bawling began again. It was louder, and more insistent.

"Ah-a-a-a-ah! Ah-a-a-a-ah! Ah-a-a-a-ah!"

It was unidentifiable, but it was a clamor for help that could be understood beyond identity or speech. It was a cry of need from the living to the living.

Farther up the deck Margaret leaned into the rain, her thighs bent against the rail, her orange cotton dress already wet. She looked down into the harbor at something just below our hull on the deck of the ship alongside. One hand on the wet rail, the other holding the straw hat bought in Athens, she was peering anxiously down at the small and untidy ship moored next to us.

"Douglas, here it is," she called through the sound of the rain. "Come and look ... Oh, the poor little thing. It's terrified out on that open deck in the storm."

Hurrying, I bumped against a short and smiling Greek. The whiteness of his moustache and of the hair sticking from beneath his odd round hat showed that he was old. His face was irrepressibly happy. He seemed unaware of the tumult in the harbor. Nothing disturbed him, neither the unexpected rain nor the bawling from the darkness below. He wanted to talk, but I brushed past him.

"Excuse me," I said, forgetting the Greek word.

"You are English, ain't you?" he asked. "I was in Austreyelia to work when I was a boy."

His speech was fluent but unusual.

"No. My wife and I are Americans," I said. Then I went on to where Margaret was staring over the side.

Her face was flushed with emotion. Her amber eyes with their brown rings looked appealingly at me. The strands of brown hair below her straw hat stuck to her pink face like melting taffy.

"Look," she said. "Isn't he pitiful?"

She nodded to the deck of the small vessel, cluttered and unpretentious, ill-designed and worn with hard use. The lights from the wheelhouse threw a lurid illumination across two closed hatches and an unused crane. It shone on the forward deck.

"He's very young. He doesn't know what's happening to him," I said.

On the open deck forward, a young male donkey was tied up. His neck was choked by two halters. The coarse lines of hemp were pulled in opposite directions and fastened to bollards on the deck. They were taut with his effort to free himself.

The frightened young animal, his hooves fixed as firmly as they might be on the uncertain wet deck, strained to move into the whipping rain and the wind. His delicate pointed ears were forward though all else about him showed that he was afraid. His tail tucked against his rump, his frail legs spread, he tried to balance his round young body against the roll of the ship in the harbor chop. The large dark eyes opened and closed, as though they would look into the terror that assaulted him if only the rain and the wind would let him do so.

"Isn't he beautiful?" Margaret said softly.

"Yes," I said.

I too was filled with compassion for the small animal. Donkeys are beautiful. There is about them a humility that endures and seems to rebuke the men who beat them with sticks. The small donkey on the deck below us had markings which, even among many donkeys, would have distinguished him. His dark gray coat was almost mauve in the rain. Above the small hooves a stocking of sooty black encased each thin leg. The same sooty mark ran from the small rump in a thinning line up the spine. There were two sooty marks, one above each eye. A soft whiteness spread about his mouth and flared nostrils. He was young. This terror was plainly his first. Something strongly appealing and moving in the very nature of the terrified young animal communicated itself.

There was a blast from the tramp steamer. The small donkey struggled and brayed in fright.

"Oh, they are going," Margaret said.

It was as though something was being taken from her. She seemed to be watching a child who was afraid at setting out for the first time alone. With her love she would have caressed the animal and kept it from too great a fear.

The lighted wheelhouse of the cargo ship seemed to be a bubble rocking slowly into the wind. The anchor chain rattled loudly as it was hauled in. With a clank the anchor hung dripping against the hull. There was a signal and the answering jangle of bells. The engines increased their rhythm. The heavy screw churned and thudded in the water alongside. The tough and untidy island ship moved slowly toward the sea.

The Greek captain left the wheelhouse and came out to the wing of the upper deck. The rain was less now; the captain did not notice it. He peered into the darkness to see that his streaked iron prow did not scrape our ship. He seemed very stern. Gray hair showed at his temples. The austerity of the bare stones of Greece was in his face as he leaned from the wing to be caught like a huge and bedraggled moth in our lights. He wore a soiled white cap and an old blue merchant officer's coat above ordinary rumpled gray trousers.

He heard the bawling of the small donkey as the ship got under way. He had heard it for the past hour, but he paid no attention to it. For him there was an inexorable duty. He would do it again and again, until he had made his last voyage along the coasts and among the islands of Greece. He came of a people who had endured the long oppression of the Turks, who had turned back the Italians and had then been overrun by German armor, bringing the Italians with them again into Greece.

Now, for a minute in history, the Greeks were free. Men who had been forced to hear the weeping of their children and still live could, without lack of pity, take a small donkey braying from fear into a stormy sea.

"Ligo aristera." The captain shouted his order to the man in the wheelhouse. "Bear left."

The rough little ship pitched and rolled as she bore past the last marker toward the unlighted sea. The small animal near the prow jerked his neck upward against the harshness of the hemp ropes. His eyes flared into white crescents. His lips curled in fear back from the whiteness of the large teeth. His shivering small body shifted uncertainly as the little hooves clattered on the wet deck in his effort to keep a footing in the pitch and roll of the ship. The frightened braying became fainter and fainter. The bulk of the small ship was lost beyond a projection of the jetty in the black sea.

"The poor brave little thing," Margaret said.

I could barely hear her.

"I wonder where they are taking him," I said.

Someone answered close beside us. We were startled.

"To one of the islands. There are hundreds of them—Tenos, Naxos, Icaria, many. Ships like that one go anywhere that they can get cargo . . . Are you going to Tenos?"

It was the little old man against whom I had brushed in coming on deck. Few Greeks need privacy. The old man traveling with us in the ship wished to talk. His square face was weathered but happy. Brown and wrinkled, he stood smiling, his arms held behind his back. His blue suit was new. So was the gray felt hat with its round crown and the brim turned up in a circle above his brows. He looked upward with innocent gray eyes, appealing to us to see that he wished only to give and to receive friendship on the uncertain journeys that men make.

"No," I said. "We are going to the next island, the one beyond Tenos."

"That one is very pretty. The houses are all white. There is a lot of weaving done there. Do you live there?" he asked.

"We are going to for a while," I said.

Margaret had dried her face with a small handkerchief. She also had become interested in the little man. He seemed, like the small donkey, to have become a part of our journey at night on the sea to an island we had seen only once.

"We found a small house up on the hill back of the town," she said. "We are going to live there. My husband is going to do some work."

"What kind of work?" the old man asked.

"With books," I said.

The answer satisfied him. He looked up at me as though to examine my quality in my face.

"Do you know any Greek?" he asked.

"Only a few words," I said.

"Doesn't matter. You will learn. The people on your island will help you ... It will be eleven o'clock, maybe later tonight before you get there."

He had become very appealing. In his gray eyes there was something enduring and sad.

"Are you from Tenos?" I asked.

"I'm from Samos," he said. "That's another island farther to the east."

"You've been to Piraeus and Athens for a trip, and now you are going back to Samos?" Margaret asked.

The little Greek looked happily at her. The question gave him the chance that he wanted, to talk about himself.

"Piraeus and Athens—that's no distance from Samos. I been farther than that. I went a long time ago ... Soon I gonna be eighty years old ..."

"Eighty years old!"

The old man looked sturdy. Margaret's unbelieving whisper delighted him. He grinned, his eyes very bright, his brown skin creased in many wrinkles.

The last passengers from Syros were on board. The rain was falling less heavily now. Our engines had started. There was a faint vibration through the ship. The old man noticed nothing but our faces as he talked.

"A long time ago when I was a young man on Samos I couldn't find no work. I wanted to marry a Greek girl I knew on Samos, and I wanted to help my people, but I couldn't find work. I went to the other islands. I went to your island. I couldn't find nothing much. I borrowed some money. I heard you could get work in Austreyelia. I didn't want to leave Greece, but I had to live . . ."

His eyes seemed to look far away. He had become very serious.

"I worked hard in Austreyelia two, three, maybe four years. Then I sent back the money I owed."

"Did the girl from Samos come to Australia?" Margaret asked.

She was looking gently at the old man, watching the lost look on his face.

"She married a man on one of the ships that come into Samos," he said. He spoke sadly and looked down at the deck. "She didn't wait for me. I never married. I got no children."

He was silent and thoughtful for a while. Then he continued with his story.

"When I got some more money, I thought I was coming back to Greece, but I bought a little store and sold groceries . . . But all those years I knew—someday I was coming back to Greece, someday I was going to bring a little money to my people and come back to Greece. Every year I would think I'm going back this year . . . Now I come back."

Margaret's lips were half open, as though she wished to speak but was uncertain what to say. Her brown eyes warmly searched the old man's face in disbelief.

"You've been back before, haven't you?" I asked.

"All my life since I left I been dreaming about coming back, but I never been back till right now," the old man said.

The ship left Syros and moved out into the darkness beyond the lights of the harbor. In an hour or an hour and a half, we were at Tenos. The little Greek went along the deck to stare at the lights of the town.

When the ship left Tenos, we knew that we would be getting off in another hour. The rain had stopped. In the clear night, the dark sea was scattered with darker shapes of other islands. In the stony folds of dark land the small lights of villages were gathered.

The sea was perfectly calm when we came to our island. We could see the luminous streak of the waterfront. We could hear men talking in the small boats as they started the motors to come out to meet the ship. They came alongside. When we followed a porter with our baggage down the ladder into one of the boats, we saw the old man above us at the ship's railing. He waved. We waved back from the boat down on the water as the engine increased its popping and we moved off toward the lights on the quay.

"I wonder what he will find when he gets to Samos?" Margaret said. "Will there be anybody left who loves him?"

She was sitting forward among the baggage looking disconsolately back at the ship. I stood, my hand on the housing of the engine, steadying myself and watching the lights and the shapes of boats rocking in the harbor.

It was after eleven o'clock. There were not many people on the waterfront. Two coast guardsmen from the coast guard station watched the passengers come ashore. Then, together, they paraded back to the station. A tourist policeman in a mustard-colored uniform looked at us. He recognized us as the Americans who had rented the small house that the Greeks thought too far up the hill back of the town. It was a ten minute climb from the harbor to the road on which our house stood. He grinned and saluted us in a friendly way. It helped us not to feel entirely like strangers.

When we found the porter, he was loading our bags on the back of a shaggy donkey. The small animal stood, its front hooves together, its dark eyes half closed.

Margaret pointed to the bags.

"Aren't they too heavy?" she asked anxiously.

The porter wore a blue fisherman's jacket and dungarees. His feet were bare. A small black beret sat tightly on his thick black hair. His white teeth showed in a fierce grin beneath his black moustache. He had understood Margaret's question. He lifted his chin in a jerk of negation. Then he pointed up the mountain to where our house was a small cube of white in the darkness.

"Sto spiti," he said.

"He says he will meet us at the house," I explained to Margaret.

As we walked away into the night toward the back streets of the town and the stone steps that led up the mountain, Margaret seemed unhappy. The doors of the small houses close together in the whitewashed stone streets were shut. The small white houses were dark.

"Do they treat them badly?" Margaret said.

"Who?"

"Do the Greeks treat the donkeys badly?" she asked.

"Some of them," I said. "The Greeks work hard to live. The animals work hard, too."

I knew that she was thinking about the young donkey on the cargo ship.

When we reached our house the porter was there. He had taken the bags from the donkey's back and piled them by the door. We paid him and said good night. Margaret watched him go back along the road toward town, a tall strong silhouette walking beside the donkey. He gave the donkey a blow on the rump with a heavy stick, and the donkey trotted faster.

On the fourth morning in our house, I woke and found Margaret dressing. She was standing in the room combing her hair.

"It's Sunday," she said.

A tumult of music came from every part of the island. All the bells of the many churches were ringing. I hurried to dress.

"Today we can have breakfast down at the harbor," I said.

When we went out into the morning, the sea and the stones of the island glistened in the sun. The waves ran one after the other from the dark blue ocean to the land, toward the square houses of the town and the little churches with their blue or red domes standing above the houses. The waves foamed white under the wind. Boats rocked in the harbor below us.

As we made our way down to the town, we saw donkeys standing against the whiteness of a wall, their bridles anchored with a stone. They waited near the open door of a small church in which candles were burning and services had begun.

In the town, men were sitting in the café. Women were standing in the doors of their houses or their shops. At the end of the harbor, we walked out on the quay. The waves slapped and washed among the rocking boats.

Margaret stood still. She was staring at the line of boats.

"Look, Douglas," she said softly.

"What's the matter?" I asked.

"That's the ship the little donkey was on," she said.

Among the fishing boats and lighters was the small, rusty, and familiar freighter we had seen in the rain at Syros.

"It certainly is," I said.

"I wonder if the little donkey is on this island," Margaret said.

In the days that followed, we always looked for him. He could have been left at some other island to which the ship had wandered, but whenever we went down to the town or passed a field of rough grasses and red and yellow flowers, we looked to see if there was a small donkey behind one of the fences of piled stones. But he was never there.

One morning many days later, we watched two shapes coming down the stony path that led to our road from the other side of the mountain. As they came near us we saw that the man was the island's baker. He was solid and young, with a red face and black brows and eyes. His trousers were rolled up from his bare ankles, above rough white shoes.

He was walking beside a small donkey hardly visible under a huge tangle of dried mountain thorn, which Greek bakers use for their fires. It bulked over him, and extended in wide bundles that bulged out from his sides. Only the gentle face with its sad eyes, the gray neck, and the legs of the small animal were visible.

"Oh," Margaret said. "It's the donkey from the ship."

We could see the sooty markings on each leg, and the sooty spot above each glistening eye. We went out and greeted the baker.

"You have a new donkey," I said.

"My other donkey was old," the baker said. "This new one came on a ship from the Peloponnesus."

Though the donkey's eyes were sad, there was no terror now. He stood, his bundle of thorns not seeming too heavy. This was the familiar Greek earth, not the unstable sea. The great journey was done. As men who wander in search of a place where they can stay, the small donkey had come to this island in the center of the blue Aegean sea, to live by laboring, like the essential Greek, who seems glad to have work to do, a little food to eat, and a place to sleep so that he may wake and look into the light that stands high above the diminished stones of the land and the endless blue of the sea.

ARTHUR MILLER
Search for a Future

(FROM THE SATURDAY EVENING POST)

I READ WHERE a great writer, just before he died, was having dinner in a restaurant, and said, "It all tastes the same." Maybe I am dying. But I feel good.

I was pasting on my beard. My mind was going back through the mirror to all the other beards, and I counted this as number nine in my life. I used to like beard parts when I was younger because they made me look mature and more sure of myself. But I don't like them as much now that I'm older. No matter how I try I can't help being philosophical on stage with a beard, and in this part I'm a loud farmer.

That night I looked at my makeup jars, the sponge, the towel, the eye pencil, and I had a strong feeling all of a sudden. That it had always been the same jars, the same sponge, the same towel stained with pink pancake exactly like this one, that I had not gotten up from this dressing table for thirty-five years, and that I had spent my whole life motionless, twenty minutes before curtain. That everything tasted the same. Actually I feel I am optimistic. But for quite a lengthened-out minute there I felt that I had never done anything but make myself up for a role I never go to play. Part of it is, I suppose, that all dressing rooms are the same. The other part is that I have been waiting to hear that my father has died. I don't mean that I think of him all the time, but quite often when I hear a telephone ring, I think: There it is, they are going to tell me the news.

The stage-door man came in. I thought he was going to announce ten minutes to curtain, but instead he said that somebody was asking to see me. People never visit before a show. I thought it might be somebody from the nursing home. I felt frightened. But I wanted to know immediately, and the stage-door man hurried out to bring in my visitor.

I have never married, although I have been engaged several times. But always to a Gentile girl, and I didn't want to break my mother's heart. I have since learned that I was too attached to her, but I don't feel sure about that. I love nothing more than children, family life. But at the last minute a certain idea would always come to me and stick in my brain, the idea that this marriage was not absolutely necessary. It gave me a false heart, and I never went ahead with it. There are many times when I wish I had been born in Europe, in my father's village where they arranged marriages and you never even saw the bride's face under the veil until after the ceremony. I would have been a faithful husband and a good father, I think. It's a mystery. I miss the wife and children I have never had.

I was surprised to see a boy of twenty-two or -three walk in. He was short, with curly hair and a pink complexion that made him look as though he never had to shave. He had a sweet expression, a twinkle in his eye. "I just wanted to remind you about midnight," he said.

About midnight? What about midnight? I was completely lost. For a minute there I even thought: My father has died and I have forgotten about it and there is some kind of procedure or a ceremony at midnight.

"The meeting," he said.

Then I remembered. I had agreed to sit on the platform at a meeting called "Broadway for Peace." My dresser's nephew, a musician twenty-one years old, had just had his eyes shot out in Vietnam somewhere, and I was sick about it. I still haven't seen my dresser, Roy Delcampo; he doesn't even call me up since it happened. I know he'll show up one of these nights, but so far there is no sign of him. To tell the truth, I do not know who is right about this war, but I know that nobody is going to remember ten years from now what it was all for—just as I know that I have had forty-three shows, forty-three openings, but who can even remember the casts, the exact kind of battles we had in production, let alone the reviews or even most of the titles? I know it all kept me alive, but it is even hard to remember the kind of actor I had wanted to be. It wasn't this kind, is all I know.

Suddenly I was a little nervous about this meeting. I have always respected actors with convictions, the people in the old days who were Leftists, and so on. Whatever people might say, those guys and girls had wonderful friendships. But I never felt it was really necessary for me to put my name on anything political; I never felt it would make any difference if I put down my name or if I didn't.

I looked at this boy and he looked at me, and I could see once again how my generation used to see things when I was his age. This meeting was more than a meeting; it was to stop the world from ending. Which I didn't believe, but for him it wasn't all the same. For him—and I could see he was an actor—every experience was some kind of new beginning. I could see that he still remembered every single thing that had ever happened to him, that he was on his way up, up.

Actually, I was quite frightened about the meeting, but I couldn't bear to say to him that it was not going to make any difference whether or not I appeared. So we shook hands, and he even grasped my arm as though we were in league, or even to indicate that he felt especially good that an older man was going to be with them. Something of that kind.

When he turned around and walked out, I saw that the seat of his overcoat was worn; it was a much lighter color than the rest of the coat. An actor notices such things. It means that he sits a lot in his overcoat, and on rough places. Like the steps in front of the Forty-second Street library, or even park benches, or some of the broken chairs in producers' outer offices. And here he is, this boy, spending his time with meetings. I thought to myself, I cannot imagine anything I would sit and wait for, and I wished I had something like that. I ended up a little glad that I was going to be at the meeting. Exactly why, I don't know.

I think I acted better that night, not that anyone else would notice, but I found myself really looking at my fellow actors as though I had never seen them before. Suddenly it was remarkable to me, the whole idea of a play, of being able to forget everything else so that we were really angry up there, or really laughing, or really drinking the cider we were supposed to drink, which is actually tea, and coughing as though it were bitter. Toward the end of Act Two some man got up from the third row and walked out. I usually feel upset about a walkout, but this night it went through my mind that it was his role to walk out, that the whole audience was acting too. After all, the whole idea of so many people sitting together, facing in the same direction, not talking, is a kind of acting.

Even the President gets made up now for his TV talks. Everybody every morning gets into costume. As we were taking the curtain calls, I thought: Maybe I never got married because it would make my life real; it would rip me off the stage somehow.

The next morning I went to visit my father at the nursing home. I had been there only four or five days before, but I felt pulled. So I went.

It was a very windy day in October, a clear blue sky over New York. My father always liked strong wind and cold weather. He would put up his coat collar and say, "Ahhh," and even as a little boy I imitated the way he exhaled and enjoyed facing into a cold wind. He would look down at me and laugh, "This is not a hot day, boy."

The old man is in a cage. But the bars are so close to his face he cannot see them, so he keeps moving, a step this way and a step that way. And finally he knows, for the hundredth time every day, that he is not free.

But he does not know why. He feels someone knows, and whoever it is means him harm. Something is going to happen. Someone is keeping him here for a long temporarily, as you might say.

The room is freshly painted and smells it. A light blue color over many coats of paint, so that the shiny surface is lumpy. A string hangs from the middle of the ceiling with a fluorescent plastic tassel on the end of it. His head strikes it whenever he moves about the room. In the dark at night he lies on his bed and goes to sleep with the bluish glow of this tassel on his retina. In the afternoons he can pull the string and make the ceiling light go on. He has never been at ease with machinery, so when he pulls the string he looks up at the ceiling fixture, a little surprised that the light went on. Sometimes after his head has hit the tassel he scratches the spot lightly as though a fly had sat on his skin. The word "stroke" is very right, like a touch on the brain, just enough.

The nursing home is an old, converted apartment house, but an extremely narrow one. The corridors on each floor are hardly wider than a man. You come in and on the right is an office where a fat woman is always looking into a thick registry book. On the left is a slow elevator. A zoo smell is always in the air as soon as you walk into the building, and it gets thicker upstairs. But it is not a filthy smell. It is like earth, humid but not diseased. At my first visit I was repelled by it, as by sewage. But after a while, if you allow yourself to breathe in deeply, you realize it is the odor of earth and you respect it.

Up one flight is my father's floor. There is always a mattress or springs standing on edge in the corridor; someone has been moved out or died. Rooms open off the corridor, most of them occupied by old women. They sit motionlessly facing their beds, some asleep in their chairs. There is no sound in the place; they are all dozing like thin, white-haired birds which do not thrive in captivity. All their eyes seem blue.

The old man's room is the last one on the corridor. Opposite his door is a widened space where the nurses have a desk. They do not look up when I open his door. Nobody is going to steal anything here or do any harm. Everyone is so old that there cannot be an emergency.

He is usually asleep on his bed, whatever time I come. I am already twenty years older than he was at my birth. I am an older man than the one I looked up at during the windy walks. My hair is gray at the sides. Mother has been dead a long, long time. All of his brothers and sisters are dead; everyone he knew and played cards with. I have also lost many friends. It turns out that he is not really too much older than I am, than I am becoming.

I stood there looking down at him and recalled the meeting the night before. About fifteen others were sitting on a row of chairs on the stage. The chairman introduced us by turn. For some reason, when I stood up there seemed to be heavier applause, probably because it was the first time I had ever come out for such a thing, and also because I have been quite a hit in this current play, and they knew my face. But when I stood up and the applause continued, the chairman waved for me to come up to the microphone. I was frightened that the newspapers would pick up what I might say, and I had no idea what to say. So I came to the microphone. There was a really good silence. The theater was packed. They said that people were jammed up outside trying to get in. I bent over to the microphone and heard my own voice saying, "Someone went blind that I knew." Then I realized that I did not actually know the boy who had been blinded, and I stopped. I realized that it sounded crazy. I realized that I was frightened; that some day there might be investigations and I could be blamed for being at such a meeting. I said: "I wish the war would stop. I don't understand this war." Then I went back to my chair.

There was terrific applause. I didn't understand why. I wondered what I had really said that made them so enthusiastic. It was like an opening night when a line you never had thought about very much gets a big reaction. But I felt happy, and I didn't know why. Maybe it was only the applause, which I didn't understand _ ...er, but I felt a happiness, and I thought suddenly that it had been a terrible, terrible mistake not to have gotten married.

"Pop?" I said softly, so as not to shock him. He opened his eyes and raised his head, blinking at me. He always smiles now when he is awakened, and the lower part of his long face pulls down at his eyes to open them wider. It isn't clear whether or not he knows who you are as he smiles at you. I always slip in my identification before I say anything. "I'm Harry," I say, but I make it sound casual, as though I am saying it only because he hasn't got his glasses on. His fingers dance nervously along his lower lip. He is touching himself, I think, because he is no longer certain what is real and what is dream, when people he is not sure he knows suddenly appear and disappear every day.

He immediately insists on getting out of bed. He is fully dressed under the blankets, sometimes even with his shoes on. But today he has only socks. "My slippers."

I get his slippers from the metal closet and help him into them. He stands on the floor tucking in his shirt, saying, "And uh ... and uh," as though a conversation has been going on. There are no immense emotions here, but deep currents without light. He is bent a little, and stiff-kneed, and plucks at his clothes to be sure everything is on. He is very interested that someone is here but he knows that nothing, absolutely nothing, will come of it. But he wants to lengthen it out anyway, just in case something might happen to free him. He is afraid the end of the visit will suddenly be announced, so he tries to be quick about everything. He says, "Sit down, sit down," not only to make you comfortable but to stall off the end. Then he sits in the one armchair, the fire escape and a patch of city sky behind him, and I sit on the edge of the bed facing him.

"I hear you went for a walk today with the nurse?"

"Ya. Awd the river. Doom days deen unden, but this here's a beautiful day. Some day."

"Yes. It's a beautiful day," I repeat so that he'll know I

understand what he is talking about, although it doesn't make much difference to him. Some things he says, though, he is very anxious should be understood, and then it all gets terrible. But I am not sure he knows he is mostly incomprehensible.

He wanders his arm vaguely toward the night table. "My glasses." I open the drawer and hand him one of the two pairs he keeps in there.

"Are these the ones?"

He puts on the wobbly frames which his incapable hands have bent out of shape. The lenses are coated with his fingerprints. "Ya," he says, blinking around. Then he says "No," and roots around in the drawer. I give him the other pair, and he takes off the first pair, opens the second, and puts the first ones on again and looks at me.

I realize as he is looking at me that he feels friendship between us, and that he is glad to see me, but that he is not sure who I am. "I'm Harry," I say.

He smiles. He is still a big man, even though he is very thin now. His head is massive, and his teeth are good and strong, and there is some kind of force lying in pieces inside of him, the force of a man who has not at all settled for this kind of room and this kind of life. For him, as for me and everybody else, it is all some kind of mistake. He has a future. I suppose I still go to see him for that reason.

I never realized before that his ears stick out, that they face front. I think I was always so busy looking into his eyes that I never really saw his ears. Because there is nothing more to listen to from him or to fear, I have time to look at his body now.

His left leg is quite bowed out, more than I ever realized. His hands are very slender and even artistic. His feet are long and narrow. He has strangely high, almost Slavic, cheekbones which I never noticed when his face was fuller. The top of his head is flatter, and the back of his neck. It was less than five years ago that I first realized he was an old man, an aged man. I happened to meet him walking on Broadway one afternoon and I had to walk very slowly beside him. A little breeze in his face made his eyes tear. But I felt then that it was not something very sad; I felt that after all he had lived a long time.

But this day I felt a difference about him. He had not given up his future. In fact, he was reaching toward his future even more energetically than I was toward mine. He really wanted something.

"Linnen, I ah gedda hew orthing. Very important."

"You want something?"

"No-no. I ah gedda hew orthing."

He waited for me to reply. "I don't understand what you're saying, but keep talking, maybe I'll understand."

He reached over toward the door and tested that it was shut. Now, as he spoke, he kept glancing with widened eyes toward the door as though interlopers who meant him no good were out in the corridor. Then he shook his head angrily. "I never in my life. Never."

"What's the matter?"

"Hew maug lee me ounigh."

"They won't let you out?"

He nodded, scandalized, angry. "Hew maug lee me ounigh."

"But you went out with the nurse, didn't you?"

"Linnen. Hew linnen?" He was impatient.

"Yes, Pop, I'm listening. What do you want?"

Something politic came over him as he prepared to speak again, something calculating. He was positioning himself for a deal. His lips, without sound, flicked in and out like a chimpanzee's as he practiced an important message. Then he crossed his legs and leaned over the arm of the chair toward me.

"Naw gen my money."

"Your money?"

"Naw gen. Yesterday she said sure. Today, naw gen."

"The lady downstairs?"

"Ya."

"She asked you for money?"

"Naw gen my money."

"She wouldn't give you your money?"

He nodded. "Naw gen. Fifty thousand dollars."

"You asked her for fifty thousand dollars?"

"For my money gen."

He was leaning toward me crosslegged, just as I had see him do with businessmen, that same way of talking in a hote lobby or in a Pullman, a rather handsome posture and full o grace. Of course, he had no fifty thousand dollars; he ha nothing anymore, but I did not realize at the time what h really had in his mind even though he was telling it to m clearly.

"Well, you don't need money here, Pop."

He gave me a suspicious look with a little wise smile; I too, was not on his side. "Linnen."

"I'm listening."

"I could go home," he said with sudden clarity. He had n home either. His wife was dead eight years now, and even hi hotel room had been given up. "I wouldn't even talk," h said.

"It's better for you here, Pop."

"Better!" He looked at me with open anger.

"You need nursing," I explained. He listened with n attention, his eyes glancing at the door, while I explaine how much better off he was here than at home. But his ange passed. Then he said, "I could live." I nodded. "I could live," he repeated.

Now came the silence, which is always the worst part. could find nothing further to say, and he no longer had a way to enlist my help. Or maybe he was expecting me to star packing his things and getting him out. All we had in th room was his low-burning pleasure that someone was her with him, even though he did not know for sure who it was excepting that it was someone familiar; and for me there wa only the knowledge that he had this pleasure.

He would look at me now and then with various expres

ions. Once it would be with narrowed eyes, an estimating look, as though he were about to speak some searching sentence. Then he would blink ahead again and test his lips. After a few moments he would look at me, this time with the promise of his warm, open smile, then once again drift into a stare.

Finally he raised his finger as though to draw my attention, a stranger's attention, and tilting back his head as though recalling, he said, "Did you St. Louis?"

"Yes, I'm back now. I was there and now I'm back." I had been in St. Louis with a show nine or ten years ago. One of his factories had been in St. Louis forty years ago.

He broke into a pleased smile. He loved cities. He had enjoyed entering them and leaving them, being well served in hotels. He had loved recalling buidings that had been demolished, the marvelous ups and downs of enterprises and business careers. I knew what he was smiling at. He had once brought me a toy bus from St. Louis, with a whole band on top which moved its arms when the bus moved, and inside it was a phonograph record which played "The Stars and Stripes Forever." He had come home just as I had gotten up from my nap. In his arms were gift boxes—this bus, and I remember a long pair of beige kid gloves for my mother. He always brought fresh air into the house with him—the wind, his pink face, and his reedy laugh.

"Well, I have to go now, Pop."

"Ya, ya."

He stood up, hiking his pants up where his belly used to be, plucking at his brown sweater to keep it properly placed on his shoulders. He hurried to stand, and even enjoyed the good-bye, thinking I had important work to do—appointments, the world's business—with which no one had a right to interfere. We shook hands. I opened the door, and he insisted on escorting me to the elevator. "This way, this way," he said in a proprietary manner as though he could not help being in charge. He walked ahead of me, bent, heavily favoring his bowed left leg, down the narrow corridor, his face very much averted from the open rooms where the old ladies sat motionless.

Outside, the wind was even faster than before, but the sky was turning gray. I had some time so I walked for a while thinking of him turning back and re-entering his room, lying down on the bed, probably exhausted, and the plastic thing on the light string swaying overhead.

It was fine to walk without a limp. I resolved again to stop smoking. I have wide hands and feet. I am not at all built like him. I crossed from Riverside Drive to the Park and caught a bus to Harlem, where I was born. But as soon as I got out I knew I had lost the feeling I had started with, and it was impossible to feel what I had felt there in my youth, forty years ago.

There was only one moment that held me: I found myself facing a dry-cleaning store which had once been one of the best restaurants in New York. On Sundays the old man would take my mother and me for dinner. There had been a balcony where a baker in a tall white hat baked fresh rolls and whenever a customer entered, the baker would look down and put in a fresh batch. I could smell the rolls through the odor of benzine on Lenox Avenue. I could see the manager who always sat down with us while we ate. He had some disease, I suppose, because the right side of his face was swollen out like a balloon, but he always wore a hard wing collar and a white tie, and never seemed sick. A Negro with a moustache was looking through the store window at me. For a moment I had the urge to go and tell him what I remembered, to describe this avenue when no garbage cans were on the street, when the Daimlers and Minervas and Locomobiles had cruised by, and the cop on the corner threw back the ball when it got through the outfield on 114th Street. I did not go into the store, nor even toward our house. Any claim I had to anything had lapsed. I went downtown instead and sat in my dressing room, trying to read.

I was just opening my pancake can when I thought of

something which I still don't altogether understand: that the old man is the only one who is not an actor. I am, the President is, and the chairman of the protest meeting is, even though his convictions are very sincere; but on the platform the other night I could tell, probably because I am an actor, that he was listening to his modulations, that he was doing what he was doing because he had told himself to do it. But he is not desperate enough, not like the old man is desperate. The old man does not know enough to listen to his own voice or to ask himself what he ought to do; he just speaks from his heart, and he has even lost his hold on the language, so all that is left is the sound, you might say, of his gut. The old man is not acting.

I wondered about the young, pink-cheeked boy who had come to remind me about the meeting—if he also was acting. Maybe in his case, with the draft grabbing for him, it was real. I started pasting on my beard and I thought again of my not being married. It was like all this agitation now, like everything I see and know about: It was a lack of some necessity. Nobody seems to *have* to do anything, and the ones who say they *do* have to, who say that something is absolutely necessary for them, may only be the best actors. Because that is what a really good actor does: He manages to make his feelings necessary, so that suddenly there is no longer the slightest choice for him. He has to scream or die, laugh or die, cry real tears or die. And at the same time he knows that he is not going to die, and this thought makes him happy while he is screaming or crying, and it may be what makes the audience happy to cry too.

I was just taking off my clothes in my bedroom that night when the telephone rang. And it frightened me, as it usually does these days. It really was the fat woman in the nursing home this time. The old man had escaped. It seems he had slipped out not long after I had left, and here it was nearly two in the morning and the police had a missing-persons alarm out but there was no sign of him yet. The worst thing was that he had gone out without his overcoat, and it was raining and blowing like hell. There was nothing more to be done now, as long as the police had an eye out for him, but I couldn't go back to sleep. I couldn't help feeling proud of him and hoping they would never find him, that he would just disappear. I have always admired his willfulness, his blind push toward what he has to have. I have admired his not being an actor, I suppose, and he was not acting tonight, not out there in that rain and wind. I couldn't sleep, but there was nothing I could do. The clock was inching up to three by this time. I got dressed and went out.

I had only walked a block when I felt my socks getting wet, so I stepped into a doorway, trying to think what to do. It was somehow strange that both of us were walking around in the same rain. But who was he looking for? Or what? I half didn't want to find him. In fact, for moments I had visions of him crossing the river to the west, just getting the hell out of here, out of the world. But how would he talk to anybody? Would he know enough to get onto a bus? Did he have any money? Naturally, I ended up being worried about him, and after a while I saw a taxi and got in.

I joke with cab drivers but I never *talk* with them, but this time I had to explain myself for wanting to cruise around. I told the driver that I was looking for my father. Cab drivers never seem to believe anything, but he believed me; it seemed perfectly natural to him. Maybe it happens quite often like this. I don't even remember what the cab driver looked like, even whether he was white or Negro. I remember the rain pouring over the windshield and the side windows because I was trying to see through them. It was getting on toward half-past four by the time I got home again, and the rain was coming down stiff. I went into my bedroom and undressed and lay down and looked toward my window, which was running with water. I felt as though the whole city was crying.

They found him next morning at about ten o'clock, and the police called me. They had already returned him to the nursing home, so I hurried up there. The rain was over and once again the sky was clear, a good, sharp, sunny October day. He was asleep on his bed, wrapped in his flannel robe. A bandage was plastered over his nose, and he seemed to have a black eye coming on. His knuckles were scraped and had been painted with Merthiolate. He badly needed a shave. I went downstairs and talked with the fat woman in the office. She was wary and cautious because they can probably be sued, but I finally got the story out of her. He had been found in Harlem. He had gone into a luncheonette and ordered some food, but the counterman had probably realized that he was not quite right and asked for the money in advance. The old man had a dollar but would not pay in advance, and they went looking for a cop to take care of him. When he realized they were looking for a cop he got up and tried to leave, and stumbled and fell on his face.

I went up again and sat in the armchair, waiting for him to wake up. But after a while one of the nurses came in and said they had given him a sedative which would keep him under for several hours. When I left just before my show, he was sitting in the armchair, eating some chicken. He looked up at me very surprised and again felt his lips with rapid fingers. I smiled at him. "I'm Harry," I said.

He looked at me without much recognition, only knowing that there was something of a past between us. I sat on the bed and watched him eat. I talked at length about the good day we were having, and how hard it had rained last night. I kept wishing and wishing that even for one split second he would look at me clearly and laugh. Just one shrewd laugh between us to celebrate his outing. But he sat there eating, glancing at me with a little warmth and a little suspicion, and finally I grinned and said, "I hear you went for a walk last night."

He stopped eating and looked at me with surprise. He shook his head. "No. Oh, no."

"Don't you remember the rain?"

"The rain?"

"You went to Harlem, Pa. Were you going home?"

A new attention crossed his eyes, and a sharpened interest. "I en home raro." He spoke the sounds with an attempt to convince me. He had one finger raised.

"You're going home tomorrow?"

"Ya."

Then he glanced toward the closed door and returned to the chicken.

Every night, sitting here putting on my beard, I keep expecting a telephone call or a visitor, a stranger, and I feel I am about to be afraid.

He was trying to reach home, where ages ago he had entered so many times carrying presents. He has a future which they will never be able to rip away from him. He will close his eyes for the last time thinking of it. He does not have to teach himself or remind himself of it. As long as he can actually walk they are going to have trouble with him, keeping him from going where he wants to go and has to go.

I'm not sure how to go about it, but I have a terrific desire to live differently. Maybe it is even possible to find something honorable without acting, some way of putting my soul back into my body. I think my father is like a man in love, or at least the organism inside him is. For moments, just for moments, he makes me feel as I used to when I started, when I thought that being a great actor was like making some kind of a gift to the people.

BRIAN MOORE

The Apartment Hunter

(FROM THE TAMARACK REVIEW)

THE VACUUM STOPPED and Ella Mae knocked on my bedroom door. "Somebody for you, the doorman say."

I went out to the hall and picked up the earpiece of the house intercom; the doorman's voice, like something coming in from a spaceship: "Jamanforya. A Misiter Pee-ee-pers." I thought of the television comedian. "Mister Peepers?" I shouted back. "What's he want?"

A pause. Then the voice, whistling up. "Come about eeee-ee-apartment."

And, oh, Sweet Mother, I'd forgotten all about him, the man who phoned yesterday about the ad Terence put in *The New York Times* about subletting the apartment for the summer. A Mr. *Peters*. I'd written his name on the pad by the phone in the kitchen. I told the doorman to send him up, then bolted back to my bedroom for a quick self-inspection. I was tidy, at least, and Ella Mae was cleaning up the place. The bell rang. And rang again. Trust Ella Mae not to answer the door when you want her to. I had to go myself.

Mr. Peters. From the very beginning there was something familiar about him, a feeling that I should know him. "Mrs. Lavery?" he asked. And then: "My card," handing it to me. I looked at it, no address, just his name: *Karl Dieter Peters*. I put it in the little silver card tray on top of the captain's chest in the hall, thinking as I did that it was the first real calling card I'd ever put there and at the same time beginning to grin goofily as though something wonderful and unexpected had happened, as though, say, I'd been out for a

201

walk and had come around a corner onto Fifth Avenue and there, in the middle of the traffic, was a great old elephant in a circus hat, ambling downtown on his only-oh. Something like that—odd, yet unexpectedly nice. Not that Mr. Peters was elephantine, far from it, he was quite small. But he was like an elephant in that he was both dignified and comic, venerable and silly, with rosy old Santa Claus cheeks and a little white Van Dyke beard, his Chesterfield overcoat beautifully tailored, but so old it was verdigris green around the shoulders. And, oh, he was all of a piece, with his silver-headed malacca cane, white chamois gloves and a hat, a wonderful old pearl-gray number which he doffed like the Laughing Cavalier when I asked him to come in, stepping over the threshold, courtly and formal, almost as though he were tracing out the first steps in a gavotte. Oh, I tell you, he was an old ducky, all right. You'd want to take him home and keep him.

So anyway, in he came, asking if he might take off his coat and thank you so much and off with it, laying the hat and gloves on top of it, revealing himself in a navy double-breasted blazer, beautifully shined brogues, white shirt and a rep tie which, like everything he wore, was almost at the point of being too worn to use, but still perfect. If you know what I mean. And he, like his clothes, very, very old, although at first I wasn't on to that because, although he kept his cane, he made it seem the action of a dandy, not a dodderer, moving toward the living room with a spry little jiggling walk, and it wasn't until he bumped heavily into the captain's chest in the hall, his old hand reaching out as though it were playing piano scales, tra-la-la-ing, searching for the edge of the obstacle, that I realized how blind he was. I switched on the hall light, hoping that would help, and he turned uncertainly into the living room, still smiling his even-dentured smile, not worried so much about *that* little accident as concerned that there might be an unseen, more dangerous obstacle still in front of him.

Well, he made it nicely and Ella Mae, for once, had the

good sense to shut off the vacuum cleaner and take herself elsewhere. He smiled vaguely at her departing back, then bent down to examine the carpet. "Haar," he said. "What a lovely Oriental that is." Which was clever of him, for the carpet, although not obvious, is the best thing in the room, it and the big French armoire which is the room's centerpiece and which he also noticed and said something complimentary and knowing about, but I forget exactly what. Then he asked if he might look at all the rooms first after which, he suggested, the two of us might perhaps have a little talk? I said perfect and off we went on a conducted tour. Already, you know, he'd won me over with the remarks about the rug and the armoire, because furniture is one of my things, I'm always getting compliments about how I've fixed up this place. Most people never guess how much of it I've done myself. Those curtains of mine, French *Empire* with a hand-tied fringe, people automatically assume they were made professionally. I did them myself, though.

So first we went into the smaller bedroom which Terence uses as a workroom, then to the big bedroom, then to the kitchen, the two bathrooms, the hall closets and back to the living room and all the time he was picking out just the right things to remark on, my collections of miniatures, for instance, and those wonderful old copper pots I picked up for nothing on the South Shore of Nova Scotia and I'm thinking isn't he nice, until, while I was showing him the kitchen, it came into my mind that it was odd, an old person like him wanting to take an apartment for just three months, old people are usually so set in their ways, was he married, why would he need two bedrooms, two baths? And so I tried to feel him out by saying that the oven has a built-in meat thermometer. "Although," I said, "I suppose that would interest your wife more than it would you?" looking at him in question marks as I said it. But he didn't pick it up at all, just nodded and moved on out of the kitchen and once again I had that nagging feeling that I knew him. He was familiar the way the old man Charlie Chaplin is familiar from his photos. You vaguely remember the old, *young* Chaplin, some distant kin to this thickening old person. Anyway, there I was, puzzling as we went back into the living room and he picked the blue Regency chair to sit on and asked if I minded his smoking. His accent was quite British, the more I listened to it, and the conversation between us went something like this.

"Haar. I hope I didn't disturb you, not putting you out too much, am I?"

"No. No."

"I thought the afternoon would be more, haar, convenient for you, but you, haar, said the morning?"

"No, this is fine. Do you—you like the apartment?"

"Yes, charming. Beautiful things you have."

"Well, that's it, I mean that's what worried us, you see we're going to be in Europe all summer and my husband feels that if we could find a suitable tenant, it would be safer not to leave the apartment empty."

"Haar. Yes, of course."

"The rent would be three hundred, which is less than we pay ourselves. And furnished, of course."

Why is it when I get involved in any business transaction I at once feel dishonest, for although everything I was telling him was true and the rent is three *fifty, un*furnished, somehow in the business of my being the seller and he the buyer I felt like a conniver, a crook, and damn Terence, I thought, why couldn't he be here, it was his idea to rent the place, why doesn't *he* handle it? And while all this was going through my mind, the old boy suddenly let a "Haar!" out of him, so loud I thought he'd begun to choke. But no, he was merely clearing his throat, an action he followed by producing a large, white handkerchief, seizing his nose between handkerchiefed finger and thumb, tweaking nose hard, then beginning a thorough old trumpeting, sneezing, waggling of proboscis and reaming of all nasal passages, an action he concluded with a flourish of the white handkerchief and a sudden smile, cheeks scarlet, eyes watering with his exertions.

"Excuse me," he began. "Haar. Well, Mrs. Lavery, as you know, that price is a bargain in this neighborhood, I might say a bargain even in a, haar, lesser neighborhood. On the West Side, for instance. Yes. Take that case last week, lawyer killed right in his own building in the elevator. Wife was, haar, waiting downstairs, waiting for the elevator and elevator came down, supposed to be carrying her, haar, her husband. But instead a colored fella ran out, ran past her and out of the building. Haar. Poor woman looked into the elevator there was her husband dead. Pool of blood. Shocking story! Well, Mrs. Lavery, haar, I happen to know that in that very building they were asking, haar, four hundred, yes four hundred for apartments not as big as this one."

I was thinking he seems well up on rents, he's well up on everything, because then he started asking all the right questions about watering the plants, defrosting the refrigerator, very sensible about it all, moving along in perfect gear, the gear of someone who has made up his mind to take the place. So, although it was ten past twelve and I was to meet Margaret Sloane for lunch at one, I felt, perhaps, I should offer him a drink. I went to the butler's tray where we keep the drinks and asked him what he would like.

"Sure I'm not keeping you?" he said.

"No, no, I have time."

"Well then, haar, a dry sherry would be very nice."

He stood up as he said this and came over toward the drinks tray. I held out a bottle for his inspection. "Haar," said he. "Wisdom and Warter. That's from Sherry Wines and Spirits. Very good buy." And I found myself laughing and saying, "You really do know everything, don't you, Mr. Peters," for to know about Wisdom and Warter, well, I mean. And he laughed too, a jolly Santa laugh. "Ho, ho, ho, I wouldn't say that, Mrs. Lavery. But Sherry, yes, that's a good wineshop."

And just then for a moment, something happened and I *did* know him, but it passed without my being able to get hold of it, and I was left, just a little angry with myself for having failed in that fleeting Indian wrestle with my memory. I stared at him as he sipped his sherry, an old man in the iron mask of anonymity. And then, thinking that if he was to be my tenant I should know who he was, I began to ask him questions, was he a New Yorker or what, and he told me he and his wife lived at Montauk Point out on the Island and they used to keep a small *pied-à-terre* in town but his wife was dead now and he'd been living all year out at Montauk and would go on living there except that he'd heard that one could rent a place out there for a lot of money in the summer and so he'd thought to make some money by renting his place and moving to town for the summer months.

Well, Hat and I once spent a summer in Easthampton: I know Montauk and it's quite true that an old boy like this could turn a tidy profit by renting his place for the summer months. It made sense. But what didn't make sense was his taking an apartment like ours with two bedrooms, two baths, three hundred a month. Surely he could find something cheaper? So, I said it out. "But won't this place be too big and too expensive? I mean, if you want to make money renting your Montauk house?"

He smiled, as the deaf smile. He twiddled the stem of his sherry glass and I wondered if I should offer him another. Old people can be a problem, they have nothing to do, most of them, and if you encourage them they'll stay for hours. I decided not. I'd better pin him down. "So," I said. "Then you want to, I mean, *do* you want to take this apartment?"

"Haar." Very carefully, he put down the sherry glass on the coffee table. "Well, let me say this. The apartment is, haar, very nice, yes, but to be fair, to be fair, there's another apartment not far from here I have it on my list to look over. Haar. Before making any final decision. Is that fair, Mrs. Lavery?"

"Of course," I said.

"Good. Well, let me see. I'll go and look at this other place now. If you don't, haar, hear from me in, haar, say two hours—then that means I'll have decided for the, haar, the other place. Fair?"

"Yes," I said. "But I may be out to lunch. You can leave a message with Ella Mae, my cleaning woman."

"Cleaning woman," he said. He nodded, felt his beard, then rose up, his hand searching for and finding his malacca cane. "Good," he said, suddenly. "That's all right then. All clear."

And so I went out with him toward the hall, waiting politely as he stopped by the drinks tray once again and picked up a Waterford glass pitcher. "Beautiful," he said. I told him it was more than a hundred years old and then said the Waterford glass factories had been closed down for seventy years and only started up again in the forties and babbled on about how this jug predated the modern Waterford and all the time while I was telling it, I was aware how pretentious and vulgar I sounded and of course the only reason I know about Waterford glass is because Terence's mother's people originally came from there and then, looking at old Mr. Peters as he listened to me, his hand twiddling absentmindedly with the white and blue silk tassel they put on the neck of each Wisdom and Warter sherry bottle, he smiling at me as though he expected me to order something from him, a sherry or a Bloody Mary perhaps, in that moment my memory, mulish, unbiddable, gave up its secret and put Mr. Karl Dieter Peters into a short white jacket and a black bow tie and supplied, as background commentary, Tom Brooks' Eastern prep school bray: "Look, look, there's the old bird I told you about, Nancy's find. Over there, at the bar."

Surreal as an early Bunuel film, I saw myself, Tom Brooks and Hat, the three of us walking in bright morning sunlight across a grassy dune, going toward the ocean, while, coming at us, bearing trays of scrambled eggs, toast, rolls and coffee were four waiters, totally incongruous in that landscape, dressed somehow indecently in dark dinner jackets and white cotton gloves. Perhaps, to be fair to Bunuel, I should blame the scene on Dali, for it was a Sunday brunch at Nancy's place and like all her entertainments, it was marred by that resolutely vulgar phoniness which is the hallmark of *Vogue* magazine and the people who appear in its pages. Of course, poor Hat was trying desperately not to see the waiters and looking around for Bloody Marys when Tom Brooks brayed out his comment about the old bird and pointed out this old waiter, standing off to the side behind a trestle table laden with bottles and set-ups: Mr. Karl Dieter Peters.

And when I remembered, I remembered completely, I even remembered the three parties I'd seen him serving at later that summer. It was a summer when it was "in" to employ Mr. Peters just as, the year before, it had been "in" to employ a certain New York faggot who cooked Chinese breakfasts. I even remembered Nancy's telling me that Mr. Peters lived in a clamdigger's shack out on the Montauk beach, and that he was a retired butler who had started, years ago, in England, as a footman to the Duke of Montrose. And that Nancy found him too old to be a really good bartender. "At least," she said, "not at my parties, not the way some of my guests drink." Which put me on the defensive, making me wonder if she was talking about Hat. And, remembering all this, I remembered one other detail, which was that when he tended bar we didn't call him Mr. Peters, we called him Dieter, old Dieter—

"But, you're Dieter," I said, out loud, and as soon as I'd said it his old face numbed as though I'd struck him. He withdrew his hand from the tasseled neck of the sherry bottle. "Haar?" he said, and this time it was a nanny goat bleat of fear.

"I mean, didn't we meet in Easthampton?" I said, hearing my voice trail away as though I were failing a *viva-voce* examination.

"Haar?"

I couldn't bear it, I rushed in, saying I must have made a mistake, he had reminded me of someone, yes, a mistake, but all the time I was saying it, I avoided looking at him and yet, at last, I *had* to. I looked and caught, as though it were a ball he threw to me, the terrified little smile on his face, caught it and returned it and, for a moment, that old man and I were trapped in awful intimacy, each of us knowing that the other knew, that there was no sense in further politicking, the results were in, Dieter is Dieter, and retired butlers who take summer jobs as bartenders and live in clamdiggers' shacks, don't have three hundred a month to spend on East Side apartments, now do they?

And then came my Down Tilt, sickening in its certainty. For this old man, old Dieter, what was he but a shill, a spy who entered people's apartments under the guise of wanting to rent them, an ex-butler trained in antiques, who knew what was worth taking. And, months from now, when Terence and I are on vacation, the smooth customers will move in, pick the locks, steal the stuff.

Caught in my smile, frightened stiff, the old spy waited my move. Should I pick up the phone?

"I wonder," I said. "Do you know Mrs. Almond? Nancy Almond?"

"Who?" He put a trembly old hand up to his beard as though to reassure himself that this part of his disguise, at least, had not slipped. "Mrs. Who?"

"Almond. Weren't you, I mean didn't you serve drinks at her parties, oh, three summers ago?"

"Haar," he cried triumphantly. "Almond on Egypt Lane. Mrs. John Bidwell Almond. Yes, I did."

And where did we go from there? He seemed to have trumped me.

He knew where *he* wanted to go. Out. "My coat," he said, moving toward the hall, picking up his overcoat, wrestling, stiff-armed and arthritic with the sleeves so that, unwittingly, I found myself helping him into it, helping him *escape*, for godsake, helping this scout for a gang of thieves, this old spy who crept out of his clamdigger's shack at dawn, took the Long Island railroad all the way from Montauk to Manhattan, took a bus uptown, politely consulted the doorman about my presence, came up in the elevator, was admitted, taken on a tour of the place, even given a *sherry*, for godsake! And now he'd leave, he'd probably take the crosstown bus to Central Park and sit on a bench outside the Metropolitan Museum, making out his inventory, my fur coat, the oriental rug, the hi-fi, the television set, my collection of miniatures, Terence's cameras, a list which, later this afternoon before taking the four-fifty back to Montauk, he, in some sepulchral Cosa Nostra bar, would pass to the smooth customers who move in, well-dressed (I read all about them in a two-part *New Yorker* article on apartment thieves) they pick the locks with plastic hotel *Do Not Disturb* signs and gut the apartment, moving the stuff out with cool efficiency, smiling at the doormen as they steal you blind.

"Well then," said the old spy. "I'll, haar, call you within the hour."

"Call?" I said, stupidly, still lost in my Mafiosan dreams.

"Yes. Call if I want the place. All right?"

I am, always have been, a fool who rushes in, a blurter-out of awkward truths, a speaker-up at parties who, the morning after, filled with guilt, vows that never again, no matter what, but who, faced at the very next encounter with someone whose opinions strike me as bigoted or unfair, rushes in again, blurting out, breaking all vows. And now, outraged by this old man's obvious lie about calling me back, the fool within me, the blurter-out, put the impossible into my mouth. "But you're not going to call, are you?" I said.

"Haa—aa—rr?"

It was too late to take it back. "I mean," I said. "I happen to know Mrs. Almond. She told me, I remember she said you live in a clamdigger's shack."

"Ah," he said. "Yes, in a shack. Yes, I used to. But not now. Now, I live here. In New York."

Well, that was it, the Perry Mason point, and I became the triumphant prosecuting attorney, swiveling to face the jury, pointing at the true culprit. "Aha," I sort of screamed. "So you live in New York, do you? Then why do you want this apartment if you already live in New York? You were lying about living in Montauk."

His fingers, touch-typing along the top of the captain's chest, found at last what they sought. His hat. Pulling it toward him, he backed in the direction of the front door. "Yes," he said, "Yes, I'll let you know, Mrs. Lavery."

"Now, you listen to me," I began. "I'm not looking for trouble. But I warn you that if anything is stolen from this apartment in the next six months, the police will be talking to you about it. You can be traced, you know."

I was screaming by now, it was horrible, my premenstrual tension had flushed into lunacy, yes, there I was, screaming, the lunatic district attorney. And he, of course he was frightened by this mad tirade and, as if to calm me, he reached out and patted my arm in such a damn theatrical way that I, furious, was just about to strike at his hand and he was opening his mouth to say something to me, but, wouldn't you know, at that very moment, Ella Mae threw the switch on the vacuum cleaner in Terence's study, making all speech impossible so, signaling to the old boy to wait, I turned and went into the study. Ella Mae switched off the machine. "Yais, Miz Lavery?"

"Hold it a moment, do something else, will you?"

I ran back into the hall but, of course, he was gone. And part of me, the normal, ordinary, shamed me, said let him go, you warned him, that's enough. But when, when you're in that mad premenstrual mood, the normal, shamed, decent you can talk all she wants to, but Mad Twin, that Mad Twin within you runs to the apartment door, opens it and runs out and up the corridor, catching up to old Mr. Peters as he hobbles toward the elevator, Mad Twin calling out in that high D.A.'s scream: "Just a moment, just a moment, there!"

He stopped. He looked at me. He took off his hat. "Please, Mrs. Lavery. Don't worry. Haar. Didn't mean any harm. Don't worry. All right?"

"No, it's not all right," cried Mad Twin within me and suddenly, oh God, it *wasn't* all right. Suddenly I was trembling again, he was going to slip away and warn the smooth customers. I was a woman, how could I stop him? "Oh, please," I said, "the things in this apartment, it's not just money, they have a sentimental value, I don't know what I'd do if anything happened to them."

"But I'm not going to steal them," he said. "What a silly thing to say, I'm going to steal, I've no intention, no, no, no, no."

"Then you mean, you mean you do want, I mean you *are* interested in the apartment, but why did you lie? I'm sorry, perhaps I misunderstood you?" (Mad Twin babbling: unable to stop.)

"I like to look at places. That's all," he said, defensively. "I like to meet people, talk to them, that's all. Maybe you wouldn't understand?"

"But I'm trying to understand. Why did you come to look at *this* apartment?"

"Because," he said, his hand reaching up to reassure his little beard. "Because, do you see, I've nothing much else to do. I get the *Times* and read the 'Furnished To Let.' Then, haar, go and look."

"Just to pass the time?"

He looked at me. "Yes," he said. And then he said that sometimes people gave him a cup of coffee, sometimes even a drink. They showed him their apartments and afterwards, sometimes, they sat down and chatted with him. His voice, as he explained, carried in it a hint of anger at my stupidity: it was as though he believed the reason he did this strange thing should be evident to anyone and I was being dense in refusing to recognize it. What he meant, but did not say, was that he was lonely. He probably lived alone in some awful little room and he'd found a way to pass some of his time. His clothes, I guess, had been given to him by various gentlemanly employers in his years as a butler. And as he talked, Mad Twin fell silent, and I knew he was no one to be afraid of, on the contrary, and so (that's the funny thing about premenstrual moods) I suddenly felt like hugging him, weeping on his shoulder, asking him back in to have another sherry. While he, caught out, waiting to escape me, trumpeted once again that he had no intention of stealing, no, no, no, no, please forgive him for wasting my time.

I said not at all, that's perfectly all right, I'm sorry, I was upset. Whereupon he fumbled off his glove and insisted on shaking hands with me, saying, "Goodbye, Mrs. Lavery. And God bless. Yes, God bless." Then fumbled the glove back on his fingers, gripped his malacca cane, its steel tip striking loud taps from the terrazzo floor of the corridor as, turning, he went away, an old man I will never see again, an old man who has become an anecdote, a story I will tell in years to come. "The Apartment Hunter." That would be its title if I ever wrote it as a story, but, oh, I'm not going to write any stories. That agony, trying to write stories, that particular search for a purpose, no. That's all over and done with.

BERRY MORGAN

Andrew

(FROM THE NEW YORKER)

THERE WAS ONLY one time in my life I had a little baby off all to myself. No kin, that is. I used to love to have my brother that drives the pulp truck bring *his,* but Mama couldn't stand too much of their commotion and they gave her colds with their everlasting sneezes till we had to wean him from it, and they grew up hardly ever stopping.

This all began with that white lady that calls me every year along in the spring to help her set her ducks. I've fooled with ducks so long now it looks like they will go on and do anything I want them to, and it has spread around the country so that I have calls for it just like a doctor. Well, it's uphill all the way from my house to this lady's house, and I was taking it nice and slow and stopping to rest every now and then and look around. I had got as far as the bluff by the corner of the old Somerset place and just looked up—I always get plums from those particular trees since nobody else seems to know about them—and lo and behold, what do I see sitting on the gallery of that old tumbled down cabin but a young girl. Her legs were hanging loose over the edge and she was swinging them back and forth and looking down at the road where I was standing. Do I know her, I thought—because I *do* know nearly everybody in King County. She might have come up from Bogue, though, and Mama always said to stay out of the way of Bogue, white *or* colored, and I have, but no, if I wasn't telling myself wrong, this was one of old lady Littell's grandchildren that they've kept sending her back from Chicago and all around for years and years.

"Are you all right, honey?" I asked her. "What are you doing way out here by yourself?"

I was sorry for saying that, because just about then I saw *him*—or anyhow an undershirt showing up white at the door. So she must be married, and that was why she was out here away from school and her grandmother in this old empty cabin.

"Yes ma'am," she said, taking time to smile with me and act sweet. "How are you, Miss Roxie?"

So she knew me. Before I could answer, I heard it—a little high crying noise behind her in the cabin. Right away I knew what had made it. They had a baby up in there, their own little baby, and most likely they were out here tending to it because back in town he had another rightful wife who would catch him and get him back. But where was their water, poor things, what did they do for water? The place didn't have enough roof left to catch any even if they had a gutter, which I disbelieved.

The gentleman must have picked it up, because the crying stopped. I knew I had to some way or other get up on that bluff and hold that little thing myself. "I don't have time right now," I told the girl, "but when I come back from setting a duck could I please see the baby? What is its name?"

She smiled and nodded her head to show manners. "Yes ma'am," she said, "you'd be welcome. Andrew. His name is Andrew."

Well, I went on up the hill to do what I'd said I'd do, and it took nearly all day. This white lady had saved up a winter's talk—wanted to tell me her frights since last spring, has two worrisome boys that she is afraid may drink a little beer. By the time I petted the duck and got it started on its eggs, she had gone on and fixed me a plate of dinner to eat on the back steps so she could talk some more.

The sun was halfway down the woods when I got back to where the cabin was, and reddening up to set because it was March and still cool. I didn't hear anything now except the birds, and I couldn't see any footholds on the outside of the cliff to climb up by. It looked a whole lot different than it had in the morning—long shadows everywhere to make me wonder if they were still up there with it.

It came into my head to give up—Mama always did hate to have me prowling too close to dark. Still I had said I was coming and they might be expecting me. Just then as the good Lord *would* have it, I caught the scent of woodsmoke. So they were still up there and even had themselves a fire. "Hello" I said every once in a while, but my voice doesn't carry and I didn't hear anything back. Just when I got to the top, though, I saw her, standing in the door with a frying pan in her hand—fixing to clean it out, I reckon, because she stooped down to a pile of moss and sticks on the gallery floor.

"How is it?" I asked her. "Is it resting well?"

"Yes ma'am," she said, knocking the frying pan on the gallery edge to clear it. "It seems like it is."

"That's good," I said. "How old is it? How long ago did you find little Andrew?"

I was afraid this had really hurt her feelings, but after a while she told me. "About a week. It's been just about a week."

"Do you have any milk to nurse it with?"

She shook her head. "It haven't come in yet."

"Well," I said, "that's what I was afraid of. It's got to have its milk, and like Mama used to say, not tomorrow or the next day but right now." I was on the gallery myself by this time, and nearly every board I set my foot on came up at the other end—loose. She tried to watch out for me that I didn't go through until she could push the old door back—it was off its hinges—to make room for me to pass. Right away I saw those foolish children had made a fire in the middle of the floor, just on a piece of roof tin—didn't have sense enough to build it in the fireplace. "Sweet girl," I said, "you're fixing to burn this old place down." And I reached and picked up a piece of rag and took the tin by the corner to pull it onto the hearth. As soon as I straightened up, she took me over to the baby. It was in an old cardboard box, and she had put all the soft things she had under it. It was sound asleep, a precious little boy baby a dark beautiful brown about the same shade, if I reckoned correctly, as Mama. "This is in God's image," I told the girl. "A sign of his love and a brand new life to be used for his glorification. Where's its papa?"

"He's about gone to get milk," the girl answered. "Leastways that's what I told him to do."

"Does he have any money?"

She bent over the box and looked hard at the baby. Oh, she was proud. You could see that. "He say he have."

I knew Mama wouldn't like me doing this but I couldn't help it. "My house is nice and warm and I have a can of Pet we can put some boiled water with and give it by an eyedropper, just a little at a time until it builds its strength. Come on with me and we will leave *him* a note if you have anything to write on."

She was still smiling all right enough, but she shook her pretty head. "He told me to stay on right here, Miss Roxie, not to leave."

"Is this a King's Town man?"

"No ma'am," she said. "It's a United States soldier."

Just drifting through then, I thought, and apt to drift on. "Well, we've got to give it milk. If you have to wait for the soldier, go ahead and wait, but let me take it on, wrap it in this fresh apron and carry it home. When it's good and strong, you can come and get it."

She leaned over the baby and looked at it again, like it might get up out of its sleep and tell her what to do.

"It's near dark," I said. "You go on and wait if you have to, but I've got to get this baby its supper. And you really ought to go with me and fix yourself up for tomorrow's school—learn something, and not stay out here in these woods with a United States soldier or anybody else." I had wrapped the baby up the best I could, and I kissed its mother and gave her the fifty cents I'd made from setting the duck. Then I was afraid of falling, going down the bluff with it, but by sitting down and sliding on a little at a time I was right down in the road and it was safe.

As soon as I started walking, I began to be happy. This was a real living baby I had to myself—God's image, like I had known it was in the cabin. "If it please Thee," I said, "let this little baby—Andrew is its name—grow strong and tall and take up Thy war against evil." It hardly weighed anything at all.

There is such a change in a house when you first take a baby into it. I put him down on Mama's bed—the first person ever laid there since the evening she passed. "Well sir, Andrew," I said, "there's so much to do and only you and me to do it, I wonder where to start." I could rock it after I put on the water—that would take a while to heat and then cool. By the time I did this, it had its eyes open and was twisting its head a whole lot, like it already knew it had changed its resting place. "Eating is the main thing," I said to it. "After you've had a few drops of weak Pet you'll sleep, and after you sleep I'll strengthen the Pet just enough to make you sleep some more. And all that time you'll be growing and getting bigger. By the time I have to give you back, you'll be looking around here like the Lord of creation—might even have caught on how to smile." If they let me keep him long enough, I could even make him apt in his books, and it made me want to cry to think of him starting to school, getting on the bus and riding off.

Andrew liked rocking. Then after I had given him the first Pet with Mama's eyedropper, I heated a sheet and wrapped his stomach good and rocked some more. He didn't cry at all except when he woke up and wanted more milk. "You are going to keep Roxie up all night," I told him, "but that's all right. When Mama was here, I never was able to sleep more than an hour at a time without her needing something, and now God has sent me a precious lamb in her place."

I would sleep and it would sleep. It felt so good to know it was lying there by me in the dark. I wished it hadn't been given a name yet, because I might name it for Mama's father, the Reverend Isaac Stoner. But you don't hear the name Isaac much anymore and I guess Andrew *was* better.

Along toward morning, even before the mill whistle, I thought I heard a car on our creek road. Who could that be, I thought. They wouldn't come for it before daylight, and besides that the girl and the United States soldier didn't have a car, and whoever this was did. When I heard it drawing up into our yard, I got up and found my wrapper. I braced the baby—it was too little to roll, but still it looked safer with something between it and the edge—and by that time there was knocking on my door.

It was Mr. Bat Becker, the sheriff's helper, and old lady Littell herself, as vexed as she could be.

"I hate to disturb you this time of night," Mr. Bat said, "but there's this little baby missing, and Eliza here's granddaughter says you're the one harboring it."

Well, I took them right in to show them it was safe and happy. But instead of being glad and taking my word, Mrs. Littell, poor old worn-out soul, snatched it off the bed and began looking at every part of it to see if it was true. Then she held it tight and began to moan and cry and kiss it so hard you wouldn't believe she already had a house full of them, all different sizes. "Mrs. Stoner always did say you were backward," she told me, "but she didn't let on you were a thief." I felt bad to hear her talk like that, but she was so old and worked up—had been afraid, I guess, that it was thrown back in the woods to buzzards—she couldn't help it. I begged her pardon over and over, and they went on out and slammed the door.

Oh, yes, I see him now and then. Twice I caught up with him at the Piggly and once at the oil station, where they have a Coke machine. And he *is* fine. I give him a nickel if I have one, and he always has a big smile for me—thank you ma'am, no idea in the world who I really am. That's all right, Andrew, I say (just to myself), because I had you for one night, you lying up there in my lap taking milk, and if I'm any judge at all of what is true, you loved me.

JOYCE CAROL OATES

*Where Are You Going,
   Where Have You Been?*

(FROM EPOCH)

TO BOB DYLAN

HER NAME WAS Connie. She was fifteen and she had a quick nervous giggling habit of craning her neck to glance into mirrors, or checking other people's faces to make sure her own was all right. Her mother, who noticed everything and knew everything and who hadn't much reason any longer to look at her own face, always scolded Connie about it. "Stop gawking at yourself, who are you? You think you're so pretty?" she would say. Connie would raise her eyebrows at these familiar complaints and look right through her mother, into a shadowy vision of herself as she was right at that moment: she knew she was pretty and that was everything. Her mother had been pretty once too, if you could believe those old snapshots in the album, but now her looks were gone and that was why she was always after Connie.

"Why don't you keep your room clean like your sister? How've you got your hair fixed—what the hell stinks? Hair spray? You don't see your sister using that junk."

Her sister June was twenty-four and still lived at home. She was a secretary in the high school Connie attended, and if that wasn't bad enough—with her in the same building—she was so plain and chunky and steady that Connie had to hear her praised all the time by her mother and her mother's sisters. June did this, June did that, she saved money and helped clean the house and cooked and Connie couldn't do a thing, her mind was all filled with trashy daydreams. Their father was away at work most of the time and when he came home he wanted supper and he read the newspaper at supper and after supper he went to bed. He didn't bother talking much to them, but around his bent head Connie's mother kept picking at her until Connie wished her mother were dead and she herself were dead and it were all over. "She makes me want to throw up sometimes," she complained to her friends. She had a high, breathless, amused voice which made everything she said sound a little forced, whether it was sincere or not.

There was one good thing: June went places with girlfriends of hers, girls who were just as plain and steady as she, and so when Connie wanted to do that her mother had no objections. The father of Connie's best girlfriend drove the girls the three miles to town and left them off at a shopping plaza, so that they could talk through the stores or go to a movie, and when he came to pick them up again at eleven he never bothered to ask what they had done.

They must have been familiar sights, walking around that shopping plaza in their shorts and flat ballerina slippers that always scuffed the sidewalk, with charm bracelets jingling on their thin wrists; they would lean together to whisper and laugh secretly if someone passed by who amused or interested them. Connie had long dark blond hair that drew anyone's eye to it, and she wore part of it pulled up on her head and puffed out and the rest of it she let fall down her back. She wore a pullover jersey blouse that looked one way when she was at home and another way when she was away from home. Everything about her had two sides to it, one for home and one for anywhere that was not home: her walk that could be childlike and bobbing, or languid enough to make anyone think she was hearing music in her head, her mouth which was pale and smirking most of the time, but bright and pink on these evenings out, her laugh which was cynical and drawling at home—"Ha, ha, very funny"—but high-pitched and nervous anywhere else, like the jingling of the charms on her bracelet.

Sometimes they did go shopping or to a movie, but sometimes they went across the highway, ducking fast across the busy road, to a drive-in restaurant where older kids hung out. The restaurant was shaped like a big bottle, though squatter than a real bottle, and on its cap was a revolving figure of a grinning boy who held a hamburger aloft. One night in midsummer they ran across, breathless with daring, and right away someone leaned out a car window and invited them over, but it was just a boy from high school they didn't like. It made them feel good to be able to ignore him. They went up through the maze of parked and cruising cars to the bright-lit, fly-infested restaurant, their faces pleased and expectant as if they were entering a sacred building that loomed out of the night to give them what haven and what blessing they yearned for. They sat at the counter and crossed their legs at the ankles, their thin shoulders rigid with excitement, and listened to the music that made everything so good: the music was always in the background like music at a church service, it was something to depend upon.

A boy named Eddie came in to talk with them. He sat backward on his stool, turning himself jerkily around in semicircles and then stopping and turning again, and after awhile he asked Connie if she would like something to eat. She said she did and so she tapped her friend's arm on her way out—her friend pulled her face up into a brave droll look—and Connie said she would meet her at eleven, across the way. "I just hate to leave her like that," Connie said earnestly, but the boy said that she wouldn't be alone for long. So they went out to his car and on the way Connie couldn't help but let her eyes wander over the windshields and faces all around her, her face gleaming with a joy that had nothing to do with Eddie or even this place; it might have been the music. She drew her shoulders up and sucked in her breath with the pure pleasure of being alive, and just at that moment she happened to glance at a face just a few feet from hers. It was a boy with shaggy black hair, in a convertible jalopy painted gold. He stared at her and then his lips widened into a grin. Connie slit her eyes at him and turned away, but she couldn't help glancing back and there he was still watching her. He wagged a finger and laughed and said, "Gonna get you, baby," and Connie turned away again without Eddie noticing anything.

She spent three hours with him, at the restaurant where they ate hamburgers and drank Cokes in wax cups that were always sweating, and then down an alley a mile or so away, and when he left her off at five to eleven only the movie house was still open at the plaza. Her girl friend was there, talking with a boy. When Connie came up the two girls smiled at each other and Connie said, "How was the movie?" and the girl said, "*You* should know." They rode off with the girl's father, sleepy and pleased, and Connie couldn't help but look at the darkened shopping plaza with its big empty parking lot and its signs that were faded and ghostly now, and over at the drive-in restaurant where cars were still circling tirelessly. She couldn't hear the music at this distance.

Next morning June asked her how the movie was and Connie said, "So-so."

She and that girl and occasionally another girl went out several times a week that way, and the rest of the time Connie spent around the house—it was summer vacation—getting in her mother's way and thinking, dreaming, about the boys she met. But all the boys fell back and dissolved into a single face that was not even a face, but an idea, a feeling, mixed up with the urgent insistent pounding of the music and the humid night air of July. Connie's mother kept dragging her back to the daylight by finding things for her to do or saying, suddenly, "What's this about the Pettinger girl?"

And Connie would say nervously, "Oh, her. That dope." She always drew thick clear lines between herself and such girls, and her mother was simple and kindly enough to believe her. Her mother was so simple, Connie thought, that it was maybe cruel to fool her so much. Her mother went scuffling around the house in old bedroom slippers and complained over the telephone to one sister about the other, then the other called up and the two of them complained about the third one. If June's name was mentioned her mother's tone was approving, and if Connie's name was mentioned it was disapproving. This did not really mean she disliked Connie, and actually Connie thought that her mother preferred her to June because she was prettier, but the two of them kept up a pretense of exasperation, a sense that they were tugging and struggling over something of little value to either of them. Sometimes, over coffee, they were almost friends, but something would come up—some vexation that was like a fly buzzing suddenly around their heads—and their faces went hard with contempt.

One Sunday Connie got up at eleven—none of them bothered with church—and washed her hair so that it could dry all day long, in the sun. Her parents and sister were going to a barbecue at an aunt's house and Connie said no, she wasn't interested, rolling her eyes to let mother know just what she thought of it. "Stay home alone then," her mother said sharply. Connie sat out back in a lawn chair and watched them drive away, her father quiet and bald, hunched around so that he could back the car out, her mother with a look that was still angry and not at all softened through the windshield, and in the back seat poor old June all dressed up as if she didn't know what a barbecue was, with all the running yelling kids and the flies. Connie sat with her eyes closed in the sun, dreaming and dazed with the warmth about her as if this were a kind of love, the caresses of love, and her mind slipped over onto thoughts of the boy she had been with the night before and how nice he had been, how sweet it always was, not the way someone like June would suppose but sweet, gentle, the way it was in movies and promised in songs; and when she opened her eyes she hardly knew where she was, the back yard ran off into weeds and a fence-line of trees and behind it the sky was perfectly blue and still. The asbestos "ranch house" that was now three years old startled her—it looked small. She shook her head as if to get awake.

It was too hot. She went inside the house and turned on the radio to drown out the quiet. She sat on the edge of her bed, barefoot, and listened for an hour and a half to a program called XYZ Sunday Jamboree, record after record of hard, fast, shrieking songs she sang along with, interspersed by exclamations from "Bobby King": "An' look here you girls at Napoleon's—Son and Charley want you to pay real close attention to this song coming up!"

And Connie paid close attention herself, bathed in a glow of slow-pulsed joy that seemed to rise mysteriously out of the music itself and lay languidly about the airless little room, breathed in and breathed out with each gentle rise and fall of her chest.

After a while she heard a car coming up the drive. She sat up at once, startled, because it couldn't be her father so soon. The gravel kept crunching all the way in from the road—the driveway was long—and Connie ran to the window. It was a car she didn't know. It was an open jalopy, painted a bright gold that caught the sunlight opaquely. Her heart began to pound and her fingers snatched at her hair, checking it, and she whispered "Christ. Christ," wondering how bad she looked. The car came to a stop at the side door and the horn sounded four short taps as if this were a signal Connie knew.

She went into the kitchen and approached the door slowly, then hung out the screen door, her bare toes curling down off the step. There were two boys in the car and now she recognized the driver: he had shaggy, shabby black hair that looked crazy as a wig and he was grinning at her.

"I ain't late, am I?" he said.

"Who the hell do you think you are?" Connie said.

"Toldja I'd be out, didn't I?"

"I don't even know who you are."

She spoke sullenly, careful to show no interest or pleasure, and he spoke in a fast bright monotone. Connie looked past him to the other boy, taking her time. He had fair brown hair, with a lock that fell onto his forehead. His sideburns gave him a fierce, embarrassed look, but so far he hadn't even bothered to glance at her. Both boys wore sunglasses. The driver's glasses were metallic and mirrored everything in miniature.

"You wanta come for a ride?" he said.

Connie smirked and let her hair fall loose over one shoulder.

"Don'tcha like my car? New paint job," he said. "Hey."

"What?"

"You're cute."

She pretended to fidget, chasing flies away from the door.

"Don'tcha believe me, or what?" he said.

"Look, I don't even know who you are," Connie said in disgust.

"Hey, Ellie's got a radio, see. Mine's broke down." He lifted his friend's arm and showed her the little transistor the boy was holding, and now Connie began to hear the music. It was the same program that was playing inside the house.

"Bobby King?" she said.

"I listen to him all the time. I think he's great."

"He's kind of great," Connie said reluctantly.

"Listen, that guy's *great*. He knows where the action is."

Connie blushed a little, because the glasses made it impossible for her to see just what this boy was looking at. She couldn't decide if she liked him or if he was just a jerk, and so she dawdled in the doorway and wouldn't come down or go back inside. She said, "What's all that stuff painted on your car?"

"Can'tcha read it?" He opened the door very carefully, as if he was afraid it might fall off. He slid out just as carefully, planting his feet firmly on the ground, the tiny metallic world in his glasses slowing down like gelatine hardening and in the midst of it Connie's bright green blouse. "This here is my name, to begin with," he said. ARNOLD FRIEND was written in tarlike black letters on the side, with a drawing of a round grinning face that reminded Connie of a pumpkin, except it wore sunglasses. "I wanta introduce myself, I'm Arnold Friend and that's my real name and I'm gonna be your friend, honey, and inside the car's Ellie Oscar, he's kinda shy." Ellie brought his transistor radio up to his shoulder and balanced it there. "Now these numbers are a secret code, honey," Arnold Friend explained. He read off the numbers 33, 19, 17 and raised his eyebrows at her to see what she thought of that, but she didn't think much of it. The left rear fender had been smashed and around it was written, on the gleaming gold background: DONE BY CRAZY WOMAN DRIVER. Connie had to laugh at that. Arnold Friend was pleased at her laughter and looked up at her. "Around the other side's a lot more—you wanta come and see them."

"No."

"Why not?"

"Why should I?"

"Don'tcha wanta see what's on the car? Don'tcha wanta go for a ride?"

"I don't know."

"Why not?"

"I've got things to do."

"Like what?"

"Things."

He laughed as if she had said something funny. He slapped his thighs. He was standing in a strange way, leaning back against the car as if he were balancing himself. He wasn't tall, only an inch or so taller than she would be if she came down to him. Connie liked the way he was dressed, which was the way all of them dressed: tight faded jeans stuffed into black, scuffed boots, a belt that pulled his waist in and showed how lean he was, and a white pullover shirt that was a little soiled and showed the hard small muscles of his arms and shoulders. He looked as if he probably did hard work, lifting and carrying things. Even his neck looked muscular.

And his face was a familiar face, somehow: the jaw and chin and cheeks slightly darkened, because he hadn't shaved for a day or two, and the nose long and hawklike, sniffing as if she were a treat he was going to gobble up and it was all a joke.

"Connie, you ain't telling the truth. This is your day set aside for a ride with me and you know it," he said, still laughing. The way he straightened and recovered from his fit of laughing showed that it had been all fake.

"How do you know what my name is?" she said suspiciously.

"It's Connie."

"Maybe and maybe not."

"I know my Connie," he said, wagging his finger. Now she remembered him even better, back at the restaurant, and her cheeks warmed at the thought of how she sucked in her breath just at the moment she passed him—how she must have looked to him. And he had remembered her. "Ellie and I come out here especially for you," he said. "Ellie can sit in back. How about it?"

"Where?"

"Where what?"

"Where're we going?"

He looked at her. He took off the sunglasses and she saw how pale the skin around his eyes was, like holes that were not in shadow but instead in light. His eyes were like chips of broken glass that catch the light in an amiable way. He smiled. It was as if the idea of going for a ride somewhere, to some place, was a new idea to him.

"Just for a ride, Connie sweetheart."

"I never said my name was Connie," she said.

"But I know what it is. I know your name and all about you, lots of things," Arnold Friend said. He had not moved yet but stood still leaning back against the side of his jalopy. "I took a special interest in you, such a pretty girl, and found out all about you like I know your parents and sister are gone somewheres and I know where and how long they're going to be gone, and I know who you were with last night, and your best girlfriend's name is Betty. Right?"

He spoke in a simple lilting voice, exactly as if he were reciting the words to a song. His smile assured her that everything was fine. In the car Ellie turned up the volume on his radio and did not bother to look around at them.

"Ellie can sit in the back seat," Arnold Friend said. He indicated his friend with a casual jerk of his chin, as if Ellie did not count and she should not bother with him.

"How'd you find out all that stuff?" Connie said.

"Listen: Betty Schultz and Tony Fitch and Jimmy Pettinger and Nancy Pettinger," he said, in a chant. "Raymond Stanley and Bob Hutter—"

"Do you know all those kids?"

"I know everybody."

"Look, you're kidding. You're not from around here."

"Sure."

"But—how come we never saw you before?"

"Sure you saw me before," he said. He looked down at his boots, as if he were a little offended. "You just don't remember."

"I guess I'd remember you," Connie said.

"Yeah?" He looked up at this, beaming. He was pleased. He began to mark time with the music from Ellie's radio, tapping his fists lightly together. Connie looked away from his smile to the car, which was painted so bright it almost hurt her eyes to look at it. She looked at that name, ARNOLD FRIEND. And up at the front fender was an expression that was familiar—MAN THE FLYING SAUCERS. It was an expression kids had used the year before, but didn't use this year. She looked at it for a while as if the words meant something to her that she did not yet know.

"What're you thinking about? Huh?" Arnold Friend demanded. "Not worried about your hair blowing around in the car, are you?"

"No."

"Think I maybe can't drive good?"

"How do I know?"

"You're a hard girl to handle. How come?" he said. "Don't you know I'm your friend? Didn't you see me put my sign in the air when you walked by?"

"What sign?"

"My sign." And he drew an X in the air, leaning out toward her. They were maybe ten feet apart. After his hand fell back to his side the X was still in the air, almost visible. Connie let the screen door close and stood perfectly still inside it, listening to the music from her radio and the boy's blend together. She stared at Arnold Friend. He stood there so stiffly relaxed, pretending to be relaxed, with one hand idly on the door handle as if he were keeping himself up that way and had no intention of ever moving again. She recognized most things about him, the tight jeans that showed his thighs and buttocks and the greasy leather boots and the tight shirt, and even that slippery friendly smile of his, that sleepy dreamy smile that all the boys used to get across ideas they didn't want to put into words. She recognized all this and also the singsong way he talked, slightly mocking, kidding, but serious and a little melancholy, and she recognized the way he tapped one fist against the other in homage to the perpetual music behind him. But all these things did not come together.

She said suddenly, "Hey, how old are you?"

His smile faded. She could see then that he wasn't a kid, he was much older—thirty, maybe more. At this knowledge her heart began to pound faster.

"That's a crazy thing to ask. Can'tcha see I'm your own age?"

"Like hell you are."

"Or maybe a coupla years older, I'm eighteen."

"Eighteen?" she said doubtfully.

He grinned to reassure her and lines appeared at the corners of his mouth. His teeth were big and white. He grinned so broadly his eyes became slits and she saw how thick the lashes were, thick and black as if painted with a black tarlike material. Then he seemed to become embarrassed, abruptly, and looked over his shoulder at Ellie. *"Him,* he's crazy," he said. "Ain't he a riot, he's a nut, a real character." Ellie was still listening to the music. His sunglasses told nothing about what he was thinking. He wore a bright orange shirt unbuttoned halfway to show his chest, which was a pale, bluish chest and not muscular like Arnold Friend's. His shirt collar was turned up all around and the very tips of the collar pointed out past his chin as if they were protecting him. He was pressing the transistor radio up against his ear and sat there in a kind of daze, right in the sun.

"He's kinda strange," Connie said.

"Hey, she says you're kinda strange! Kinda strange!" Arnold Friend cried. He pounded on the car to get Ellie's attention. Ellie turned for the first time and Connie saw with shock that he wasn't a kid either—he had a fair, hairless face, cheeks reddened slightly as if the veins grew too close to the surface of his skin, the face of a forty-year-old baby. Connie felt a wave of dizziness rise in her at this sight and she stared at him as if waiting for something to change the shock of the moment, make it all right again. Ellie's lips kept shaping words, mumbling along with the words blasting in his ear.

"Maybe you two better go away," Connie said faintly.

"What? How come?" Arnold Friend cried. "We come out here to take you for a ride. It's Sunday." He had the voice of the man on the radio now. It was the same voice, Connie thought. "Don'tcha know it's Sunday all day and honey, no matter who you were with last night today you're with Arnold Friend and don't you forget it!—Maybe you better step out here," he said, and this last was in a different voice. It was a little flatter, as if the heat was finally getting to him.

"No. I got things to do."

"Hey."

"You two better leave."

"We ain't leaving until you come with us."

"Like hell I am—"

"Connie, don't fool around with me. I mean, I mean, don't fool *around*," he said, shaking his head. He laughed incredulously. He placed his sunglasses on top of his head, carefully, as if he were indeed wearing a wig, and brought the stems down behind his ears. Connie stared at him, another wave of dizziness and fear rising in her so that for a moment he wasn't even in focus but was just a blur, standing there against his gold car, and she had the idea that he had driven up the driveway all right but had come from nowhere before that and belonged nowhere and that everything about him and even about the music that was so familiar to her was only half real.

"If my father comes and sees you—"

"He ain't coming. He's at a barbecue."

"How do you know that?"

"Aunt Tillie's. Right now they're—uh—they're drinking. Sitting around," he said vaguely, squinting as if he were staring all the way to town and over to Aunt Tillie's back yard. Then the vision seemed to get clear and he nodded energetically. "Yeah. Sitting around. There's your sister in a blue dress, huh? And high heels, the poor sad bitch—nothing like you, sweetheart! And your mother's helping some fat woman with the corn, they're cleaning the corn—husking the corn—"

"What fat woman?" Connie cried.

"How do I know what fat woman, I don't know every goddam fat woman in the world!" Arnold Friend laughed.

"Oh, that's Mrs. Hornby ... Who invited her?" Connie said. She felt a little light-headed. Her breath was coming quickly.

"She's too fat. I don't like them fat. I like them the way you are, honey," he said, smiling sleepily at her. They stared at each other for a while, through the screen door. He said softly, "Now what you're going to do is this: you're going to come out that door. You're going to sit up front with me and

Ellie's going to sit in the back, the hell with Ellie, right? This isn't Ellie's date. You're my date. I'm your lover, honey."

"What? You're crazy—"

"Yes, I'm your lover. You don't know what that is but you will," he said. "I know that too. I know all about you. But look: it's real nice and you couldn't ask for nobody better than me, or more polite. I always keep my word. I'll tell you how it is, I'm always nice at first, the first time. I'll hold you so tight you won't think you have to try to get away or pretend anything because you'll know you can't. And I'll come inside you where it's all secret and you'll give in to me and you'll love me—"

"Shut up! You're crazy!" Connie said. She backed away from the door. She put her hands against her ears as if she'd heard something terrible, something not meant for her. "People don't talk like that, you're crazy," she muttered. Her heart was almost too big now for her chest and its pumping made sweat break out all over her. She looked out to see Arnold Friend pause and then take a step toward the porch lurching. He almost fell. But, like a clever drunken man, he managed to catch his balance. He wobbled in his high boots and grabbed hold of one of the porch posts.

"Honey?" he said. "You still listening?"

"Get the hell out of here!"

"Be nice, honey. Listen."

"I'm going to call the police—"

He wobbled again and out of the side of his mouth came a fast spat curse, an aside not meant for her to hear. But even this "Christ!" sounded forced. Then he began to smile again. She watched this smile come, awkward as if he were smiling from inside a mask. His whole face was a mask, she thought wildly, tanned down onto his throat but then running out as if he had plastered makeup on his face but had forgotten about his throat.

"Honey—? Listen, here's how it is. I always tell the truth and I promise you this: I ain't coming in that house after you."

"You better not! I'm going to call the police if you—if you don't—"

"Honey," he said, talking right through her voice, "honey, I'm not coming in there but you are coming out here. You know why?"

She was panting. The kitchen looked like a place she had never seen before, some room she had run inside but which wasn't good enough, wasn't going to help her. The kitchen window had never had a curtain, after three years, and there were dishes in the sink for her to do—probably—and if you ran your hand across the table you'd probably feel something sticky there.

"You listening, honey? Hey?"

"—going to call the police—"

"Soon as you touch the phone I don't need to keep my promise and can come inside. You won't want that."

She rushed forward and tried to lock the door. Her fingers were shaking. "But why lock it," Arnold Friend said gently, talking right into her face. "It's just a screen door. It's just nothing." One of his boots was at a strange angle, as if his foot wasn't in it. It pointed out to the left, bent at the ankle. "I mean, anybody can break through a screen door and glass and wood and iron or anything else if he needs to, anybody at all and specially Arnold Friend. If the place got lit up with a fire honey you'd come runnin' out into my arms, right into my arms an' safe at home—like you knew I was your lover and'd stopped fooling around. I don't mind a nice shy girl but I don't like no fooling around." Part of those words were spoken with a slight rhythmic lilt, and Connie somehow recognized them—the echo of a song from last year, about a girl rushing into her boyfriend's arms and coming home again—

Connie stood barefoot on the linoleum floor, staring at him. "What do you want?" she whispered.

"I want you," he said.

"What?"

"Seen you that night and thought, that's the one, yes sir. I never needed to look any more."

"But my father's coming back. He's coming to get me. I had to wash my hair first—" She spoke in a dry, rapid voice, hardly raising it for him to hear.

"No, your Daddy is not coming and yes, you had to wash your hair and you washed it for me. It's nice and shining and all for me, I thank you, sweetheart," he said, with a mock bow, but again he almost lost his balance. He had to bend and adjust his boots. Evidently his feet did not go all the way down; the boots must have been stuffed with something so that he would seem taller. Connie stared out at him and behind him Ellie in the car, who seemed to be looking off toward Connie's right, into nothing. This Ellie said, pulling the words out of the air one after another as if he were just discovering them, "You want me to pull out the phone?"

"Shut your mouth and keep it shut," Arnold Friend said, his face red from bending over or maybe from embarrassment because Connie had seen his boots. "This ain't none of your business."

"What—what are you doing? What do you want?" Connie said. "If I call the police they'll get you, they'll arrest you—"

"Promise was not to come in unless you touch that phone, and I'll keep that promise," he said. He resumed his erect position and tried to force his shoulders back. He sounded like a hero in a movie, declaring something important. He spoke too loudly and it was as if he were speaking to someone behind Connie. "I ain't made plans for coming in that house where I don't belong but just for you to come out to me, the way you should. Don't you know who I am?"

"You're crazy," she whispered. She backed away from the door but did not want to go into another part of the house, as if this would give him permission to come through the door. "What do you . . . You're crazy, you . . ."

"Huh? What're you saying, honey?"

Her eyes darted everywhere in the kitchen. She could not remember what it was, this room.

"This is how it is, honey: you come out and we'll drive away, have a nice ride. But if you don't come out we're gonna wait till your people come home and then they're all going to get it."

"You want that telephone pulled out?" Ellie said. He held the radio away from his ear and grimaced, as if without the radio the air was too much for him.

"I toldja shut up, Ellie," Arnold Friend said, "you're deaf, get a hearing aid, right? Fix yourself up. This little girl's no trouble and's gonna be nice to me, so Ellie keep to yourself, this ain't your date—right? Don't hem in on me. Don't hog. Don't crush. Don't bird dog. Don't trail me," he said in a rapid meaningless voice, as if he were running through all the expressions he'd learned but was no longer sure which one of them was in style, then rushing on to new ones, making them up with his eyes closed, "Don't crawl under my fence, don't squeeze in my chipmunk hole, don't sniff my glue, suck my popsicle, keep your own greasy fingers on yourself!" He shaded his eyes and peered in at Connie, who was backed against the kitchen table. "Don't mind him honey he's just a creep. He's a dope. Right? I'm the boy for you and like I said you come out here nice like a lady and give me your hand, and nobody else gets hurt, I mean, your nice old bald-headed daddy and your mummy and your sister in her high heels. Because listen: why bring them in this?"

"Leave me alone," Connie whispered.

"Hey, you know that old woman down the road, the one with the chickens and stuff—you know her?"

"She's dead!"

"Dead? What? You know her?" Arnold Friend said.

"She's dead—"

"Don't you like her?"

"She's dead—she's—she isn't here any more—"

"But don't you like her, I mean, you got something against her? Some grudge or something?" Then his voice dipped as if he were conscious of a rudeness. He touched the sunglasses perched on top of his head as if to make sure they were still there. "Now you be a good girl."

"What are you going to do?"

"Just two things, or maybe three," Arnold Friend said. "But I promise it won't last long and you'll like me the way you get to like people you're close to. You will. It's all over for you here, so come on out. You don't want your people in any trouble, do you?"

She turned and bumped against a chair or something, hurting her leg, but she ran into the back room and picked up the telephone. Something roared in her ear, a tiny roaring, and she was so sick with fear that she could do nothing but listen to it—the telephone was clammy and very heavy and her fingers groped down to the dial but were too weak to touch it. She began to scream into the phone, into the roaring. She cried out, she cried for her mother, she felt her breath start jerking back and forth in her lungs as if it were something Arnold Friend were stabbing her with again and again with no tenderness. A noisy sorrowful wailing rose all about her and she was locked inside it the way she was locked inside this house.

After a while she could hear again. She was sitting on the floor with her wet back against the wall.

Arnold Friend was saying from the door, "That's a good girl. Put the phone back."

She kicked the phone away from her.

"No, honey. Pick it up. Put it back right."

She picked it up and put it back. The dial tone stopped.

"That's a good girl. Now you come outside."

She was hollow with what had been fear, but what was now just an emptiness. All that screaming had blasted it out of her. She sat, one leg cramped under her, and deep inside her brain was something like a pinpoint of light that kept going and would not let her relax. She thought, I'm not going to see my mother again. She thought, I'm not going to sleep in my bed again. Her bright green blouse was all wet.

Arnold Friend said, in a gentle-loud voice that was like a

stage voice, "The place where you came from ain't there any more, and where you had in mind to go is canceled out. This place you are now—inside your daddy's house—is nothing but a cardboard box I can knock down any time. You know that and always did know it. You hear me?"

She thought, I have got to think. I have to know what to do.

"We'll go out to a nice field, out in the country here where it smells so nice and it's sunny," Arnold Friend said. "I'll have my arms tight around you so you won't need to try to get away and I'll show you what love is like, what it does. The hell with this house! It looks solid all right," he said. He ran a fingernail down the screen and the noise did not make Connie shiver, as it would have the day before. "Now put your hand on your heart, honey. Feel that? That feels solid too but we know better, be nice to me, be sweet like you can because what else is there for a girl like you but to be sweet and pretty and give in?—and get away before her people come back?"

She felt her pounding heart. Her hand seemed to enclose it. She thought for the first time in her life that it was nothing that was hers, that belonged to her, but just a pounding, living thing inside this body that wasn't really hers either.

"You don't want them to get hurt," Arnold Friend went on. "Now get up, honey. Get up all by yourself."

She stood.

"Now turn this way. That's right. Come over here to me—Ellie, put that away, didn't I tell you? You dope. You miserable creepy dope," Arnold Friend said. His words were not angry but only part of an incantation. The incantation was kindly. "Now come out through the kitchen to me honey and let's see a smile, try it, you're a brave sweet little girl and now they're eating corn and hot dogs cooked to bursting over an outdoor fire, and they don't know one thing about you and never did and honey you're better than them because not a one of them would have done this for you."

Connie felt the linoleum under her feet; it was cool. She brushed her hair back out of her eyes. Arnold Friend let go of the post tentatively and opened his arms for her, his elbows pointing in toward each other and his wrists limp, to show that this was an embarrassed embrace and a little mocking, he didn't want to make her self-conscious.

She put out her hand against the screen. She watched herself push the door slowly open as if she were safe back somewhere in the other doorway, watching this body and this head of long hair moving out into the sunlight where Arnold Friend waited.

"My sweet little blue-eyed girl," he said, in a half-sung sigh that had nothing to do with her brown eyes but was taken up just the same by the vast sunlit reaches of the land behind him and on all sides of him, so much land that Connie had never seen before and did not recognize except to know that she was going to it.

DONALD RADCLIFFE

Song of the Simidor

(FROM THE LITERARY REVIEW)

GOD'S BLESSING OF rain would reach even this remote and arid island, the bearded bush priest knew, but he could not help hoping that it would be less precipitous this year than last when the thinly rooted crops were washed down the side of Morne Vidé, the Mountain of Emptiness.

The small bag of grain on the back of the burro might be too late for the growing season this year, depending on the weather. Even worse, his natural generosity had made him distribute more than he should in earlier visits on his island circuit, lost in the Caribbean and forgotten by all but God.

"If only there was more, bourik," the priest said, the burro responding with a lazy flap of the ears. "Fortunate beast, you do not have to stretch His blessings as far as I—a cup of seed corn where there should be a cartful, a tiny medicine kit to cure the mountainside. Oh bourik, I might as well try to budget God's love."

The priest, known along his circuit as Father Jesus, moved up the trail. He became more and more a *père savanne*, father of the fields, in the ageless anonymity of stone wilderness and clay. The figure of the priest took on the protective coloration of the land as he trudged forward in distance, strode backward in time.

Midway up Morne Vidé, the man leading the burro did not so much as startle the kolibri into flight or disturb the timid field mouse. The farms were scattered clearings of leprose land on which the native farmers had scratched scars of a primitive fight for survival against the earth, still parched from the dry season.

The tropical sun fired the clay-colored brush in withered effigy. Forbidding stood the thorny sabliers. The longest shadows were cast by the sacred spiked mapous, but even those tree-giants were being strangled in the death grip of the parasitic liana vines.

The trail rose against his step, but Father Jesus took heart at the sight of a lone farmer who worked the steep-sloping soil with a rope tied to his waist. The rope was anchored, not to the giant sacred mapou, but to the serpentine liana vines.

And Father Jesus could just imagine how that one loved to tell of the time he was hurt falling out of his red bean patch!

"So you see, bourik, the road is not so steep. It is the eyes that become cowards."

The handful of huts called la Misère, last stop on his circuit, was reached just before the sudden eclipse of tropical night. At this height, the arid earth was scarlet-veined as though nourished by the blood of the dark farmers. The tear-shaped village was deserted, but Father Jesus could hear drumbeats from the Vodun ceremony on the mountainside even above the village height.

"Perrault is ever at work," Father Jesus spoke to bourik of the Vodun priest. "No doubt he has undermined much of the work of our last call. The thorn in the flesh that is Perrault will serve to keep us humble."

Though he could point to great gains in the visits of twenty years, he still needed a bridge between himself and the villagers. Ruefully he conceded the truth of a frequent remark of the haughty Perrault:

"Father Jesus, the village is mostly yours, but all of it is mine."

Once in his early eager years in la Misère, Father Jesus had tried to make the villagers choose; he had given them a kindly ultimatum, *la renonce*. The next morning he had found the natives' crucifixes stacked neatly at the door of the church-hut.

But he had learned, and now the villagers attended the church-hut as well as the houmfort. Gradually the Vodun rituals had been moved out of the village to the plateau above. Amulets were seen, but crucifixes were also in view. The sacred and profane were still woven together in the common fabric of a primitive world, but who could demean the achievements under the circumstances?

In dusk Father Jesus cared for bourik, put his own personal effects in order and attended to devotions. In truth his eyes looked beyond, farther up the mountainside, even higher than the plateau reserved for Perrault and the Vodun—up, up to the remote marô country.

The marô country! It was Father Jesus' greatest regret that he had not been able to take the word of God into that untamed region at the very peak of Morne Vidé, so near, yet a world away.

But there were so many scattered miles of clay, so many stops along the way. Time was short. The seasons were capricious as the rains were fickle. Back on the main island, he said each year the marô country was not too far a goal. Once here, he did not deny that to have reached even the height of la Misère, all things considered, was creditable in itself.

So comforted he prepared to sleep. Despite the hard journey, first nights on the rough-woven sisal mat were always restless. The incisive fibers bit into his flesh in unaccustomed places, and bourik never seemed to recognize this stop, even after all his years. The restive burro and the drum-voices of Vodun disturbed the priest far into the night.

Just before dawn he was half-awakened by the incantation of a pleading Creole voice in the clearing at village center. He dismissed it as one carried down from the mountainside. A moment later he was startled awake by the unmistakable swish-swish of rain-wind against the thatched roof.

"Grên! Grên!" Father Jesus gasped. "The seed! The grain!"

He peered out into the eerie-shadowed clearing, to judge the force of the rain against the crop seedlings.

In the clearing, arms upraised, Perrault assaulted the skies. In the glare of lightning, the dark figure loomed larger than life. The rain-wind's response was to beat back, pasting against his skin the black coat and trousers, both ragged. Against the backdrop of night, the figure shrank and faded.

His voice rattled like a ceremonial gourd as the houngan pleaded with his loa: "Legba, Master of the Crossroads ... Simbi of the water ... Put the rest of the rain on the back of the burro by the church-hut and send them all away."

Angry thunder answered his voice. The heavens replied with torrents of rain. Even the self-sure Perrault trembled as he cried out against the impending disaster:

"O Grav! Grav!"

His eyes turned back to the earth. A flash of lightning framed the crucifix hanging above the door of the church-hut. Perrault approached within the reach of Father Jesus, tore loose the crucifix, and raised it to the sky with one hand. With the other, he touched his head, lips and heart in a clumsy, uneasy genuflection.

"Little Jesus," the houngan called, "Son of the Holy Ghost, Blessed Virgin Mary, and Head Bishop, shut down the skies that wash away our crops." A raging deluge interrupted his Christian petition. He paused to plead with Simbi. He called again to the Little One in the bulrushes. Finally he kneeled in the downpouring rain and the fear-shadowed dawn, clutching both a cross and ouanga amulet.

Were it windshift or prayer-answer, the storm abated. A moment of calm passed through the village, long enough for Father Jesus to be heard:

"Perrault!"

The giant Negro arose, holding the crucifix behind his back.

"Father Jesus, welcome return. You find us in trouble with the gods again."

"You are never in trouble with God, Perrault. He will help

us. Bring your people together. We must pray for the crops."

"My need is yours," the houngan conceded. Soon an unseen drum summoned the villagers to the church-hut, but not until it had first asked Legba to open the gates. In a few minutes, a farmer arrived from the sun-struck ridge not far from the village center.

"Honor," Antoine said as he entered.

"Respect," replied Father Jesus.

"Honor," each villager said on arrival.

"Respect," Father Jesus replied to each. Most he could call by name, and the others received an appropriate welcome, for he had marked those in his mind with a little nickname: kòk, whose rooster-walk could be singled out halfway down the mountainside; jij, the self-appointed judge of village ways; ti-satâ, the little devil of ten who always disrupted services; bourik, a worry-stricken old man who carried the burden of the mountain on his back; tété, whose natural endowments were thrust upon his reluctant notice.

He was most cautious that the welcome did not reflect the source.

Even sooner than expected, Ginou from farthest down the mountainside was seen at the edge of the village. He labored under a heavy burden and might have faltered, were it not for his family who followed in a respectful, urging procession. The children shouted ahead excitedly:

"Blâch moun! Blâch moun! A white! A white!"

Altar and candles were overturned in the rush to the door. Ginou forced his way through the crowd and laid a wet, inert figure on the floor before the two priests.

The man, in his forties, was dressed in street clothes far beyond the means of most of the main island. His hands were white, uncalloused and meticulously manicured. His pulse was fleeting; his bruised forehead was hot to touch.

"The bag!" Ginou shouted. "Give us the bag, stupid wench!"

With a defiant toss of her head, the wife of Ginou waited

for the attention of the crowd. Then, with a flourish, she laid a black leather kit down beside the man.

The bag bore the name *Jean Pierre Gide* and a tiny medical insignia.

What mission of mercy, Father Jesus wondered, had brought the good Doctor Gide, whose name in Creole meant to guide, so near to death?

Gide felt the body that had been his poise at a crest of the welling, spongy sea. The grave that had sought him out was not the cold and wormy earth; the tomb of water was buoyant, dry. The body, now as free as the mind, rested at the top of a pulsing upward rush.

Moments or hours before, the doctor in the body had been near escape in the small boat, a breaker away from the island shore. The end of the eyeless flight was a step away. But then, a hand had reached out the miles from the mainland. The boat had wavered, then torn loose from the grasp. On release, the reef was heard tearing, ever so slightly, at the underbelly of the boat, like flesh against knife.

Gide permitted himself curiosity but never fear. He had not called out as the water rose. He had stood motionless, measuring the rise of the draught line with his eyes as the broken boat settled, ever so gently, beneath his feet.

He had not accepted the sinking of the boat as fact until he saw the bag, the improvised provisions and the money spilling into the sea, washing back to the mainland in the fierce undertow. Even to the last, it had not been himself he had tried to save.

Now the upward rush was ended. Body and mind rested at the crest of a black wave, a reach beyond the past, a leap away from the mainland shore. The sea-grave was quiet. This rest was dark and immobile, pleasing but for the vague feeling of one hand being raised.

His mind, demanding orientation, ruled that he was feet-forward and face to sky. But damn reason! He could not drown with one hand raised, and he should not hear that soft voice from the fleeting break in black. It was not scientific!

Safe, he heard the soft voice say.

He shrank from the voice and the purblind figures just out of focus above, contours of a circle of black savages and a strange white man. He would return to the black eddy, but it still carried the cry from the mainland.

The whisper from above: "You're in fever, doctor."

He heard his own voice scream: "The blacks! Get them away!"

The white man replying: "Ginou saved your bag."

The bag! There was comfort there. He felt himself striving to contain this moment of clarity that he knew was prelude to deep shock and fleeting. He found he had achieved a sitting position and was saying: "I can do it."

He saw the needle enter flesh; his eyes shifted from the hair on arm to occult lights to the left of the white man ... candles, of course, flickering ... and to the right of a black, a shimmer of softer light, a cross, of course. He heard himself say: "Oh, you're one of those."

Wide-eyed blacks stared at him, at his hands, the syringe. He dropped it into his lap. Strength resurged, rolling back the arid, swelling sea. He felt the weight of the syringe just before his hands dropped it into the bag.

The circle of figures shuffled back.

He found the strength to hurl the weight of the bag aside.

Startled figures stumbled back. He heard a jabber of crude country Creole from beyond his sight, "The rain is dry." A chant in unison, he heard, "The rain is dry; the rain is dry!" And they were gone.

He clutched at the solitary form. His fingers closed on flesh. The arm was white, then it was gone.

When your enemy's beard is on fire, it is time to wet down your own.

So Perrault crouched in the thicket beneath the breadfruit tree in a look-line to both the church-hut and the hut that housed the new one. The visit of Father Jesus meant no more this year than any other, but that new one, who had caught the look of the village, needed the eye of the houngan.

He was more stooped than crouching; he had no one to hide from or spy on. He who could control the dogged Father Jesus all these years could handle one who was washed up by the sea, whoever he was.

To ease the ache in his bent back, Perrault thought forward an hour to when the shadow of the thorn acacia would reach the step of the church-hut. Then Mister Sun, blinding down at that late afternoon slant, would strike directly into the eyes of anyone leaving the hut that housed the new one. It would be easy to watch then.

Behind him, he heard the voice of the young and ragged villager, Fleury: "Perrault! The chicken that watches the kernel doesn't see the hawk, or is it the other way around?"

"My bent back serves the village better than your gusty tongue, ungrateful youth. I watch the hut that houses the new one who came in from the water so you others can tend your crops."

"The hoe is always left to me, that is true," observed Fleury.

"We both have our work; mine is to find what reason brings him here."

"Was it not to stop the rain? I was one of the first to see that the rain had stopped."

"So why do his cries set fire to the night? His sleep is not as sure as yours."

Fleury moved closer and leaned over so he might whisper in the ear of the houngan: "You have heard Father Jesus speak of a coming-again. Surely we should not chance to offend such an event."

Eyes still in the look-line, Perrault said: "Father Jesus is a good man. He brings seed grain and the good wishes of his gods, but the things of which he speaks were long ago or still yet to be."

"We look first to the houngan," Fleury hastened to assure

him, "but each year we also welcome the père savanne. Why not the new one as well?"

"A devil would take your hand if you held it out. You must learn to trust only your eyes that have seen the père savanne to be a friend and your heart that leaps back to Dahomey."

"The new one is on the tongue of the village though."

"They had best speak of Simbi, who guides the rain and is its master, but for the whim of Erzilie. Trust what you know to be, Fleury. You know which loa live in the trees and the stones, just as you show respect for the cave or waterfall that houses a loa. When you are possessed on the mountainside, your own blood runs back to Guinea."

"At the risk of sin, I must say I have more gods than goods," replied Fleury.

"The dog has four paws, and yet he moves as his heart must go."

"But do I not follow my father's heart? And the heart of his father? Each had but little, and I have less."

Perrault risked standing up, to make a gesture of despair. "Oh, the young, the young, who think they know too much for the old life."

"No, no," replied Fleury. "We fear to know too little for the new."

Out of the fevered wandering of Gide's mind, a single phrase torturously fashioned itself. Born of the need for some simple ordered thought to cling to, the mind had strived to work it out before the body's recovery:

For a man who is used to the best, this thatched hut is indeed strange fare. It seemed profound, and once his mind had worked it out, important. The simple rote of repeating the words brought comfort. To the exclusion of all else, his mind could center on the phrase for hours. *For a man who is used to the best, this thatched hut is strange fare indeed.*

He scorned the weakness that hungered for the phrase, but he thought the words as he choked down the few grains of tasteless gruel offered by the one in the collar who wore none. He nurtured the syntax as he rested on the woven sisal mat that induced nightmares of memory in deeper sleep.

Best . . . strange fare . . .

In the phrase he could find the promise of escape, and even that the money might still be there in the wrecked boat or the sea. Not that there was any earthly use for money here.

And, oh God, he needed comfort, he caught himself thinking, in this alien land, against those enemy eyes. He had ventured no more than a few feet from the hut, but he could see that disease hung in the air, infested the seed corn. The fear of it ate at the very rocks of the land. Even the children, bloated and bony and black, ugly and unappealing, had not the decency to keep out of his sight!

The natives could feed their bellies with boiled plantain, millet, a handful of red beans and their souls on the nocturnal orgy on the mountainside!

"Look at them," he said to the priest. "Why aren't they out working?"

"The fields bake in the sun," answered Father Jesus.

"By whose direction, the mountain or the sky?"

"By the order of the seasons, which you know as well as I."

"But the idleness."

"At the moment there is no work."

"Impossible! I never knew a time when I had no work." Gide shouted out through the door: "Get to work!"

As if at his command, the village center began to empty; in a few moments, the huts were deserted. Gide looked out, not knowing whether to expect the sound of hoes or the breaking through of crops. The lights had dimmed in preface to some primitive nightplay. The stage was set, empty-black.

"It's just the dusk, the coming of dark," observed the priest.

As if in agreement, the mountain came alive, voicing a drum and a call, barely discernible. Of course! The clavilux of nocturnal moods was all in his mind, Gide knew. But later, near sleep, his mind entertained the thought that sounds were coming closer. He spoke sharply to himself, as once he might have reprimanded a frightened patient: "Increased aural acuity, perfectly natural. You're becoming acclimated, that's all."

He said it again, between waking and sleeping, as he sought rest on the sisal mat, after the sounds had invaded the village: "Heightened hearing, perfectly normal."

He said it about the slow maddening drum, the whispered voice two huts away, and the step outside the door. He said it about the beat, beat, beat, echoing out of mind and out of time as he fought to wake himself ... too late, too late, too late ... it beat, beat, beat ... the drum in his mind ... and the nightmare-rage congealed in a memory-web of the mainland, and he woke up screaming: "Butcher! Butcher!"

The muffled cry of the doctor startled Father Jesus from sleep. He forced himself awake. Perhaps the doctor would cry out again, for the heavy breathing was labored. The hut scarcely could contain the breathless echo the doctor could not subdue.

The doctor did not cry out again, and Father Jesus felt justified in permitting himself a moment of annoyance, even anger. After all, he had been understanding, even about the doctor's injuries that were minimal. He had been more than reasonable, even the day before, when Gide had spent the entire day repairing the broken wing of a fallen bird.

Not that any of God's creatures should lack care, but it infuriated him to see Gide waste hours that could be better spent in helping the villagers. The work of a doctor was desperately needed now, and Father Jesus was angry!

"Gide, I need my sleep!"

There was no response, save the mocking resonance of his own words.

"You're faking, Gide. You are awake. You're trembling too."

"You do feel it then," Gide replied at last. "The night, I mean, and the air."

"I am more near despair, at the damage to the work on the island."

"These dry ruins are beyond damage, to my mind. Utter destitution cannot be made more poor."

"You've managed to impoverish the spirit of the village."

"I eat little; I keep to the circle of the hut; I speak to no one but you. How much smaller can I make myself?"

"A cocklebur doesn't depend on its size. In years past when the village went to the mountainside, they left behind only Father Jesus, a friend. Now two white men stay in the village."

As if in emphasis, the cadence of a chorus of drums from the mountain increased. The beat of the drums ebbed and flowed, ebbed and flowed, and for a moment, the two white men seemed to be projected upward, up toward the Vodun plateau, toward the pagan rites and the clear, measured voice of the mambu priestess singing the pure tones of a plaintive chant.

The Creole patois was barely discernible to Gide, because of the distance and dialect, but Father Jesus repeated the words half aloud, as much from memory as from hearing:

> Great Loa, Great Loa, Simbi of the water!
> Maîtresse Erzilie has made a sign to me.
> Will you too make a sign to me?
> O, when will you make a sign to me?

The voice died out. On the echoing wave of silence, the two white men were swept back to reality, back to la Misère, to the night sounds of whirring bats in the trees and the last tired cry of the toco bird.

"Simbi, a water god," Gide said. "That's easy."

"Who sometimes walks as a white," Father Jesus added. "Even many Christian symbols have gotten mixed up in unholy matrimony with Vodun, like Maîtresse Erzilie as the

Blessed Virgin Mary. In some of her aspects, she's the wife of Simbi."

"Superstition and sex orgies. That's what I've heard about voodoo."

"Vodun," the priest corrected him. "A religion as remote to us as the moon it rhymes with, and sometimes, I fear, as far a goal in my work."

"With proper planning, there's a means to every objective. This voodoo is common enough, even back on the mainland."

"Morne Vidé is not the main island, and these rituals are not for tourists. Perrault confides in me a little—professional courtesy, you might say—but there's always a point at which he says the affairs of the sheep are not the business of the goat."

"Or perhaps, like the snake, he feels biggest in his own house."

"Perrault is haughty, but he is cautious too. He would be turned away if he incurred the disfavor of the loa, or if the villagers thought he had."

"In twenty years you've never learned to compete with that witchcraft? I'm surprised at you, Father Jesus. I could do it in twenty minutes."

"Ignorance begets the easy answer."

"It's the only one," Gide countered. "You must work in their terms, talk their language."

"What is the tongue of a hungry man?"

"The empty belly has ears for all."

"I work. I plead. I teach. When the time is right, I have no fear, they will respond."

"But now they hear only the call of a racial heritage?"

"It is that and much more—the legends, the ceremonies, the companionship of the rites—the beauty part of their lives in a drab and downcast land."

"Crutches! They reach for crutches when it's work they need!"

"Even the strong can't stand alone on shifting sand," said the priest.

"A crutch for a crippled people. Kick the crutch out from under them, I say. Make them walk, and they will learn to run."

"Cruel, cruel, cruel," whispered the priest.

"You did not make them cripples," Gide said. "Why should you be kinder than God?"

The next morning Gide awoke to find the usual breakfast pot still warm over a smoldering coal. Dusty gesture, he thought. He wished the priest had put out the fire and left the pot cold or empty. Then at least, he'd have shown the guts of anger.

The sticky gruel was cold before he finished, as he sought to prolong the time in eating. He dressed slowly, straightened up the hut, and an hour later, stepped outside.

He was momentarily blinded by the unaccustomed light. He lowered his line of vision and caught sight of a wild onion plant growing near the path; it had somehow escaped notice by the hungry natives. The odor was strong; the juice was slimy to his touch; he did not risk the taste.

A full belly says the ripe guava is wormy; an empty belly says, "Let me look." Right now, his belly was full enough, but his attention was drawn to the intricate structure of the overlapping layers of tissue.

He sat down on a bench in the shade and began to pick at the plant with his fingers. He lifted off the two outer layers, but the third was more tightly bound. The medical kit, which he must have left near the entrance to the hut, was there at his feet. He reached into the bag and, by feel, found the proper scalpel. He reduced the onion to half its size, with the risk of cell breakage growing at each succeeding stratum. The interweaving was becoming tighter and more intricate, but his own dexterity was increasing.

At last he reached the kernel. The plant had been reduced to its parts, an inedible pile of skins, some wet, others shriveling in the sun. His task finished, he kicked the refuse up against the hut, and faced the empty afternoon.

Lacking other occupation, he now faced an apology to the priest. He realized he should not diminish another in his area of work, the one arena he respected, even in the church-hut.

There, he found Father Jesus and Perrault in earnest conversation. Had the two priests been less agitated, he could have followed their patois more closely. Even so, he was able to garner bits and pieces of meaning from their dispute.

Perrault: "Idle seed, idle hands."

Father Jesus: "Dry land, waste seed."

"Idle hands, useless lands."

"Time for planting is wrong."

"And so the time for going to the church-hut."

Gide, with little interest and no occupation, idly began to examine the projector that illustrated the services. He fingered a box of small colored picture slides, each about the length of a culture plate, and flexible. He flicked one between his fingers.

He had used a similar device in his student years to train his fingers. Back and forth, the slide appeared and disappeared. He found the fingers sluggish. He directed his mind to make the movements fluid; he commanded an adjustment in the response of his hands; he decreed the lead of the line of his eyes.

In a matter of minutes, he could manipulate the slide by the cardboard edge with increasing dexterity. He took another from the box, flicked it rapidly between his fingers, then held it up to the light. Not a fingermark had reached the film! The Blessed Virgin Mary appeared, and disappeared.

Of the two priests, it was Perrault he noticed first, standing silent before him, following the movements of the slide to and from view. On an impulse, Gide said, in his own crude Creole: "Maîtresse Erzilie." He palmed the card. "And now it is not Maîtresse Erzilie."

With another quick motion, he cast the card aside. His

own eyes caught the telltale streak of light that traced its path to the side of the church-hut. When he extended his open hands for inspection, only Father Jesus was there to look. Perrault had fled.

"Blasphemy!" the priest shouted. "Devil! Get out!"

"I was only trying to help. I would have made her reappear to call the village to the church-hut. In another minute, I'd have had the hut filled with worshippers," Gide said, picking up the slide that had lodged against the medical kit in the corner.

"Don't you think I could use cheap theatrics too? You profane a house of God with such abortions of trust."

"Don't use that word! Don't use that word to me!" Gide shouted from the door of the church-hut.

"Not kinder than God. More cruel than man!" the priest shouted after him.

Outside, Gide wandered without purpose through the village. The tropical sun with its narcotic heat brought the blessing of anonymity to all but him. He could not associate the night-worshipping voices from the mountain and these sun-poor savages who planted disease with the urine they spilled in the fields. Simbi of the night could be any of a dozen ragged farmers, struggling with the earth. The mambu Maîtresse might be any of the fat women with a trail of children, struggling with life.

Near the edge of the village, he picked up the pieces of a calabash gourd, lying on the ground like a child's broken toy. Scattered about were a few snake vertebrae that had given the ritual gourd its voice. He bent down to pick one up, and his glance caught a dark object on the ground. It was his own medical kit. The sun and this strange land left nothing to surprise.

But he had no stomach for grotesque games. If the natives expected him to treat them, they were mistaken. He had no intention of midwiving blacks or husbanding the strength of those who could have given him instruction in that. Such a village as this had lived at the brink of epidemic and disaster for generations.

Even now, as he walked, he saw the eyes of the natives, listless. Hoes, abandoned in the fields, lay idle around the perimeter of the village. Machetes, stuck point-down in the earth, rusted. The doctor, without employment, walked past the tiny squares of dry earth.

Good God, the waste of it all!

At the shared hut, there was nothing left to do but turn in. It was too early for sleep, but he could avoid the awkward confrontation with Father Jesus. The sisal mat bit into his flesh with vigor. It was not the discomfort, but the lack of any need for it, that infuriated Gide. Any self-respecting native could make a comfortable bed of banana straw, drought or rainy weather.

But, of course, Father Jesus must have his nightly penance!

Hours later Gide half-awakened from a restless daysleep to hear twilight sounds outside the hut—gossipy farmers released from the soil until dawn, shrill women escaped from the children, young voices free until dark. The sounds were outside his door, miles away; the voices were in the village, a world apart.

Then, at a signal he must have missed, like the simple rising of the moon, soft scuffling footsteps emptied the village. Gide lay back, prepared to feign sleep when the priest returned. He nurtured the rare stillness, the quiet pause. He reached out, hoping to stem the flow of time, not for its passing, but to physically block the onrush of another day. In half-sleep he grasped infinity.

"Simbi ... Simbi ..."

From far away the call whirled into Gide's consciousness. He sat bolt upright and looked out into the village clearing. It was deserted, but for the flickering lights in the church-hut where the reassuring figure of Father Jesus could be seen quietly reading.

Gide crept outside and stood in the brooding darkness,

listening. The drum he awaited was choked off; a black wall of silence confronted him. He did not fear the barrier of death—as a doctor, he had lived with it all his life—but this was void of waste, idleness, doubt and ignorance ... all despicable.

The words from the mountain were now so clear that even his own sketchy Creole served him:

> The boar in the thicket bars the road;
> The boar in the thicket bars the road;
> Seven times I cannot enter.

The plaintive voice that he remembered as that of the mambu Maîtresse invaded the night like a miasmic fog, slowly swept the plateau, clung to the ravines and lingered among the deserted huts. It crept serpentlike into Gide's mind and echoed:

> He will come,
> He will come,
> He will come.

A great lure twisted and writhed before Gide. It was not the pagan lode of Morne Vidé, or the lust of his body, or even the suddenly recurrent memory of the mainland. It was the desperate driving desire to know the true from the false, the sum from the parts, back on the mainland, here in the island huts, and there on the mountain.

How could a man stand not knowing for twenty years?

> He will know,
> He will know,
> He will know.

The startled cries of Father Jesus were lost to his hearing at the edge of the village. That serpent in his mind, the silent drum, pointed the way. At the first step into the darkness, his feet signaled the elevation of the path. Without hesitation he plunged headlong through the corridor that opened up ahead.

He scratched his way up, his fingers touching ground at the steepest sloping points. His feet responded to the side elevation of the worn path at the turns. The beacon in his mind was clear. He never once groped for direction. Only when he burst into the open area was he stopped, and then by the very lack of resistance.

There it was, the ritual clearing. His mind, as his eyes, faltered for a moment at the blurred, occult, and flickering scene. The first object to focus in the dim light was the silhouette shape of a huge mountain goat hanging grotesquely from a tree at his right. Singly, other objects defined themselves, a light as a lamp, a cross as a primitive wooden altar. The dominant circular sweep of light resolved itself as a ring of white-hooded figures. Perrault, the only one he recognized, restrained two subpriests who held back the wild tusked boar. The tableau was stopped in time.

Then Gide saw her, outside the circle at the edge of darkness, a young quadroon with a rare strain of bloodline that gave her skin a golden tone. He could not say if she was real, so motionless she stood, dressed in majestic white. Even at that distance, though, he could see that the hem of one sleeve showed wear.

He became aware of the antiphonal chant of the voices and drum now breathing life into the dormant air. How long had it been stilled before his arrival? When was this stage last alive? Was it real even now?

Yes, the sounds could invade the mind. The scene could seize the senses. The nails of his clenched fists broke flesh. Therefore, the girl was real. So, too, the voice of Perrault: "Erzilie, Erzilie, make a vêvé for me!"

From the perimeter of the circle that now enclosed him, Gide heard the voice of the girl respond:

> The cock lies in its sacrifice,
> The goat hangs high in the mapou.
> My spirit is still disunited;
> Simbi must call to me.

"Erzilie, Erzilie, will you make a vévé for me?" The voice of Perrault was pleading.

> The boar in the thicket bars the road,
> And Legba alone cannot prevail;
> It is Simbi must summon me.

Perrault's body seemed to atrophy and collapse in a death-montage. Gide read in his eyes the flight of his soul. The plea denied, the struggle was over. The broken Perrault moved toward oblivion. With a last look to the girl, he broke through to the edge of his world.

Toward the fleeing figure, Gide called out: "Perrault!" And to the girl: "Maîtresse!" And by the sound of the name, the voices and drum were strangled.

Born of the silence, or in response to the name, there appeared in the circle of flickering lights an Afro-Indian figure of white-clothed bronze. Maîtresse or Mary, Madonna or Erzilie, she moved in tempo with a slow, raspy calabash gourd from beyond his hearing. Or did she glide so slowly to control the broken seam of her robe?

From an altar she carried a bowl of white flour. Her slender legs and bare, expressive feet carried her to within a step of Gide. From her fingers trickled a fine stream of flour, but it was the youth of the girl that held his attention.

"The vévé, the vévé, look to the vévé," the chorus directed him.

Gide's gaze freed itself from the grace of the girl; he saw she had traced on the ground a design of striking beauty. If it was phallic, he would not have known. If it was sterile, he would not have cared. If it was a call, he could not have answered, for how could he know what was expected?

What was his role, his mind demanded to know, *and was she real?* This, at least, he could determine. He reached out and grasped the girl by the wrist. There was flesh and pulse, regular and measured. She neither resisted nor advanced. She gave no sign that she noticed, but the gesture brought life to the voices and drum.

The lambent lights flared up; white-robed figures defined themselves; shadows fought for survival against the light. The abrasive voice of the ceremonial gourd was racing the drumbeat to the ear. The chanting chorus must have shouted alarm, but it was the surge of the blood beneath his fingers that warned him that the boar had been released an instant earlier.

"Maîtresse!"

Had his voice startled her, or was it the split second she had taken to free her wrist from his grasp that delayed the motion toward the knife in the folds of her dress? Or, he would always wonder, had she even tried to avoid the charging animal?

The boar raced through the circle and into the darkness as the young Maîtresse crumpled to the ground. Gide was at her side in an instant. Mainland or la Misère, he was conscious only of the body before him and the torn flesh. The blood was real, the blood was red, and it spurted from the wound. With a swift, reflexive motion he opened his medical kit that had been dropped at his side. Without looking up, he surveyed the trauma; within seconds, he had controlled the bleeding; soon he had closed the wound.

The young girl lay quiet and still, the hemorrhage stopped. Now that he felt certain he had done all he could, the doctor rested. He granted himself a feeling of pride in the work; he admitted relief that the skill in his hands had not atrophied.

Around him, the natives stood erect like stringed puppets and as obscure. They stared fixedly at the doctor as he crouched beside the girl Maîtresse. For the moment, they seemed to demand no more of him, but he wondered, was the price of Perrault's life the birth of his own or its death?

In posing the question to himself, his own certainty failed him, and instinctively he felt her pulse.

She was alive. She was alive.

"I've done all I can! I've done all I can!"

His voice rang across the plateau, echoed down the mountainside, and died out in the valleys far below. The faces around him were still fixed and expressionless, revealing nothing. They stood like cataleptics, in the immobile and timeless tropic night, waiting for her to live, or die.

The meaning of the grim masque was yet to be revealed, but the stoic masks could not conceal the clutch of starvation, the scars of the yaws, the fevers of malaria. Back on the mainland, he had seen the same symptoms, disease, decline. He had treated the same scars, fevers, sores. He remembered them clearly as faceless studies in a medical text.

His glance fell on an old woman, a withered vine hovering in a dark shadow of the clearing. He felt an uncommon sympathy, then excitement. Here was clearly a case of degenerative cachexia, of a type never seen back on the mainland.

"Vié-fâm!" he called. "Old woman!"

She took a step in his direction. Then she hesitated, framed in the transient light. She could not survive the summer, but it was not out of fear that she stepped back, vanishing into the shadows. Here was one who had less to fear from death than life. The last trace of her presence was the residual image of the look in her eyes, a look he had acknowledged but once before ...

... back on the mainland, in the eyes of the somber-skinned girl who had come to his office that day, weeks before. As always, he had glanced up to note the patient's entering posture. He had seen only her beauty.

He did not permit distraction, and immediately he directed his attention to the girl as a patient. There was no time for conjecture beyond the medical implications. He did treat them competently, for he could not ask less of himself. He never asked less of himself than he demanded of others, and his own.

He caught himself wondering if she might be of the elite, but one never could be sure. It was common to hear: "A rich Negro is a mulatto, but a poor mulatto is a Negro." It was clear that she was no burden-laden, child-worn peasant, to this point at least.

When he directed his eyes to those of the girl, it was her look that was searching. She had never been in his office before, but she took command with her first step inside. It was he who turned away. Mute for the moment, he stood at the window, looking away. His mind raced on, silently screaming: *Say it! Say it!*

She spoke, in her own good time: "We loved."

He had feared most those simple words. Now he pretended not to have heard.

"But we did love," she insisted.

"Like animals," he shouted.

"As man, as woman."

"The whole city knows I never do what you will ask."

"This time you must. This one time, you will."

He found that impulsively he had reached for the telephone.

"He will tell you it is true," she said.

"He must tell me it is false. He must!" But the words were hollow in his own ears. He dropped the telephone back in its holder. "If it were not true, he would be here," he admitted, more to himself than to the girl.

In silence, he stood at the window for several minutes. My child is the child of your blood, she had meant, the child of the sin of your son ... the sin he could condone in anyone else, but never forgive in his own ... the son he had raised himself, without the courage to come with her ... the one *he* had raised, a *coward!* ...

But the decision was not yet made. There were ways out, at least for a white doctor of prominence. He turned to face the girl.

"There are practitioners who are expert in what you ask. Why come to me?"

"You and I are thrown together in silence. My father would kill me if he knew it was a white."

He had no reason to doubt her word, and what she asked was simple enough. Any butcher could do it. He could be done with it in a matter of minutes, the girl in a matter of hours, and his son forever. If it be wrong, he scorned weakness as much.

He commanded his hand be steady. He demanded his mind be sharp. He brought every nerve to bear, and he was ready. In a matter of minutes, he could put back in place the disorder to his life, put out the memory of his son, and ease the burden of the girl and her family. A life in the hands of the doctor was nothing new to him.

But a death? Even before he could start, the tremor was in his fingers. Even before he began, the image was in his mind, born in some dark nidus of the soul. The embryo blood of his own making was darkly growing.

In the mere consent of the act, he had held his life up to the light. The shimmer of the flaw caught his eye, and now it was blinding. The glow of paste burned in his mind.

In flight, the strong outrun the weak.

* * *

After three days Father Jesus sought to fulfill his duty to the missing doctor. Back on the main island, he would have considered the service perfunctory at best, but here it would have to do. At least, he had been able to ask forgiveness for Gide, despite the damage to God's work on the island.

Even so, Father Jesus could not entirely suppress a feeling of satisfaction at the justice of this simple island world. He was sincere in his prayers for Gide, but he was never more sure that God's ways were wise. Justice, to be complete, must be final, and surely no alien white could long survive the mountainside wilderness above.

Now Father Jesus began to prepare himself for disappointment. The *diablerie* of the doctor would not be lost on the village, even after his disappeareance. Despair was not new, and he was ready.

Strangely enough, when his spirits were lowest, the natives returned to the church-hut. When he least expected a miracle, even of a minor order, the entire village turned out, explaining that it was clearly the wish of the blâch loa.

Father Jesus was pleased that they had returned, but it was disquieting that they could still confuse his role after all these years. If only they would accept him for what he was, a humble bush priest. However, only a fool throws stones into his own bed, and for the time being, he chose not to labor the point.

And the village, too, was better blessed. There were more able-bodied men in the fields. The malarial epidemic began to subside. The marks of the yaws were seen less frequently. For the first time in years, there might be a harvest worthy of the name. This was truly a village of hope regained. La Misère was becoming la Renet.

Each morning more men left the village for the long day in the fields. Each evening they returned exhausted, but one scant step closer to survival. Each evening at vespers they all thanked God, and rightly so, but Father Jesus admitted that even He was not entirely without help.

A man might say to his wife: "The grove is distant, and I can see from here that the mango is green."

"It will be sweet when the work is done," she would reply and hand him a hoe, with authority.

True, the rituals of Vodun flourished as well. If only Perrault would return, he would know how much. Now he realized how he had depended on the houngan who, even now, could make the work more fruitful and easier too.

Meanwhile, he was busy. There were services to be arranged, families to be visited, and workers to be helped in the fields. He visited the sick, his greatest concern.

He did stay behind when the natives gathered in a coumbite to work the fields of those unable to work. He felt a stranger to the special intimacy of the coumbite, just as he could not have intruded on a Vodun rite. He did, however, take pains to indicate his own approval of the coumbite.

Better help your neighbor than go to pray in Guinea, was often said of the coumbite.

The work of the coumbite was directed by the simidor, who led the songs that gave the beat to the hoes. The songs were sparked by the mood of the moment, most often commenting on the friendly rivalry between competing teams of workers. Or again, the refrain might bear the stamp of gossip, and then an affair that was guessed at was as good as a fact. Sometimes the songs were laced with logic, telling the sad story of the brilliant chicken that argued down the stupid hawk.

One day the coumbite was so close to the village that Father Jesus could hear the words of the workers distinctly:

> The simidor's work is leading the way,
> And that is enough, enough for all.

Father Jesus was startled by the answering voice of the simidor:

> The simidor is a worker too,
> And he must strike the hardest blow.

The traditional role of the simidor as song-leader and spectator to the work had been altered by those few words. The fierce pride in the voice of the simidor was accented by the dull, determined thud of hoes against the earth.

At that moment, Father Jesus knew the time for leaving had come. In his years on the mountain he had learned patience and the fact that there was a time to stand aside and wait. He packed the few belongings on the back of the burro and, with the song of the simidor still ringing in his ears, left the austere and ageless la Misère.

He made his way slowly down the twisting trail through

the giant mapous, sacred trees of the Vodun, and the forbidding thorny sabliers. The fertile outlying fields that clung to the face of the mountain were a testament of the faith of the farmers. The burning sun that beat down could only hasten the harvest now.

Halfway down he encountered one of God's toads, blinking placidly in the heat, in the middle of the path. Though the chances were few that bourik might step on the tiny beast, Father Jesus held back the burro until, with his foot, he could gently nudge the puffy creature to the side of the path.

Soon the land began to lose its lenten look. A sudden red sea of immortelle blooms sprang out from a twist in the road. The bougainvillea vines reddening the roadside and the burst white puffs of the mapou pods lent an air of fleshiness to the land never seen in la Misère.

For a moment he chided himself for being reminded of the relative luxury of the main island, but knowing that comfort delayed was pleasure enhanced, he permitted the burro to make the rest of the trip at a leisurely pace.

Too soon he caught sight of krabié, the crabfisher, carrying food to his nest under the watchful eye of malfini, the hawk. At a narrow bend in the road, two peasants wrangled, with great satisfaction, over priority of passage. The road was soon crowded with carts, people, and dogs. He found he had to caution himself against annoyance at the press of bodies and obstructions in his way.

At the base of the mountain, he returned the borrowed burro to the stable of his owner. It was but a short walk to the improvised pier where, in time, the small boat arrived on its capricious schedule. First to step ashore were two jâdams of the main island police.

Lapolis might have arrived on this island a month before or a year later. Like water against earth, they could be expected to reach every level in their own time, but it could never be certain where sand would be found or rock.

Father Jesus stepped forward to broach the subject of the

missing doctor, for he was sure the interest of the police in Gide's destiny was as real as his own.

"Oh, so much trouble he causes us," the first jâdam complained, squinting in the sun so that his eyes were like scars.

The second and junior officer was round-eyed and wondered: "With the richest of patients and the best of life, why would he run away?"

Father Jesus did not wish to appear idly curious, but before they could be separated, he must resolve one question: "Was the doctor charged with crime?"

"No, but he has influential patients who insist he be found," the scar-eyed one replied.

The junior jâdam tucked in the uniform shirt that was continually rejected by his billowy waist and conceded: "It is much trouble, but at least the search is more pleasant duty than most back on the main island."

The senior jâdam relaxed a bit, and his face eased at the prospect of an open search throughout the islands. "Yes," he said, "it could take a long time to locate the good doctor."

Father Jesus could see that they must be told. Gide's presence and disappearance near la Misère was no longer his responsibility alone. The fingers of petit officialdom necessarily must now reach into both their lives.

He spoke as forthrightly as he knew how, but both jâdams stood looking away. He wondered if they were even interested. Clearly the two officers were not yet eager to encounter the facts; even less were they prepared to challenge the rigors of the climb up Morne Vidé.

Suddenly the one with big eyes brightened: "Father, you really only saw him disappear from the village. Now, presuming that he is still up there, would you not say that he has surely departed his life by now?"

"I doubt that any white man could survive alone on that mountain," Father Jesus conceded. "Without native help, at least."

Now even the squinter saw the light of reason: "And if he

were to be found alive, which is our mission, it could not be on the mountainside. If he lives as of this day, he must have made his way down to the sea or on to some other island."

The junior officer risked taking the arm of his senior and said: "You are correct. It is better that we search for a live doctor on the islands than a deceased one on the mountain."

"Let us begin with this pleasant beach then," said the senior one, and they were off arm-in-arm, with the eagerness of young men in search of a career, in a lateral direction along the island base. The last words to reach Father Jesus might have been shouted by either one: "Be assured, Father, we will add your words to our report!"

Perhaps it was as well they were gone. He could not have argued further, for he had only time to step aboard the boat as it moved away from the shadow of Morne Vidé. The voyage was short, and it was his custom to stand at the railing, exalt the clear blue sky and bask in the work completed. For twenty crossings the balm of quiet sea between the islands had capped the achievements of a circuit made.

This trip the new captain had chosen the safer course in the deepest channel, but an unexpected current rolled the craft awkwardly in the running sea. By the time the boat was turned into the wind, she had lost much of her dignity. Wet to his knees, Father Jesus could see far to his right a tiny koralê, built for the reefs, skim impudently in and out among the rocks, mocking the larger boat.

At least the task of locating dry shoes would give him time to work out in his mind just the right way to ask that someone else be assigned to la Misère next year.

He must be fully prepared to meet the objections that would be raised. He could show that even a younger man might work out, for life in la Misère was always easier after a good harvest. He could argue that the new père savanne would need fewer farming and medical skills than those demanded of him. He had broken the ground, so the young one would never even know what a bush priest had faced, especially in the early years.

Father Jesus had made up his mind. At that very moment, he began to plan the next year's work in the marô country, already too long deferred. The mere anticipation of goals waiting to be achieved up there made him wish the boat could be turned back toward Morne Vidé. That, of course, was not possible, and so resolved, his mind was at rest with the sea. A longer, more leisurely trip would not have been unwelcome, but already the main island loomed ahead.

Along the rail toward the stern, a boisterous worker had begun to sing, with embarrassing abandon. Almost against his will, Father Jesus smiled in the man's direction. He was dressed in work clothes, but his occupation was not readily apparent. He seemed to be at home with the sea, but a fisherman would have sailed his own small boat. He could not have been a farmer, for there was no escape from the fields at this season. Nor did his clothing show the markings of a lime pit.

Most likely he was a worker on a sugar or sisal plantation, Father Jesus concluded. Perhaps he was between jobs, or he might be going to or returning from a family emergency on one of the islands, a birth or death perhaps.

But sing he did, full-throated as the boar at bay or the hawk in flight and in a voice that would do credit to bourik:

> O, my troubles will be through when I have a horse;
> O, I'll sure thank God if He sends me a horse;
> O, I'll make God a present but I'll need a dog
> To call that horse so my troubles are through.
>
> O, I'll make God a present if He sends me that dog;
> O, I'll sure thank God but I'll need a cat
> To wake the dog that calls the horse
> That He sends me so my troubles are through.
>
> O, I'll make God a present if He sends me that cat;
> O, I'll sure thank God but I'll need a tree

To save the cat that wakes the dog
That calls the horse that He sends me
So my troubles are through.

O, I'll make God a present if He sends me that tree,
O, I'll sure thank God but I'll need rain
To grow the tree that saves the cat
That wakes the dog that calls the horse
That He sends me so my troubles are through.

O

But if He sends rain my house will leak;
My wife will talk, and talk, and talk,
And talk, and talk, and talk, and talk,
Till I fix that leak or the sun comes out,
Or I make God a present so the rain will stop.

So, if He wants a present, He'll keep that horse,
O, if He wants a present, He'll keep that horse
And the dog and the cat and the tree and rain
And the talk of my wife so my troubles are through.

HENRY ROTH

The Surveyor

(FROM THE NEW YORKER)

IT WAS WITH an air of suppressed excitement that the slight, middle-aged man with the unruly gray hair put down the box he was carrying, snapped open a tripod, and drew out of the box a small surveyor's transit. He swiftly mounted the transit on the tripod. He seemed to work as though he were doing something he was not thoroughly practiced at but something he had rehearsed, adjusting the legs of the tripod and the leveling screws with a certain nervous haste. A short few minutes ago, he and the woman who accompanied him had gotten out of a taxi with their equipment. He had paid the driver and had led the way at once to the spot they were now on. This, too, he had done with an assurance that indicated the location had been decided on beforehand. In a little while, he had the transit leveled to his own satisfaction and was steadying the plumb bob beneath. The woman, who was also middle-aged, but taller and more slender than the man, with a gentle face and a high forehead, was carrying a telescoped leveling rod, which she now extended part way.

They were on the west walk of the short, very wide Avenida del Cid, in Seville, and the man had set up his transit in the middle of the entrance to the Fábrica de Tabacos, a huge, gray edifice, rising only two stories high but sprawling out immensely in length and width. Cigarettes had once been manufactured there; now the building housed the University of Seville. On both sides of the surveyor and his assistant stretched a low stone wall that fronted a deep, wide, waterless moat, overgrown with grass, which ran parallel to the façade of the Fábrica de Tabacos behind them.

"The exact center of the gate. Right?" asked the man, straightening up and adjusting his spectacles. The woman nodded. She seemed more self-possessed than he, not so much because she was under less strain as by temperament. The man drew out of his jacket pocket a small notebook. "No, I don't need that now," he muttered, and thrust the notebook back into his pocket impatiently. "The tape. No, the rod. You've got the work to do."

"I'm ready," she said.

"OK. You pace off about fifty steps along the wall," he said. "When you've gone that far, just turn around. Keep snug to the wall."

Obediently, the woman walked away from him with steady, measured stride, holding the leveling rod as she went. She stopped, turned, and planted the foot of the rod on the ground.

"OK. Now hold it up so I can sight it." She held the leveling rod erect; he swung the transit around rapidly, sighted through the telescope, and began making adjustments. "Lean the stick toward me. Good. Hold it there. Right there. OK. Now come back." Swiftly, he drew out his notebook, leaned over the protractor of the instrument, and jotted down some numbers. The woman, holding the leveling rod upright before her like a staff, came back to join him.

About them, a Sunday morning quiet prevailed. Most of Seville had probably not arisen, and the Avenida del Cid was almost empty of people. Few automobiles or buses were in sight. At one end of the wide avenue was the *glorieta*, or traffic circle, of Don Juan de Austria, where the waters of a large fountain glinted intricately in the morning sunlight as they played from periphery to center and splashed from basin to basin. A short distance beyond the *glorieta* a large radial crane stood like a red, ungainly cross in the midst of new government buildings under construction. At the other end of the Avenida was the *glorieta* of San Diego, an open space encompassed by the María Luisa Park and buildings left over from the Spanish-American Exposition of the nineteen-twenties. Trees lined the Avenida, and a number of streets entered the *glorietas* from different directions. Dominating all this was the central figure of the area, the monumental equestrian statue of El Cid Campeador, semi-legendary hero out of eleventh-century Spain. Horse and rider were poised on a massive granite pedestal that stood in the middle of an oval traffic island on the Avenida. Around the base of the pedestal, there were flower beds surrounded by grass and filled with plants no longer in bloom. High above, El Cid stood in his stirrups and brandished his bannered spear. There was no mistaking what the bronze statue was meant to portray: Spain's martial valor and audacity, the prowess that had rewon the peninsula from the Moors and later subjugated a new world.

There were one or two people waiting for buses at various *paradas* along the Avenida. All of them by now were watching the activities of the surveyor and his assistant. A man walking by, the lone stroller on their side of the avenue, stopped to stare with unabashed curiosity.

"*Buenos días,*" he said

"*Buenos días,*" said the surveyor shortly. "Now begins the tough job, Mary. You cross. I'll compute the angle."

A woman with a leveling rod crossing a thoroughfare would have been a strange sight anywhere, and Seville on Sunday morning was hardly an exception. A man left one of the *paradas* and sauntered over. A couple of strollers across the street changed course and directed their steps toward the surveying operations. A cyclist teetered on his wheel a moment without making any forward progress, then dismounted and brought his bicycle up over the curb. The tall, particolored staff seemed to be attracting people from a greater and greater distance.

Ignoring all this, the man at the transit worked intently at his computation, swung the instrument in the direction of the woman, who was now standing on the traffic island below the statue of El Cid, and began adjusting the vernier. "A little to the left, Mary," he called. "About two short steps."

"*Qué es esto, señor?*" inquired a young man in the white shirt and tie of Sunday.

"*Un momento.* Mary, a little more left!" he shouted to the woman across the street. "*Por favor, señor,* do me the favor of standing to one side." The surveyor immediately crouched before his instrument. His spectacles had apparently fogged. He snatched them off. "A little more," he directed. He looked up from the telescope. "Where are you? Good! Mark it right there." The woman crayoned a cross at the base of the leveling rod. "Come on back," he called. "I can't leave the transit."

"*Fotógrafo?*" a woman in black asked him.

"*No, no,*" he replied. "*Agrimensor.*"

"*Por qué? Es extranjero,*" she said. The man shrugged his shoulders.

"*Señor.*" One of the bystanders, a man in a Basque beret, came forward. "*Qué está usted haciendo?*"

"Measurements," the surveyor replied in Spanish. His assistant was approaching. "OK. I'll take it," he said to her, and stepped forward to relieve her of the leveling rod. "Now," he said grimly, handing her the tape. "Fifty-six and three-fourths meters."

"Yes, I know the number. Don't get rattled, Aaron." She was already backing away from him, unreeling the tape, one end of which he continued to hold.

He laid the leveling rod down, hurried back with his end of the tape to the transit, and knelt at the plumb bob beneath it. "Are you there, Mary?" he called.

The tape was now across the highway, and the woman had reached the traffic island and was aligning the tape with the mark she had previously made. The bystanders' wonder increased, and so did their numbers. Newcomers began to ply those already there with questions. "*Ingleses? ... Me parecen americanos ... Qué hacen?*"

"A car!" The woman's warning cry came from across the Avenida.

"Lower the tape!" the surveyor yelled from his stooped position. "Lower the tape, Mary. Wave him on!"

The woman, at her end of the tape, smiled pleadingly at the driver of a small Seat that had stopped before the narrow ribbon of metal. *"Por favor! Pase, por favor!"* The driver proceeded reluctantly.

"Where are you?" said the man at the plumb bob.

"Fifty-five and one-half!"

"It has to be fifty-six and three-quarters!"

"That's the flower bed!"

"Oh, hell! Note the number! Mark the edge!" The woman quickly made a cross where the pavement of the traffic oval met the grass border of the flower bed. With one accord, they arose, the woman reeling in the tape, the man walking toward her. "Did you have the tape tight?" he asked her. He was perspiring.

"Yes. I made two marks, one behind the other."

"Wonderful," he said, a little breathlessly. "There. Let's scoot out of here." He had already taken the reel from her, and was winding in the ribbon of tape with a rapidity that made it writhe and slither on the ground. He shoved the reel into his pocket. "Telescope the rod. I'll dismantle."

With the small crowd still watching them, as puzzled as ever, the pair packed their equipment, and in a few minutes they carried it to the curb. "Taxi!" the man called, and waved.

The driver of a cab going by on the other side of the traffic island waved back, circled about the oval, and came their way. The surveyor swung the transit box into the cab as soon as it came to a stop. The driver, who appeared to be accustomed to the strange ways of tourists, got out and helped him mount tripod and leveling rod on the carrier above the cab. "Hotel Inglaterra, *por favor*," said the surveyor, and then, settling in his seat, whistled with relief. "I wasn't any too soon, you know."

"Why?" the woman asked.

"Look back. I think you can still see him."

At one of the corners of the Glorieta de San Diego stood a gray-clad member of Spain's Policía Armada.

"What rashness!" Aaron Stigman reflected aloud as he and his wife approached the Avenida del Cid once more, this time on foot. "Why didn't I pace it off and let it go at that? No, I had to find the very spot. As rash as anything I've ever done. Was it my passion for accuracy, do you think? Or am I turning into an absurd old man?"

"No, I just think it's Seville," she replied.

"Why?" He was carrying a raincoat over his arm, and reached under the coat to adjust something beneath it.

"Too many cathedrals, too many *retablos,* stained-glass windows, saints, crucifixes, Virgins—Virgins! Even a Protestant mind like mine rebels at it." She laughed. "It's just too much."

"Yes, too many martyrs of their faith. None for mine—or what used to be mine. Why shouldn't there be some acknowledgment?"

"Well, of course, Aaron. That's why I approved."

It was now about two hours later, and the Avenida del Cid presented a livelier appearance. Amorous couples, the young man's hand often resting in Spanish fashion on his sweetheart's shoulder, strolled along in and out of the shade of the acacias. Short, robust infantrymen in their coarse khaki uniforms mingled with sober Sevillians returning from Mass. On one corner, before the Fábrica de Tabacos, a street vendor had opened his little stand and was arranging his candy and loose cigarettes. Tourists in a yellow-wheeled, horse-drawn cab gazed diffidently about while the coachman leaned sideways to comment on points of interest. Three tall, obviously Scandinavian youths, their bare heads shining like brass in the Sevillian sunlight, turned the dark heads of the Spanish *señoritas* who passed them. All the *paradas* on the Avenida now had their queues of people waiting for the bus.

Traffic moved in all directions to and from the *glorietas;* jaunty little Seats droned along, interspersed with buzzing scooters and suddenly outdistanced by snarling motorcycles. From his traffic island in the midst of all this, the monumental El Cid still stood in his stirrups, brandishing his bronze spear.

"I'm sure no one will notice," said Stigman as they waited at the curb.

"I'm sure no one will."

"I could have triangulated it to be absolutely certain, but I guess one measurement was enough. All we had time for." He took his wife's arm. "We can cross now."

"I was only afraid the measurement would end at that catch basin over there."

"Oh, no! What a grisly thought! And yet you know they *have* found bones in the most unlikely places. Anybody watching?" They had reached the traffic island and were standing by the marks his wife had made on the pavement earlier.

"No, I don't see anyone," she said.

"I'll just lay it here. All right?" He had stepped over the grass as far as the flower bed. "OK?"

"OK."

He took a small wreath of fern and boxwood from beneath the raincoat over his arm and placed it on the flower bed. "There! I've done it." He stepped back to the pavement. "A little tribute where it was due. It's scant enough, isn't it?"

"I'm surprised how much I feel about it, Aaron. I didn't think I would."

"Yes?" He stood looking at the flower bed. "What kind of flowers are those?"

"Canna lilies, I think. They've been cut."

"Canna lilies—I don't know them." There was an expression of contemplative sadness on his face. "The gardener or somebody will find a wreath here and wonder why. He'll probably move it to El Cid, but there's nothing I can do about it. There's little one can do against oblivion, anyway." He was silent. "And now?" He finally turned toward his wife. "Where shall we go now?"

"Anywhere. María Luisa Park?"

"All right. Let's find a bench there and sit down."

They skirted the base of the monument—and saw, walking toward them, a gray-clad policeman. He still had a few steps to go before he reached them. *"Buenos días, señores,"* he said, and saluted.

"Buenos días," said Stigman.

"Are you by any chance the same English couple who were seen surveying here this morning?"

"We are Americans, not English," said Stigman, speaking in Spanish. "But we were surveying."

"In that case, I have a few questions to ask you."

"Yes?"

"I am sure you can answer them easily. Can you explain why you were surveying?"

"Yes. I was attempting to locate a spot of some sentimental value to myself," said Stigman. "A place no longer shown on the maps of Seville."

"What place is that, *señor?*" The policeman was a stalwart figure. Gray hair showed under his scarlet-ribboned military cap. The skin of his large face was pink, as though freshly shaven. His competence and good judgment were manifest.

"It is a—well, I would rather not say. It is a private matter."

"Señor, surveying in public places among public establishments is no private matter. I could point out further that you laid a measuring tape across a highway, impeding traffic—"

"It was only for a minute."

"A minute is enough for an accident. You attracted a crowd."

"I could not very well help that."

"No, but these are not private matters. Do you have a permit from the proper authority to do this kind of work?"

"I did not know I needed one," said Stigman.

"It is customary to have a permit from the proper authority to avoid difficulties such as those I have just mentioned. However, you are a tourist, and sometimes we overlook what tourists do. But what is this surveying about?"

"Well . . ." Stigman took a deep breath. "I said I tried to locate a place of some sentimental value to myself. I had no other reason for doing so. In fact, I have just laid a wreath over there."

"A wreath?" The policeman turned and looked at the flower bed.

"Yes. Do you want me to remove it?"

"Naturally. I would like to see it." All three of them moved toward the flower bed. Stigman picked up the wreath and showed it to the policeman, whose face gave every indication of extreme perplexity. *"Señor,* you realize that you have not yet explained yourself."

"I have tried to."

"But what you have told me is no explanation. I have asked you what the surveying was about."

"I have already told you what the surveying was about. What explanation do you want me to make?"

"Aaron . . ." his wife cautioned.

"No, I haven't anything more to say to him." Stigman reverted to English. "I told him all I could. What does he want?"

The policeman showed signs of impatience. *"Señor,* once more, will you explain what you were doing?"

"I have already told you what I was doing."

"You have told me nothing. Nothing I can understand."

"That is not my fault!"

"Señor!" The policeman raised the hand that held his gloves. "Please accompany me."

"What for?" Stigman braced his legs against the ground.

"There are too many private matters involved here. Too many things that need explanation. This way, *por favor.* The *señora* too."

"Well, for God's sake," Stigman said, looking bleakly at his wife.

They crossed the Avenida to the low wall before the Fábrica de Tabacos, and there the policeman turned to lead the way toward Menéndez Pelayo, the main thoroughfare. Two monks who were at that moment striding toward them, vigorous, bearded young men with bare feet in sandals and white cord about brown robes, noted the wreath in Stigman's hand and looked at the trio alertly. It was evident they thought the policeman was escorting two tourists bent on a commemorative act. And so others appeared to think—those they met strolling along the Paseo, and those sitting among the colored tables and chairs of the outdoor cafés. Street photographers arranging their miniature horses and black bulls nodded in deference, and a chestnut vendor halted his stirring of the chestnuts to peer at the wreath through the white smoke. Between the traffic and the wall—between the rumbling of vehicles on Menéndez Pelayo, reverberating against stucco buildings and store fronts across the street, and the ancient wall of the Alcázar deploying its series of pyramidal caps—the three passed the double pillars of the monument to Columbus and drew near the orange trees of the Jardines de Murillo. In the distance, above the Cathedral, the weather vane Giralda, frail and diaphanous against the blue sky, seemed to accompany them as they walked. Stigman glanced at his wife as if seeking reassurance. With parted lips, she seemed to be drinking in the scene. She seemed to be enjoying it.

There were two men behind the railing in the drab *comisaría*, one man at the desk and one standing. The man at the desk wore a blue sweater and large tinted glasses. His head tapered, and this, together with the large glasses and his heavy torso in its dark sweater, gave him a froglike appearance. There was a touch of the forbidding about him. The man standing wore a business suit and a white shirt. He was uncommonly tall for a Spaniard, and the way he stood, in a stooped, hollow fashion, was even more uncommon. Under thick, iron-gray hair, his features seemed to wince, as if his face were too close to a hot fire. Behind the two men hung a fading portrait of Francisco Franco, in which the Caudillo looked out at the newcomers with benign eyes. Below the portrait, a large map of the district was tacked up. A ring of heavy ancient keys on one wall had scored an arc in the plaster; on the opposite wall, the hands of a new electric clock neared noon. The two men on the other side of the barrier stopped talking.

"*Buenos días*," said Stigman mechanically. His wife repeated the salutation.

"*Buenos días*," the two men before them replied.

The policeman saluted the man at the desk. "Señor Inspector," he began. "On two occasions today, I was at the Glorieta de San Diego when I saw this gentleman and his wife doing what seemed to me very strange things. On the first occasion, they left in a taxi before I had an opportunity to question them."

The two men behind the railing regarded Stigman and his wife noncommittally. The policeman went into a detailed description of what he had observed and the information he had gathered: that the couple had used surveying instruments on the Avenida del Cid for purposes they refused to disclose; that they had carried out this activity in a hurried and surreptitious manner; and that later in the day they had allegedly placed a wreath on one of the flower beds near El Cid, a wreath that he had not even seen them bring. "The Señor is carrying the wreath," he concluded.

Stigman held it up.

"May I see it?" the Inspector asked. Stigman handed over the wreath; the Inspector examined it briefly and then set it down on the desk.

"And the surveying instruments—where are they?"

"They are at our hotel, the Inglaterra."

"You travel with surveying instruments?"

"They are not mine. I rented them. If you wish ..."

Stigman brought out his wallet, produced a slip of paper, and passed it across the railing. "This is the voucher for my deposit for the use of the instruments."

The Inspector examined the voucher and laid it on the desk. "And your passports?" The documents were produced and surrendered. After a glance at each booklet, the Inspector placed them on his desk.

"You have been conducting surveying operations on a public thoroughfare in Seville, *señor*. What is their purpose?"

"Their purpose was to find the place for that wreath."

"And that place was the flower bed beside El Cid. What lies in the flower bed?"

"Nothing that I am sure of, Señor Inspector."

"What did you think was there?"

"That is something I do not care to discuss."

"Come, *señor*."

"No, I do not care to discuss it," Stigman said. "If there is a fine attached to what I have done, I am prepared to pay it. If the case is more serious, I demand my right to speak to the American consul."

"We are not at that pass, *señor*. I am asking for clarification of certain mysterious activities that you have been conducting in public. The police have a right to inquire into their meaning."

Stigman moved his head abruptly to one side and looked up. "Señor Inspector, what would you think of a person who was a guest in your house and insulted you—a guest who insults his host?"

The Inspector made a deprecating gesture. "Obviously, I would feel contempt. What has this to do with you?"

"I am attempting to refrain from insulting the country I am visiting."

"Let us not worry about insults, *señor*. All I ask for is a little clarification. Why were you surveying? What lies in the flower bed? What are the facts?"

"I have already told you all the facts that are pertinent,"

Stigman said. He gripped the railing. "The rest I refuse to tell you. I have done no one any harm."

The Inspector sat back. "What is your occupation?" he asked quietly.

"I am a general science teacher, retired," said Stigman. "My wife gives music lessons in private."

"I note that you speak Spanish very well."

"We have spent many summers in Mexico."

"And what possible reasons can you have, *señor*, for refusing to tell me what was the object of your surveying?"

"I did tell you. It was to place a wreath. Nothing more."

The Inspector looked up at the man beside him as if at one with greater authority. Wincing and unwincing, the tall man's difficult face seemed to belong at times to two different individuals. He had studied Stigman for a while and then Stigman's wife. Most of the time, his eyes rested on her, and when they did his features became lighter. He now addressed a question to the policeman. "Where, once again, was this wreath laid?"

"There, Señor Abogado, at this end of the oval." The policeman leaned over the railing and pointed at the wall map. "The end toward the Glorieta de Don Juan."

"Ah."

The Inspector swiveled about. "There is nothing there of importance," he said, pointing to the wall map. "The Capitanía, the Portuguese Consulate—nothing more. The Palace of Justice is only in its foundation."

"Right here?" The tall man put his finger on the small end of the oval and looked at the policeman.

"*Sí, señor.*"

The lines in the tall man's face cleared. "You need not detain them any longer," he said to the Inspector.

Not the slightest shade of expression came over the seated man's face. He picked up the passports and the voucher and handed them over the railing to Stigman. "I would caution you against continuing to use surveying instruments in public without a permit," he said.

"Then we may go?"

"*Sí, señor. Adiós. Adiós, señora.*" They were free to leave.

The tall man had brought the wreath through the gate of the wooden barrier. He handed it to Stigman. "You know your way back?" he said.

"Oh, yes," said Stigman. "The way we came."

"It would be a privilege if I could accompany you for a while."

"By all means, if you wish," Stigman said.

The three paused for a moment outside, under the red and yellow flag of Spain over the doorway. "I am Miguel Ortega," the tall man said. "I am a state attorney."

"I understood as much," said Stigman.

"We can go to the Inglaterra this way"—he indicated Menéndez Pelayo—"or this way, through the Barrio de Santa Cruz. It is more picturesque." His face unkinked as he spoke to Mary Stigman. "Every Sevillano fancies himself a guide."

"We shall need a guide, Señor Ortega, if we go through the Barrio de Santa Cruz," she said.

"And I shall be delighted to conduct you."

"I am sure that no one will mind if I throw this raincoat over my wreath," said Stigman.

The little café to which the lawyer had invited them was, as he said, something more like old Seville than new. The *espresso* machines were there, as they were in all Seville cafés, and the barrels of wine and sherry as well as the ranks of colorful bottles on the shelves in the rear. The usual paper wrappers of sugar cubes littered the floor. But the atmosphere in the place was more neighborly than in any of the cafés Stigman and his wife had been to. To the right of the bar, in the rear of the establishment, was a small provision shop. Aging hams covered with gray mold hung from a pipe near the ceiling, and next to them was an assortment of smoked sausages equally aged. There were basins of chickpeas visible on the small counter, lentils, rice, a large slab of brown quince jelly, and a crock of olives. A youngster with a fresh roll in his hand stood before the counter while the proprietress cut russet slices of *chorizo* for a filler. Three or four men were leaning on the bar in the café, one of them quietly shaking a dice cup. There were only three tables in the place; at one of them a bespectacled old man was busy filling in some sort of form. He had a large glass of white wine and a bundle of lottery tickets in front of him. On the wall behind the bartender hung a slate with the appetizers for the day chalked on it.

"Yes, I do like it," Stigman's wife replied to the lawyer's question. "It has all the appeal of something long lived in."

The lawyer nodded. "Ever since my youth and long before," he said.

The waiter brought the three cognacs they had ordered. *"Salud,"* Ortega said, and lifted his glass. Stigman and his wife lifted theirs, and they drank.

Ortega put his glass down. "You know, Señor Stigman, I quite appreciate your feelings," he said. He tilted his head slightly toward the wreath, which Stigman had put on a chair under the table. "In fact, if you wish, I will escort you back to the Avenida del Cid. Would you like to leave it there?"

"Oh, no," replied Stigman shortly. "I have made my gesture, for whatever it was worth."

"You found this place to your satisfaction? I mean, you are reasonably satisfied with the accuracy of your location?" Ortega's face knit and darkened.

"Oh, yes. Shall I say, within a half meter?"

The lawyer shook his head. "You intrigue me enormously."

"Why?"

"That any man would be so—I hesitate to use the word—so naïve. I do not know what word to use."

"I was determined that I was going to make my gesture. I made it."

"Of course." The man's face, wrinkling and unwrinkling, must have been a formidable thing to confront from a witness stand. "Señor Stigman," he went on, "I have old maps on the wall of my study. They are not maps, no. They are old views of Seville. Have you seen such views?"

"I have seen reproductions."

"I have three. In two of mine there is shown a certain landmark of the city, outside the walls. Where El Cid now stands. Approximately."

Stigman sat back listening.

"It is no longer there."

"No, it is no longer there," Stigman conceded.

"And this is the *quemadero,* where criminals were burned to death."

"That is where I laid the wreath."

"So I concluded."

In the pause that followed, only the dry rattle of the dice in the dice cup could be heard, and the scratching of the pen of the man doing his accounts at the table nearby. The café door opened, and three well-dressed patrons walked in— Spaniards with placid faces. They ordered *café con leche* and looked about. A hum of conversation began. A hissing sound came from the *espresso* machine.

"That is where I laid the wreath," Stigman repeated. "Your conclusion is correct. But do you know why I laid the wreath?"

"Yes. Because this was the same *quemadero* where heretics found guilty by the Holy Inquisition were burned—among others, relapsed *conversos,* those Catholics who secretly clung to their old Judaic faith."

"They were men and women who were put to death because they would not renounce their faith," Stigman said. "They were martyrs. I honored them because they deserved to be honored, because of their heroic constancy in the hour of trial. I honored them because no one in Spain honors them."

"I understand," said Ortega. "I am not offended, if that is what you were concerned about. All this is part of the Spanish heritage, along with her age-old greatness."

"I am happy to hear it," said Stigman. "I am happy you

were not offended. It was a small enough tribute I paid—but, even so, it seems to have had some consequences."

Ortega's squint might have been a smile. "Among them, I have had the pleasure of meeting you and your charming wife."

"Thank you. It has been a pleasure for us, too."

Again there was a pause, this time an awkward one.

"Señor Ortega," Stigman said finally, "it seems to me a strange thing that a gentleman in your position, even with such views of Seville as you have on your walls, should have fixed so immediately on the *quemadero*—should have focused on that spot at once. No one else realized what it was. Not the crowd around us this morning, not the policeman, not the Inspector." He hesitated. "You say this is part of the Spanish heritage. Why is everyone ignorant of it but you?"

"There may have been personal reasons. An idiosyncrasy."

"What, for example? I am eager to know how you could locate a thing like that so quickly. I had a good deal of research to do before I could be sure."

Ortega grimaced. He seemed to be deliberating. He brushed a small flake of cigarette ash from the table. "You have a point," he said.

"But how?"

The Spaniard clouded his eyes briefly with his hand. "Señor Stigman," he said, "what if I informed you that my grandfather told me that his father, when he became very old, would light a candle on Friday nights—would do it as a matter of compulsion? Would light a candle and put it in a pitcher?"

"Ah, so that is why," Stigman said. "That is why you knew where the *quemadero* was."

"In part. I knew where the *quemadero* was because I feel the same way about the people who died there that you do. Because I cannot forget their heroic constancy, as you call it. It was the heroic constancy of Spaniards who were also Jews."

"Spaniards!" Stigman looked at the other man with a

startled expression. "It was the heroic constancy of Jews who were also Spaniards!"

Ortega sat motionless. For once, his uncertain face seemed at rest.

"And do you light a candle on Friday nights?" asked Stigman.

The lawyer shook his head, almost as if disdaining the thought. "A candle in consciousness is enough, is it not? And you?"

"Oh, no," Stigman said. "I left the faith of my ancestors many years ago."

Their glasses were empty. Ortega signaled the waiter, who brought three full ones and removed the others.

"I think the word now should be *'l'chaim,'* " said Mary Stigman.

"Do you know it?" asked Stigman, lifting his glass.

Ortega lifted his. "Of course. It is the equivalent of our Spanish *'salud.'* "

From some open window or café door, a male voice hovering in a flamenco quaver reached the Stigmans as they walked through a cramped street of the Barrio. A thin reek of urine emanated from the unsunned cobblestones. Huge doors supporting other doors within them and studded with brass nipples in showy array opened on the flagstones of tranquil patios. Inside, copper salvers gleamed amid the potted plants; there was a courtyard well in one patio, vases and conch shells in another. Above their heads hung the shallow balconies of the houses, glassed in or laden with greenery, and above these the very roofs grew moss and weeds among their curved tiles.

"This is charming," said Mary Stigman. She was walking close to her husband's side along the narrow pavement.

"Are we going all right?"

"Yes, I think so. The next should be Mateos Gago, and then we should see the Cathedral."

"Quite a remarkable man, Señor Ortega, isn't he?" Stigman

observed. " 'Spaniards always pay,' he said when I tried to pay the waiter. *'Los españoles siempre pagan'*—as if it were a tradition." He looked at his wife. "I'll think you're remarkable, too, if you can find a way out of this maze," he said, smiling. "I wish you hadn't been so insistent with him about our ability to find our way without his help."

"I've got the city guide to Seville in my purse."

"So you have. I don't know whether there's something wrong with my sense of reality or my sense of direction," Stigman said. He took his wife's arm. "It must be those two cognacs," he added lamely.

They reached the corner and turned into Mateos Gago. The orange trees that lined the street were in the way for a moment, and then they saw it—the Giralda, *la Fe*, the weather vane. Faith stood on her high pinnacle above the Cathedral, pointing at every wind with her palm branch of triumph. A few more steps and the lofty Moorish minaret that supported her came wholly into view, rearing high its small balconies and sinuous arches, its marble pillars from whose capitals delicate brickwork tracery rose like spreading smoke from a brazier.

"Yes, there it is. You found it," said Stigman. "Now I know where the hotel is." They walked confidently ahead. "Wait a minute!" he said, and arrested his stride.

"What is it?" Involuntarily, his wife looked back.

"Oh, no, no one is following us. Do you know what I did?" Stigman held up his raincoat. "I forgot the wreath."

DAVID RUBIN

Longing for America

(FROM THE VIRGINIA QUARTERLY REVIEW)

BEFORE HE WENT to Bombay four years ago he had never left Zero Road for more than a day at a time. The second summer after that he came home for six weeks, but the following May, despite his promises, he stayed on at the University to get ready for graduate work, then let another year go by until this second difficult returning. He was aware that during all this time Zero Road was there, nine hundred miles away across the plains and rivers, and with an ache of affection he often remembered his father and mother, his younger brothers, and even the older sisters who had died. But they were vague, obscure, without geography until this moment when, after walking from the station, he stopped dead, his eyes overwhelmed with Zero Road.

It was the morning of Divali. From the station, down Leader Road, he had seen the streets jammed with throngs celebrating the four days of the festival, regular mobs squeezing in around the shops to buy statues of Lakshmi, new things for the house to honor her, lamps to light her to their doors. If she could find your home she would bring prosperity, she was prosperity. He had forgotten how seriously Divali was celebrated in Allahabad, forgotten the Divalis when his father and mother performed the rituals and threw away their few spare annas on clay lamps, mustard oil, and foolish gifts. Lakshmi had never found them.

Distressed, he began to grasp how far he had strayed from Zero Road, with his daily life in Bombay and his eyes and his heart set on further shores he would have thought unattainable three years before if he could even have dreamed of them. Now he felt a pang of anguish, then a hardening of his resolution until quite unexpectedly his whole mood softened and he stood in the clear, dry November sunlight drinking in the smells he had missed, almond rice with onions, pickled mangos and lemons, minty pakoras, the sweets in the Bengali stalls, sizzling twisted jalebis, frosted cake squares, all the homely smells of Zero Road blended with flowers from the garland-makers' booths, the last of one kind of jasmine, the first of another, bridal wreath, marigolds, and roses. More slowly, he began to walk again, down the road, until he saw his corner.

It was not much of a house to come back to. At least there were two rooms, one for the women and one for the men in the traditional fashion—even when the two sisters died his father had left his wife to occupy the other room by herself, for there was no one more traditional than Pundit Tivari. Two rooms and two windows perched not quite parallel to the ground over a bicycle repair shop, a Brahman restaurant, and a kind of closet, the dwelling of a disreputable Muslim tailor who pretended he was persecuted and sang love songs in the night when he was high on *bhang*. It was only a two-story building so his family had some of the roof for themselves on hot nights. There was electricity but no water apart from the tap in the street in front of the bicycle shop where tanners and Muslims and dogs and women of no caste constantly defiled it—a problem for his father and a hardship for all of them who had to walk to a temple for the water. He had forgotten the tap after all this time in a hostel in Bombay where he shared a bathroom with Christians and Muslims.

He stopped, tried to recall how he had planned his arrival, how he would tell his father that he meant to go to America though it meant defilement, how he would have prepared them with his cigarettes and his slacks and bush-shirt, which they had never seen him wear. He could not concentrate on it now, he felt the pang returning, compounded with the disquieting knowledge of his father's illness that had called him home, for it was not precisely to celebrate the holiday that he had come.

Impatiently he pushed through the crowd to his door, found himself all in a moment running up the stairs, where his feet in their Bombay shoes managed to skip the broken step and the sagging step and the step that was no longer there as deftly as when he ran barefoot. Halfway up he stopped; with his eyes just clear of the landing he could see through the open door. His father sat on a mat near the window, a book open on his lap, over his shoulders his gray Kashmir chuddar, the family's most precious article of clothing. He was not reading but staring at the floor, half asleep perhaps and dreaming as he had dreamed most of the time while they stayed poor (the poorest Brahmans, he remembered, stung with quick anger, ever known in Allahabad). Mr. Tivari had never seemed to mind being poor. Lakshmi would find them one day, he would say, perhaps she had already, for prosperity was not what the vulgar conceived it to be. He lived by teaching scriptures and the sacred epics in temples, on street corners and lately, since his illness, at home. He appeared smaller, frailer, his balding head very large on the narrow shoulders but with a certain quizzical humor in its sleepy tilt, as though he had withdrawn only temporarily from waking life to store up some new laughter against the wise world.

From the street a holy man called up for alms. Mrs. Tivari, walking swiftly with her swaying motion, came before his eyes. He had not remembered that his mother was so big, her hair so shiny, her face so silly in its speechless anger against her husband's idleness, her eyes so beautiful.

"Arrey!" she called down to the sadhu, "did we not give to you ten minutes ago?"

"Stop it," Mr. Tivari said, catching her hand to draw her back from the window. "He asks again, we must give again. Since when have we become so stingy?"

"Ha!" Mrs. Tavari exclaimed and walked into the next room.

"Wait," Mr. Tivari called down. Then he coughed hard, his shoulders shaking, and while he coughed he fumbled in his kurta pocket until he found a square silver two-anna piece. He held it up to the light, leaned over the sill and tossed it out, saying, "With blessings, but do not move in with us, someone here would make you give it back!"

The holy man gave a tinkling laugh and called up in a high voice, "I did not mean to ask of you again, Punditji, I wished only to shame the bicycle shop!"

"Ha!" Mrs. Tivari said and came out of the other room and then, glancing toward the stairs, gave a little gasping cry as her son rushed up the rest of the steps and through the door, flung himself down to kiss the ground at his father's feet and would have done the same for her had she not caught him up and embraced him.

"Hari Lal, Hari Lal!" she said, squeezing him.

"The train was late," he said just as his brothers scampered into the room. Mahesh was eleven, Triveni ten, but they seemed half their age to their brother as he gave them each the Cadbury's chocolate bars he had brought. They shrieked with delight. Mr. Tivari coughed, rolled his eyes in dismay at their barbarism, while Hari Lal sat down facing him.

"First tell me, son, why you were not home for the summer and not for Dushehra, when you had two weeks, and not for Divali last year when you had an extra day and Dushehra last year when the conflict of calendars gave you two weeks extra."

"That is no way to begin," Mrs. Tivari said. "Are you hungry, son? There is cold rice and dal. I am saving the fuel for tonight."

"I am not hungry now." He looked at his father and waited in an agony of suspense.

"Have things gone well?" Mr. Tivari said more gently. "I am pleased you are in the first division. Do you like your professors? Do you respect them? How many of them are foreigners?"

"Only one," Hari Lal said. "The professor of American literature."

"He is American?"

"She is American."

"She? A woman teaching in the University?"

"There are women who teach in the University here," Hari Lal said. But he knew they were not like Barbara Ford, for whom he had the strangest feeling of love without desire, or anyway, not the ordinary desire, but a sense that she was more than herself, more than a striking face and figure and more than an image of freedom from convention (though not restraint, Dr. Ford was certainly restrained); she was America walking through the corridors of the University, conversing with her students or anyone who cared to talk to her, America in Bombay since last July and until next April. He had heard others lecture on Emerson and Fitzgerald but they had not been able to bring out the charm, the romance of the writers and the country, qualities he knew were there even before Dr. Ford so expertly made them manifest. And it was she who had encouraged him, told him how, if he did well in his examinations, there should be no difficulty in getting a fellowship for a year or perhaps longer, with the proper backing—hers, for example. She was his Lakshmi from now on.

It was not the moment to explain. He felt trapped, the silence grew intolerable until Mr. Tivari continued his questions: "And this year what did you do for Dushehra?"

"I went to Delhi."

"Hm! Almost fifty rupees up and down, unless you went on the Mail, and that is still more. I asked Mr. Shukla downstairs. And either way, it is more than it would cost to come home."

"I rode in a car with people I know. It cost nothing."

"In a car? Very good! And why did you go to Delhi?"

"To see the Ramlila at the Cricket Grounds."

"Very commendable!" Mr. Tivari said. "A religious observance converted into a spectacle with wiggling girls and people dressed up as monkeys."

"It is the same poetry of Tulsidas that you taught me."

"I do not ask you to argue. Stand up, let me look at you. You too are a spectacle. When you left with your scholarship a kurta and dhoti were good enough but now you look like a deputy collector's second clerk. And your hair is short, you have cut off your topknot."

"Be calm," Mrs. Tivari said from the next room and there was a rattling crash as a tray was knocked over in the restaurant downstairs.

"The world outside is different," Hari Lal said, sitting down again.

"The world *outside?* The world is one, inside, outside, upside down." He laughed, but gently. "You are just past eighteen and you tell me about the world."

"I have been to Bombay and Delhi and you have never left Allahabad."

"In this house we call it Prayag, we do not use Muslim names. It was Prayag three thousand years before Islam was invented, why should we use their name?"

"The world calls it Allahabad and you would know this if you had left it only once in your life."

Mr. Tivari was speechless. Mrs. Tivari came from her room.

"You must not speak to him that way," she said. "No son may speak to his father that way, and do not tell *me* about the world either, your father is right and I know what I know." She looked down at her husband over the rim of her bosom. "It is your fault, you should have greeted him properly and not tried to show he was wrong at the very beginning—remember, Prakashji is coming, so be calm!"

Mr. Tivari did not appear to have heard her. "Once," he said softly, "I went to Varanasi. Well, child, you have changed. How shall I call you now: Punditji?"

"I'm sorry, father."

"I'm glad of that. Did they teach you in Bombay to be disrespectful?"

It was going much worse than Hari Lal had anticipated. He looked toward the window as though Barbara Ford might be there to encourage him and heard his father say:

"Well, what is it they teach you there?"

"I study only English now. There are papers in Shakespeare and eighteenth century and the Romantics and contemporary ..."

"And there is the paper in American literature," Mr. Tivari said, but more to himself. "But no philosophy! No study of truth. How can a University teach the truth anyway? The truth is one, you see it in a moment or never. It is darker than falsehood, its face is covered with a disk of gold and you cannot find your way past that with your Bombay professors. Only I can lead you past the sun glow of falsehood." He sighed, then laughed. "And you tell me I have never been out of Prayag! What of that? Do we not have Sungam here where Ganga and Yamuna and invisible Saraswati flow together, the confluence of the holiest rivers? I have been everywhere, across the world to the court of Indra and the land of the Gandharvas."

"There are no such places, father. They are imaginary."

"How you contradict yourself! And where did you learn this?"

"In the Ramayana. I mean, in ... a footnote."

"In a footnote?" Mr. Tivari doubled over with laughter. "That is altogether too simple! Tell me what other wisdom you have acquired."

Hari Lal stiffened with anger but he answered quietly. "I have talked to people from England and America—"

"Very good—footnotes to America—I hope that exists, at least. Have they tried to make you a Christian?"

"No. I don't know if they are Christians. To them their scriptures are poems. They recite it like poetry."

"Excellent; they are not so simple. Have you learned any of their scripture?"

"A few lines."

"Recite!"

Overcome with shyness, Hari Lal began, fighting a stammer:

"The Lord is my shepherd, I shall not want."

"Hm!" Mrs. Tivari said softly and they realized that she was still standing over them. She looked at her husband as though in triumph and walked away.

"The Lord is my shepherd," Mr. Tivari repeated, then said it over in Hindi. He looked out the window. "The Lord is my teacher. Though I may want, yet I shall know the truth."

There came a call from the street.

"Is he back?" Mrs. Tivari demanded from her room.

Mr. Tivari placed his chin on the sill and looked out. "A different one," he said. "Blessings!" He threw down a coin.

"Have you forgotten it is Divali?" Mrs. Tivari demanded. "How shall we buy lamps and oil? Ours will be the only house in the Chowk without a light for Lakshmi."

Mr. Tivari began to cough. When he stopped, Hari Lal saw that he was laughing. "Hear your mother," he said. "It is a joy to see her affection for the right way. We must have lights for Lakshmi, and by good fortune I have a few annas for the purpose. I shall get them now on my way to the Fort—I am to talk there on holy Rama as son, husband, brother, and father. I like going to the Fort ghat these days for I can see the rivers come together and I think of the inevitable transformation we must all undergo to attain the true prosperity of deliverance."

"The Fort is too far for you," Mrs. Tivari said, invisible in her chamber. "You cannot walk to the Fort."

"I can, I must, I shall."

"I'll go with you," Hari Lal said. "If you wished it, I might go for you."

Mr. Tivari smiled. "Yes, I know you would go for me. You will have your chance for that soon enough. Today I want to go alone, and you must talk to your brothers, only do not exaggerate too much when you describe the splendors of that outside world you love." He folded his hands and inclined his head, elaborately ceremonious, to say, "Ram Ram." Then he stood up, drew his chuddar around his shoulders and walked slowly to the stairs.

Was there mockery in that valediction? Shamed at his suspicion, Hari Lal called his brothers, who came running into the room at once, and with a feeling of relief he began to tell them about Dr. Ford and America and the bright promise of the future. They could not, he realized, he expected to understand very precisely, but that was for the moment the least of his concerns.

Mr. Tivari was very tired when he came home. By then it was time for the evening meal and he made the ritual offering of food, sang the verses, and lit the lamp before the little statue of Vishnu in the corner and then the new clay lamps filled with mustard oil along the sills. After that they sat down to eat. Although Mrs. Tivari had prepared as much of a feast as their finances would allow, her husband scarcely touched his food. During the afternoon Hari Lal had questioned her about his health. He had been ill since the rains stopped, she said, with something like a cold that did not improve; quite often he stayed on his charpoy all day. The Ayurvedic physician had prescribed the usual herbs but they did not help. She could not say more; she was prepared for anything. She had written to Hari Lal because she had thought it might be good for his father; now (she looked at him steadily and without reproach) she was not so sure.

He thought about these things while they ate their vegetables and wheatbread. The America he longed for flickered in his consciousness, utterly preposterous, first, then utterly dark. His father spoke only once, to ask him if he had tasted meat in Bombay.

"No," Hari Lal said, wounded that his father could conceive of such a thing, and they finished their meal in silence. He was relieved when the visitors arrived until he began to suspect what their business was. Prakash was a very old and feeble man, magnificently attired in an embroidered shirt with a white flowered chuddar draped regally over his shoulders; he wore his sacred thread outside his garments like a uniform braid and in his hands, wound around with rosaries, were three books. He was apparently an astrologer and he had come, obviously, to plan a wedding. Hari Lal shivered with angry excitement and studied the other man, a fat bald-headed Brahman with bulging eyes; he was not presented, he said nothing, and as he looked around him, his features expressed a monstrous distaste for everything in the room. He was doubtless an observer for the prospective bride's family and he would certainly bargain hard.

The preliminaries were long; it was all preliminaries. Prakash, who addressed only Mr. Tivari, muttered obscure explanations, opened his books, pored over fantastical charts, chanted mantras to himself. At length he proposed a day for next September. The other man cleared his throat.

"You have computed by the wrong calendar," Mr. Tivari said. "There are three, not two, calendars to consider—lunar, solar and solar-lunar."

"No, no, no, no, no!" said Prakash, grinning wickedly around toothless gums.

"What then?"

"No, no, no!" Prakash repeated with the same inexplicable grin.

"But you've scheduled my son's wedding to coincide with Janmashtami."

"Janmashtami will be in August, as it always is," the astrologer said.

"But August is not the problem, the month of Ashvin is the problem!"

Mrs. Tivari, who was sitting by the fire, laughed softly. To no one in particular she said, "I have a calendar from the newspaper with all the holidays for next year clearly indicated."

They droned on. Chilled, Hari Lal listened. It was incredible, he told himself (though he ought to have expected it, this after all is why they had dragged him home), incredible that in this day and age astrologers (and even fathers) could control one's fate, his fate.

The horoscope of a girl was set on the floor beside another, his own. There was talk of money, the stranger communicating only by nods, winks, and flickering fingers, bargaining for terms, impatience on both sides, and finally, near midnight, when the noise in the street began to subside, an agreement was reached. Prakash, silent at last, drank tea with Mr. Tivari and the stranger. Then they rose and the astrologer bowed and grinned for the last time before he tottered down the stairs after the other man.

"Now, my son," Mr. Tivari said, "we must talk. We shall go on the roof."

"No," Mrs. Tavari said in her sharpest tone. "It is too cold on the roof. You can talk as well in here."

"The boys have been kept awake long enough and I have my chuddar. Come, Hari Lal."

Mrs. Tivari handed her son her shawl; embarrassed, he put it back around her and followed his father to the roof. He was aware while he left the room of her eyes and scowling brows in the glow from the embers.

"The girl is fifteen and fair," Mr. Tivari said, "of an acceptable family though not rich. If she were—enough of that. Tripathi, her father, is a scholar and a good man. Her mother was brought up in Bengal and somehow that has given her ideas about herself. The girl does not appear to have been spoiled by her. She is strong and is reported to have a good disposition and a sweet tongue. That is most important. Her name is Maya. She knows a little English, she sews well, and she has studied the sitar for two years. She writes Nagari clumsily and I hope you will help her with that. Do you have any questions?"

Hari Lal gazed around him from their dark perch. Half the lights had burned out by now. Along the square some of the buildings had chains of electric lights instead of lamps.

One string of bulbs went out and there was laughter above the buzz of conversation in the Brahman restaurant. The Muslim tailor squatted on his doorstep and moaned an old song off key. Hari Lal felt cold, his tongue had gone dry. He wished he had not come home.

"How can I marry?" he managed to say. "I have a year and a half before I sit for the M.A. examinations."

"That is not so difficult. You will marry and Maya will stay with us or with her family, if she wishes, until you return. Then, when we are all together, we will try to find a place with three rooms—"

"I could not do that. What is the point of marrying now if we cannot live together for so long a time?"

"You are going on nineteen, your prospects are good, and this is the time to negotiate. You might even give up the University and stay with us from now on."

Amazed, Hari Lal stared at his father. "What would I do here?"

"What have we always done?"

"You mean, sit at the window and throw coins to beggars and dream about the court of Indra?"

"If that is how you wish to put it—why not? We have had a good life. We do not need much money to live. We have been happy."

Hari Lal thought of his mother. Mr. Tivari seemed to follow his thoughts.

"Do you think any of us would change it if we could? Your mother would be lost if she did not have me to scold and to cherish. That is more than money to her. These years she has been happier than you can imagine."

"And does that mean that I ... and ... Maya, this girl I've never seen, could be happy with such a life?"

"Of course. You are intelligent and you have our example."

"Father, when I marry I do not think I would live with you and mother, even if I stayed in Allahabad."

"Not live with us?"

"That is no longer the way."

"In the 'outside world'? I am beginning to see what the University has done to you. There *is* no other way, of course you would live with us. Still ... perhaps that is not the most important thing. First is the marriage."

Hari Lal said, "I know people in Bombay who go to America to study and leave their wives and sometimes children behind. That seems to me to be a sacrifice."

"People who go to America? But you are not going to America."

"You have not asked me."

"What is there to ask? To leave India is defilement. Pundit Pandey's daughter went to London and she has never come back. She is married to a Christian, she eats meat, even beef, she smokes, she drinks—"

"I would not go to America to get married. I want to go to study more—"

"You want to go?"

"—to learn. The universities here are looking for teachers of American literature and history—"

"You want to go to America? Are you not to consider our happiness?"

"Why should your happiness depend on my unhappiness?" Hari Lal asked, almost pleading.

"It does not, that is only your illusion. You still have much to learn. The first law of happiness is to accept the world as it is and things as they have to be. The circumstances of the world and the way things are have very little importance so long as you know the truth behind and above them. When you know the truth, you obey your dharma, you respect your father, accept his judgment, and life is simple, life is tranquil, and you are happy."

"You used to teach me that each one of us is alone responsible for himself."

"And our happiness, then?" Mr. Tivari said with such an air of bereavement that Hari Lal felt his resolution waver. He tried to summon up the image of Dr. Ford, but she would not come and once again America flickered out. He looked at the street. Below them the tailor sang, "The whole world does nothing but fall in love. How is it that you don't know what love is?" An early poem of Firaq, who was still living in the city. How had the tailor gotten on to it? He obviously had a different scripture, a different dharma. Love: all the films were about romantic love, learned from other films, American films, and everyone who flocked to see them considered them make-believe, all the while they loved them, for that was the word, one loved that vision and longed for it where freedom was the dharma—or was it only make-believe in America too? His own father and mother were what love could be, could do. They had not met even once before their wedding. And it was true: they had been happy.

"Is she pretty?" he asked.

"Maya? What a question!" Mr. Tivari broke into his clear, happy laugh. "She has two eyes, a nose, a mouth—of course she is pretty. What girl is not at fifteen?"

"The whole world," sang the tailor, hiccuping.

"You, Hari Lal, you are the dreamer. You say I waste my time in dreams at the window, but it is you who are the dreamer. America!"

Hari Lal felt tired. " . . . fall in love," the tailor said, no longer singing. Suddenly aware that his father was shivering, Hari Lal pleaded the cold as an excuse to go to bed.

In the night he heard his father snoring over the light breathing of his brothers. He could see Mahesh's forehead and fists in the glimmer from the street light, the rest of him and Triveni beside him shadows. Not only America but even Bombay vanished in the realm of fantasy. In this house there was an odd kind of peace; with the silence, all that was preposterous faded. His father (he turned his head to note the vague outline of the charpoy in the darkest corner) was as he had to be, his mother too; they knew their place, their way, their world. It was wisdom, surely, and tempting to be wise.

But Maya: she had become real in his father's sparse description. Marriage in this way was medieval. What did Maya have to do with the truth? She was more likely the disk of gold in front of it. Her name meant illusion. Though it also meant Lakshmi, prosperity. And perhaps they were the same. Poor Maya, a frightened child, probably, afraid to leave her father and mother to sleep under a stranger and find herself heavy and ungainly with a mysterious growth inside her. Or perhaps she was a prisoner, mooning over her sitar, wild to be delivered at any cost from Zero Road or wherever she lived. Or just a girl who would become a woman, a wife, a mother without any fuss, like his own mother, and scold and cherish him . . .

The temptations of wisdom increased instead of diminishing. Still, she was only a mirage and so long as he did not really know her he would be able to resist.

In the morning his father did not rise from his cot. "Not ill," he said. "Tired, nothing more. Do not trouble me with questions, any of you, I want to dream. Of Indra's court and Gandharva land." He laughed and turned his head to the wall.

Hari Lal had given ten naya paisa to each of his brothers (God knew what they could buy for the house with that, but it was all the change he had). Alone with his mother in her room, he was ill at ease. Since his Bombay transfiguration, she regarded him with a respect he could not understand; she kept a distance. He asked her again about his father's illness, suggesting that they call a doctor.

"We have had a doctor," she said.

"I mean a modern doctor with medicine, not herbs."

"How are we to pay a modern doctor?"

"But you can't let a few rupees stand in the way if he's seriously ill."

"Could we not? What do you suppose all of us do at such times, my dear Hari Lal? We let it stand in the way and we grow more ill and then we die."

"But I could get the money."

"How? Desire is not enough, and anyway, your scholarship is a pittance, I wonder how you live on it. And then, he would never consent to see anybody but our old physician—who is very ill, too. It may be wrong, but he cannot be changed and he must be true to what he believes. Be thankful we are not on the ground floor: here, at least, it is dry. What did you say," she went on abruptly, "when he told you about Maya?"

"I ... didn't agree to it."

"Or disagree?"

"Well, almost, it wasn't clear."

"But you will marry her, Hari Lal, you must. She is a beautiful girl and already in love with your picture and for a poor family they have managed a very decent dowry since she is luckily the only girl. Here she is," she added, taking a snapshot from her sari. "Your father would never think of this when he had all his solar-lunar calendar to calculate."

He saw an oval face, the eyes wide open and not at all shy, as he had expected, a rather long fine nose and a small chin which hinted at stubbornness.

"Yes," he said. "She's pretty. That was not what concerned me."

"What is it then?" In his mother's serene patience for the first time he suspected a sense of unshakable superiority to himself, even to his father; her new regard for him was only toleration of his Bombay eccentricities.

"I mean, this is no way to marry in the modern world."

"What has the *modern world* to do with it?" she demanded, using his English phrase, which sounded even stranger in her homely Hindi speech. "The world changes only superficially, history makes that obvious."

He had to smile, wondering what she knew of history except legends from the epics and chronicles.

"Is there a better way?" she went on. "Do you think I have not been happy with your father? We married in this way; our betrothal was even much earlier."

"What does that have to do with us, Maya and me, I mean?"

"What doesn't it have to do with you?"

Mahesh and Triveni came in and solemnly offered their mother two tiny clay images of Lakshmi, horribly painted, too small to be more than lumps.

"Good boys," Mrs. Tivari said. "Only let your father sleep. Very good boys. I thought you would buy sweets for yourselves." She sighed. "This is the only way Lakshmi will enter this house," she said to Hari Lal.

"Son," Mr. Tivari called from the other room. Hari Lal went in and saw his father sitting by the window. He beckoned and asked him to sit beside him.

"Look into the street and tell me what you see."

"Zero Road," Hari Lal said, smiling despite himself.

"Lord Indra's court!" Mr. Tivari's answering smile was mysterious.

"The street?"

"Perhaps. I said only Lord Indra's court and you jump to conclusions. Can't I say whatever I please?" He laughed more gently than usual. "The University must be responsible for your muddled head these days. Surely I am not, nor your mother, who is the most sensible woman in the world except when perversity tempts her to oppose me. I meant only that Zero Road is all the world—can anything be more obvious? I suppose I am more attached to it than I ought to be. And you—not enough. But this is where I have taught the epics, this is ..." He paused, put his hand on Hari Lal's. "How fortunate we have been, my dear Hari Lal. Except for when the girls died, our lives have been ... I do not know how to say it. If only you do not disappoint us, then ... Well, I have given you a muddled talk. If it has meant anything, remember it this afternoon when you meet Maya."

"This afternoon?" Hari Lal could not conceal his dismay. Mr. Tivari smiled, an ordinary smile this time, and said:

"You will go this afternoon to Shri Tripathi's to meet his daughter. I think it will be better if I am not there. Your mother will accompany you." He looked out the window, wistfully, Hari Lal thought, and he wondered if his father were missing this most important occasion because he was so ill. "I have decided not to go," Mr. Tivari went on, "because I want you to feel that it is entirely your affair, since that is so important for you. I do not ask you to promise anything. You must make your own mistakes, you must find the truth for yourself. You must promise me only this."

Hari Lal waited. "Yes, father?"

"No," Mr. Tivari said, "what is the point of promises? Are you going to wear that clerk's suit? Lord, Lord!"

And Hari Lal was startled to realize that, whether suddenly or by imperceptible degrees, he had capitulated to his father, and his father knew it.

It was out of the question for them to speak. Maya stayed beside her mother all the while they walked in the largest of the Tripathis' four rooms in New Katra on the other side of the city. Shri Tripathi and his four sons were hearty and full of sympathy for Hari Lal's nervousness; he found them detestable. Mrs. Tripathi, voluminous and bulging-eyed (like her brother, the stranger who had accompanied Prakash— and both of them were there too), was endlessly inventive on the subject of the grandeurs of Burdwan Junction, the superiority of Bengali manners despite the Bengali arrogance, the decline of Allahabad, since independence, since the new cinemas opened, since ...

Hari Lal caught a smile from Maya, very discreet but plain enough: she did not take her mother seriously. He tried to move closer to her; both mothers expanded at once and he found himself still farther from her. It was infuriating. He decided that he had once and for all to show his independence. He had barely had a clear glimpse of Maya, though he could see she was even prettier than the photograph and very graceful in a terrible flower-print sari which had doubtless been magnificent thirty years before in Burdwan Junction.

"Maya," he said, and stepped around the mothers to the side of his fiancée (for his presence there, he suddenly understood, amounted to betrothal), and when he took her hand, for only a second while they stared at one another, there was scarcely a person in the room who did not gasp, but Maya, braver than he could have hoped, returned the pressure of his fingers and did not draw away until he let her hand fall free and stepped back; Mrs. Tripathi, frowning terribly, and Mrs. Tivari, inscrutable, intervened again. He sipped his tea, sighed, saw Maya smile over her cup, and suddenly tea was over, he was walking in the street with his mother.

"You were rude," she said. "Poor Maya must have thought you a boor."

He was surprised at how much this possibility troubled him and how swiftly he refuted it—there was the warmth of her smile and her hand to reassure him. They were walking past Muir College by now and he saw a band of University students sauntering along smoking and laughing with girls in pigtails, one of them flourishing a film magazine. He was all in a moment ashamed at how easily he had surrendered to his father and mother, to Maya, how easily his longing had been supplanted by a new one. He summoned his forces for a battle, but then he looked at his mother, so impassive in her steady swaying walk, the sari bunched around her thick waist with peculiar grace, and just as suddenly he put away his hopes of freedom, let his longing go for good.

The two boys met them in the middle of the stairs, their faces frightened. There was chanting in the room. About twenty minutes before Mr. Tivari had died quietly while looking into the street, with his head propped above the sill.

In the evening the barber came to shave Hari Lal's head. He worked very fast, leaving only a strand in back for the ritual top-knot. Hari Lal was aware of a humiliation in his grief, more troubling than his grief. The humiliation warned him that his surrender might be a mistake, after all. He was no longer reconciled; he felt merely trapped.

The boys had their turn next and they recovered their spirits a little for the first time since the afternoon. Hari Lal looked at their bright shiny skulls and burst into tears.

"Enough of that," Mrs. Tivari said. Her face was swollen with weeping but her voice held steady now. She had first taken it calmly but broke down when the old physician gave his opinion: Mr. Tivari's heart, exhausted by illness and work, had stopped. He spoke in a thin cracked voice that somehow provoked her fury. She had ordered him to leave, waved her arms at him, screamed, and then gone sobbing to the other room. The physician had not flinched; he sat beside the body and looked around him with a sweet and patient smile as though to say that he knew what to expect on such occasions.

"We must plan everything," Mrs. Tivari said. "I will go tomorrow afternoon to Sister's in Jaunpur with the boys. The train leaves at twenty-five minutes past four. We will take what we can carry, the rest I will leave with Maya for the two of you, and the books are yours. There is nothing more to that. Mrs. Sen at the third door down above the spice shop has been a widow for eight years; go to her and borrow a white sari, she must have many. There is nothing more to that. Stop weeping now, it is of no use. Your father will find a better lodging in the world next time, I hope, but Lord, though he was a good man he was too full of imperfection to escape the mortal world once and for all. Then you must go to bed, for it is a long journey to the Rivers and the procession will start at dawn. Go to Mrs. Sen now and do not cry, for what have you to fear, what have you to mourn? Go now."

It was a surprise when he woke in the middle of the night and realized he had been sleeping comfortably. He looked at his brothers huddled together as though they were frightened. Why shouldn't they be? He was afraid too. The way, so simple to follow, was perilously easy to lose. Once he had given up his freedom he was lost at the prospect of regaining it. His affection for his father, his conflict with him, he told himself now with an echo of the anguish he had first felt when he stepped into Zero Road, his affection and his conflict had nothing to do with the darkness of truth or the splendid glow of illusion. Nothing. He blinked at the streetlight's pale glimmer, rounding on the floor. He had not yet told his mother he would give up the University—pride still rebelled at that—but of course she would have guessed it and it would be a consolation for her. The astrologer could be talked into setting the wedding date a few months earlier; if he would not, then another astrologer would have to be found. He would tell her after the funeral; she would go to Sister's anyway with the boys for a few weeks, it would be good for her, then Maya would come from her four rooms to his two, his mother would come back with the boys and take her old room, he and Maya his father's, and farewell to Bombay, he would not even think of what beside Bombay, and then nothing but verses from holy Ramayana, verses by holy Tulsidas, restive children and the books molding in the rains and crumbling to dust in May.

Then he heard his mother weeping softly in her room and he shut his eyes.

He wore a dhoti and a kurta for the first time in months; it did not feel so strange as he had expected. With three brittle old Brahmans he shouldered the bier at sunup for the three-mile walk to the burning ghats. He wanted to walk fast but the old men angrily ordered him to slow. He resented their weakness before he was touched by their devotion, for they had been his father's friends. With a mongrel crowd of acquaintances and idlers behind them, while someone chanted, they stumbled along the dusty road toward the Fort and Ewing Christian College and the funeral ghats under a cloudless dark blue sky. Because it was almost winter flowers were plentiful and cheap; the bier was smothered in red and yellow blossoms. He wondered how his mother had seen to it all, where she had gotten the money for everything, and he winced, thinking how hard she must find the walking. He turned his head to see her, caught a glimpse of Mahesh tempted just then to linger to watch some urchings playing tipcat, but he could not find his mother. Then he tripped and after that did not look back.

The trees thinned, the plain fell away to the rivers, still high from the rains, the Ganges and Jumna spilling gray-blue and green waves together, the holiest spot in India, holier even than Banaras itself. The burning ghats appeared festive. All along the wide flight of steps mourners who looked like revelers stood watching another funeral; the pyre still blazed at the bottom landing beside the river. Mr. Tivari had to wait. The other fire seemed almost finished but it flamed up again. There was nothing sad about it. Hari Lal had been to a lot of funerals: he knew that the corpse was nothing, the funeral only a consolation for the living, a distraction. The singing sounded joyous, like the conch blasts and the bells and the laughter. Mr. Tivari would have approved, it was absolutely proper. And suddenly it was his turn. The new pyre was ready; the body was placed on it, scarcely visible under the flowers. The purohit chanted holy mantras and at the right moment Hari Lal recited the verses of his Brahmanhood:

> Pray that we attain the high glory of the divine sun:
> May he guide us in our prayers.

Then the new verses he did not know which he had to repeat after the priest:

> Ganapathi, beloved of Shiva, of Prajapati,
> Bring peace to the heavens and to man
> And to all the visible worlds.

It was only the beginning, it seemed intolerably long, and while he repeated the prayers he recalled unexpectedly when he had learned the Gayatri, those lines about the glory of the divine sun which he had since spoken every morning and every evening and every time he ate, even in Bombay. It was an afternoon when Zero Road was flooded and Mr. Tivari, unable to go out, had decided it was time to teach his son, and they had talked about the Gayatri while Mrs. Tivari cooked rice and dal, casting fragrant herbs in the pots, and the rain spattered on the sill and Mr. Tivari had laughed at his son's mistakes in Sanskrit. Hari Lal thought he was going to cry. The torch was put in his hand. He lit the pyre.

In the smoke of the kindling and fresh flowers he watched his father reposing on the bier, lightly, it seemed, with his winsome smile playing behind the transparent sooty swirls. The blaze took, flames leaped skyward, and Hari Lal's eyes followed them up to where they fused with the sun. He was mastered by devotion to his father, he felt a sudden joy in that devotion. When he turned he saw Maya standing on the top step far above, then his brothers with faces lost between terror and curiosity, his mother solemn, an old man laughing very gently and sweetly as he whispered to a friend. Hari Lal fancied he heard the hermits singing from across the river. The tears came to his eyes.

It was not a very elaborate pyre. It took little time to burn. Hari Lal was grateful that it did not go out, as they often did, leaving some of the corpse unconsumed. When the flames spurted up for the last time before they subsided in smoke, while the fire smoldered (for others were waiting, one could not delay), he reached in for ashes to scatter in the river to symbolize the return of the individual to the absolute, the all, the One. A noise overhead, a roar, and he faltered. He looked up to the top of the ghat. Maya was gone—had it been Maya? He was no longer sure. There was an airplane flying over, trailing a long banner with some new film title on it. The heat of the sun and the pyre burned into him. He began to sweat. A sudden spurt of unreasonable resentment coursed through him. He reached again for the ashes and with them picked up a hot coal; he gasped, flung it with the ashes into the river and fought the temptation to bring his scorched palm to his mouth. The plane buzzed more faintly in the distance, invisible in the sun's glare. The resentment vanished, he felt an unfamiliar relief.

"We must go," his mother said. "There is much to do and this is finished."

He looked at her, the tears rising again, and saw the rivers stretch into blind infinity, a golden ocean driving him in its westward tide, and he said, "I cannot marry Maya, I cannot do what I do not believe in, I cannot sacrifice myself."

She regarded him with her old serenity for some time before she spoke. "No one asks any of these things of you. You have heard your father read, 'Man is the altar, man is the sacrifice.' Come now, we must take your brothers away from here."

In the afternoon he saw her and the boys off at the station. It was crowded with holiday travelers, the windows of the train bristled with hands, waving and clinging or merely grasping for pan or fruit juice or comic books or film magazines from the vendors' carts. Mrs. Tivari smiled once at Hari Lal, then turned her head away and did not look at him again, though the boys grabbed his hands as though they would pull him through the window, even when the train had started, and then he watched with a sinking heart as it disappeared.

A half hour later, longing for the old two rooms, for his father and mother and for Maya too, he caught the Kashi Express and began the night and day of journeying that would bring him back to Bombay.

JESSE STUART
The Accident

(FROM THE SATURDAY EVENING POST)

"How would you like to go for a ride with your Aunt Effie and me?" Uncle Jad said. "It's a nice Sunday afternoon and we won't have many more such days before snow falls."

Uncle Jad Higgins ran the Ranceburg Men's Clothing Store in Ranceburg. He had inherited this store from his father, and there was a sign above the door which read: SEVENTY-SEVEN YEARS IN BUSINESS. The Higginses were without posterity, and I was Uncle Jad's sister's son; it was understood that I would take over the store someday after Uncle Jad retired or was deceased. Since my father was a farmer, Uncle Jad had invited me to live with him and Aunt Effie while learning the business from A to Z, and of course I couldn't let an opportunity like that pass. Naturally, if Uncle Jad asked me to do something, I did it. If he wanted me to take a drive with him and Aunt Effie on a sunny fall afternoon, I went along. I'd seen enough of the Lantern County hills to do me a lifetime, but if they wanted me with them, then that was all right with me.

"It's a nice idea to take a drive, Uncle Jad," I said. "You are so right. We won't have many more afternoons as pretty and as sunny as this one."

"Yes, and your Aunt Effie and I have seen more seasons—winters, springs, summers, autumns—than we will ever see again," he said. "The years take their toll. But it's always nice just to get out and drive around."

"You want me to drive so you and Aunt Effie can relax and look at the countryside?" I asked.

"No, Tom, I'd rather have my own hands on the steering wheel," he said. "You know I have faith in you. But this is just my nature. I've never had a wreck in my life. And I've been driving since I was sixteen."

Aunt Effie came into the room dressed like she was going to church. Aunt Effie was a big woman, with twinkling blue eyes. She was always smiling and she always had something to say. She dressed in the latest style, wearing big hats and dresses with frills and laces. No wonder Uncle Jad and Aunt Effie were considered the best-dressed couple in Lantern County. They spent a lot of money for clothes, and took plenty of time getting properly dressed for an occasion. Uncle Jad warned me about wearing the right clothes when I took over his store after he was gone. He said I'd be selling men's clothes, and young men would be watching what I wore, so I'd have to be a living example of the well-dressed man. Uncle Jad was himself a living example of the well-dressed man in Lantern County.

Uncle Jad was not tall, and he was big around the middle and little on each end, which made him hard to fit, but he wore the kind of clothes that made him look good. He wore small hats with broad brims, and pinstripe suits to give him height. On this particular fall Sunday afternoon he wore a pair of gloves, not because he'd need them in the car, but just to accent the positive. He never missed a trick when it came to wearing clothes or selling them. He wouldn't wear a pair of shoes out of his own house onto the porch unless they were shined.

"Effie, you look real well," Uncle Jad said. "You look real nice in that blue suit and that white blouse with the lace collar. It's most appropriate for early winter wear."

"Well, Poppie, *you* look wonderful," she complimented him. "Yes, I've got the most handsome man in Lantern County." She pulled him over to her and kissed him. She was always very affectionate with Uncle Jad.

Well, they were telling each other the truth with their compliments, I thought as they walked toward the garage. I got ahead of them and raised the garage door. Then Uncle Jad opened the car door for Aunt Effie and, after she got in, pushed the door shut gently behind her. Then he walked around to the other side, got in, started the engine, and backed the car out. He waited for me to pull the garage door back down and get in the back seat. This was our regular routine.

"Well, which way shall we go, Mother?" he asked Aunt Effie.

"Let's drive up Kinney Creek Valley and over to Taysville," she replied quickly. Aunt Effie always knew where she wanted to go. All Uncle Jad had to do, if he was undecided, was to ask. She could soon make a decision.

"Then up Kinney Valley and over to Taysville we will go," Uncle Jad said.

"The valley will be beautiful this time of year," I said. "I am glad, Aunt Effie, that you have chosen this route. There'll still be autumn leaves on many of the oaks."

"You are so right," Aunt Effie said.

Uncle Jad drove slowly and carefully down the street. When he came to the railway crossing at the edge of Ranceburg, he stopped and looked carefully this way and that, though he could see for a mile either up or down the tracks.

"It always pays to be careful," he said. "Never had a wreck or hit a person. I can certainly boast of my record."

"I've not been driving very long, Uncle Jad," I said. "But I've never hit a person or had a wreck either."

"You're a careful young man, Tom," he said. "That is why I'm turning everything over to you someday. You're a lot like my father and me. By looks and by nature you could well have been my son!"

"Thank you, Uncle Jad," I said.

"I've got security in life," he said. "Mother and I could live to the end of our days without my working anymore. Mother and I have had a good life. We go to our church, vote for our party, belong to a few organizations. We are somebody in Ranceburg now, and remember, Tom, it *pays* in this life to be somebody. So be a somebody when your Aunt Effie and I are no longer around. Marry a nice woman. Drive a nice car and wear good clothes. Make your life a safe adventure."

We were in Kinney Valley now. There had been a few killing frosts, and the grass on the pasture fields was brown, but the oaks in the wooded areas were still filled with multicolored leaves. As we passed farmhouse after farmhouse, Uncle Jad called out the name of the man who lived there, and told how many sons he had and if they traded at the store. Uncle Jad also mentioned which men he had to ask for cash, and which could be trusted to buy now and pay later.

There were green areas on the Kinney Valley bottoms where winter wheat had been sown. When the wind swept through the valley, the wheat bent and rose up again after the wind had passed. The sun was bright, and when a crow flew over, though we didn't always see the crow, we could tell where he was flying by his shadow on the brown grass of the fields.

"Life is just so wonderful, Poppie," Aunt Effie said with enthusiasm. And she put her arm around Uncle Jad's neck, pulled him over, and kissed his cheek.

"Do be careful, Mother," Uncle Jad said. "You could cause me to have my first wreck." Actually, he liked for her to do him this way. He was just pretending that it could be dangerous.

"Yes, I have a fine automobile, fine store, fine home, prettiest wife in Ranceburg," Uncle Jad said. "When a man gets old enough to have security and enjoy life, the tragedy is he's about old enough to die and leave this world. Not a very pleasant thought, but how true it is!"

If life could shape up for me, I thought, like it had shaped up for Uncle Jad and Aunt Effie, then I'd be a happy man. They had everything they wanted. They had security. And they would go to the end of their days like this!

"Look out, Poppie," Aunt Effie screamed, and covered her

face with her hands. Uncle Jad slammed on the brakes. The car skidded, tires squealed, and there was a thud. I saw a man fly up and hit a tree.

"Where did he come from?" Uncle Jad said. "I didn't see him until he was in front of the car."

"I saw just as you hit him!" I shouted.

"I wonder if I killed him," Uncle Jad said. His face was extremely white. He had lost that redness of color that made his cheeks pink. He sat with his hands on the steering wheel, looking out of the car at the man who lay at the foot of a large oak close to the highway.

"Oh, Poppie!" Aunt Effie wailed. She kept her hands over her face. "We bragged too soon! Life has been too good. We couldn't go on until the end with all this good fortune we have been having."

"He's not dead," Uncle Jad said. "He's trying to raise his head up to see what has happened. He's looking at the car. The poor fellow is looking at me! He's looking at me and trying to smile."

When Uncle Jad got out of the car, I got out with him.

"I never saw you," Uncle Jad told the man. "I'm sorry. How bad are you hurt?"

"I don't know," he answered softly. "Lift me upon my feet."

Uncle Jad got on one side and I got on the other, and we lifted him up. The man put his arms around our shoulders.

"See if you can bear your weight," Uncle Jad said.

The man tried one foot and then the other, and took two steps.

"Thank God!" Uncle Jad said. "No broken legs."

"It knocked the wind from me," the man said. "It jarred me to my foundations!"

Well, I knew that the big car had done that much and more too. The man had hit the side of the tree about six feet up and then fallen to the ground in a crumpled mass of humanity. Such a lick should have killed him outright.

"And where do you live?" Uncle Jad asked.

"Mort Simmons.' He sighed softly. "I'm John Simmons' boy."

He was a less-than-average-sized man who looked like he weighed about one hundred and thirty pounds. He was wearing a work shirt and jeans, and brush-scarred brogan shoes without socks. His face was unshaven, with a growth of stubbly black beard.

"And where do you live?" Uncle Jad asked again.

"On Shelf's Fork of Kinney."

"I thought I knew about everybody in Lantern County," Uncle Jad said, "but I'm sorry to say I don't know you or your father. Have you ever traded in my store in Ranceburg?"

"No, but I will in the future," the man replied.

"Poppie, let's take him to Doctor Raike and have him checked," Aunt Effie said.

"Not a bad idea, Mother," Uncle Jad said, and sighed.

We helped Mort Simmons to the car. When we took his arms from around our shoulders, he stood up all right, and although we helped him to get on the rear seat, I think he could have done it by himself.

"I feel much better," he said.

"What about going back to Ranceburg with us and letting Doctor Raike see you before we take you home?" Uncle Jad asked him.

"That will be all right," he said. "Yes, I'd like to go see how bad I'm hurt."

"You watch over him now, Tom," Uncle Jad told me. "If he gets dizzy he might just pitch over! Watch him!"

"I will, Uncle Jad," I said as I got in the car. "Don't you worry!"

"No, I've got a lot to worry about now," he said.

Aunt Effie, who couldn't stand much excitement, was trembling like a leaf on a November oak. Uncle Jad was still pale, and his hands shook so on the steering wheel that the car swerved back and forth. But there was very little traffic on the country roads this time of year, and we made it safely back to Dr. Raike's office in Ranceburg.

"I'm glad you are here, Doctor Raike," Uncle Jad said. "I hit this man and knocked him upon the side of an oak tree. I never saw him until my car hit him. Seems like he just came up out of the ground. Mort Simmons. You ever have him for a patient before?"

"Can't say that I have," Dr. Raike said. "No, I don't know that name Simmons in Lantern County."

Dr. Raike, who was almost as old as my Uncle Jad, was a little man with blue eyes and a kind face. He had once had golden blond hair, but time had turned it white.

"I'm John Simmons' boy, and we live on Shelf's Fork of Kinney Valley," Mort Simmons said.

"Well, I wouldn't know all the people who live on Kinney Valley any more," Dr. Raike said. "Now, let me see about you."

Dr. Raike went over Mort Simmons' head and arms and legs. Then he had Mort strip off his shirt so that his back could be examined.

"You've been shaken up," Dr. Raike said, "and you've got a lot of minor bruises. But you don't have any broken bones. I can release you, all right."

"Doc, how much do I owe you?" Uncle Jad asked.

"Not anything, Jad," Dr. Raike said. "Glad to do it. I hope everything will be all right for you."

"Thank you, Doc," Uncle Jad said, with a worried look.

Mort Simmons walked out of the office under his own power, though he limped and moved his legs very stiffly, and Uncle Jad wasn't as nervous on the drive back to Kinney Valley as he had been when he drove Mort in to Ranceburg. He had more self-composure.

"Let me out here," Mort Simmons said at last. "You can't drive up Shelf's Fork. The road is too bad. I don't want you to hurt your fine car."

"Sure you can make it all right?" Uncle Jad asked. "I'll try to take you on. I don't mind hurting my car."

"I can make it," Mort Simmons said. "Thank you for taking me to the doctor, and thank you for bringing me back."

"I'm so sorry this happened," Uncle Jad said. "I truly am."

Mort Simmons smiled and walked up a narrow little slit of a road alongside a small stream. Uncle Jad drove back toward Ranceburg.

"Well, Mother, our pleasant Sunday afternoon didn't turn out too well," he said. "It seems like I've dreamed what has happened! But when I wake up in the morning, I'll know it *did* happen. We might be sued for everything we have. We might not have any more security in this life."

"See John as soon as we get back," Aunt Effie said.

"John Lovell is a good lawyer," Uncle Jad said. "I'm glad we have him."

He asked Aunt Effie and me if either of us had seen where Mort Simmons came from at the time of the accident, and we said we never saw him until he was in front of the car and it was making contact with his body.

"I'd just climbed a rise," Uncle Jad said. "I wasn't going fast. If I had been going fast, he wouldn't have known what struck him. I am a lucky man."

"It's worked out for the best," Aunt Effie said. "I believe what is to be will be."

That evening Uncle Jad told John Lovell what had happened and how it had happened. John Lovell said that one bit of luck Uncle Jad would have if he were sued was that he would have two witnesses while Mort Simmons would only have himself. Uncle Jad told John Lovell how pleasant the man was and about his good manners. He told how Mort Simmons had been thankful for being taken to Dr. Raike and examined, and for being brought back to the Shelf's Fork road that led to his home. But John Lovell admonished Uncle Jad that Mort Simmons might nevertheless be thinking he had a good chance to sue, for everybody in Lantern Valley was pretty sure Uncle Jad had plenty of money.

When Uncle Jad came back from the lawyer's house, he told Aunt Effie about how he had been warned, and that night he was so worried he had to take medicine to put himself to sleep. The next morning he said to Aunt Effie, "Mother, yesterday is still a bad dream."

"I can't believe it either," she said. "But all three of us know that it *did* happen."

After breakfast Uncle Jad and I walked to the store, only two blocks away. We always opened at seven to catch the early morning trade of men on their way to work. It didn't seem like anything special was going to happen that day, but that afternoon I looked out of the office at the back of the store and saw Mort Simmons looking at some shirts. "See what he wants," Uncle Jad said when I told him. "I'll stay out of the way. I think I know what he wants. He wants to know more about this business before he sues me."

I went out to Mort Simmons and said with a smile, "Good afternoon." He smiled and said, "Howdy." Then he said, "I've come for some work shirts. We've been working in the tobacco, and I've got glue from the tobacco on all my shirts. I want a couple of clean shirts to go against my body. But I can't pay you until tomorrow. Our tobacco sells today in Taysville, and Pa will fetch the money home. So I'll pay you tomorrow, if that will be all right?"

"It will be all right," I said.

I knew Uncle Jad was in the back listening, and I knew he wouldn't want me to contrary Mort Simmons. I hoped I was doing things the right way, and decided that I would make the debt good if it didn't get paid.

I showed Mort Simmons all the work shirts we had, and he ended up buying two, size fifteen with a thirty-two-inch sleeve length. He smiled when he left, and I smiled and thanked him for purchasing in this store. When Mort Simmons was gone, Uncle Jad came out of the little office where he had kept himself hidden.

"You played it just right," he said. "You are a good diplomat, Tom! I feel sure he's going to sue, but it doesn't hurt to soften him up. We've let him know how friendly we are. We have built our business here because the people know we are friendly and reliable. We serve the public! And this will be the first time a Higgins has ever been sued. My father before me, Abraham Higgins, was never sued. And I have never been sued."

"I can't figure that man out," I said.

"Well, I can't either," Uncle Jad said. "But I don't think he will be back to pay for the shirts. I think this is the last time we will see him before he sues me. The friendly man that looks at you and smiles and asks some little favor, that is the man who will sue you quicker than you can bat your eye."

At home that evening we told Aunt Effie what had happened, and Aunt Effie, who had always been good at judging people, said she didn't know what to think. She said she was puzzled.

The next day went along very quietly until the early afternoon. I was restacking some shirts when I turned around, and there stood Mort Simmons again. I looked back and saw Uncle Jad scurrying into his office.

"Pa is here with me," Mort Simmons said. "And four of my brothers have come too."

I thought I was going to sink through the floor! His father and his brothers! They had come for Uncle Jad and me! It ran through my mind that this was the way with the people who lived among the high hills and in the deep hollows. Do something to one, even if it is an accident, and his blood kin will never stop harassing you as long as you live. Uncle Jad and I were in a lot of trouble!

"We've come to get some orders filled," Mort Simmons said. "It's shoe and clothes time before real winter sets in."

"All right," I said.

"Come and meet Mr. John Simmons, my pa, and my four brothers," he said.

I said hello to the five big men standing over by the door. And then I filled the biggest order I had ever filled for one family since I came to work in Uncle Jad's store. They took two pairs of shoes each; they took socks, underwear, handkerchiefs, work pants, work shirts and Sunday shirts. And all five brothers picked out suits. I handed out almost five hundred dollars' worth of clothes and shoes, and I was sure there would be no mention of paying till Mort Simmons got through suing Uncle Jad.

After they had everything, John Simmons said to me, "Where is your uncle? I would like to see him."

Here it comes, I thought. I knew that Uncle Jad couldn't run from trouble. He would have to meet this Simmons family and tell them he had an attorney to represent him. They would have to consult his attorney. Or his attorney could talk to them.

I went back to the office and told Uncle Jad that John Simmons and his sons were asking for him, and that they had ordered almost five hundred dollars' worth of merchandise. Uncle Jad's face lost its color just like it had when his car hit Mort Simmons and flung him upon the side of the big oak.

"Guess I'll have to go and face them," he said. "You with me, Tom?"

"Of course," I said.

We went back to where the Simmonses were standing with bundles of merchandise in their arms, and more bundles around them on the floor. Uncle Jad was shaking. His lips were twitching nervously, and he kept jerking his head.

"Mr. Higgins, I wanted to meet you," John Simmons said. "You are a fine man. That's the reason my son Mort was in here yesterday. And that's why I brought my other sons here today to get new Sunday suits and winter clothes and shoes."

"Thank you, Mr. Simmons," Uncle Jad stammered. He couldn't understand why he was being called a fine man.

"We've got our tobacco money now," John Simmons said. "No charging anything. Here is what we owe you, including the cost of those shirts Mort bought yesterday."

Uncle Jad and I stood there, so surprised we couldn't speak, and John Simmons handed over the money, every cent. "As I have said, Mr. Higgins," he said, "we know from what happened last Sunday that you are a fine man."

"Last Sunday? You mean the accident?" Uncle Jad was still stammering.

"It was not the kind of accident you mean," John Simmons corrected him. "You see, my son Mort has a fault. He's as absentminded as can be, never thinks what he's doing or looks where he is going. I have warned him many times about that fault, but he keeps walking out in front of cars, and he tells me he just can't think why it's so hard for him to remember not to do it. He will be marked by a car one of these days."

Uncle Jad was beginning to recover himself. Color was coming back into his face.

"You see, Mr. Higgins," John Simmons said, "my son Mort has been struck by cars half a dozen times, and you're the only man who ever picked him up, took him to the doctor, and was even nice enough to fetch him back toward his home. I just want you to know that his mother and I appreciate what you did. And buying from you is a good way to thank you from now on. Thank you."

Uncle Jad and I shook hands with all the Simmonses, and they smiled and we smiled. I have known my Uncle Jad since I was a little boy big enough to remember anything. And I never saw him so happy as he was right then, though he still had a puzzled look on his face.

CAROL STURM
The Kid Who Fractioned

(FROM PRAIRIE SCHOONER)

FROM FAR DOWN the block Rose McGworski spotted the church spire tall against the dusky sky. She plodded toward it eagerly, leaning backward a bit to offset her unaccustomed weight. Maybe I shouldn't be goin' if it's gonna mark the baby, she thought, frowning at the bulge beneath her maternity jacket. But I just *had* to get outta that apartment and watchin' Gus drinkin' beer all the time!

In front of the old red brick church, Rose drew a hurried breath, then picked her way over the cracked sidewalk, past the scrawny rose bushes and lilacs to the side door. Above it hung a bare light bulb and a hand-lettered sign: BINGO. Inside the building it was dim and hot. She stood on the landing listening to the sounds from the basement while her eyes gradually made out the stone stairway. In her throat she felt the same queasy tremblings that always came when she went to a place for the first time. She swallowed once and followed the stone steps down to the basement.

The large room was crowded with women drinking grape soda, smoking filter-tipped cigarettes, and talking to no one and everyone simultaneously. Toddlers chased each other around crying infants in strollers. At last Rose's eyes settled on a table loaded with lamps, steak knives with imitation bone handles, toilet bowl brushes, home hair-cutting sets, and fluffy throw rugs. At least they got good stuff for prizes! she thought, her eyes lingering long on the assortment.

At the head of the farthest table Rose noticed a man whirling a wire cage of dice. Faster and faster he whirled the cage as Rose watched in growing fascination. At the peak of his frenzy, a woman in a pink linen sheath yelled, "Let's go already," and instantly the room's noises drifted down to murmurings.

Then one of the women spotted Rose. "Come on in and grab a chair, honey."

Rose waddled over eagerly.

"My God, kid, you're preg!" The woman shoved the green-visored cap farther back on her perspiring forehead.

Rose giggled as she sat down on the wooden folding chair next to the woman.

"I'm Mary Murphy." The woman shot a blast of smoke over Rose's head. "But everybody here calls me Fat Mary. Guess you can see why." She nudged Rose and chortled once. "Lemme get ya started."

Fat Mary shoved a handful of corn kernels to Rose and thumped the table for someone to bring over the bingo cards.

"You gotta be careful ya pick lucky ones," she hissed confidentially to Rose, alternately squinting and grunting at the cards. "Here. These are sure shots for four corner wins."

Rose looked at the three dog-eared cards before her and faltered. "I don't know if I can—I ain't never—"

"That's okay, kid," Fat Mary grinned benevolently. "I know ya ain't never been here before. I'll keep 'em in the corner of my eyes."

Rose blinked at the solid block of cards stacked in front of Fat Mary. "Okay, but I don't wanna make you miss your—"

Fat Mary laughed hoarsely. "That's okay, kid. Tell ya the truth, that's why I called ya over when I seen ya come in the door. 'Beginner beside ya, luck won't deride ya.'" She cackled again.

Rose said, "Well, I—". But a boy with a canvas money pouch tapped her on the shoulder.

"Lemme get 'em this game for ya," Fat Mary rasped. "You can get 'em next game for both of us. 'Even Steven,' huh?" She grabbed a quarter from her wallet and tossed the wallet back onto the table. "Smart to play three," she confided in a hoarse whisper, " 'cause you're gettin' one for a nickel. Ten cents apiece, three for a quarter."

Rose said, "I—" But the man at the front of the room started calling bingo numbers.

All evening Rose lost herself in the bingo cards, the shouts of the winners, and Fat Mary's rasping commentary. When the lights on the stage flicked on, she looked up at the wall clock in surprise. My gosh, I been happy all night, she marveled. I ain't even thought about Gus once!

"Sure goes fast, don't it, kid?" Fat Mary hollered over the din. "Father always talks at the end."

Rose turned toward the stage. A priest she thought looked like Tyrone Power stood in the center of the stage. Behind him a canvas curtain made up of flashy square advertisements for the local drugstores, meat markets, and insurance agencies swayed lightly in the gentle summer breeze, making Rose feel a little dizzy.

The priest gripped the microphone. "Good ladies," he intoned with obvious sincerity. The loudspeaker shrilled once and from then on Rose could only watch the priest's lips moving.

"Don't worry, kid," Fat Mary consoled. "Father's just tellin' us how glad he is we had us a good time. Tells us every time." She turned and noticed Rose's flushed face. "You like bingo, kid? You want me to tell ya the other places?"

Rose nodded.

"Mondays and Fridays at St. Ben's, Holy Angels on Tuesdays and Saturdays, and Wednesdays and Sundays here."

Rose silently rehearsed the nights as she left the church basement arm-in-arm with her new friend.

"You wanna come home with me and—have a beer?" Rose dared ask once they were outside. " 'Course if Gus is still there the beer'll all be inside him!" She laughed nervously.

"Who's Gus?" Fat Mary inquired suspiciously.

"I married him," Rose said simply.

"A drinker, huh?" Fat Mary asked indignantly.

"Yeah. Some people might think Gus ain't so much, but when I first met him he looked sorta like this here picture of Ernest Hemingway I seen in a magazine once. I thought Gus was really something." She snorted, remembering how Gus had courted her by waiting until she left work and tapping on his auto horn from halfway down the block until she gradually worked up enough courage to speak when she passed his gray Chevvy coupe. "Looked like Ernest Hemingway on account of he don't shave most days."

"God!" said Fat Mary.

Then, afraid lest she had given the impression she had married blindly, Rose sought to convey some of the magic of her husband. "Before we were married, Gus used to tell me about the water tanks he painted and the ceilings and all the high dangerous places, and I could just see the faces of all them ladies where I work when I said I was married to the guy who done all that." Rose sighed, remembering how she had imagined all the good things that marrying Gus had never brought.

Fat Mary seemed to understand. "Where ya workin'?" she asked.

"The Beauty Nook on North Michigan," Rose said proudly. "It ain't bad, with all them classy ladies comin' in for washes and sets and all that." Rose smiled mysteriously, failing to mention that her chores were restricted to shampooing customers' daughters, cleaning the brushes and combs, and sweeping up after haircuts.

"I guess when I started workin' there I figured I'd get to be like them ladies, all with fancy clothes and stuff, if I was with 'em enough," she said soberly. "They sure got class! I can spot a dentist's wife a block away. But you know, after bein' with 'em, I found somethin' out. They're all stuck-up! I wouldn't even *wanna* be like 'em!"

"God, ain't it the truth!" Fat Mary exploded.

"I'm thinkin' of gettin' me another job. I just haven't decided where yet," Rose said mysteriously.

"You been to college?"

"Well, not exactly. Who'd want to go, anyway?"

"God, I know what you mean," Fat Mary grunted.

"High school was bad enough. Always hearin' about stuff that nobody cared about, or sittin' in some dark auditorium watchin' them stuck-up ones gettin' called on the stage to get awards that nobody'd care about havin'."

Fat Mary pursed her lips and nodded knowingly.

"After a while I left high school and started working. That was right after my father died and my mother and sister went to New Jersey to live with my aunt. Then Gus and me got married. Right after that, Gus falls off a ladder on to this here radiator and now he says it hurts him to lift a paint brush." Rose made a face. "So all I do now is work and evenings watch him drink beer."

"My God, kid," Fat Mary said, "you've sure had it."

"No," Rose said seriously. "I learned about life and people. I know what the whole thing's about now. Sure, I had me some rough times, but *now* things are gonna be different. The baby'll make everything better. You wait and see."

"My God, kid, you're a good one!" Fat Mary thumped Rose across the butt.

They reached Rose's apartment building and Rose led Fat Mary up the narrow stairs.

"Watch them loose pieces of stuff," Rose warned. "Them pieces is always comin' off the stairs."

Rose opened the apartment door. Gus was sprawled on the couch staring at the television, a beer can balanced on his bare chest.

Fat Mary sat down at the kitchen table and looked around at the two-room efficiency.

"Gus got some paint wholesale and done the walls when he first moved in here with me," Rose said in a loud voice, jerking her head significantly toward the battleship-gray enamel paint. "That's *all* he's done since the honeymoon." She turned away from Fat Mary suddenly, still having to choke down disgust about her honeymoon, when she had had to cash her own paycheck their first night away.

Gus turned his large bristle-haired head toward them and waved a twenty-dollar bill. "See this? Won it today bettin' some guys I could make a cat pick up a beer bottle."

"That tavern again," Rose said scornfully, sliding the porcelain sugar bowl deftly over the tear in the oilcloth on the kitchen table. "Always that tavern. And me gettin' close to my time."

"Say," said Fat Mary. "Why don't I see if I can get Gus workin' nights at the place I work at days?"

Rose brightened. "Hey Gus, ya hear that?"

Without looking away from the TV, Gus touched his forearm and winced.

The following week Rose quit the Beauty Nook and Gus started bartending nights at the Pennsylvania Bar and Grill.

To show her gratitude to Fat Mary, Rose missed only six nights of bingo when the baby came.

Gus first saw his son the night Rose arrived home from the hospital.

"I picked him out a name already," she told him proudly.

Later that week Rose took the skinny infant to church and had him christened Ernest Hemingway McGworski.

At last Rose fancied the tide of her fortunes had truly changed. No longer an observer of life's benefits, she felt herself beginning to be a participant, and at times, even a star. Now that she no longer worked at the Beauty Nook, she slept late each morning, got up and got herself dressed and her face put on extra special. Then she tended little Ernest, cooing over him: "You gotta wear somethin' different and cute every day, honey, so's the people will notice us."

Things ain't never been like this before, she thought triumphantly while she paraded the streets with her new son. I'm *somebody* now! These people look at me and even *smile*. Everybody notices me when I tell 'em Ernest's name!

Rose sometimes went back to the Beauty Nook to show Ernest to the ladies. Sometimes she pretended to examine merchandise so she could talk about Ernest to the clerks in stores. But always on Fridays she attended the matinee at the Ritz.

Now I can see all the first-run movies in town, she thought happily. Babies are *sure* good to have. Only I just wish Ernest didn't pee on me so much at the movies.

At night Rose and the baby met Fat Mary at the church basement. Soon Ernest graduated from the secondhand baby buggy to the floor around Rose's feet, and spent his evenings mouthing corn kernels and sucking on the ends of Rose's sandal straps.

One night after bingo while Rose plucked corn kernels from her son's mouth, she saw that the bows on her black patent leather flats had something else on them besides the usual slobber. Teeth marks!

"Hey, look," Rose shouted. "Ernest Hemingway's got teeth!"

Fat Mary stuck her fingers into Ernest's mouth and found out for herself. "By God, he sure does!"

In the midst of this unique attention, Ernest spoke his first word. He looked up at Rose, drooled from both corners of his mouth, and gleefully bubbled, "B—in—go!"

"God, ain't that cute! Hi, ya little Bingo," Fat Mary burst out.

"Bingo, bingo, bingo," he repeated.

Nothing else distinguishable passed over his lips until he was nearly three.

Untroubled by his bumbling gushes of sounds, Rose continued showing Bingo off unceasingly.

"This is *my* boy," she beamed. "*My* boy. And he's good and smart and's gonna be *somebody*. I *know* it."

Rose repeated it so often that she came to fully believe it herself, and her unfaltering belief served as reason enough to say it many more times.

Things, indeed, had never seemed better to her.

Then one night when she returned from the church basement with little Bingo, she found a note from Gus saying his arm hurt him so bad that he was going to California because he heard that was where the best doctors were.

After the first shock, Rose brooded about Bingo. "How'm I gonna tell poor Bingo he ain't got no more Daddy?"

But the four-year-old reacted calmly to her explanation of Gus's departure, merely questioning, "Man go bye-bye?" whenever he saw a beer can.

Now I gotta go back to work, Rose thought. She left Bingo with a lady in the same apartment building and returned to the Beauty Nook.

"Why, my kid's so smart he knows more in his little finger than them other kids in their whole head," she told the customers.

She swept away her disappointments about Gus with the fallen wisps of hair. She daydreamed about her son constantly while she washed the hard-rubber combs. Someday Bingo'll *build* water towers like Gus *said* he painted. Or maybe he'll write books better'n the other Ernest Hemingway.

When it came time for Bingo to start school, Rose's pride knew no bounds. Imagine, she marveled. Me! Me! The mother of a first-grader!

She bought Bingo the best clothes she could afford, slicked down his straight yellow hair with perfume, pinned his name onto the front of his shirt, and proudly sent him off to school with four unsharpened colored pencils.

The phone call came during the second week of school. It didn't surprise Rose. She had been impatiently waiting for the school to recognize Bingo's talents.

"Don't be alarmed," the voice said. "But Dr. Higgins, our school psychologist, examined Ernest yesterday, following the request of his first-grade teacher. He would like to discuss Ernest's abilities with you."

Rose considered this a minute. "Sure. Fine. I could come

talk to him." Imagine! she thought after she had hung up. My Ernest being promoted *so soon!*

She triumphantly told her news to Fat Mary that night at the church basement.

"Bernice Hatenburg had a conference about her kid, too," Fat Mary said glumly. "Somethin' about him bein' ready to read and all that. He went three years to the first grade."

Rose frowned. "I'd just *die* if Bingo wasn't *somebody*, and *me* bein' his mother."

"Don't worry, kid," Fat Mary assured her. "Bingo's a good boy."

Thus assured, Rose traveled through the week before her conference with the school psychologist. Rather a good week, too, she concluded. Three money wins and a porcelain lamp with blue violets.

She got to school early on Friday. Outside Dr. Higgins' door she stopped and made sure her seams were straight. For herself, it didn't matter, but she wanted the school people to know Bingo had a good mother.

"Dr. Higgins?" she asked. The young man behind the gray metallic desk arose.

"Mrs. McGworski, I asked you to come in today because the first-grade teacher isn't sure Ernest belongs in her room," Dr. Higgins said as Rose sat down.

Sure Bingo's real smart, she thought, swelling proudly and looking around her at all the books.

"Since testing Ernest I can say I heartily agree with her. Do you have any idea of Ernest's I.Q.? I mean, do you realize he's—"

"Well, no," she interrupted him modestly. "If you mean, do I *know* about him, all my lady friends say he's a real good boy."

"Yes, I'm sure he must be an obedient child," Dr. Higgins said gingerly.

Rose watched him impatiently while he toyed with a pencil. Just tell me what grade you want Bingo to be in and let me go back at the Beauty Nook, she thought.

"Did he do good for you in the tests?" she asked finally to break the silence.

"The truth of the matter," said Dr. Higgins in a rush, "is that Ernest's I.Q. is about 47. Now I know that this might come as a—"

"Forty-seven!" exclaimed Rose. "Imagine that! And him bein' only six years old!"

Dr. Higgins opened his mouth and closed it without speaking. "I don't think you quite understand what I'm trying to say," he said, swallowing several times. He pointed to a sheet of paper in front of him. "Listen to this. I asked Ernest to name four colors. He said: 'Yellow goes to orange, orange goes to red, red goes to blue, blue goes to green.' I must confess I don't see what—"

"He's right!" Rose laughed delightedly. "Fat Mary, she's at bingo after she gets through work at the tav—the sal—the place where she works, and she tells Ernest about the juke box. It goes just like he said. Yellow, orange, red, blue, green. Then the yellow again. He's right!"

"Oh," said Dr. Higgins. He pushed aside the papers, laid his chin in his hands, and stared at the woman facing him. "Mrs. McGworski, sometimes there are certain aberrations—" He stopped as soon as he saw the woman's expression cringe. He pulled the papers back in front of him and reread a line. He tried again. "The child doesn't seem to know the same things that the rest of the first-graders know. For example, numbers."

Rose half-stood in her excitement. "Oh, then you know about his fractioning?"

"His WHAT?"

"His fractioning. He fractions real good. He—" Her sentence stopped midway as a young lady opened the door, rolled her eyes ceilingward, and pushed Bingo into the room.

"That," said Dr. Higgins reverently after the woman had left, "was Ernest's first-grade teacher."

Bingo ignored Dr. Higgins and trotted over to Rose.

"Hi, honey," she said, giving him an affectionate pat on the head. "Let's show the man how good you fraction."

She scooped Bingo up onto her lap and faced him around toward the psychologist. "Now Bingo," she said sweetly, "listen to Mama. He's real good at fractioning," she confided to Dr. Higgins. "Now Bingo, if me and this other lady the both of us goes to bingo and wins the same game, and the winner's s'posed to get fifteen dollars, you tell the man here how much Mama'd get."

Bingo's eyes glistened. "Seven-fifty."

"That's good, honey. *Real* good." She gave him another pat on the head. "Now you see, Dr. Higgins, he's real good at fractioning."

Dr. Higgins recovered from choking and asked, "Could you have him do another? I mean, is he getting tired?"

"Tired! F'heaven sakes, no! He fractions all night at the church basement, don't you, honey? Let's do another one, okay? Now, if me and two of them other ladies all shouted at the same time, and they had the jackpot a hundred dollars, you tell the man here how much we'd take home."

Bingo gurgled once and slid off Rose's lap. "Thirty-three dollars and thirty-three cents and one for the beer can."

Rose laughed. "What he means, if the money's not even, we put the extra in this little can, sorta like a beer can."

The psychologist cleared his throat, his eyes wide. "Mrs. McGworski, I suppose the term 'idiot savant' is strange to you?"

"I never learned no foreign tongues," Rose admitted.

The psychologist waited a moment. "Then let me explain. I know you want Ernest to be happy."

Rose nodded enthusiastically.

The psychologist drew a deep breath and plunged. "I think, in view of Ernest's—his fractioning—that he would be very happy at the State Training School."

"The what?" Rose asked.

"A Training School. They have boys living there who are

his same age. Boys who are slower learners, ones who need special help in their—their academ—their fractioning."

Rose hesitated. The memories of the combs she had cleaned, the never-realized promises of Gus, the hopes of Ernest—but her own selfishness must not stand in the way of Ernest's happiness—all merged into a generous certitude. She pulled herself up erectly. "Sure. Sure, doctor." She nodded rapidly, ignoring the tears that formed automatically in her eyes. "Sure, I'd let Ernest go there and live with them other kids. He'd be glad to go there and live." She jabbed Bingo with her elbow. "Wouldn't you go live there, honey?"

Bingo sat down on the floor, drew the soles of his shoes together, and fingered the fly on his pants.

"Good," said Dr. Higgins. "Ernest can enter the school as soon as we make certain arrangements."

Rose beamed. "Sure, doctor." She stood up. "But with Bing—Ernest at this other school, the money—I work, but—"

"Don't let money bother you. We'll work out satisfactory arrangements."

Rose left his office glowing, with Bingo tagging after her.

That night she bought a bottle of Mogen David and invited Fat Mary to the apartment. "This here's a celebration," she said, waving toward the bottle of wine. "Bingo's goin' to a special school."

"God!" Fat Mary gasped.

"Yeah," said Rose modestly. "That doctor at school didn't say too much about it, but I figured out that them boys at the school *need* Bingo to teach 'em fractioning."

"God!" Fat Mary gasped again.

"Them boys are 'slow learners,'" Rose said in a reverential whisper.

"Really, kid?"

Rose smiled serenely. "Yeah. I wouldn't have to work, what with Bingo's money from teachin'. But I'm thinkin' of goin' ahead and workin' anyway, so's I don't miss him too much."

Fat Mary nodded emphatic agreement.

In the days before Bingo was to leave, Rose sang delightedly through the two-room efficiency. "This is even better'n what I thought," she grinned at Bingo. "You on the stage, fractioning, the other boys sittin' there watchin' you." She could almost hear the boys stomping and whistling as Bingo fractioned for them. Bingo tellin' them how he fractioned, learnin' them all to fraction. Other schools wantin' Bingo—

Saturday morning Rose trimmed Bingo's hair and dressed him and tied his new shoes and gave him a new little blue school bag with a magazine in it to carry. She called a cab to take him to the bus depot, and told the driver how to put him on the right bus.

When at last she saw Bingo leaving, tears slipped down her face. She hugged her son hard against her, then slammed the cab door and waved until he was out of sight.

"*My* son," she excitedly began improvising the conversation with the lady who always acted so high and mighty about *her* children. "*My* son—"

ROBERT TRAVERS

The Big Brown Trout

(FROM ARGOSY)

CLAY MILLER LEANED against the slope of his spring-green pasture and watched the Co-op milk truck spiraling down the road toward the city. The city was a long way from the Schoharie hills; it was at the faraway end of the truck route. And that's the way Clay Miller wanted it. At this end of the route—Clay's end—was the farm. The farm was the way he wanted it, too.

Turning toward the higher acres, he saw his spread of Ayrshires drifting away from the patches of early morning sun. By noon, they would be under the maples, hunched together in the shade. The late afternoon would nudge them easterly again toward the high red barn and the milking stalls. The Ayrshires moved with the sun and the seasons, and Clay Miller moved with them.

Near the barn was the hundred-year-old house he had restored with his own hands and his own tools. It also operated on the time of sun and season. Right now, Clay knew, his wife would be in the kitchen, pushing the buttons on the electric stove. The boys, both of them towheads, would be coming down for breakfast; they'd eat and run for the school bus. Then the chores, the orderly pattern of the day's labor, until the sun moved all the way across the sky.

To Clay Miller, there was nothing more important than the routine of house and farm. He didn't have time left over for the city or for the world, either. In politics, he supported the objectives and the involvements of the free world without paying too much attention to what was going on in Vietnam or in Cuba. He was a dairy farmer. His world was enclosed by the rim of the Schoharie hills. As he headed for the house, he was thinking about the things that were closest to him, things such as bacon and eggs and, after a couple of cups of coffee, the repairs to be made on one of the milking machines.

His wife, Helen—she was as towheaded and blue-eyed as the two boys—met him at the kitchen door. "They phoned a telegram from town," she said.

"Those tractor parts finally arrived?" he asked.

"No. It's signed 'Sergeant Sales.' " Then she read the words she had scribbled on the telephone pad: "In New York for a sales conference. Any chance for a weekend reunion with Corporal Hayfoot? How is the fishing up there?"

"That's Harry Larkin!" Clay said. And just saying the name took him back a long, long time. Clay and Harry had been in the same infantry company, in the same squad and often in the same foxhole throughout the Korean War. They were young then, perhaps too young to understand what it was all about. They concentrated, instead, on survival. Clayton Miller, from upstate New York, and Chicago-born Harry Larkin were tossed together in a bleak village in southern Korea, and they learned how to stay alive as they moved north over the alien plains and rocky steeps.

After the truce, Clay returned to Albany and tried to readjust to civilian life. It wasn't easy; he had no goal or direction. What he did have, though, was a small legacy left by his father and a driving need to make his own, and separate, peace. He finally found the place he was looking for—an old farmhouse surrounded by eighty grassy acres in the Schoharie hills. His inheritance covered the down payment, with a little left over for enough Ayrshires to build a herd. Then, starting along the way he wanted to go, he married the girl he'd known before Korea. They settled on the land, and Clay learned dairy farming the hard way.

Harry Larkin went back to Chicago, joined a high-powered manufacturing firm and lit into his new job as if he were still fighting a war. After five years, he was sales manager and, after three more, vice-president in charge of sales. He was smart and ambitious. He got around. His Christmas cards, expensively engraved, and the occasional letters were postmarked from every industrial city west of the Mississippi. Now, for the first time in twelve years, he had come this close to the Army buddy he used to call Corporal Hayfoot.

"I've told you about him," Clay said to his wife. "We were in Korea."

While she put his breakfast on the table, he phoned a telegram to Harry Larkin's hotel: TAKE ROUTE 145 TO SCHOHARIE. GET DIRECTIONS TO OUR PLACE AT FEED STORE THERE. HAVE SET OUT THE JUG, AND THE FISH ARE BITING IN THE CREEK.

Harry Larkin arrived at the farm the following Friday evening in a Cadillac, bringing with him a cowhide traveling bag and a handful of beat-up fly rods. He was older, of course; the gray was starting to show around his temples. But he still looked strong and very sure of himself.

Harry took one look at Helen Miller, grinned, and said something about old Corporal Hayfoot being a lucky guy. Helen liked him; when she went out to the kitchen, Clay could tell she was going to dig the best steaks out of the freezer. The boys liked him, too.

Later, when Clay and Harry were alone with a bottle between them and the quiet house like some kind of a cover around them, they talked about the Army. It was nostalgic talk. They didn't recall any of the tough times; they remembered only the sunny days. Soon, since there hadn't been many sunny days in Korea, they were talking about their peacetime careers.

"Old Corporal Hayfoot," Harry said, grinning. "I was

afraid you'd end up pushing a plow. What happened to you?"

"Happened?" Clay asked. "What do you mean? Man, I've got it made!"

Harry wasn't so sure about that. "I thought you were going into electronics. You had the head for it."

"I changed my head."

Harry laughed. "I guess a real campaigner can get used to anything."

"Depends on what you want to get used to," Clay said.

"Well ..." Harry glanced around the living room. There was a stack of magazines, farming and animal husbandry journals, on the table. Also, a few books and a country newspaper, creased and unread.

"It's kind of quiet," he remarked. He let it go at that and shifted to a discussion of what was going on in the world. But, on that subject, Clay didn't have much to say.

"I'm not getting to you," Harry said.

"I'm not a debater," Clay replied. "I'm a farmer."

"And that's enough for you?"

"Sure is. Tomorrow, I'll show you around the place. You'll see what I mean."

"Okay," Harry said. "After I get back from the creek."

Harry left right after breakfast the next morning, wearing grimy flannels, a felt hat decorated with hand-tied flies and a nicely blackened briar pipe. The older Miller boy, ten-year-old Tommy, went with him.

Clay called after them: "Good luck!"

Harry signaled the all-okay sign. As he swung the Cadillac around, he shouted: "Tell Helen we'll bring fish for supper."

They did get back in time for supper, but Harry didn't have any fish.

"I thought Schoharie Creek was a real trout stream," he said. "There's nothing in it bigger than your hand!" He glanced at Tommy. "Even an experienced guide, the best one I ever had, couldn't get me a good strike."

Tommy grinned. He'd had a fine day; he learned something about fly-casting and heard a lot of good stories. But Clay could see that Harry was disappointed. To Harry, taking a fish would be like landing a new account. He'd hate to lose.

"You can try it again tomorrow," Clay told him. "Your luck will change."

Harry shook his head. "It's not luck. The water's too high; the big ones just aren't hitting."

Later on, as the sun was starting to touch the top of the hills, Clay took Harry out to the barn and showed him the gleaming equipment racked up under massive oak beams. They inspected the milking stalls, the feed bins, the cooling room. Finally, they went up the back path and looked at the Ayrshires standing philosophically in the dusk. There was a breeze with the new-grass smell in it, and the birds were as busy and noisy as they always were just before sundown.

"It's peaceful," Harry admitted. "But what the hell, Clay. You're cut out for more action."

"What kind of action?" Clay asked.

"There's a job opening with my outfit. On the management side. You'd be good at it. You'd save more in a year than you'll make here in ten. And you'd be *doing* something."

"I *am* doing something," Clay pointed out. He couldn't quite find the words for the way he felt about his eighty acres. He kicked out a bit of pasture dirt. "This is my land," he said. "I'm working it."

Harry wasn't convinced. "I'm not just talking about a job," he said. "Or about money. Things are going on, Clay. Over in the Pacific. In the Caribbean. Even in Europe. The people in Washington, the ones who know the score, are saying we're in a fight for our lives. You know—our national lives. We're fighting for everything we are, everything we stand for. It's a lot bigger than Korea ever was. A lot bigger. And everything we have depends on how it turns out."

"I know it," Clay said.

"Sure, you know it." Harry was talking fast, like a salesman selling something he really believed in. "But you're not in it. You're way back in the hills. You're ducking away from the front lines—something you never did before."

"That's kind of rough talk," Clay said.

"It's straight talk," Harry said.

Clay looked at him. They were friends, good friends; they had covered a lot of ground together. In Korea, they had talked bluntly about what they thought and believed. They were still talking that way—as though the time between this hour and the hours in Korea hadn't changed anything at all.

"See if you can get this through your head," Clay said. "Right here is the front lines for me."

"No," Harry said. "You're on the sidelines; you're sitting it out."

"What does your company make?" Clay asked. "Machine parts?"

"Right."

"And that's more important than running a dairy farm?"

"It might be," Harry said. "We're ready to convert to essentials, to weapons, in twelve hours. But that's still not what I mean. I mean the thinking part of it. You're ... well, you're isolated. You're not part of what's going on."

"You think what I'm doing doesn't count?" Clay asked.

"It's not just doing something, Clay. Plenty of people aren't doing anything. I mean, they're not up in the front lines. But they're *still* involved. Even in just thinking. They're part of what's going on."

Clay used one of the phrases they had tossed around in Korea. "You figure I've been brainwashed?"

"Something like that," Harry said.

"Let me tell *you* something," Clay said. "All this is part of what's going on, too." He motioned toward the darkening stretch of his acres. "The land is what the shooting is all about in the first place. It gives men something to fight for. Don't you see that?" There was passion in his voice. "This farm went through the Revolution. And the Civil War. And all the rest of them. And the people on the land went through those wars. They were in them just staying here, just *being* here. That meant as much, in the long run, as joining up with a regiment." He paused. "The land is in the war. In any war, a cold war or a hot one. Remember how we held those hills in Korea? Now I'm holding these hills. The way the families living here before us held them. You understand what I mean?"

"Let me think about it," Harry said. He was starting to turn away. "Anyway, we better knock it off for awhile— before we start slugging."

They didn't talk any more as they crossed the meadow. The evening was quiet, too. They could hear the water tinkling in the pool long before they elbowed through the fringe of laurel.

When Clay Miller bought his eighty acres, the pool wasn't much more than a trickle of water coursing along an old stream bed. But after the house and barn were in shape, he found time to build a timber dam along the downgrade end of a little valley. Thereafter, the mud of several Aprils and the leaves of October chinked the dam. It became as solid as stone; the water, flowing steadily from a hillside spring, collected and spread out against it and deepened into a broad pool. There was a screen of laurel around it, and the birches had grown and leaned their branches toward the water.

Harry had forgotten his salesman's pitch about the cold war. He was looking at the pool with a fisherman's eye. "Nice," he said. "Ever think of stocking it?"

"There's some bluegills in it," Clay said. "And a few perch."

"I mean *fish*," Harry said.

As he spoke, the big brown trout—which Clay Miller knew was also in the pool—started to feed. There was a dimpling of the darker water near the dam as he rolled over lazily and scooped up a hatch of insects. Then he broke water, leaping, throwing a lot of spray.

"That's a trout!" Harry shouted.

Clay didn't say anything.

"How'd a buster like that get in there?" Harry asked. He was excited.

"I don't know," Clay said.

That was a fact. Clay didn't know where the big brown trout came from. Perhaps when he was a fingerling, he was washed down in the flood waters following a late winter thaw. Perhaps some bird picked him up out of the creek and, on the way to his nest, dropped him into the widening pool. There were a lot of possibilities. But who could tell now where the trout came from? And what difference did it make? He was there.

Clay Miller first saw the trout two years after the dam was built. During the following years, he watched him grow, and he developed a real feeling, a kinship, for him. Sometimes, in the summery dusk, he stood by the pool and heard the trout finning near a submerged root. It occurred to Clay that the fish lived in water which was as calm, on its surface anyway, as the farm. You wouldn't expect to find so big a fish in such a placid pool. And you wouldn't believe he'd be content to stay there—he had a heritage linked to the freedom of a running stream. But there he was; he had adapted to the backwaters. Even so, he was still close to his origins. The water the trout lived in came down from the hills. Before that, it came from a river. And, before that, from the sky.

Harry was saying: "Nothing to match him in the Schoharie."

"I suppose not," Clay said.

"You ever cast for him?"

Clay shook his head.

The trout jumped again. After a moment, Harry said, "I'd sure like to try a couple a' lures on him."

Clay hesitated. Then, as heartily as he could, he said, "It's okay with me. I'll give you an early call."

Sunday was Harry's last day. He was up, dressed and at the pool by sunrise. Clay took a lot of time over a cup of coffee and then joined him there.

Harry cast and retrieved skillfully, until the sun was an hour high. Handling the four-ounce rod as though he'd been born with it, he worked the sides and then the center of the pool. He showed more patience than one might suspect he had. He was surely a match for the big brown trout. They both were wise and wary. And they both could play the old waiting game.

Clay watched and said nothing. He knew the trout did most of his feeding in late afternoon. Harry must have realized it, too. "I'll try again," he said. "Later."

It was a pleasant day, but neither Clay nor Harry were with it. They were thinking, in different ways, about the pool. And, at five o'clock, they were back there.

"This is it," Harry said. "Last round."

After he cast a fly into the center of the pool, Clay sat down, put his shoulders against one of the birches and took it easy. He wasn't worrying much. He knew Harry would never catch the trout that way.

Harry switched to a silver-colored streamer, a Gray Drake, and then to one of the flies he had tied himself. But nothing happened.

"Other side may be better," he decided.

Sitting silently, facing into the last slants of the sun, Clay watched Harry cross the log dam. Standing well back from the opposite shore, he cast again into the center of the pool.

Clay got out a cigarette and struck a match. There was less than half an hour's fishing time left, and he was beginning to think the big brown trout was safe because he never fed in the center of the pool. He stayed close to a deep hole at the base of the dam, and even the most expert angler probably couldn't coax him away from it. That was one thing Harry didn't know. And Clay didn't tell him. He was neutral.

He was giving both Harry and the trout an even break. He leaned against the birch, waiting to see what would happen.

As he watched the smooth cast and retrieve, cast and retrieve, Clay's thoughts wandered back to a particular night in Korea. In a darkness torn with flares and shell bursts, they were starting the long journey to the crest of some nameless ridge. It was a position they had taken and lost, and taken and lost again. This time, they had to go up and stay there. And they went up, and they did stay there. But not all of them made it all the way. Clay Miller was one of them. A few crouching steps from the top, he stumbled into a blinding flash that was half hit and half concussion. Panic and fear flooded into every part of his mind. He retreated away from it into something even darker than the night. Then, Harry Larkin was bending over him, pulling him back to consciousness. As he got his eyes open, he heard Harry talking, telling him to hang on until the medics came.

During the next half hour, Harry kept talking, talking and holding onto him. And when he couldn't think of anything else to say, he talked about a trout stream he had fished years before he ever heard of Korea. He told Clay how it felt to wade in the stream and cast and get a strike. He described the water, the cool feel of it, the warmth of the sun, the sound of a breeze in the weeds along the shore.

That's how Clay Miller first learned Harry was a fisherman. He was a good deal more than that, of course. He had ideas about how to get through a war and what to do afterward. Maybe he had different notions about things. Maybe there were some things, such as a feeling for eighty acres and a remote farmhouse, which he didn't understand. But he *was* a fisherman. More than that, he was a friend.

Clay rubbed his cigarette out and stood up. He looked at Harry, still on the far side of the pool. There wasn't much light left. "Come on back over here," he called.

Harry made a fast retrieve and crossed the dam.

"You see that snag over there?" Clay said, when Harry

was standing beside him. He was pointing to the spot above the deep hole, where he knew the big brown trout lived.

Harry nodded.

"That's the best place," Clay said. "There's some old roots down there. If you drop a fly easy, you might raise him."

Harry was glancing at Clay and smiling a little—a good smile, a warm one. "I noticed that spot myself," he said. He hesitated a moment. "But I figured I better stay away from it. Just casting is sport, too." He hesitated again. "I'll tell you the truth. I get the idea you don't want anyone to take that trout."

"You're crazy!" Clay said gruffly. "Work around that snag. Go ahead!"

Harry cast deftly, in exactly the right place. On the third delicate, tantalizing retrieve, the fly disappeared in a sudden scoop of water. Harry flipped up the rod, bending it almost double, and set the hook. The brown trout reacted like lightning. He came out of the water in an explosive leap.

The reel zipped. Harry let it go, just for a few seconds, and then put on the pressure. If the trout got enough line, he'd wrap it around half a dozen roots and rocks and snap it like cotton thread. He was feeling the drag now, and he fought it, breaking out again, curving and twisting, and then running back toward the base of the dam. But Harry judged the run nicely and checked it, gaining a few feet of line. The trout's next leap wasn't as high. He arched slowly, showing his full length, the streamline form, the spotted sides, the wild head shaking in a frantic effort to throw the barb.

"A four-pounder!" Harry shouted. "A real fighter! Look at him!"

Clay looked. He was a fighter, all right. Harry was a fighter too. It took him ten pulse-pounding minutes to work the trout close to the bank. He worked carefully, gaining slowly and steadily, wearing the trout down until he couldn't surge any more, until he was quiet and beat at the end of the line.

Harry held up the rod tip. He was stepping into the

shallows. The trout made a final, stout-hearted run, and Harry yielded some line. "Still game," he said admiringly. He won the line back and led the trout closer, bringing him in under the shadow of the trees.

There was a landing net swinging on Harry's belt. He groped for it with his right hand and started to unhook it. His fingers stopped moving, though, before the net was clear. He was remembering the trout's final run, and then he was glancing back over his shoulder at Clay. Since Harry was a fisherman, he understood—and respected—the trout. And he could understand, now, some of the same things about Clay. He could express it best in angler's language: the fish, in a way, was part of the fisherman, but this trout had a stronger bond to the pool. It was the same kind of deep-going, fiercely loyal bond that held Clay to his land.

Clay watched, surprised, as Harry turned back toward the pool. He hadn't unhooked the net. Instead, he clamped the handle of the rod under his arm and leaned over to wet his hands in the pool. "This way it won't harm the scales," he said.

"Use your net!" Clay told him. "That's what it's for!"

Harry reached toward the water. Swiftly, with a sure touch, he held the trout for a flailing instant and backed the hook out of his lip.

There was a moment when nothing happened, a complete stop, with Harry still bending over, hands outstretched, and the trout motionless beyond his fingers. Then, action again; a new start. Harry straightened up. The big brown trout moved, too. He rolled, steadied and finned away, heading back toward the deep hole by the dam. His shadow, blurred by the water, went deeper. Then he was gone.

"Why didn't you take him?" Clay said. "He was yours! You had him!" His voice was strained. He hadn't said anything while Harry played the trout, but his throat felt as though he had been shouting.

Harry was staring after the fish. "Be a long time before he strikes another hook," he said. "A long time."

"Why didn't you take him!"

"Remember what you were telling me last night?" Harry said. "About the land?" He was smiling. "I see what you mean. That trout belongs here. The same as you."

Clay swung away. He didn't want Harry to see his eyes. "We better go up to the house and get some coffee," he said. "You got some miles ahead of you."

"We both have," Harry said, coming along after him, unjointing his fly rod. "You stay here and hold onto these hills." He added, "Sure. You're right. This is important, too. And as long as you don't let anyone talk you out of it, I guess everything will turn out okay."

WILLIAM WISER
House of the Blues

(FROM THE KENYON REVIEW)

WALKING THE PONT NEUF I walked past old Vert Galant's statue all slimy green wet in the rain—but he's brass and won't get warped like a guitar will, or melt, like me. Tried to poke my guitar up under my Army surplus jacket but no go, me and it just got all the wetter. Didn't it rain? Here I was out in the freezing French rain trying to locate my buddy Roger-D Rogers who wasn't nowhere to be found. Roger-D's the one that first give me the money to go down to Spain. He's got a prostitute works for him and that's about the best paying job you can get in Paris. I was just back from Spain and broke again. Maybe old Rog—if I could find him—would let me have franc number one, to get me started. All I wanted was money enough to get dried off some place. April in Paris, Jesus.

It was like I was some kind of private eye out looking all over Paris for this missing person. What you do, you *cherchez la femme,* like a detective would, but I already walked all up and down Rue St. Denis twice and couldn't find a woman in a doorway anywheres. Back before I went to Spain Rue St. Denis used to be the prettiest girl-street: girls' faces blooming at every café window and girls standing out around swinging their shiny pocketbooks at you, dressed bright as butterflies, ready to wrap you right up in their silky wings.

But Paris is getting all cleaned up of late. De Gaulle's out scraping the buildings down and he's gone and got the cops after the St. Denis girls. What's the use of nice white houses to look at if you can't have pretty girls standing out in front of them?

Anyway, from the looks of things, Roger's woman didn't hang out around Rue St. Denis anymore.

Figured I'd try his old hotel on Rue de la Harpe over on the Left Bank, but I didn't have no great confidence I'd find him there. People I know don't stay more'n three months at the same hotel, and addicts—like Roger—don't leave their forward addresses. I went over there anyway, soaked to the bone by the time I ducked in the lobby. Nobody behind the deck. That was good luck for me or I would've probably got chased outside for dripping rainwater all over their downstairs rug.

I climbed up five flights, and that's tough climbing with your lungs all waterlogged. He used to live right next to the WC, so I held my nose and knocked next door to the john. The door finally opened a crack, but no Roger. It was Lulu, his prostitute.

Right away the door started shutting closed again. I'm what's called Colored—which always gets you a poor reception at people's doorways. Lucky I got my surplus Army boot in before she got the door all the way shut.

"N'est pas là," she told me, one evil eye looking out at me through the crack.

"I'm his buddy that went to Spain." I said that so she wouldn't think I was the cops. "I'm back."

"Fous-moi le camp," she said, which sort of means bug off.

"I'm the one brought you that package that time, remember?"

She opened the door a half inch off of my big toe. You could see her other eye. She studied me a minute, mean, and finally remembered. "You owe him some money, is what I remember."

"No, I don't. He give me that money."

She opened the door some more—all the way the chain would go—and stuck her whole face out at me.

"How much he give you? What was he giving you money for? We're broke, he needs that money."

"Well, I'm broke myself. He give me that money to keep. I did him a job and he paid me. He said to take a package over to you that night and I took it and he paid me the money to do it."

"How much he give you?"

Women, when they get on the subject of money, you can't budge them. Especially whores.

"100 francs."

"100 *francs?*" Her pencil eyebrows shot up. Her big painted eyes got twice as big. "He could've hired an armor car for 100 francs. That was just a *note* he sent over to me, with some *chocolate* in it."

"How did I know what was in it?" I said, acting like I never knew what was in it. "I thought it was dope and I was taking a big risk to carry it around Paris."

"*Risk?* That wasn't no risk. That was *chocolate* in that package."

"Well, Roger never told me what it was. I thought it was dope."

"Roger's off dope."

I didn't answer nothing to that. I believe that when I see it myself.

"He's off dope and he's gained over four kilos already. We got married in January and I'm taking care of him."

You could've knocked me over with a broomstraw. She stuck her hand out over the door chain to show me her wedding ring. It was true. The hinges went out of my jaw. I had to steady myself against the door frame. I should've knew something was up the minute I first sneaked a look into the hotel room. Everything was all changed around from the last time I was here: somebody painted the place blue-green with a high polish rose-print linoleum on the floor. There was a stuffed chair in there now, with doilies all over it to hide the cigarette burns, and a new brass bed from the flea market where Rog's cot used to be. There was shelves all over the place with knickknacks from Monoprix on them and a red-and-white checkerboard oilcloth on the table and a goldfish bowl full of goldfish and an empty wine bottle full of wax flowers. Lulu had even put up polka dot curtains on the airshaft window. Whores are great that way for Interior Decoration.

Not counting the evidence on Lulu's finger. You can't argue with a wedding ring. So there it was: Roger-D Rogers had gone and married his prostitute and lost his self a good income.

When I could work my mouth again I said, *"Tiens, tiens,"* which sort of means, "My, my," or something just as foolish, and that's when she took advantage and put a spike heel down on my big toe and got the door slammed shut. Damn. And I didn't even find out where Roger was at.

"Wait a minute! Where's he gone?"

I could hear her through the door: "He don't see nobody but me. He's in a hospital and he's gained back four kilos already."

"But I'm his buddy . . ."

"Fous-moi le camp."

So I did.

That was a very careless hotel for Paris because somebody had went and forgot to put the lock on the downstairs telephone dial. So I sneaked behind the front desk like I belonged there and called up. I called up this American lady living in Paris that was very big with all kind of various organizations. Somebody come on in French and I asked for Madame Price-Loftus and they said, *"Ne quittez pas,"* and then somebody else come on in English.

"Good afternoon. This is Miss Beardsley, secretary to Mrs. Price-Loftus. May I help you?"

I told her who I was. I said Mrs. P-L told me to call up if ever I needed help, and I was broke right now and needed help.

"Excuse me, are you of the colored race?"

People always excuse theirselves when they ask you color

questions, but I just said, "Yes ma'am." I'm honest as daylight on the subject.

"I'm terribly sorry but on March third of this year Mrs. Price-Loftus was set upon by two members of your race at the intersection of Rue des Pyramides and Avenue de l'Opéra. A report of this unfortunate episode appeared in the Paris *Herald Tribune* . . ."

"I been away."

". . . cut and bruised and was only saved from further injuries by the fortunate intervention of a passerby. She was robbed of her purse and a double strand of matched pearls, the latter of considerable sentimental value. Mrs. Price-Loftus has since withdrawn all aids and supports from any non-white individuals as well as any organizations purporting to represent these individuals."

I started to argue that it could've been Algerians—rich people never stop and look close at different colors of black—but the telephone had already went click.

This other buddy of mine, André, lived on a beat-up old barge tied up next to Piscine de Ligny, which is an actual swimming pool right out in the Seine. André made a steady living stealing suitcases out of cars parked around the Gare de Lyon. He was home, because I passed his rusty motor scooter chained to a dock post and there was smoke coming out of his smokestack.

Inside was wet clothes hanging all over everywhere and the portholes shut and André sitting in front of the coal stove wringing out a pair of socks in a bucket of river water. As soon as he sees me he dropped the socks and come over and give me a big French bearhug full of Supersuds.

"When you back in Paris, man? Hey, that's the greatest, see your ugly mug again. Man, I'm glad to see a friendly face. Since eversince Saturday the cops're staking me out to put a finger on me for heisting tires off Army trucks over at Châtelet. *Truck* tires for crying bloody murder. Can you feature it? And Châtelet ain't even my territory."

That's the way he talked, only he couldn't pronounce nothing right. He talked American and wanted to go to America in the worst way and be an American gangster.

"... got bour-glar alarms built into every damn' *petite voiture*, so help me Jesus, that you turn on air raid sirens just to jimmy an honest window. Sweetcases is for the birds this year. Look at me what I got to do, I got to go and wash all these duds I heisted 'cause fences won't touch dirty duds this year, the bastards. The fences have reducted me to a washer-woman to make a franc."

He was hopping barefooted around stacks of jimmied empty suitcases, ducking under clotheslines, popping mothballs out of a paper sack into suitcoat pockets hanging up on hangers amongst the wetwash.

"... the fences find a bughole they knock ten francs—how much is that in bucks?—ten whole francs off the pay-off, so help me Jesus." He went numerating all the different thieveries a fence pulls on a thief, popping mothballs as he went, cussing out cops when he picked up a little extra breath. I asked him why he didn't just quit and go legitimate.

"I want to make my bundle, man, before I blow this town."

Since he was on the subject of bundles I figured I could hit him for a little loan of money.

"Can you let me have, say, twenty francs till I get on my feet?"

He stopped popping. He asked me how much was that in bucks. (Not even five bucks.) "... anyway, I ain't got the scratch. I had to pay off this goddamn' *criminel* in Clichy so Françoise wouldn't have that baby she almost had." Françoise was his girl that wrote poetry in her spare time. "I didn't want to go to America with no goddamn' kid."

"Can you let me have ten then?"

He reached in his jeans and let me have five, which is only about a buck, smelling of mothballs. A buck's a buck, and anyway that's a buck more'n I started with. So I said *merci* and tucked it in my pocket. I asked him if he heard any news about Roger-D Rogers.

"That cat's had it, man. He married some *poule* he knew. Can you feature it?"

"Yeah. She told me about it herself. She said she put him in a hospital where he's getting cured and I'm trying to locate where the hospital's at."

"*Drogues?* It's the Maison Bleue. They put all the dips in the Maison Bleue. All those bughouse hospitals, they're out in Vincennes."

The Maison Bleue. That's a good name for it, named for the Blues, I guess. And that's where Roger-D Rogers was at. I wanted to see that old boy again, I don't know. Maybe he was a changed man and wouldn't even recognize his buddy anymore. Since he was married. Married and off H and winning his angel wings. Maybe not. I just wanted to see him. He used to be a jazz piano player, you know. He played very cool piano for a white boy. Very cool. But he was way downhill when I saw him last. I made a mental remembrance to go out to the Maison Bleue next chance I got.

André was boiling coffee on the coal stove. Looked like he poured river water in the coffee pot, but I don't care. Those coffee grounds smelled real good. I sat down on an empty steamer trunk and wished he'd open at least one porthole.

He give me a bowl of coffee about as black as me and a rusty pair of shears and asked me would I mind trimming his hair some around the neck where he couldn't reach it. He needed a haircut back there in the worst way. I said sure. He said Françoise wouldn't never cut his hair herself: "... you know how she talks, man. Claims it's too superstitious and a doll could capture a guy's soul that way. But she wants me to always cut hers."

While I was chopping his hair with one hand and drinking my coffee with the other one I explained him some female psychology: "A woman, especially that writes poetry, don't give that much of a damn if a guy captures *her* soul. She just don't want to be responsible for nobody else's soul on her conscience."

"Baloney, man. What about Roger-D's woman?"

He was right. Lulu had went and knocked Rog out of his natural habits and brainwashed him right into a hospital. There's all kind of female psychology. It changes from female to female. I wanted to really find that old boy and find out what come over him. Or turn in my badge.

Hair was flying every which way. The trouble was to keep the hairs out of my coffee. André started having this terrific idea.

"Listen, man, I got this *terrifique* idea. I got these puppets. Me and Françoise was going to work them, but I'm going to cut you in. You going to make some real loot with us and our puppet show."

"Puppet show!"

"Yeah, man. Dig this." He jumped up right in the middle of when I was trimming his sideburns and nearly got his ear cut off. He went and dug down in one of his ratty old suitcases and dug up these two puppets. One was a girl and one was a boy.

"Here's the pitch . . ." He looked comical as hell standing there with his hair only half cut trying to untangle puppet strings to make them dance. Here was a guy that could open any make car door with a bent wire hanger and rifle your glove compartment in twenty seconds flat, here he was acting a fool in the middle of washday, daydreaming to go into show business. ". . . you and your guitar to get up a crowd, me, I show the suckers a puppet show." His eyes was shooting off sparklers, his plans blowed up bigger than he was: "When everybody's hands're busy clapping bravo, Francoise goes around frisking all the back pockets for their billfolders. You get the picture? Germans, Belgians, Limeys—all the tourists all over Paris. They all start coming in from Easter on."

I said sit down and I'd finish his haircut.

He come back with the puppets and played with them on

his lap, still talking: "I learn how to make a little *tableau pornographique*, the Germans go for that stuff, you know." He figured out all different positions to put the puppets in while I trimmed off his other sideburn. "But I got to learn how to make them make love with the strings."

I never said nothing. He was too busy playing dolls to pay no attention to me anyway. Count me out, but I never told him. He was too excited to listen to any sense. In the first place Françoise wouldn't hold still for no pickpocketing. She didn't mind if her boyfriend was a thief, but she wasn't about to let him talk *her* into stealing. Not for love nor money. As for me, I operate solo only. I play strict guitar and sing for myself and take up my own collection at the end. Steer clear of corporations is my motto. Especially white people's. I don't mind borrowing money off of white people, but I don't want to go into partners with them. Only thing I wanted right now was a dry place to sleep tonight.

I dusted the hairs off his shoulders with my surplus Army khaki handkerchief—it was a damn' good haircut, if I do say so myself—and asked him, casual, "I was just wondering if you happen to have a spare bed I could sleep on the boat any place?"

He let the puppets slide and all of a sudden went down to brass tacks. "Sorry as Jesus, man, hell, but Françoise my girlchick's coming over tonight ... you know?"

French people are shyer about privacy than you'd think, but I don't blame them.

Over on the Right Bank by the Samaritaine Department Store the bums were sleeping out on the subway gratings, covered over with copies of *L'Humanité*, which is about all the good a Paris bum ever gets out of a Communist newspaper. I almost wished I could crawl in there with them; the rain already quit raining and there's always a nice warm steam comes up out of the Metro tunnel. But there wasn't no room for me, and I don't want to get caught sleeping under

L'Humanité. They'd send my picture to the FBI sure and I'd get my U.S. passport took away.

Anyway, what I wanted was to find my sculptor buddy Marcel that worked over at Les Halles and slept in the back of a cheese warehouse, and maybe he'd let me sleep in there with him. I slept there before. It's nice. Cheeses big as cotton bales and Marcel's sculptures he makes out of cratewood all around and you go to sleep smelling Gruyère and Port Salut and that way you don't dream about going hungry.

Les Halles was all lit up with spotlights so the unloaders could see to work and all around was piles of crates with spinach and celery leafs sticking out of the slats and big neat pyramids of melons trucked up from the springtime south (where I should've stayed, instead of coming home to freeze my ass in Paris) and artichokes and whole piles of grapefruits—mountains of them—waiting to be sorted for size. Those big Les Halles ladies in their half a dozen sweaters and wearing rubber boots was out hosing down seeds and peelings where the rotten stuff was tossed off to one side, and beggars with ratty shopping bags went picking through the mounds of ruint oranges to go and try to sell them to poor people tomorrow, and the thickest built huskies I ever saw east of the U.S. waterfront out hauling crates and whole treeloads of bananas on their backs with burlap shoulder pads to soak up the sweat, their big fat faces strained tomato color under the weight and hot breath steam clouds blowed out in the cold where they was heaving around, setting up the Paris France dinner table under the spotlights.

There was fires built around to stop and get warm at, and I went over to a bonfire of splintered-up cratewood in an oil drum to ask some old biddy roasting her fingers if she saw Marcel lately. She said no, she didn't know him, and to ask this guy sitting in his truck across the street by the sheds; he knew everybody.

He was reading *France-Soir* newspaper murders under the big lights.

"Artist-type, ain't he?"

I said *oui*.

"Carves out statues in the daytime, right?"

I said *oui*, said he only worked fruit-hauling nights.

"Curly-headed kid trying to grow a moustache?"

I said that's right, that's him.

"Drafted." Marcel drafted into the Army, broke my heart to hear. What they want with sculptors in the military for? "They'll send him off to fight Turks some place. It's the goddamn' government." He went back to his *France-Soir*.

And Roger-D Rogers married to a whore, in a hospital. Seemed like all my best civilized buddies gone down the drain.

Just then the sky popped open and a cloudburst of crystal marbles fell down out of the black, right on top of everybody. Hailstones big as mothballs, bouncing around hard and beaning everybody. And *sting*, Jesus. People looked up from their fruitstacks to see what hit them. I ducked across the street to Saint Eustache church, hailstones pelting hell out of me all the way across. Old God was shaking his fist at me, god only knows what for.

Saint Eustache was still open, some old people inside praying late. I could still hear hailstones rattling against the church windows so I stayed inside, out of it. But pretty soon the guard came by running people off, right in the middle of their beads.

I hid off in a corner behind a statue of Saint Somebody in the shadows, out of the candlelight, and stayed there and the guard never saw me, passed me right by. But I saw somebody else come by, janitor or somebody, so I ducked behind a curtain and I found myself inside a confession box, so I sat down.

It had a little window with bars, like a jail cell, where you talk through to a priest—or where the priest talks through to you. I wasn't sure whether I was sitting on the confess side or the forgive. All I know is it smelled like onions and sour tobacco and general halitosis in there, but it was halfway warm, and as private as you can get. I listened and heard the guard shut the big heavy front door shut and slam the bolt home. Then he shuffled down the stone walkways turning out lights, snuffing candles, shutting the incense off and such last minute closing-time stuff till he shuffled on up some stone steps some place, just his echoes all over that whole entire church, then quiet.

In a little while I must've went to sleep and snored out confession revelations to every saint in the place because next thing I knew three big tremendous organ pipe notes rocked me and Saint Eustache awake both. Daylight was coming through the color windows.

To get to the Maison Bleue you have to take a Metro train at Châtelet and go all the way to the end of the line at Vincennes and then you find out you got to take a bus the rest of the way. There's different hospitals out there named the Rose House and the White House and all, and I had to be sure to get the right bus for the Blue House.

Big lawns all around with spider-leg sprinklers and flower gardens where when the weather got better some blue flowers would spell out MB, for Maison Bleue, but right now they was just dried stalks and buds and a few new leaves. The hospital was back behind a high wall trimmed all along the top with different-colored broken bottle glass to cut your hands to pieces if you tried to climb over. I don't know if it was to keep people out or keep people in.

Bicycles and cars parked in a sideways row against a wall and people going through the gate carrying get-well candy and flowers and clean laundry and I was glad I had sense enough to remember to bring old Roger some fruit I bought cheap at Les Halles out of André's five francs. A guard in a little stone concierge house told me which building to go to, Building B, and a nun met me at Building B with a string of keys tied around her waist instead of a crucifix. She unlocked for me into a white hallway. I followed her down the hall to another door where she talked through a peephole to somebody until that door opened up and there was a nurse all starched up, waiting. I said who I wanted to see and the nurse let me in and the nun stayed outside. She checked the fruit. The system was something on the line of Alcatraz.

Everything was white, white—white walls, ceilings, white lights hanging down, and white enamel beds with white sheets over them. Like to snow-blinded me. I was the only shadow in the whole place.

Two rows of beds like in the Army, with mostly old men sitting on them and the visitors sitting next to the beds on stools or standing around leaning against the white walls talking. When you got up close you saw it wasn't all that clean as it was white. I noticed where the paint was chipped off the enamel beds and saw slop jars poked out from under the mattresses. Down at the far end of the bed row was Roger-D Rogers his self, sitting in bed propped up on a pillow with an old guy sitting next to him, playing checkers with him.

I gave a yodel and went down to handshake him but all he said was, "Well. Look who came down to see Roger-D in his sickbed. My ace number one favorite guitar player, back from the wars, never even sent me a postcard."

With Roger you never knew if he was glad to see you or wished you was dead or what.

". . . came all the way out to our private bughouse to play us a folk song."

I was carrying my guitar with me on account of I didn't have no safe place to leave it at. Everything he said, it always turned out sarcastic, because he never liked to let down on his cool. That was just his way, it didn't mean nothing personal. He called me a folk singer to make fun of me playing guitar, but I wrote my own songs and played them and he knew it.

Yes, it was the same old Roger-D for sarcasticness, but he was changed a lot in the face, blowed up twice his previous size like he'd been sucking on an air hose, cheeks puffed out full of apples. I told him how good he looked.

"I'm off stuff, you know. I'm cured from that scene."

All that stuff, benny, horse, hash, big O, he called it Stuff. "I saw Lulu yesterday. I heard."

"... they got this new addicts' treatment they call the *traitement de sommeil*. They put you to sleep and feed you through a hose. You only wake up once a day to go to the john. The rest is sweet dreams, baby. They keep giving you shots of something. You never feel a thing. You're asleep. Doc talks to you while you're under and tells you what a famous guy you are, to build you back your confidence." He started fingering thin air, playing the whole story out for me, like playing piano. "That's my exact problem, you know, lost confidence in myself. Lulu read about the treatment in the French *Reader's Digest* and found out a doctor to do it and signed me in here instead of us going on a honeymoon. I'm a goddamn' new man."

He stopped moving his fingers at me and held his hand out over top of the checkerboard to show me how steady he was. Looked to me like it still shook anyway, but he was a hell of a lot better, I admit.

I noticed the old guy was just sitting there listening to us talk English, polite, not making a sound, so I said in French, "Don't let me bust up your checker game."

The old guy smiled at me with his mouth open and I saw he didn't have tooth one, just a lot of gums and an old man's big old tongue. He went on smiling like that till he drooled down on his hospital pajamas. That's the trouble with old men.

"Don't pay any attention to Checkers. He's nuts, you know." Roger was still holding his hand out to show me how steady it was. "I play checkers with the bastard to keep him happy. He makes my moves for me and I play all his for him."

Old Checkers nodded and drooled and moved one of Roger's red checkers to show me how.

"Whores always make the best wives, you know," says Rog, out of the blue, hand still out trying to show me how steady a hand whores make you, too. "Look at that hand, would you."

Me and Checkers looked both.

"That's the sleep treatment does that, you know."

Roger kept all the time saying "you know" everything he said, which gets monotonous but keeps you up answering.

"That's an awful steady hand," I said, and the old boy nodded and held *his* hand out for good measure. It was steadier than Roger's if you ask me.

Then he finally put his hand down and the old man did the same and they both belched a little dinner gas like twins.

"Food's lousy here."

Which reminded me what I brought. I heaved my sack of pears and cherries up onto Rog's bed.

"What the hell's that?"

"Just some fruit. I figured you might like to get some fresh fruit. It's fresh right out of Les Halles."

Roger smiled his tricky jazzman smile at me and said, sly, "You didn't by any chance smuggle me some Stuff in there in that bag, did you?"

I smiled back and said, "No. Just fruit."

Roger chuckled way low in his belly and acted relaxed and said, "I'm off Stuff, you know. Permanent."

Old man backed him up, nodding yes.

"That's what Lulu told me. Congratulations." I was congratulating for the cure, not Lulu.

I noticed he went pawing through the pears and sorting cherries looking careful for any kind of a little surprise that could maybe turn out to be Stuff. Then when he saw all there was was just fruit he really relaxed and reached in and give me and the old man each a pear. He didn't eat none of it, his self.

There was a long time of quiet of just me and Checkers munching pear and all around visitors buzz-buzzing in different patients' ears and somebody way off in Solitary someplace screaming regular as heartbeat, to remind you what kind of a hospital you were at—but it was far enough off you didn't feel it too personal. Then Roger-D asks me, "You still banging hell out of that banjo?"

It was a guitar, and he knew it. "Yeah, still."

"You're nuts, you know that?"

"Can't help it."

"Yes you can, man. You can wise up and quit. Look at me. I quit, didn't I?"

I never had a sermon out of Roger-D Rogers before, so I never said nothing and just listened, kind of interested.

"I'd still be nuts playing piano, shooting Stuff, dying out by inches the way I was. You saw me, how I used to be when I was hung up on H, and music. But I found out I knew when to quit. I'm a new goddamn' man."

He was, too. He'd put on some baby fat, mostly under his eyes, and had an extra new chin to rest his face on. His hair was mostly all gone but what was left was neat combed and a neat shave to back it up. Nurse or somebody, maybe Lulu, clipped his fingernails down clean for him and he smelled like Lysol and after-shave.

And he had him a wife now too and a sweety-bird nest hotel room to go home to when he went home out of the Maison Bleue. Yes, and he was getting fatter and sassier than I ever saw him before. He might even sometime up and have kids and be a father. I wouldn't put nothing past him, that's how brand-new hospital changed and dry-cleaned he was.

The old man was quiet reaching in the sack for cherries and slipping them between his gums, swallowing cherry stones and stems and all. Then while Checkers was working on the cherries Roger-D leaned over to me and whispered, confidential, like he wanted to keep the old man out of it: "I'm really off Stuff for life, you know. I'm to where I could even take a little pinch now and then, maryjane or something mild, and get the good of it and have a little Technicolor once in a while and let up whenever I want, and quit. I mean I can *handle* it now, you understand what I mean?"

His littleboy eyebrows went all up into wrinkles looking question marks at me, wanting me to back him up. "I was one time a famous guy, you know . . ." he whispered behind his fingers, even his fingers was fat, those same fingers that used to be thin as pretzels and played the fartherest-out jazz piano in Parisville. There was little drips of honest-to-god tears in his eyes when he said to me, "So what do I need Stuff for?"

I had to look out the window. White people are just like innocent little kids when they're like that. To make a buck I might lie, but not to make a sick man sicker. When I never said nothing and couldn't look him in the eye he must've finally knew I knew. He saw I saw right through him.

He reached out, mad, and took the sack away from the old man and took a pear to eat.

"When you going to wise up and shut down that stupid music box of yours?"

He was back goofing off again; tears dried, sarcastic, mouth full of pear.

"I like guitar."

He poked the old man with his elbow, winking at him: "He *likes* guitar for christsake," then back to me, ". . . goddamn' amateurs are coming in the windows, crawling out of the woodwork, cluttering up the profession."

I come in this place a happy man, now I wished I had my fruit money back. Roger-D Rogers could switch quicker'n anybody I ever saw from night to day, good guy to bastard. I knew I wasn't no Andrew Segovia, but I wasn't no amateur either. And I wrote music, too, even if I never wrote it down. I was as much music as Roger was and I never took no Stuff to prop it up with. Okay, so I never was great like him but at least I was always independent me.

"Guitar's all I know."

"Learn something else. Learn how to shine shoes and make yourself a buck. Or be a bellboy. You never get anywhere in music, you know that, don't you? Look at me, and I was *good*."

He was, too.

"If you want to bang guitar, bang it private and don't go

messing around with the shitting public. Public'll whip you good. Public'll put you in a nut house getting cured from living, like they did me."

Spit his pear out all over the checkerboard. His face was almost blue from being so mad and he had to scratch his neck with both hands where it was a big blotchy red rash, and itched.

I kept quiet. Old man cleaned up where he'd spit out the pear, sad to see a good pear wasted. I kept quiet and shut up. Didn't want to get him worked up worse.

But all of a sudden he calmed down to earth and his eyes went blazy staring down the bed rows where a door opened up. I stared down there too, and it was Lulu, just now strutting through. She came onstage with every man jack's eyeballs on her, she was used to it.

Her dress was plain enough but she was strapped into it pretty tight, and she had went all out on makeup to make up for the dress being only black and white. Her legs are all hard muscle from standing around St. Denis so many years and she wore black fishnet stockings on them. French girls never shave their legs and black mesh stockings never works out too terrific on hairy legs. She didn't wear no hat because she was only about fifteen minutes out of the beauty parlor where some madman must've back-combed her hair with a waffle iron. You can take the girl out of the cathouse, as the saying goes, but you can't take the cathouse out of the girl. One thing, she had her décolleté buttoned up tight to match her wedding ring, so you had to give her credit. She brought Roger a tissue paper full of red roses and a stack of comic books.

I tried to stand back out of the way behind the old man but she saw me right off and give me a look full of daggers. She never said nothing, though. Changed her mouth back to smiles for Roger to reach up and kiss it. Then she planted him in roses and tucked the comics under his pillow. The old man had his tongue out again and he slid back with his checkerboard to make room for Lulu to perch up on the bed swinging her muscly legs like she was on a barstool.

First thing Roger did was slip her purse out from under her arm, out of habit, and give it a run-through. His fingers have got fat but he's still got prime use of them—he could've been a cardshark if he never got hooked on piano—and no more wrist motion than a curtain rod. The old man was backed up against me so I couldn't see too good what Rog dug out of her pocketbook, but he give me a sly wink which could've meant anything.

Then, funny thing, Roger picked up my bag of fruit and stuck it back in my hand and said to Lulu: "My friend here, my ace number one favorite guitar player, was just saying he has to take off."

That was my hint to say good-bye, so I said it. But what was Roger giving me back my fruit for? Lulu never even let on she knew I was standing there. Rog give me a wave with the back of his hand and said, "So long, sport. Don't join no hillbilly bands. And promise me one thing, promise me you'll eat them pears and get fat and happy like me."

I didn't know what to say so I just said okay. The old man was the only one looked sad when I left, sorry to see the fruit sack go with me.

I caught the same bus back to Vincennes, passing up all the different hospitals full of everybody sick, and passed through suburbs like suburbs any place, big brick apartment house projects going up, brand new windowpanes whitewashed with X's, slender little scraggly trees planted in the concrete and braced with wire braces. Even a shopping center where you could get your TV dinner without having to go into Paris anymore. It could've been the Bronx, New York.

My spirits slid way down just thinking how downhill things are getting. But when I saw two painters painting silver paint on a whole kilometer of chain fence to where they was painted silver theirselves, like saints—that someway cheered me up again. I reached into my sack to draw me out a pear and make some lunch out of it, but guess what I drew out instead. It was a 50-franc note, so help me Jesus!

Ten bucks, out of the blue. Out of Lulu's purse, rather, and now I knew why Roger-D was winking at me when I went out. Didn't I tell you he was changeable as the weather? My feelings shot way up and I almost busted right out of myself. Wanted to throw pears at those X windows, for kicks. (Maybe Roger-D and Mrs. Lulu Rogers would be moving into that brick pile next month, maybe André and Françoise moving in next door if their puppet show made a hit. Everybody, if you ask me, is going to end up in a project or a hospital bed before long.) I looked at my money again and I could've done a soft-shoe right down that bus aisle, but I made myself sit still and hold it in.

50 francs in one hand and my guitar in the other, don't talk to me about security for a long time yet.

BIOGRAPHICAL NOTES

BIOGRAPHICAL NOTES

ETHAN AYER was born in South Hamilton, Massachusetts, in 1919 and was educated at Trinity College in Hartford and at Columbia University. In 1951 his novel *The Enclosure* was published. His short stories have appeared in *The New Yorker, The Literary Review, Voices,* and other magazines, and he was the editor of *Voices* from 1953 to 1965. His off-Broadway productions include *Claude* and *The Great Western Union,* and he wrote the libretto for an opera based on Henry James' novel *Wings of the Dove,* which was produced by the New York City Opera in 1962.

GEORGE BLAKE currently teaches at Rockland Community College in Suffern, New York. His work has appeared in *Mutiny, The Canadian Forum, Prism-international, December, Aspects, The Literary Review, Colorado State Review, Literary Artpress, Xenia,* and *Vagabond.*

KAY BOYLE, who was born in St. Paul, Minnesota, now lives in San Francisco, where she is a professor in the English Department of San Francisco State College. The years between Minnesota and California were spent in New York, New England, and Europe. Although she never ceased writing fiction, she has undertaken such assignments as being a foreign correspondent for *The New Yorker* from 1946–1953. Miss Boyle won Guggenheim Fellowships in 1934 and in 1961; she was awarded the O. Henry Memorial Prize for the best short story of the year in 1934 and 1941. She has lectured widely in universities and is a member of the National Institute of Arts and Letters. Her current writing project is a history of Germany.

RAYMOND CARVER was born in Clatskanie, Oregon. He received a B.A. in English at Humboldt State College in California and went on to do graduate work at the University of Iowa. He has had stories published in *The Western Humanities Review, December,* and *The Carolina Quarterly.* His poems have appeared in numerous magazines and reviews, and a book-length collection of his poetry, *On the Surface,* is ready for publication. He is currently working on his first novel.

H. E. FRANCIS was born in Bristol, Rhode Island, but claims Long Island and Mendoza, Argentina, as his spiritual homes. Educated at the University of Wisconsin, Brown University, and Pembroke College, Oxford, he has held Fulbright scholarships in both England and Argentina. A collection of his stories was published in Buenos Aires in 1966 in Spanish. His stories have also appeared in England, France, the United States, and South America. He now teaches Creative

Writing at the University of Alabama and is the editor of *Poem*, a new poetry magazine.

MACDONALD HARRIS was born in South Pasadena, California, and now lives in Newport Beach on the coast south of Los Angeles. During the Second World War he sailed in the merchant marine and later served in the Navy as a deck officer. His first published story appeared in *Esquire* in 1947. Since then he has published frequently in magazines ranging from *Harper's* and *The Atlantic Monthly* to the quarterlies. His most recent novel is *Mortal Leap* (1964).

ROBERT HAZEL, born in Indiana in 1921, studied with Elliot Coleman and Karl Shapiro in the Writing Seminars at Johns Hopkins University in 1950–1951. He is the author of two novels, *The Lost Year* and *A Field Full of People*, published in 1953 and 1954, as well as a book of poems, which appeared in 1961. In 1955 he was the Eugene Saxon Memorial Fellow in Fiction. At present Mr. Hazel is a professor of English at Washington Square College, New York University.

HUGH ALLYN HUNT was born and grew up in Nebraska. At the age of seventeen he went to Los Angeles, where he eventually enrolled in the University of Southern California, majoring first in fine arts and then in journalism. After two years he left and worked at various jobs, went to Mexico, married, and was drafted into the Army. While stationed in Georgia he attended the University of Georgia. Since then he has worked mainly in public relations and advertising. Two years ago he and his wife returned to Mexico where they intend to stay for some time to come.

LAWRENCE LEE, born in Alabama, is now a professor in the Humanities Division of the University of Pittsburgh. He has had five volumes of poetry already published and a sixth, *The Cretan Flute*, is now in preparation, as are a novel and a collection of short stories. His two dramatic poems, "Prometheus in Pittsburgh" and "The American as Faust," have been performed on television and the stage. He and his wife Musier, who is a painter, lived for several months on the Greek island of Mykonos. In August 1967 he lectured at the Yeats International Summer School in Sligo, Ireland.

ARTHUR MILLER was born in 1915 in New York City. His first success came in 1945 with *Focus*, a best-selling novel; he followed this up with *All My Sons* which won the 1947 Critics Circle Award. *Death of a Salesman* won the Pulitzer Prize for drama in 1949. In 1953 *The Crucible* won the Antoinette Perry Award, and in 1955 *A View from the Bridge* won the New York Drama Critics Award. His most recent works for the stage are *After the Fall* and *Incident at Vichy*. Mr. Miller is now serving as president of the International P.E.N.

BRIAN MOORE was born and educated in Belfast, Ireland, emigrated to Canada in 1948, and now lives in the United States. His first novel, *The Lonely Passion of Judith Hearne*, was published in 1956 and immediately acclaimed. He has written four other novels: *The Feast of Lupercal* (1957), *The Luck of Ginger Coffey* (1960), recently released as a film, *An Answer from Limbo* (1962), and *The Emperor of Ice-Cream* (1965). Mr. Moore has received a Guggenheim Foundation

BIOGRAPHICAL NOTES

Fellowship, an award from the National Institute of Arts and Letters, and the Governor General of Canada's Award for Fiction.

BERRY MORGAN was born in 1919 in Port Gibson, Mississippi, of a family who settled there in 1798. She still lives there, on a large plantation, with her husband, who is an oil geologist, and their four young children. She attended Tulane University and Loyola in New Orleans, and has been writing ever since she can remember. She and her husband spend a part of each month in New Orleans, and summer on their farm in Virginia. Mrs. Morgan was awarded a Houghton Mifflin Literary Fellowship for *Certain Shadows,* a projected series of novels, the first of which, *Pursuit,* was published in 1966.

JOYCE CAROL OATES has had stories published in *The Kenyon Review, Southwest Review, Mademoiselle, Cosmopolitan, MSS, Prairie Schooner,* and other magazines. Her work also appeared in the O. Henry Award volumes for 1964, 1965, and in *The Best American Short Stories* for 1963 and 1966. Her first book of stories was published in 1963, a novel in 1964, and another story collection, *Upon the Sweeping Flood,* in 1966. Her latest novel, *A Garden of Earthly Delights,* is scheduled for publication in the fall of 1967. She is now an associate professor of English at the University of Windsor in Ontario.

DONALD RADCLIFFE was born in Belle Plaine, Iowa, in 1920, and was educated first as a youthful hobo on a tour of the country and then as a college student at Ames College. He served with the Navy in the Pacific and the Caribbean during World War II. He has worked as a Morse telegrapher in railroading and the grain market. Two years with the City News Bureau in Chicago led him to start Sidebar/Chicago, a free-lance writing service. "Song of the Simidor" is his first nationally published short story. At present, he is working on a play set in the newspaper world, *Remember Me in the Morgue, Man.*

HENRY ROTH was born in Tysmenica, Austria–Hungary, in 1906. He received his B.S. from the City College of New York in 1928 and has engaged in a variety of occupations — high school teacher, tutor, precision metal grinder and waterfowl farmer. He is perhaps best known for his novel *Call It Sleep,* which has had a resurgence of popularity in recent years. Mr. Roth left his Maine homestead after twenty years to spend a year in Spain, and it was in Seville that he wrote "The Surveyor." He and his wife are now living in Mexico.

DAVID RUBIN has taught English at various colleges and universities, including the universities of Allahabad (1958–59) and Jaipur (1963–64) in India. He is currently a member of the Literature Department at Sarah Lawrence. His first novel, *The Greater Darkness,* published in 1963, received the British Writer's Club Award as "the most promising first novel published in England in 1963."

JESSE STUART, born in Kentucky, started his career in teaching in a one-room school in the Kentucky mountains at the age of seventeen. Thereafter he added to his experience at the University of Indiana, the University of Nevada, and the American University in Cairo, Egypt. In 1962–63 he toured the world for the USIS giving 372 lectures on education, creative writing, and American literature. Mr. Stuart has published hundreds of short stories in this country and in Europe, the Near and Middle East, and the Orient. He has also written many books, the latest of which, a novel, is entitled *Mr. Gallion's School*.

CAROL STURM was born in Indiana and received her B.S. and M.S. degrees from St. Louis University. Several of her stories have appeared in *Prairie Schooner, Minnesota Review, Phylon, Reflections,* and other magazines. She is currently living in Roseburg, Oregon, with her husband and ten-year-old daughter.

ROBERT TRAVERS, a native of Somerville, Massachusetts, is a graduate of Antioch College, and before and during World War II was a seaman on merchant ships. He has been an editor and writer on newspapers and magazines and with public relations agencies. Mr. Travers has had published two novels and a collection of stories.

WILLIAM WISER has lived in Kentucky, Georgia, Florida, Belgium, and France, and at present is a resident of New York City. His wife, whom he married in Paris in April 1962, is Belgian, a painter. Mr. Wiser has published stories in *Cosmopolitan, Playboy, The Kenyon Review,* and *Antioch Review*. In 1963 he and his wife spent a year in Mexico on a writing fellowship granted by the Centro Mexicano de Escritores during which time he completed his first novel, *Troubadour*. In 1964 he received a fellowship grant from the Mary Roberts Rinehart Foundation.

THE YEARBOOK
OF THE
AMERICAN SHORT STORY

January 1 to December 31, 1966

Roll of Honor, 1966

I. *American Authors*

ALLEN, JOHN HOUGHTON
Horse Cavalry. Southwest Review, Spring.

AUCHINCLOSS, LOUIS
Sabina and the Herd. Saturday Evening Post, Jan. 29.
The Secret Journal of Waring Stohl. Saturday Evening Post, Apr. 23.

AYER, ETHAN
The Promise of Heat. New Yorker, Sept. 3.

BLAIS, MARIE-CLAIRE
A Season in the Life of Emmanuel. Tamarack Review, Spring.

BLAKE, GEORGE
A Place Not on the Map. Literary Review, Fall.
The Heart Line. December, Fall.

BODE, WINSTON
Summer Skies. Southwest Review, Winter.

BORENSTEIN, WALTER
The Other Cheek. Phylon, Winter.

BOYLE, KAY
The Wild Horses. Saturday Evening Post, Apr. 9.

BROWN, JEFF
Incident on the Tenth Floor. Saturday Evening Post, July 30.

CARVER, RAYMOND
Will You Please Be Quiet, Please? December, Fall.

CONAWAY, RAY
If You Need Me, Let Me Know. Saturday Evening Post, July 16.

CONROY, FRANK
Hanging On. New Yorker, Dec. 10.

CORRINGTON, JOHN WILLIAM
To Carthage Then I Came. Southwest Review, Spring.

DAVIS, OLIVIA
Constance. Virginia Quarterly Review, Autumn.

DEGNAN, JAMES P.
An Existential Experience. Virginia Quarterly Review, Summer.

DE MOTT, BENJAMIN
The Other Man. Massachusetts Review, Winter.

DUNOVAN, CASS
Fair Is for Games. McCall's, April.

DURANT, MARY
Messenger, What Tidings? Esquire, Feb.

ENRIGHT, ELIZABETH
An Hour in September. Ladies' Home Journal, Sept.

EVANS, ROBERT O.
A Visit to Lily. Virginia Quarterly Review, Winter.

FRANCIS, H. E.
One of the Boys. Southwest Review, Spring.
All the People I Never Had. Transatlantic Review, Summer.

FRIEDMAN, PAUL
The White Man's Burden. Prism International, Autumn.

GALLANT, MAVIS
Bonaventure. New Yorker, July 30.

GARDNER, JOHN
Nickel Mountain. Southern Review, Spring.

GOLD, HERBERT
  My Father, His Father and Ben. Playboy, Aug.
  The Ancient Company. Playboy, Nov.
GORDON, ROBERT
  About Chicken Little. Western Humanities Review, Summer.

HARRIS, MACDONALD
  Trepleff. Harper's Magazine, Dec.
HARTER, EVELYN
  A Kingly Exit. Prairie Schooner, Fall.
HAZEL, ROBERT
  White Anglo-Saxon Protestant. Hudson Review, Winter.
HEINEMANN, ARTHUR
  The Visible Surface. McCall's, March.
HOFFMAN, WILLIAM
  Sea Tides. McCall's, Sept.
HOOD, HUGH
  Looking Down from Above. Prism International, Autumn.
HUNT, HUGH ALLYN
  Acme Rooms and Sweet Marjorie Russell. Transatlantic Review, Spring.
HURST, JAMES
  The Summer of Two Figs. Transatlantic Review, Spring.

KITTREDGE, WILLIAM A.
  The Waterfowl Tree. Northwest Review, Fall-Winter.
KNICKERBOCKER, CONRAD
  Diseases of the Heart. Kenyon Review, March.
KUNASZ, PAUL
  All the Little Swingers. Redbook, Sept.
KURTZ, M. R.
  Waxing Wroth. Carleton Miscellany, Summer.

LARSEN, ERIC E.
  Skirmish. South Dakota Review, Winter.
LAVIN, MARY
  The Patriot Son. Georgia Review, Fall.
LEE, LAWRENCE
  The Heroic Journey. Michigan Quarterly Review, Spring.
LIEBER, JOEL
  Eat a Sour Grape. Literary Review, Autumn.

MADDEN, DAVID
  Love Riding. Southwest Review, Summer.
MENDOZA, DURANGO
  Summer Water and Shirley. Prairie Schooner, Fall.
MICHAELS, LEONARD
  The Deal. Massachusetts Review, Winter.
  Going Places. Transatlantic Review, Winter.
MILLER, ARTHUR
  Search for a Future. Saturday Evening Post, Aug. 13.
MITCHELL, DAVID
  The Voices of Spring. Redbook, Sept.
MONTGOMERY, MARION
  A Mess of Partridges. Georgia Review, Winter.
MOORE, BRIAN
  The Apartment Hunter. Tamarack Review, Autumn.
MORGAN, BERRY
  Andrew. New Yorker, July 2.
  The Organ Piece. New Yorker, Aug. 13.
  Miss Idella, the Travelling Hoe Lady. New Yorker, Dec. 10.
MOUNTZOURES, H. L.
  The Music of the Tree. New Yorker, Jan. 8.

NABOKOV, VLADIMIR
  An Affair of Honor. New Yorker, Sept. 3.
NEMEROV, HOWARD
  The Nature of the Task. Virginia Quarterly Review, Spring.

OATES, JOYCE CAROL
  Dying. Transatlantic Review, Spring.

In the Region of Ice. Atlantic, Aug.
The Thief. North American Review, Sept.
Where Are You Going, Where Have You Been? Epoch, Fall.
The Four Seasons. Virginia Quarterly Review, Winter.

PRATT, JONATHAN
Girl on a Dark Road. Saturday Evening Post, Dec. 3.

PURDY, KEN W.
Chronicle of an Event. Playboy, April.

RADCLIFFE, DONALD
Song of the Simidor. Literary Review, Winter.

ROTH, HENRY
The Surveyor. New Yorker, Aug. 6.

RUBIN, DAVID
Longing for America. Virginia Quarterly Review, Summer.

SAROYAN, WILLIAM
The Swimmers. Playboy, Nov.

SINCLAIR, ANDREW
The Atomic Band. Transatlantic Review, Summer.

SINCLAIR, THOMAS
Champion Red Archer. Yale Review, Winter.

STEWART, EDWARD
The Barefoot Soprano. Esquire, March.

STUART, JESSE
The Accident. Saturday Evening Post, Nov. 19.

STRUM, CAROL
The Kid Who Fractioned. Prairie Schooner, Fall.

TRAVERS, ROBERT
The Big Brown Trout. Argosy, April.

TRILLIN, CALVIN
Barnet Frummer Hears a Familiar Ring. New Yorker, July 2.

TURCO, LEWIS
Hillsdale Epistles. Carleton Miscellany, Summer.

UPDIKE, JOHN
Harv Is Plowing Now. New Yorker, April 23.

WELTY, EUDORA
The Demonstrators. New Yorker, Nov. 26.

WILNER, HERBERT
No Medal for Sonny. Saturday Evening Post, Nov. 5.

WISER, WILLIAM
House of the Blues. Kenyon Review, March.

WOIWODE, L.
Beyond the Bedroom Wall. New Yorker, Mar. 5.

WOLITZER, HILMA
Today a Woman Went Mad in the Supermarket. Saturday Evening Post, Mar. 12.

II. Foreign Authors

AHLIN, LARS
Polluted Zone. Literary Review, Winter.

BÖLL, HEINRICH
So Ward Abend Und Morgen. Vagabond, Vol. I, No. 1.

CLARKE, AUSTIN C.
Give Us This Day; And Forgive Us. Tamarack Review, Winter.

FEJES, ENDRE
Engagement. Literary Review, Spring.

GLENNON, MAURADE
My True Love's Face. Texas Quarterly, Spring.

GORDIMER, NADINE
  Say Something African. New Yorker, Aug. 20.
GRIFFITHS, SALLY
  Ferrets for Friends. Transatlantic Review, Spring.

IONESCO, EUGENE
  Slime. Evergreen Review, June.

JHABVALA, R. PRAWER
  In Love With a Beautiful Girl. New Yorker, Jan. 15.

LITVINOFF, IVY
  Sowing Asphodel. New Yorker, Apr. 23.

MANNES, VICTOR
  Joshua's Day. Transatlantic Review, Spring.
MEHTA, VED
  Ram, Ram, Ram. New Yorker, Jan. 29.
MUSIL, ROBERT
  Grigia. Partisan Review, Winter.

O'CONNOR, FRANK
  The School for Wives. New Yorker, Nov. 5.
O'FAOLAIN, SEAN
  The Heat of the Sun. Atlantic, Sept. 6.
ÖRKÉNY, ISTVÁN
  There Is No Pardon. Literary Review, Spring.
OTTLIK, GÉZA
  Love. Literary Review, Spring.
PRITCHETT, V. S.
  The Honeymoon. Harper's Magazine, Feb.
  The Skeleton. New Yorker, Mar. 5.

SHRUBB, PETER
  The Swagman. Transatlantic Review, Summer.
SPARK, MURIEL
  The House of the Famous Poet. New Yorker, Apr. 2.
SPENCER, ELIZABETH
  Tall Boy. New Yorker, Dec. 31.
STRANGER, JOYCE
  The Running Foxes. Saturday Evening Post, May 7.
SZABÓ, LÁSZLÓ
  King Solomon. Literary Review, Spring.

TEMPLETON, EDITH
  Equality Cake. New Yorker, Nov. 12.
TREVOR, WILLIAM
  The Hotel of the Idle Moon. Transatlantic Review, Winter.

VAJÁY, SZABOLCS
  The Pot. Literary Review, Spring.

WARNER, SYLVIA TOWNSEND
  A Winding Stair, A Fox Hunt, A Fulfilling Situation, Some Sycamores and the Church at Henning. New Yorker, Sept. 26.

Distinctive Short Stories in American Magazines, 1966

I. *American Authors*

ACKERSON, DUANE
  The Dust of August. Phylon, Summer.

ACKLEY, DAVID
  All of You, All of Us. Greensboro Review, Dec.

ALGREN, NELSON
A Ticket on Skorouski. Saturday Evening Post, Nov. 5.

ALLEN, JOHN HOUGHTON
Horse Cavalry. Southwest Review, Spring.

ALLISON, P.
The Fulfilling of the Law. Transatlantic Review, Spring.

AUCHINCLOSS, LOUIS
Sabina and the Herd. Saturday Evening Post, Jan. 29.
The Secret Journal of Waring Stohl. Saturday Evening Post, Apr. 23.
The Wagnerians. McCall's, July.

BAIL, JAY
Lament. North American Review, March.

BALLARD, JAMES
Wild Honey. Atlantic, Jan.

BARTH, JOHN
Night Sea Journey. Esquire, June.

BEAUFORT, BOWMAN
The Game. Greensboro Review, Dec.

BENDER, ELEANOR
The Judgment of Madame Charpentier. Carleton Miscellany, Fall.

BERRIAULT, GINA
The Search for J. Kruper. Esquire, Oct.

BLAIS, MARIE-CLAIRE
A Season in the Life of Emmanuel. Tamarack Review, Spring.

BLAKE, GEORGE
A Place Not on the Map. Literary Review, Fall.
The Heart Line. December, Fall.

BLYTH, MYRNA
The Lovers. Redbook, Nov.

BODE, WINSTON
Summer Skies. Southwest Review, Winter.

BONGARTZ, ROY
The Whoo-ee Egg. Transatlantic Review, Winter.

BORENSTEIN, WALTER
The Other Cheek. Phylon, Winter.

BOSSE, M. J.
The Boy Who Loved Shakespeare. North American Review, Nov.

BOWERING, GEORGE
The Elevator. Tamarack Review, Summer.

BOYLE, KAY
The Wild Horses. Saturday Evening Post, Apr. 9.

BRENNAN, MAEVE
I See You, Bianca. New Yorker, June 11.
The Twelfth Wedding Anniversary. New Yorker, Sept. 9.

BRODEUR, PAUL
The Spoiler. New Yorker, Jan. 8.
The Siphon. Michigan Quarterly Review, Spring.

BRONER, E. M.
The Woman Who Lived for Ten. Epoch, Fall.

BROWN, JEFF
Incident on the Tenth Floor. Saturday Evening Post, July 30.

BURCH, EMILY
The Children's Game. Vagabond, Vol. I, No. 1.

CABLE, MARY
We and They in Rhodesia. New Yorker, Feb. 19.

CALIN, ANNE
The Adventure. Literary Review, Autumn.

CARDWELL, GUY A.
Pig and Mouse. Carleton Miscellany, Fall.

CARVER, RAYMOND
Will You Please Be Quiet, Please? December, Fall.
A Child's Christmas in Utah. Carleton Miscellany, Winter.

CHARYN, JEROME
  The Man Who Grew Younger. Paris Review, Spring.
  "Sing, Shaindele, Sing." Transatlantic Review, Summer.
COBURN, ANDREW
  The Heir. Transatlantic Review, Spring.
COLTER, CYRUS
  A Gift. Northwest Review, Winter.
CONAWAY, RAY
  If You Need Me, Let Me Know. Saturday Evening Post, July 16.
CONROY, FRANK
  Nights Away from Home. New Yorker, Oct. 22.
  Hanging On. New Yorker, Dec. 10.
CORRINGTON, JOHN WILLIAM
  To Carthage Then I Came. Southwest Review, Spring.
CURRAN, MARY DOYLE
  Mrs. Reardon's Gamble. Massachusetts Review, Winter.

DAVIS, OLIVIA
  Constance. Virginia Quarterly Review, Autumn.
DEAL, BABS H.
  Lemmings Are Lonely. Cosmopolitan, May.
DEGNAN, JAMES P.
  An Existential Experience. Virginia Quarterly Review, Summer.
DE MOTT, BENJAMIN
  The Other Man. Massachusetts Review, Winter.
DESSART, GINA
  Nemesis in the Cornfield. Literary Review, Autumn.
DI DONATO, PIETRO
  The Hayloft. Playboy, May.
DINEEN, JOHN E.
  The Gods of Rome. Transatlantic Review, Spring.
DIXON, STEPHEN
  The Neighbors. Atlantic.

DOHAN, MARY HELEN
  End of Innocence. Redbook, August.
DUNOVAN, CASS
  Fair Is for Games. McCall's, April.
DURANT, MARY
  Messenger, What Tidings? Esquire, Feb.
DURSIN, MARGARET
  An Off-Campus Love Story. Harper's Magazine, Jan.

EASTLAKE, WILLIAM
  There's a Camel in My Cocktail. Harper's Magazine, April.
ELLIOTT, GEORGE P.
  Something to Want. Northwest Review, Spring.
ENRIGHT, ELIZABETH
  An Hour in September. Ladies' Home Journal, Sept.
EVANS, ROBERT O.
  A Visit to Lily. Virginia Quarterly Review, Winter.

FATKA, JAMES
  George's Place. North American Review, Sept.
FAUST, IRVIN
  Simon Girty Go Ape. Transatlantic Review, Summer.
FISHER, M. F. K.
  The Changeover. New Yorker, May 14.
FRANCIS, H. E.
  One of the Boys. Southwest Review, Spring.
  The Moment. North American Review, May.
  All the People I Never Had. Transatlantic Review, Summer.
FREE, WILLIAM J.
  Caleb and the Iron Monster. Georgia Review, Winter.
FRIEDMAN, PAUL
  The White Man's Burden. Prism International, Autumn.

GALLANT, MAVIS
  Bonaventure. New Yorker, July 30.
  A Report. New Yorker, Dec. 3.
GARDNER, JOHN
  Nickel Mountain. Southern Review, Spring.
GOLD, HERBERT
  My Father, His Father and Ben. Playboy, Aug.
  The Ancient Company. Playboy, Nov. 6.
GORDON, ROBERT
  A Lovely Ring. Transatlantic Review, Summer.
  The Last of the Frontier. Prism International, Autumn.
  About Chicken Little. Western Humanities Review, Summer.
GRACE, NANCY
  The Thief. Carleton Miscellany, Spring.
GRAU, SHIRLEY ANN
  Wind Shifting West. Cosmopolitan, Aug.
GROSSMAN, ALFRED
  The Beauty Contest. Transatlantic Review, Winter.
HACKEL, GLORIA
  Williamsburg. North American Review, Sept.
HALE, NANCY
  Family Ties. Southern Review, Spring.
  Animals in the House. Harper's Magazine, Sept.
  The Most Elegant Drawing Room in Europe. New Yorker, Sept. 17.
  Waiting. Virginia Quarterly Review, Autumn.
HARNACK, CURTIS
  The Mistake. North American Review, July.
HARRIS, MACDONALD
  Trepleff. Harper's Magazine, Dec.
HARTER, EVELYN
  A Kingly Exit. Prairie Schooner, Fall.
HAZEL, ROBERT
  White Anglo-Saxon Protestant. Hudson Review, Winter.
HEINEMANN, ARTHUR
  The Visible Surface. McCall's, March.
HILL, JUDITH BRENNER
  The Health Scheme. Literary Review, Autumn.
HOCHSTEIN, ROLAINE
  Child of Delight. Redbook, Oct.
HOFFMAN, WILLIAM
  Sea Tides. McCall's, Sept.
HOLDITCH, KENNETH
  In November the Nights Come Early. Phylon, Fall.
HOOD, HUGH
  Looking Down from Above. Prism International, Autumn.
HOYER, LINDA GRACE
  The Burning Bush. New Yorker, Oct. 1.
HUNT, HUGH ALLYN
  Acme Rooms and Sweet Marjorie Russell. Transatlantic Review, Spring.
HURST, JAMES
  The Summer of Two Figs. Transatlantic Review, Spring.

IGLAUER, EDITH
  The Beautiful Day. New Yorker, Mar. 19.

JACKSON, GLENN F.
  Gibraltar. Literary Review, Winter.
JOHNSON, DOROTHY M.
  The Ten-Pound Box of Candy. McCall's, April.

KITTREDGE, WILLIAM A.
  The Waterfowl Tree. Northwest Review, Fall-Winter.
KNICKERBOCKER, CONRAD
  Diseases of the Heart. Kenyon Review, March.
KNOWLTON, ROBERT A.
  The Couple Across the Street. Good Housekeeping, May.

KOLLING, WANA
  The Taste of Oranges. Carleton Miscellany, Fall.
KUNASZ, PAUL
  All the Little Swingers. Redbook, Sept.
KUNTZ, M. R.
  Waxing Wroth. Carleton Miscellany, Summer.

LAMOTT, KENNETH
  The Kangaroo Lottery. Saturday Evening Post, Mar. 26.
  Gatsby and the Sea Gull. Harper's Magazine, Oct.
LARSEN, ERIC E.
  Skirmish. South Dakota Review, Winter.
LAVIN, MARY
  The Patriot Son. Georgia Review, Fall.
  A Glimpse of Katey. Georgia Review, Winter.
LEE, LAWRENCE
  The Heroic Journey. Michigan Review, Spring.
LELCHUK, ALAN
  Sundays. Transatlantic Review, Summer.
LICHT, FRED
  Touch-for-Luck. Carleton Miscellany, Fall.
LIEBER, JOEL
  Eat a Sour Grape. Literary Review, Autumn.
LOESER, KATINKA
  The Life and Death of Little Children. New Yorker, Aug. 27.
  How I Spent My Summer Vacation. Redbook, Sept.
  To All a Good Night. Redbook, Dec.
LORD, RUTH K.
  Oh, Lord, Remember Me. Ladies' Home Journal, April.
LYON, RUTH M.
  The Train Don't Stop Here Anymore. Texas Quarterly, Spring.

MADDEN, DAVID
  Lone Riding. Southwest Review, Summer.
MADDOW, BEN
  The Wind Machine. Harper's Magazine, Aug.
MALOFF, SAUL
  The Limits of Sound. Northwest Review, Winter.
MALONEY, RALPH
  The Best Man. Atlantic, May.
MAROPHIS, PETRO S.
  Saturday Night. Esquire, Nov.
MATTHEWS, JACK
  Inviolate on Shawnee Street. North American Review, July.
MAYER, TOM
  The Eastern Sprints. Playboy, May.
  A Green-Broke Stud. Atlantic, Oct.
  My Father and the Fighter. Saturday Evening Post, Oct. 22.
MAZOR, JULIAN
  Rock Creek, New Yorker, Dec. 17.
MENDOZA, DURANGO
  Summer Water and Shirley. Prairie Schooner, Fall.
MICHAELS, LEONARD
  City Boy. Paris Review, Fall.
  The Deal. Massachusetts Review, Winter.
  Going Places. Transatlantic Review, Winter.
MILLER, ARTHUR
  Search for a Future. Saturday Evening Post, Aug. 13.
MILLER, WARREN
  The Spanish Suit. Saturday Evening Post, Nov. 19.
MINOT, STEPHEN
  I Remember the Day God Died Like It Was Yesterday. Carleton Miscellany, Summer.
MITCHELL, DAVID
  The Voices of Spring. Redbook, Sept.

MONTGOMERY, MARION
A Mess of Partridges. Georgia Review, Winter.

MOORE, BRIAN
The Apartment Hunter. Tamarack Review, Autumn.

MORGAN, BERRY
Andrew. New Yorker, July 2.
The Organ Piece. New Yorker, Aug. 13.
Miss Idella, the Travelling Hoe Lady, New Yorker, Dec. 10.

MORRIS, WRIGHT
Lover, Is That You? Esquire, March.

MOUNTZOURES, H. L.
The Music of the Tree. New Yorker, Jan. 8.
The Pigeon. New Yorker, July 16.
The Beating. New Yorker, Aug. 20.

MURDRICK, MARVIN
Cleopatra. Hudson Review, Spring.

McCORMICK, JAMES
Father's Keeper. Transatlantic Review, Summer.

NABOKOV, VLADIMIR
An Affair of Honor. New Yorker, Sept. 3.

NEMEROV, HOWARD
The Nature of the Task, Virginia Quarterly Review, Spring.

NEUGEBOREN, JAY
The Zodiacs. Transatlantic Review, Spring.

OATES, JOYCE CAROL
Dying. Transatlantic Review, Spring.
In the Region of Ice. Atlantic, Aug.
The Thief. North American Review, Sept.
Where Are You Going, Where Have You Been? Epoch, Fall.
The Four Seasons. Virginia Quarterly Review, Winter.

O'HARA, JOHN
Leonard. New Yorker, Feb. 26.
Yostie. Saturday Evening Post, June 4.

OLSEN, HANK
As Fair Flowers Fade. Prism International, Autumn.

PETRAKIS, HARRY MARK
The Gold of Troy. Playboy, Sept.

PIERCY, MARGE
Going Over Jordan. Transatlantic Review, Summer.

POTTER, NANCY A. J.
The Happiest You've Ever Been. Massachusetts Review, Summer.

PRATT, JONATHAN
Girl on a Dark Road. Saturday Evening Post, Dec. 3.

PURDY, KEN W.
Chronicle of an Event. Playboy, April.

RADCLIFFE, DONALD
Song of the Simidor. Literary Review, Winter.

REYNOLDS, LAWRENCE JUDSON
One Dominique'r Hen. Greensboro Review, Dec.

RICHLER, MORDECAI
St. Urban's Horseman. Tamarack Review, Autumn.

ROBERTS, PHYLLIS
The Way to the Lions. Ante, Winter.

ROBINSON, BARBARA
Someone to Love. McCall's, March.

ROCK, E. S.
Home. North American Review, Summer.
Storm. Western Humanities Review, Summer.

ROGIN, GILBERT
The Indoor Bird Watcher. New Yorker, April.

ROSENBERG, ELSA
Abraham Muscovitch's Michael. Saturday Night, March.

ROTH, HENRY
  The Surveyor. New Yorker, Aug. 6.
ROTH, PHILIP
  In Trouble. Atlantic, Nov.
  "O Beautiful for Spacious Skies." Harper's Magazine, Nov.
RUBIN, DAVID
  Longing for America. Virginia Quarterly Review, Summer.
RUTSALA, VERN
  Night Driving. Southwest Review, Winter.

SAROYAN, WILLIAM
  Don't Laugh Unless It's Funny. Playboy, July.
  The Swimmers. Playboy, Nov.
SAYRES, WILLIAM
  A Countryman's Hands. North American Review, July.
SINCLAIR, ANDREW
  The Atomic Band. Transatlantic Review, Summer.
SINCLAIR, THOMAS
  Champion Red Archer. Yale Review, Winter.
SINGER, ISAAC BASHEVIS
  The Prodigal Fool. Saturday Evening Post, Feb. 6.
  The Needle. Cosmopolitan, Aug.
STACTON, DAVID
  An Old Man Crosses the Border. Southwest Review, Winter.
STAGER, CAROL
  C'est la Guerre. Trace, Winter.
STEIN, GERALD
  Have Another Cupcake, Jack. Redbook, May.
STERBA, MONICA
  Love and Hate and Dr. Tisch. Reporter, May 6.
STEWART, EDWARD
  The Barefoot Soprano. Esquire, March.
STUART, JESSE
  The Accident. Saturday Evening Post, Nov. 19.
STURM, CAROL
  The Kid Who Fractioned. Prairie Schooner, Fall.

TAYLOR, HARRY H.
  The Guards. South Dakota Review, Winter.
THOMAS, DOROTHY
  Joy Cometh in the Morning. Redbook, Dec.
THOMPSON, PAUL
  The Last Laugh. Transatlantic Review, Spring.
TOPEROFF, SAM
  A Spoonful of Nothing. Atlantic, Aug.
TRAVERS, ROBERT
  The Big Brown Trout. Argosy, April.
TRILLIN, CALVIN
  Barnet Frummer Hears a Familiar Ring. New Yorker, July 2.
TRUDELL, DENNIS
  Penance. Prism International, Autumn.
TURCO, LEWIS
  Hillsdale Epistles. Carleton Miscellany, Summer.
TYLER, ANNE
  As the Earth Gets Old. New Yorker, Oct. 29.
  Two People and a Clock on the Wall. New Yorker, Nov. 19.

UPDIKE, JOHN
  Avec la Bébé-Sitter. New Yorker, Jan. 1.
  Marching Through Boston. New Yorker, Jan. 22.
  Harv Is Plowing Now. New Yorker, Apr. 23.
  During the Jurassic. Transatlantic Review, Summer.
  The Witnesses. New Yorker, Aug. 13.
  The Pro. New Yorker, Sept. 17.
  Bech in Rymania. New Yorker, Oct. 8.

VAN LARE, B. CANARY
　Who Will Save the Evergreens? North American Review, July.

VIVANTE, ARTURO
　The Room. New Yorker, July 10.
　Lesson in the Dark. Southern Review, Autumn.
　The Little Ark. New Yorker, Nov. 19.

WELTY, EUDORA
　The Demonstrators. New Yorker, Nov. 26.

WHEATCROFT, JOHN
　Image of Departure. Georgia Review, Fall.

WHITE, ELLINGTON
　The Hant Watchers. Southern Review, Autumn.

WHITEHILL, JOSEPH
　The Round Brass Elevator. Hudson Review, Spring.

WILNER, HERBERT
　A Gift Every Morning. Esquire, Aug.
　No Medal for Sonny. Saturday Evening Post, Nov. 5.

WILSON, MARTHA
　The Plain Brown Bird. Redbook, Aug.

WILSON, ROBERT
　The World Outside Illinois. December, Dec.

WISER, WILLIAM
　House of the Blues. Kenyon Review, March.

WOIWODE, L.
　Beyond the Bedroom Wall. New Yorker, Mar. 5.
　The Visitation. New Yorker, Sept. 10.

WOLITZER, HILMA
　Today a Woman Went Mad in the Supermarket. Saturday Evening Post, Mar. 12.

II. Foreign Authors

AHLIN, LARS
　Polluted Zone. Literary Review, Winter.

BABEL, ISAAC
　Shabos Nahamu. Atlantic, Mar.
　You Must Know Everything. New Yorker, Apr. 9.

BELLOCCHIO, PIERGIORGIO
　Not Guilty. Chelsea Review, June.

BÖLL, HEINRICH
　Si Ward Abend und Morgen. Vagabond, Vol. I, No. 1.

BRADBURY, MALCOLM
　The Adult Education Class. Transatlantic Review, Summer.

BROBOWSKI, JOHANNES
　Stranded in a Capital. Transatlantic Review, Winter.

CLARKE, AUSTIN C.
　Give Us This Day; And Forgive Us. Tamarack Review, Winter.

DAVIE, ELSPETH
　Traveller. Transatlantic Review, Winter.

DELIUS, ANTHONY
　Nothing Personal. New Yorker, Mar. 19.

FEJES, ENDRE
　Engagement. Literary Review, Spring.

GLENNON, MAURADE
　My True Love's Face. Texas Quarterly, Spring.

GODDEN, RUMER
　The Kitchen Madonna. Ladies' Home Journal, April.

Distinctive Short Stories, 1966

GORDIMER, NADINE
Say Something African. New Yorker, Aug. 20.

GRIFFITHS, SALLY
Ferrets for Friends. Transatlantic Review, Spring.

GYLLENSTEIN, LARS
Sunday Outing. Literary Review, Winter.

HAZZARD, SHIRLEY
The Meeting. New Yorker, July 23.

IONESCO, EUGENE
Slime. Evergreen Review, June.

JHABVALA, R. PRAWER
In Love with a Beautiful Girl. New Yorker, Jan. 15.
The Man with the Dog. New Yorker, Nov. 19.

KARINTHY, FERENC
Ante, Apud. Literary Review, Spring.

LEVINSON, DEIRDRE
Crouch. Commentary, May.

LITVINOFF, IVY
Sowing Asphodel. New Yorker, Apr. 23.

MÁNDY, IVÁN
An Ordinary Member. Literary Review, Spring.

MANNES, VICTOR
Joshua's Day. Transatlantic Review, Spring.

MEACOCK, NORMA
In Marriage. Transatlantic Review, Winter.

MEHTA, VED
Ram, Ram, Ram. New Yorker, Jan. 29.

MUKHERJEE, BHARATI
Debate on a Rainy Afternoon. Massachusetts Review, Spring.

MURTHY, V. R. ANANTHA
Initiation. Transatlantic Review, Summer.

MUSIL, ROBERT
Grigia. Partisan Review, Spring.

NARAYAN, BADRI
The Silver Plate. Transatlantic Review, Summer.

NEIH, HUA-LING
The Several Blessings of Ta-Nien Wang. Atlantic, Dec.

O'CONNOR, FRANK
The Corkerys. New Yorker, Apr. 30.
The School for Wives, New Yorker, Nov. 5.

O'FAOLAIN, SEAN
The Jungle of Love. Saturday Evening Post, Aug. 13.
The Heat of the Sun. Atlantic, Sept. 6.

ÖRKÉNY, ISTVÁN
There Is No Pardon. Literary Review, Spring.

OTTLIK, GÉZA
Love. Literary Review, Spring.

OWEYELE, DAVID
The Beggars' Tree. Transatlantic Review, Summer.

PIS'MENNYI, ALEKSANDER
Vaska and Vasilii Vasil 'Yevich. Prism International, Autumn.

PRITCHETT, V. S.
The Honeymoon. Harper's Magazine, Feb.
The Skeleton. New Yorker, Mar. 5.

QUARTESAN, SERGIO
The Apartment House. Chelsea Review, June.

RADSTRÖM, PAR
The Story of Jock. Literary Review, Winter.

SHRUBB, PETER
The Swagman. Transatlantic Review, Summer.

SPARK, MURIEL
The House of the Famous Poet. New Yorker, Apr. 2.

SPENCER, ELIZABETH
The Pincian Tale. New Yorker, Apr. 6.
The Absence. New Yorker, Sept. 10.
Tall Boy. New Yorker, Dec. 31.

STRANGER, JOYCE
The Running Foxes. Saturday Evening Post, May 7.

SZABÓ, LÁSZLÓ
King Solomon. Literary Review, Spring.

TAMÁSI, ÁRON
The Golden Mouse. Literary Review, Spring.

TAYLOR, ELIZABETH
The Devastating Boys. McCall's, May.

TEMPLETON, EDITH
The Weary Titans. New Yorker, Oct. 15.
Equality Cake. New Yorker, Nov. 12.

TREVOR, WILLIAM
The Hotel of the Idle Moon. Transatlantic Review, Winter.

VAJAY, SZABOLCS
The Pot. Literary Review, Spring.

WARNER, SYLVIA TOWNSEND
Oxenhope. New Yorker, July 9.
A Winding Stair, A Fox Hunt, A Fulfilling Situation, Some Sycamores and the Church at Henning. New Yorker, Sept. 26.

Addresses of American and Canadian Magazines Publishing Short Stories

Ante, Box 22915, Los Angeles, California
Antioch Review, 212 Xenia Avenue, Yellow Springs, Ohio 45387
Ave Maria, Notre Dame, Indiana 46556
Argosy, 205 East 42nd Street, New York, New York 10017
Arizona Quarterly, University of Arizona, Tucson, Arizona 85721
Atlantic Monthly, 8 Arlington Street, Boston, Massachusetts 02116
Canadian Forum, 30 Front Street West, Toronto 1, Ontario, Canada
Canadian Home Journal, 71 Richmond Street, Toronto, Ontario, Canada
Carleton Miscellany, Carleton College, Northfield, Minnesota 55057
Catholic World, 304 West 58th Street, New York, New York 10019
Cavalier, 67 West 44th Street, New York, New York 10036
Charm, Glamour, 420 Lexington Avenue, New York, New York 10017
Chicago Review, Reynolds Club, University of Chicago, Chicago, Illinois 60637
Colorado Quarterly, University of Colorado, Boulder, Colorado
Commentary, 165 East 56th Street, New York, New York 10022
Contact, Box 758, Sausalito, California 94965
Contemporary Fiction, Box 1323, Milwaukee, Wisconsin
Critic, 180 North Wabash Avenue, Chicago, Illinois 60601
December, Box 274, Western Springs, Illinois
Descant, Texas Christian University, Fort Worth, Texas 76129
Edge, Box 4067, Edmonton, Alberta, Canada
Ellery Queen's Mystery Magazine, 505 Park Avenue, New York, New York 10022
Epoch, 252 Goldwin Smith Hall, Cornell University, Ithaca, New York 14850
Esquire, 488 Madison Avenue, New York, New York 10022
Evergreen Review, 80 University Place, New York, New York 10003
Fantasy and Science Fiction, 347 East 53rd Street, New York, New York 10022
Four Quarters, LaSalle College, Philadelphia, Pennsylvania 19143
Gentleman's Quarterly, 488 Madison Avenue, New York, New York 10022
Georgia Review, University of Georgia, Athens, Georgia 30601

Good Housekeeping, 959 Eighth Avenue, New York, New York 10019
Greensboro Review, University of Greensboro, Greensboro, North Carolina
Harper's Bazaar, 572 Madison Avenue, New York, New York 10022
Harper's Magazine, 2 Park Avenue, New York, New York 10016
Holiday, 641 Lexington Avenue, New York, New York 10022
Hudson Review, 65 East 55th Street, New York, New York 10022
Husk, Cornell College, Mount Vernon, Iowa 52314
Inland, P.O. Box 685, Salt Lake City, Utah
Kenyon Review, Kenyon College, Gambier, Ohio 43022
Ladies' Home Journal, 641 Lexington Avenue, New York, New York 10022
Laurel Review, West Virginia Wesleyan College, Buchhannon, West Virginia 26201
Lillabulero, P.O. Box 1027, Chapel Hill, North Carolina 27514
Literary Review, Fairleigh Dickinson University, Teaneck, New Jersey 07666
McCall's, 230 Park Avenue, New York, New York 10017
MacLean's, 481 University Avenue, Toronto, Ontario, Canada
Mademoiselle, 420 Lexington Avenue, New York, New York 10017
Mainstream, 832 Broadway, New York, New York 10018
The Malahat Review, University of Victoria, Victoria, British Columbia, Canada
Manhattan Review, 229 East 12th Street, New York, New York 10003
Massachusetts Review, University of Massachusetts, Amherst, Massachusetts 01003
Michigan Quarterly Review, University of Michigan, Ann Arbor, Michigan 48104
Midstream, 515 Park Avenue, New York, New York 10022
Minnesota Review, Box 4068, University Station, Minneapolis, Minnesota 55414
Motive, P.O. Box 871, Nashville, Tennessee 37202
MSS, 670 Fifth Avenue, Chico, California 95926
New Campus Review, Metropolitan State College, Room 608, 250 West 14th Avenue, Denver, Colorado
New Mexico Quarterly, University of New Mexico, Albuquerque, New Mexico 87106
New Yorker, 25 West 43rd Street, New York, New York 10036
North American Review, Cornell College, Mount Vernon, Iowa 52314
Northwest Review, Erb Memorial Union, University of Oregon, Eugene, Oregon 97403
Paris Review, 45-39 171 Place, Flushing, New York 11358
Per Se, Box 2377, Stanford, California 94305
Perspective, Washington University Post Office, St. Louis, Missouri 63130
Phylon, Atlanta University, Atlanta, Georgia 30314
Playboy, 232 East Ohio Street, Chicago, Illinois 60611
Prairie Schooner, Andrews Hall, University of Nebraska, Lincoln, Nebraska 68508

Addresses of American, Canadian Magazines 399

Prism International, University of British Columbia, Vancouver, British Columbia, Canada

Quarterly Review of Literature, Box 287, Annandale-on-Hudson, New York 12504

Queens Quarterly, Queens University, Kingston, Ontario, Canada

Redbook, 230 Park Avenue, New York, New York 10017

Reflections, P.O. Box 109, Chapel Hill, North Carolina 27514

Reporter, 660 Madison Avenue, New York, New York 10021

Rogue, 1236 Sherman Avenue, Evanston, Illinois

San Francisco Review, P.O. Box 671, San Francisco, California

Satire, State University College, Oneonta, New York 13820

Saturday Evening Post, 641 Lexington Avenue, New York, New York 10022

Seventeen, 320 Park Avenue, New York, New York, 10022

Sewanee Review, University of the South, Sewanee, Tennessee 37375

Schenandoah, Box 722, Lexington, Virginia 24450

Sound, 15918 60th West, Edmonds, Washington 98020

South Dakota Review, Box 111, University Exchange, University of South Dakota, Vermillion, South Dakota 57069

Southwest Review, Southern Methodist University, Dallas, Texas 75222

Tamarack Review, Box 159, Postal Station K, Toronto, Ontario, Canada

Texas Quarterly, Box 7527, University Station, Austin, Texas 78712

Transatlantic Review, Box 3348, Grand Central P.O., New York, New York 10017

Vagabond, Collierstrasse 5, 8 Munich 12, Germany

Virginia Quarterly Review, 1 West Range, Charlottesville, Virginia 22903

Wagner Literary Magazine, Grymes Hills, Staten Island, New York

Weird Tales, 9 Rockefeller Plaza, New York, New York 10020

Western Humanities Review, University of Utah, Salt Lake City, Utah 84112

Yale Review, P.O. Box 1729, New Haven, Connecticut 06520

Yankee, Dublin, New Hampshire 03444

MORE BALLANTINE BOOKS
YOU WILL ENJOY

THE GOLDEN NOTEBOOK, Doris Lessing $1.25
The scorching novel of a woman who dared to live with the freedom of a man. "Brilliant . . . places Doris Lessing in the forefront of present British women novelists."—*Saturday Review Syndicate*

HELL'S ANGELS, Hunter S. Thompson $.95
The strange and terrible saga of the outlaw motorcycle gangs. Every word of the Random House best seller. "Superb and terrifying!"—*Chicago Tribune*

THE WORLD IS NOT ENOUGH, Zoé Oldenbourg $1.25
The boldly beautiful novel of chivalry and war in Medieval France—by the author of *The Crusades*. "Exciting and dramatic . . . the finest historical novel that has come my way."—Orville Prescott, *The New York Times*

DIBS IN SEARCH OF SELF, Virginia M. Axline $.75
The deeply moving true story of a five-year-old boy's successful struggle for identity, by the author of *Play Therapy* and the originator of the dramatic new technique for aiding emotionally disturbed children.

ZORBA THE GREEK, Nikos Kazantzakis $.95
The famous best seller that became a smash-hit film, Kazantzakis' fiery novel of a modern pagan. "Alive with energy. . . . Earthy and Rabelaisian."
—*Saturday Review*

complete list of Ballantine Books, or to order write to: Dept. CS, Ballantine Books, 101 *ue*, New York, N.Y. 10003